The Charmer

MANDASUE HELLER

The Charmer

HODDER &
STOUGHTON

First published in Great Britain in 2005 by Hodder and Stoughton
A division of Hodder Headline

A Hodder & Stoughton Book

1

A CIP catalogue record for this title is available
from the British Library

Hardback ISBN 0340 838280
Trade Paperback ISBN 0340 896949

Typeset in Plantin Light by
Palimpsest Book Production Limited, Polmont, Stirlingshire

Printed and bound by
Clays Ltd, St Ives plc

Hodder Headline's policy is to use papers that are natural, renewable
and recyclable products and made from wood grown in sustainable forests.
The logging and manufacturing processes are expected to conform to the
environmental regulations of the country of origin.

Hodder and Stoughton Ltd
A division of Hodder Headline
338 Euston Road
London NW1 3BH

To Win

For giving me the seed of a storyline which grew it into this – and for the best bit of advice ever when I got stuck. The end result is very different from your original idea, but I hope you like it anyway?!

AAF
X

Acknowledgements

As usual, I give my sincerest love and thanks to my fantastic family: my mum, Jean Heller; my sons and daughter, Michael, Andrew, and Azzura; my sister, Ava, and my nieces and nephews Amber, & Kyro, Martin, Jade, and Reece; Auntie Doreen, Pete & Ann, Lorna & Cliff, Chris & Glen; Natalie & Daniel Ward. And not forgetting the rest of the family, and the great friends who have supported me. I love you all.

My professional gratitude goes – as always – to all at Hodder for their unstinting support and belief in me, not least Carolyn Caughey, Emma Longhurst, Lucy Hale, and . . . well, everybody. (And welcome to Isobel Akenhead, who has already been most helpful.)

My agents, Cat Ledger, and Faye Webber.

Special thanks to Nick Austin; Norman Brown; Betty and Ronnie Schwartz (and their ever expanding family!); Wayne Brookes; Martina Cole; Carole, Julie, & Linda.

Fiona Gregory and Doreen Lovatt, for advice on wills and investments.

And, lastly, everybody who has been buying (& selling) the books and giving such great feedback. You make it all worthwhile!

Prologue

Burglars!

Switching the desk lamp off, he eyed the bottom of the door, waiting for the reception light to go on, which would have told him that it was someone with authority to be there. It stayed dark.

Shaking now, he reached for the heavy Blue John paperweight and edged his way out from behind the desk. Using the faint glow of the street lamp leaking in through the slatted blind to guide him to the door, he pressed his ear to the wood.

A minute passed, then two . . . Hearing nothing after three full minutes, he dared to peer out through the small glass panel. He could just about make everything out in the muted light coming through the smoked-glass street doors – couches, coffee machine, reception desk . . .

There was nobody out there. He must have imagined it.

Exhaling loudly, he flipped the overhead light on and glanced at his watch. It was almost three a.m. No wonder he was so spooked.

Time had a way of running away with him when he got stuck into something – but *boy* was he glad he'd got stuck into this. It had been incredibly revealing. The shit was really going to hit the fan come the morning.

Yawning, he shivered and rubbed at his arms. He should go home and get his head down. Knowing who he was up against, he needed a crystal-clear head to tackle this.

Putting the Blue John back, he locked the paperwork he'd been working on away in his briefcase. Pulling his jacket on, he took one last look around, then opened his door.

Still nervous despite knowing that there was nobody out there, he snaked an arm out to flip the reception light on, locked his office, set the alarm, and let himself out of the building.

Market Street was deserted but for a lazy breeze rifling through the litter bins and scattering loose food-cartons around the walkway. After the bustle of daytime, it felt eerie and abandoned, and the strange orangey glow of the lamps made it look other-worldly. Locking up, he hurried around to the car port at the rear of the block.

Acutely aware of the sound of his own footsteps, he felt the fear prickling the hairs on his neck when he heard a second, slightly out of sync set.

It's just an echo, he told himself, quickening his pace. And that shadow he'd just seen from the corner of his eye was only that – a shadow: a nothing piece of missing light.

Reaching the car, he fumbled to get the key out of his pocket, cursing himself for not having it ready in his hand.

Damn! He was all fingers and thumbs.

The shadow took solid form. Feeling the breath on his neck, he dropped the key and turned around, wide-eyed with fear.

'What the hell are *you* doing here?' he gasped when he saw who it was.

Pressing himself back against the car when the hooded shadow reached for his briefcase, he shook his head and gripped the case tighter.

'Give me the fucking bag!' the shadow snarled.

'There's no p-point,' he stuttered. 'I know *everything*. This is the end of the line.'

'For you, maybe,' the shadow hissed, pulling a knife out of nowhere.

'Don't be stupid . . .' His voice was shaking as much as his body now as the blade glinted in the dark. 'Put it away. That won't solve anything . . . *No!* . . . *Noooo* . . .'

PART ONE

I

Davy Boyle skidded his bike to a halt beside the fence and stuck his nose through the chain links. It was gone five and the afternoon sun was dipping behind the spindly trees, making the wreck look bleaker than ever as the wind snuffled through the sparse brown undergrowth. Spotting his sister Vicky's gang messing about on a home-made raft on the cut down by the croft, he stuck two dirty fingers in his mouth and gave a shrill whistle.

'Maria!' he yelled when heads turned his way, his voice high and thin on the chill air. 'You'd best come. The pigs is knocking on at yours.'

'Pigs?' Maria Price repeated with alarm. Jumping off the raft she scrambled up the slippery mud bank. 'What do *they* want?'

Squinting up at her from her tyre throne in the middle of the raft, Vicky gave her a sly grin. 'What you been up to, you sneaky cow? Been on the rob without us again, have you?'

'As if!' Maria tutted, wiping her wet hands on her jeans, adding to the dirt already streaking them. Her mum was going to have a fit when she saw them. Please *God* don't let her be in trouble with the coppers as well. She'd get a proper roasting.

'Wait on,' Vicky said when Maria turned to go. 'I'll come with you. Later, you lot.' Jumping across to the bank, she linked her arm through Maria's and they ran across the field to where Davy was waiting by the fence.

'Hurry up,' she moaned when Maria went over ahead of her. 'I need a piss.'

'Go behind that bush,' Davy said, pointing to an anorexic pile of twigs.

'Behave!' Vicky snorted. 'You think I want everyone seeing me arse? I'll wait till we get to Maria's.'

'What's up with yours?' Maria asked, dropping down to the pavement with a thud. Her mum wasn't overly fond of Vicky, and wouldn't like her using their loo when her own was just one floor down.

'There's nowt wrong with it,' Vicky said, climbing over and jumping down beside her. 'But me mam'll be at the pub by now.'

'So? You've got a key, haven't you?'

Snatching the cigarette that Davy had just sparked up, Maria took a drag and blew the smoke in his face. She grinned when he grimaced, making out as though he didn't like it. He adored her, and she got a buzz out of teasing him. But nothing was ever going to come of it. He was nine – she was eleven. It wasn't decent.

'*Duh!*' Vicky sneered, looking at her like she was thick. 'Knob-head Brian will be in on his tod.'

Passing the fag to her, Maria frowned. 'I thought you was gonna tell on him?'

'I tried, but she never listens, so what's the point?'

'She's your mum, she's *got* to listen.'

'Yeah, and he's her live-in shag, so whose side do *you* reckon she'd take?' Taking two aggressive puffs on the cigarette, Vicky handed it back to Davy, muttering, 'The sun shines so far out of his arse I'm surprised the stupid bitch ain't got an all-over tan!'

Maria would have laughed if they'd been talking about anybody else, but her best friend was suffering and she didn't find that remotely funny.

'I reckon you should try again,' she said firmly. 'She'd have to kick him out if she knew what he was up to.'

Vicky and Davy gave a simultaneous snort.

'Would she fuck,' Davy scoffed. 'She'd just kick the shit out of our kid then go and get pissed again.'

'Yeah, and I'd *really* cop for it off Brian,' Vicky added. 'Only he'd be twice as bad 'cos I'd grassed him.'

Hawking up loudly, Davy spat at the fence. 'I'm gonna do for him one of these days,' he muttered darkly as the phlegm slithered slowly down the links. 'You watch.'

Exchanging an amused glance, Vicky and Maria laughed.

'Yeah, whatever!' Vicky said, ruffling his dirty brown hair with rough affection. He was so small and cute, but if anyone tried to hurt her, he flipped out good-style. Which would have been great, if it didn't always end with *him* getting his head kicked in. 'Anyhow, come on,' she said, linking her arm through Maria's again. 'I'm gonna wet myself in a minute.'

Maria was quiet as they headed back to the estate. She felt really sorry for Vicky sometimes. Fancy not wanting to go home to use your own toilet in case your mum's lecherous boyfriend ambushed you. And it wouldn't be so bad if he was even nice, but he wasn't – he was fat and ugly, and he reeked of BO. But for some strange reason, Vicky's mum wouldn't hear a word against him, preferring to kick holes out of her own kids than admit what a filthy loser she'd shacked up with.

Maria thanked God *her* mum was nothing like that. Maria couldn't remember her ever having a boyfriend, never mind a dirty one. If she ever went out it was usually to the bingo with her mates from work, but she was always back by eleven, and *never* drunk. And if she *did* meet men, she didn't inflict them on Maria.

Pedalling furiously as they neared the estate, Davy rode

ahead to Brook House. Circling back a few seconds later, he
said, 'They're still there, Maria, but your mum ain't letting
'em in so they're just hanging about outside.'

Maria frowned. They must have been there for a while
already, given how long it had taken for Davy to see them,
ride to the wreck to fetch her, and come back again. They
should have sussed that no one was in by now, so why hadn't
they gone?

'What do you reckon they're after?' Vicky asked.

'No idea.' Shrugging, Maria pulled her arm free and ran
around the corner. Shielding her eyes against the late-
afternoon sun, she peered up to the fifth floor. Two uni-
formed police officers were standing at her door, one male,
one female. There was another woman with them, wearing
a smart black jacket and clutching a thick briefcase.

Catching up, Vicky hooked a lock of lank hair behind
her ear and frowned. 'God, they look serious. They're like
them what come for Uncle Franny that time, aren't they,
Davy?'

'When he stabbed that bloke and hid under me bed,' Davy
affirmed, nodding sagely. 'You should have seen them when
they nicked him, Maria – they was *proper* rough. Dragged
him down the stairs by his hair, then snapped his arm in
half shoving it up his back.'

'Shut up,' Maria hissed, her worried gaze darting back up
to the coppers when she heard a fresh burst of knocking.

'They don't look like they're gonna give up any time soon,'
Vicky said. 'Best go and see what's up, eh?'

Feeling sick, Maria nodded. 'Yeah, all right, but come with
me – and don't leave me on me own.'

'I won't,' Vicky assured her – praying that whatever it
was it wouldn't take too long, because she *really* needed
the loo.

Following the girls, Davy hooked his bike over his shoulder

as they set off up the stairs. 'Wonder why your mam hasn't answered?' he said thoughtfully. 'You don't reckon she's robbed a bank and gone on the run, or something, do you?'

'Why are you always saying menky stuff like that?' Maria snapped, tossing a warning glare back over her shoulder. 'She'll still be at work, you dickhead.'

'*Sorry*. I was only saying.'

'Yeah, well, don't!'

When they reached the fifth floor, Vicky groaned when she saw who the officers were.

'God, it's them who nicked me mam when she kicked off in the pub the other night,' she muttered. 'She's all right, but *he*'s a git.'

'Should I leg it?' Maria asked fearfully.

'Probably, yeah.' Vicky shoved her backwards towards the stairs. 'We'll go to mine and keep an eye out till they've gone.'

It was too late. PC Aiken had already spotted them.

'Just a minute, kids . . .' he called, too loud for them to pretend they hadn't heard. 'Any of you know the girl who lives here – Maria Price?'

Stepping protectively in front of Maria, Davy swung the bike down onto the landing with a thud. 'Who wants to know?' he demanded cockily.

'Pack it in, you little mong!' Vicky hissed, giving him a sharp dig in the ribs with her elbow.

'I'm Maria,' Maria admitted, clutching at Vicky's arm as she approached the adults. Now she knew that they were definitely looking for her, she was petrified. 'I haven't done nothing wrong, though.'

'Don't worry, Maria.' The woman with the briefcase smiled a little too brightly. 'My name's Tanith; I'm from social services. Do you have a key so we can go inside for a little chat?'

Maria didn't answer. She couldn't. Her mouth was too

dry, and the clammy hand of dread was gripping her by the throat.

'Your key's in your pocket,' Vicky prompted, nudging her. Then, turning to the policewoman, she said, 'Her mam must still be at work. D'y' want me to run and fetch her?'

'No, I'll go,' Davy offered. 'I'll be quicker on me bike.'

'You wouldn't know who to ask for,' Vicky said.

'Yeah, I would,' he argued. 'Maria's mam.'

'You wouldn't get past the gate.'

'Wanna bet?'

'Thanks, kids, but there's no need for either of you to go,' WPC Lennox said, ending the debate. 'Just get off and leave it to us, eh?'

'I can't go nowhere,' Vicky blurted out, remembering her promise. 'I'm stopping at hers tonight – aren't I, Maria?'

Maria nodded mutely.

'No, you're not,' Aiken grunted, his voice brooking no argument as he stepped between the girls and began to herd Vicky away. 'You'll have to find yourself somewhere else to go. You too, son,' he added, placing a firm hand on Davy's back.

'Get off me,' Davy spat, struggling to keep a hold on his precious bike while trying to squirm out of reach. 'I'll have you for harassment.'

'Zip it up, gobshite,' Aiken drawled, propelling him along the landing.

'But you don't understand,' Vicky protested, craning her neck to look past him to see if Maria was all right. 'We can't go home. Our mam's in hospital. We've got no key.'

'I'm sure you'll manage,' Aiken replied unsympathetically, not believing a word of it.

'Pig!' Davy muttered, shooting him a poisonous look. 'You can't *make* us go.'

Losing patience, Aiken seized him by the grimy neck of

his T-shirt. 'Carry on like that,' he snarled, lowering his face, 'and you'll be getting yourself locked *up* for the night, never mind locked *out*.'

'Leave him alone!' Vicky yelled, grabbing Davy's arm and trying to yank him free. 'I'll report you to Child Line, you big bastard!'

'And you'll be going with him if you're not careful,' Aiken warned her. 'Now, hop it, the pair of you!' Letting go of Davy, he wiped his hands on his trousers as if he'd touched something nasty. 'Go on! Piss off before I change me mind.'

Knowing they'd get nowhere but into trouble, Vicky said, 'All right, we're going.' Taking one last look back at Maria, she gave Davy a shove. 'Come on, you. We'll come back later when this lot's pissed off.' Tossing a defiant glare at Aiken, she stalked away with her nose in the air.

Folding his arms, Aiken stood with his feet apart, watching until they disappeared down the stairs. They amused him, these little estate rats. Being dragged up in squalor made them tough, and you had to admire their fierce sense of loyalty, but you had to show them who was boss from the get-go or they'd walk all over you.

Back down the landing, Maria's hands were trembling wildly as she slotted her key into the lock. Almost falling over the step, she led the women inside.

Lennox's radio began to crackle. Moving out of earshot, she spoke quietly into it and listened to the muffled reply. Turning back after a moment, she said, 'Why don't you show Ms Ryan into the lounge, Maria? Through there, is it?' She gestured towards an inner door.

Gazing back at her wide-eyed, Maria nodded.

Giving a questioning jerk of her chin, Tanith's heart sank when the policewoman raised her eyebrows grimly in reply, telling her exactly what she hadn't wanted to hear.

'Come on, lovey,' she said, opening the door and ushering

Maria through the small hallway. 'Let's go and make ourselves comfortable while we're waiting, eh?'

Sitting beside Maria on the settee, Tanith was surprised by how clean and cosy everything looked. She'd expected dirt and mess, but this was a real home, with all the loving touches that showed somebody really cared about the place; little things like cushions, plants and ornaments, which most civilised people took for granted, but which were almost unheard of in some of the disgusting hovels she'd had the misfortune to visit on this estate.

Numerous photographs of Maria at various ages graced the walls, and there was a portrait of both her and her mother on a shelf above the fire; heads touching, faces wreathed in happy smiles. Saddened by the obvious affection in their eyes, Tanith folded her hands tightly in her lap. This was never easy, but it was so much harder where love existed. She wished the officers would hurry up so they could get things moving. The sooner this was dealt with, the better for all concerned.

Watching Tanith out of the corner of her eye, Maria chewed on her lip and fiddled with her fingers as she waited for the axe to fall. She'd been racking her brain but, apart from wagging it, she couldn't think of anything she might have done that was bad enough to get arrested for.

Apart from throwing that brick through Mrs Felix's window the other week.

Shit!

That *had* been an accident, though, and Mrs Felix had promised not to grass on her. She could have changed her mind, but Maria doubted it. Not after she'd apologised *and* taken Mrs Felix's piss-stinking clothes to the wash-house to make up for it.

Other than that, she genuinely didn't think she'd done anything wrong lately. But she'd find out soon enough. And whatever it was, it had to be pretty bad, because this felt *way* heavier than the time when she'd been nabbed for shoplifting. She'd only got a warning from the coppers who brought her home that time, but this felt a thousand times worse. Her mum was going to *kill* her.

After a while, Aiken came in and sat awkwardly down on a chair across from the couch. Resting his elbows on his knees, he clasped his hands together and stared down at the recently vacuumed carpet. He hated shouts like this involving kids. They always cried and expected someone to hug them, but sympathy didn't come naturally to him. Sure, he *felt* for them, but it didn't show on his face, and the comforting words sounded false on his lips. No, he was quite happy to let his partner and the social worker deal with it – as long as they didn't drag it out. He had a darts match at The George tonight, and he didn't want to miss it.

Lennox came in then and exchanged a hooded glance with Tanith before sitting down on the other side of Maria.

'Maria,' she said, her voice soft and low. 'We need to talk to you about something really important. But before I start, I want you to know that you needn't be scared, because you're not in any trouble . . . Okay?'

Scared more by the insistence that she *shouldn't* be, Maria felt the room closing in on her. They were being too nice, and it just didn't feel right.

'I want my mum,' she croaked, her voice just a whisper as her throat constricted with dread. 'Can you get my mum, please? She'll be scared if you take me away while she's out. I don't even know what I've done.'

'You haven't done *anything*,' Lennox assured her quietly. 'That's not why we're here, sweetheart.' Sitting forward, she reached for one of Maria's hands and patted it reassuringly. Like Rob Aiken, she, too, hated these shouts. It was absolutely the worst part of the job that she otherwise loved. At times

like this, she wished she were a waitress or a meter-maid –
anything but the person about to destroy a child's life. 'There's
been an accident,' she said at last. 'Your mum—'

'What about her?' Maria's head jerked back, her eyes wide
with fear. 'What kind of accident? What's happened?'

'I'm so sorry,' Lennox went on gently, 'but she was hit by a
car when she left work today. She was taken to the infirmary,
but I'm afraid she didn't make it.'

'No!' Maria gasped, wrenching her hands free as if they'd
been burned. 'No, you're wrong!'

'I wish I was,' Lennox sighed. 'But that call I got just now,
that was the station, confirming that she's been positively
identified by two of her workmates.'

'They're lying,' Maria spluttered, refusing to believe it. 'It
wasn't her – I *know* it wasn't.'

'It was, my love.' Lennox's brow was deeply furrowed with
pity. 'She had benefit books in her bag, with her name and
national insurance number on them. She also had her works'
photo-security card pinned to her jacket. And, apart from
the two who did it officially, *all* of her workmates who were
coming out at the same time said it was her. There's absolutely
no doubt.'

'This is where *I* come in,' Tanith interjected softly. 'It's my
job to find a place for you to stay – preferably with family.'
Taking a notepad from her briefcase, she flipped it open and
took a pen out of her pocket. 'Now, we've been told that
Dad doesn't live with you, but I need to know if you have
a contact number for him?' She looked at Maria expectantly.
'His work number will do, but a mobile would be better.'

'I haven't got a dad.' Maria heard the voice, but it didn't
sound like her own. It sounded alien, disembodied, as if it
was coming from the corner of the ceiling, drifting further
and further away. 'Never had one. He's dead.'

'Grandparents, then?' Tanith probed gently. The last thing

this child needed was to be placed with strangers. At a time like this, she needed the love and comfort of people who had rejoiced at her birth. 'Aunts or uncles?'

'No.' Maria shook her head as the tears fell over her lower lashes like bright diamond chips and tumbled down her cheeks. 'There's only me and Mum. I want my *muuum* . . .'

'There must be *some*body?' Tanith persisted. 'Come on, Maria, *think* . . . I know it's hard, but this is really important.'

When Maria shook her head again, Tanith gave a small helpless shrug. This was the last thing she wanted to do, but she had no choice. Getting up she walked to the door and, taking a mobile phone from her pocket, tapped in a number.

Motioning to Lennox while she waited for an answer, she said, 'Could you help her get some things together, please?'

'Yeah, sure,' Lennox agreed, getting up and joining her at the door. 'What's happening?'

'I'm arranging an emergency placement at one of the units for tonight,' Tanith told her quietly. 'I'll see if I can locate any family when she's settled, but we need to get her out of here before it hits home. I've got a feeling she's going to take it very badly.'

Maria didn't hear any of this. Nor did she hear a word Lennox said as she allowed the kindly policewoman to lead her to her bedroom to pack a small bag. Numbed by grief and shock, she retreated into a cocoon of silence – and stayed there long after they had bundled her into the back of the police car and driven her far away from the only home she had ever known.

PART TWO

2

It was freezing in the flat. Huddled beneath the quilt, Maria watched as the weak morning sunrays danced off the spirals and iridescent baubles of the sea-horse mobile dangling down from the curtain rail. It was a birthday present from Beth. She'd brought it round last night and forced Maria to open it there and then – too impatient to wait until it was official.

Leanne and Sharon's presents were still sitting wrapped on the table. They had insisted that she *did* wait, even though she already knew what they had bought her: *Louvre Letters*, from Leanne – a book of prints from the gallery; and the D & G scarf they had found in the pocket of a jacket at the local Oxfam shop from Sharon. Not much to mark the passage into true adulthood, but it was more than enough for Maria.

Hearing the morning post dropping onto the lino in the hall below, she reached for her dressing gown and shivered her way down the stairs. It was supposed to be an Indian summer, but this was definitely early winter. The thin sheen of ice that coated the inside of the windows for half the year was already evident. But there was no point moaning; the landlord refused to replace the windows *or* update the heating.

'It's a listed building,' he chanted whenever anyone complained about the lack of central heating or double glazing. 'I'm not allowed to modernise.'

That was bollocks, because Maria had gone to the town hall and checked the records, and it wasn't listed at all.

But there was no reasoning with a dickhead like Ken Greenbridge. If you argued, he told you to put up and shut up – or pack up and piss off. And, bad as it was, the place was still the cheapest and best of the slums-by-the-sea. So she stayed put, using the extra money she'd have to pay to live somewhere nicer to save for the trip to Australia that she and the girls had been planning since leaving uni. Their last girly holiday before they settled into their *proper* lives: full-time jobs; marriage; mortgages; babies.

That was what the girls were aspiring towards, anyway. Maria would be happy just to have a full-time job, but they were few and far between in this dead little backwater. She was job-sharing with Beth, teaching art at the local primary school at the moment, but half a job meant half the pay, and while that was fine for Beth who was still living at home, Maria was having a harder time of it. But there weren't too many opportunities for art graduates here, so, unless she fancied trying her hand at one of the new lap-dancing clubs in one of the tourist Bays, she was stuck on the work-to-survive hamster wheel – living in squalor and saving her butt off.

Tiptoeing across the freezing lino, Maria scooped up the mail. Flipping through it, she took her own and dumped the rest on the ledge. She had three cards, and two letters.

Back in her room, she opened the first card. It was from Ian, a lad she'd dated briefly in her first year at uni. They'd split when he moved to Wales, but he never forgot to send birthday or Christmas cards. Which was kind of sweet, considering she'd been pretty cold about the break-up.

The second was a hand-painted fairy from a girl called Sam who had stayed on to specialise in fine art after the rest of them graduated. The card was so gorgeous that Maria thought she would frame it and keep it, on the off chance that it might be worth something one day.

The last card was a jokey one from Beth, with a lovely

silver wrist chain sellotaped to the inside, alongside the words: *'Thought you said I couldn't surprise you?'*

Peeling the chain off, Maria looped it around her wrist and held it up at the window to admire it. It was so delicate – and so typical of Beth: always making that extra bit of effort, because she knew that no one else would.

Standing the cards alongside the others on the mantelpiece, she smiled. Seven – her lucky number.

Washed and dressed, she opened the letters, groaning when she saw that the first was an electricity bill. Bang went the *lucky* theory. Apart from the holiday money, which she had vowed not to touch, she had just about enough in the bank for this month's rent and the minimum payment on her credit-card bill, and her wages weren't due for another two weeks. Great!

She almost binned the second letter, sure that it would be another bill. But then she figured that she'd rather know if the bailiffs were planning on booting the door in. Not that they'd get much. She doubted whether even the tramp who lived in the arcade doorway near the Den would want her ancient Sanyo portable, and the kettle was a death trap in training. The furniture was the landlord's, so they were welcome to that. But, apart from her clothes, she didn't actually own much else.

That was the legacy of growing up in the so-called *care* system. Someone invariably stole whatever you had, so you learned not to get too attached to anything. And you kept everything to a minimum so it was easy to pack when you were being shunted from home to home, and easy to replace if – *when* – it went walkabout.

Opening the second envelope with a resigned sigh, she frowned when she saw the letterhead: *Wilkins, Grayson & Cobb Solicitors. 326 Market Street. Manchester.* Why on Earth would a solicitor be contacting her?

Oh, God, she hoped it wasn't the catalogue!

She hadn't *meant* to stop paying for those boots, but they'd been so unreasonable when she missed a couple of instalments, demanding the whole lot in one go even though she told them she didn't have it, that she'd stopped opening their letters. And then she'd forgotten all about it.

There was a tap on the door, then Beth's grinning face appeared around it, singing, 'Happy birthday to you! Did you get it?' she asked then.

'Er, yeah . . . thanks.' Still frowning, Maria waved her to come in.

'What's up with your miserable face?' Beth asked, unwrapping the scarf from around her neck and draping it over the back of the couch. 'Oh, you didn't snap the chain, did you?'

'Course not,' Maria said, holding her arm up so that Beth could see that it was fine. 'I love it.'

'Knew you would.' Leaning over the back of the couch, Beth kissed her on the cheek. 'So, what *is* up?' she asked, dumping her coat on top of the scarf and taking three steps back into the square-foot space that the landlord laughingly called a kitchen.

'This.' Maria flapped the letter. 'It's from a solicitor.'

'Saying?' Beth switched the kettle on and swilled two cups out under the tap.

'Don't know, I haven't read it yet. I was just about to when you came.'

Snorting softly, Beth shook her head as she spooned coffee into the cups. 'You haven't even read it, but you've already convinced yourself it's bad news, haven't you? You need to sort that pessimistic streak of yours out before it eats you alive, girl. You could have won some big competition, for all you know.'

'Yeah, right. Like I can afford to enter competitions.'

'Give it here – and get that look off your face before I slap you,' Beth said bossily. Striding across, she snatched the letter and pulled Maria to her feet. 'You finish the brews, and I'll read this. No sugar for me, though – I'm on a diet. Right, let's see what's going on . . .

'"Dear Miss Price,"' she read aloud, '"I am contacting you on the occasion of your 21st birthday as per the instructions of our client, Miss Elsie Leonora Davidson. As the only surviving relative of said client – now deceased – it is my pleasure to inform you that you are the sole beneficiary of the estate as detailed in the . . ."' Reading the rest to herself, she glanced up excitedly. 'God, Maria! You've inherited a *house!*'

Maria had a confused frown on her brow. 'What do they mean – only surviving relative? I've never even heard of her.'

'Who cares?' Beth grinned. 'She's left you a house, and some money. You might be *rich.*'

Maria thought about it for a moment, then shook her head. 'They must have got the wrong person. I haven't got any relatives. It was only ever me and my mum.'

'Well, apparently, there *was* someone else,' Beth said, rereading the letter. 'It's definitely your name and address, and it *is* your birthday. How would they have known that if it wasn't you?'

'*I* don't know.' Maria shrugged. 'From the electoral register, or something. It's too easy to get people's personal details these days.'

'Well, they want you to get in touch to set up an appointment,' Beth said, handing the letter back to her when she brought the coffees over. 'Ring them and find out what's going on.'

'No way.' Maria dropped the letter on the couch between them as if it was on fire. 'I think it's the catalogue after me over those boots. They're just trying to lure me into a false sense of security by making me think I'm coming into money. But they're blagging the wrong person, because I haven't got any relatives.'

'Don't talk such utter *rubbish*,' Beth scoffed. 'They'll have given up on them ages ago.' Sipping her coffee, she grimaced. 'God, that's horrible without sugar. How long is it since you last heard from them?'

'About a year.'

'Exactly.'

'Yeah, but they won't just let it go, will they?' Maria reached for her cigarettes.

'Maybe not,' Beth conceded. 'But they wouldn't go to *these* lengths for – what? Thirty quid? Getting a solicitor to write a letter would cost them more than that. Nah. This is nothing to do with them, I guarantee it. Just give them a ring. What have you got to lose?'

'You do it if you're so sure,' Maria said, *almost* convinced but still wary.

'Take your cig over there and I'll think about it,' Beth said, wafting the smoke away with her hand. 'You know I'm trying to give up.'

'Sorry.' Getting up, Maria went to sit by the window. 'It's hard to remember *what* you're giving up. If it's not cigs, it's chocolate. Or you're going veggie, or something.'

'Yeah, well, I'm back on meat at the moment,' Beth said, reaching for Maria's phone and tapping in the solicitor's number. 'And if that coffee's anything to go by, I'll be back on sugar before the day's out, too. Shush now . . . it's ringing.'

'Don't stay on too long,' Maria whispered hurriedly, conscious of not running up yet more bills. 'And don't forget to say you're me or they might not tell you anything.'

'Oh, hello, yes . . .' Beth said, waving her to be quiet. 'My name's Maria Price. I got a letter from you this morning asking me to ring a –' she ran a finger down the letter, '– Nigel Grayson. Yes, I'll hold.'

'You should have told them to ring back,' Maria hissed.

'Oh, so you *want* me to give them your number, do you?' Beth asked, covering the mouthpiece. 'What if it *is* the catalogue?' Flapping her hand just as Maria was about to reply, she said, 'Mr Grayson? Hi, yes, my name's Maria Price. I got your letter this morning. Something about an inheritance . . . ?'

Listening to whatever was being said, Beth made *mmmm hmmm* noises for several minutes, then said, 'Could you just give me a minute, please?' Covering the mouthpiece again, she whispered, 'This sounds genuine, Maria. But he reckons you need to go to the office because there's too much information to tell you over the phone, and a ton of paperwork. What should I tell him?'

'I don't know.' Maria shrugged. 'I still don't think I'm the right person.'

'Well, someone obviously thinks you are,' Beth hissed impatiently. 'And if they want to give you a house, does it *matter* if they've made a mistake? Just go and *talk* to the man.'

'But it's in *Manchester*,' Maria moaned.

'Oh, shut up!' Beth scolded dismissively. 'I'll come with you if you're scared. We'll book ourselves into a hotel and go shopping. It'll be great.'

'With what? I'm broke.'

'Not for long, by the sound of this,' Beth said, grinning now. 'Come on. Let me tell him you'll go. You can dip into your holiday money.'

'No way.' Maria shook her head adamantly. 'If it turns out not to be me, I'll be buggered. The girls would never forgive me.'

'Well, I'll lend it to you, then,' Beth said impatiently. 'You can pay me back when you're rich.'

'And what if it's *not me*?' Maria said again, feeling desperate now.

'We'll sort something out.' Beth flapped her hand. 'Can I tell him yes, or what? Come on, girl – take a chance for once in your boring life!'

Taking a deep breath, Maria nodded. 'Okay. Go on, then. But if I end up in the shit, I'll blame you.'

Making an appointment for one week's time, Beth hung up with a whoop of jubilation.

'Sorted! All you need is your passport for ID, and he'll do the rest. Oh, crap!' she said then. 'I should have asked him about hotels. Oh, sod it, you must remember some. Make sure you pick a *good* one, though, 'cos I'm not staying in a B&B.'

'I don't remember anything,' Maria said, stubbing the cigarette out and coming back to the couch. 'Oh, hang on,' she said then. 'There was one called the Britannia. Me and my mates used to hang about outside in the summer holidays, winding the fat doorman up. We thought everything must have been made of solid gold inside, 'cos we used to see all these women in furs and diamonds going in, and men smoking big fat cigars.' Sighing wistfully, she smiled. 'I'd love to go there, but I bet it's way too expensive.'

'Only one way to find out,' Beth said, tapping the Directory Enquiries number into the phone.

'What are you *doing*?' Maria yelped, making a grab for it. 'I can't afford it!'

'I've already told you I'll lend you the money,' Beth said, holding her at bay. 'You can pay me back when you've claimed that – Oh, hello . . . Manchester, please . . . The Britannia hotel.'

Tapping the number in when she had it, she said, 'I'd like to book a room, please. Single, in the name of Price . . .'

'*Single?*' Maria hissed. 'We can't share a single bed! Are you mad?'

Shushing her, Beth gave the date and reached into her bag for her credit card.

'That wasn't too bad,' she said when she'd finished. 'It's only fifty-five quid for the night. The way you were going on, I thought it would be more than double that.'

'I'm glad *you* think it's so cheap,' Maria grumbled. 'I can't wait to see your face when you find out they've got the wrong person. I won't be able to pay you back for years.'

'Yeah, whatever,' Beth drawled, taking a crumpled transport timetable out of her bag and dialling the booking office.

Maria was beginning to wonder what she'd let herself in for, but there was no stopping Beth when she got like this. She was so organised, it was frightening.

'Right, that's all sorted,' Beth said with satisfaction when she'd booked the ticket. 'Just pick it up from the station on the day, and off you go. Now, let's see what you owe me . . . ?' Pursing her lips, she worked it out in her head, then delivered the news.

'A hundred and eighty *quid*?' Maria repeated, her eyebrows puckering with dismay. 'Oh, Christ, that's almost all my savings. You *own* me! I'm your slave.'

Wrinkling her nose, Beth said, 'I'd rather take cash, if you don't mind.'

'You'll be lucky. And what's with the single room, by the way? Don't you think they'll notice two of us going in?'

'Ah, about that . . .' Beth grinned sheepishly. 'I, er, won't actually be able to go.'

'Beth!'

'Sorry, babe, but it's my mum and dad's anniversary that day. I only remembered after I'd already set the date with the solicitor, and I didn't tell you straight away because I knew you'd bottle out. But you can't now, can you?'

Narrowing her eyes cynically, Maria said, 'You knew you weren't coming from the start, didn't you?'

'Don't know what you're talking about,' Beth replied innocently.

'Yeah, well, don't think I'm inviting you round to dinner when I'm living in my mansion.' Maria laughed softly. 'You're far too devious for my liking.'

3

The knot in Maria's stomach tightened as the train rolled into the station and came to a rumbling, squealing halt beside the Oxford Road sign.

Manchester.

It had been ten years since she'd been here, and she'd never planned on coming back. Beth had bullied her into it, making her believe that it would be fun, but now that she was here she just wanted to turn around and go back home.

God help the solicitor if he *had* got this wrong and she'd come all this way for nothing, because she hadn't had a proper night's sleep since his letter arrived for worrying how she was going to pay Beth back and still go on the holiday. Maria was shattered, and her nerves were screaming after so many hours on this cramped, stinking, heap-of-shit train. If she had to listen to one more mobile-phone-obsessed wanker telling anyone who'd listen about the *ever-so-important* meeting he was having when he got to the city, she would *kill* before the night was out!

Scowling at the wankers now as they jostled their way down the aisle, Maria gathered her stuff together and waited until the coast was clear before stepping out onto the platform. She shivered when an icy breeze gusted up from the tracks and swirled around her legs – just the welcome she should have expected from this dump!

Walking briskly out into the sunlight, she made her way

down the sloping approach road to the revamped Cornerhouse
Cinema. She gazed around with genuine surprise. She'd
expected everything to be exactly the same as when she'd last
seen it, but ten years was a long time, and a lot of new buildings had sprung up since she'd last been here: modern glass-
and-steel monstrosities that towered over the faded old-timers
like lanky, sneering teenagers.

Maria felt a little tug of nostalgia when she saw the blue
and yellow sign above the scarred black doors of The Ritz
club. She and the gang used to queue beneath that sign every
Tuesday night for the under-twelves' disco. They'd thought
it was so glamorous back then, but now it looked as grotty
as it probably always had.

The Palace Theatre looked shabby too, with its neglected
paintwork peeling and its billboards a disgusting mess of
pigeon crap. And the BBC building, where she and Vicky had
spent many a freezing Saturday hyperventilating over the pop
stars coming out after recording the weekend chart shows,
was equally dated and dirty.

Brought back to the here and now by a shuffling sound
behind her, Maria saw a scruffy man loitering in the shadows
of the cinema doorway and eyeing her bags. Gripping them
tighter, she gave him a fierce *Just try it!* glare and stalked
away in disgust. They might have cleaned the place up, but
it was still the same shitty old scene.

Reaching the hotel a few minutes later, she felt a flutter of
excitement as she made her way up the wide stone steps.
They had *so* wanted to know what it was like behind those
doors when they'd been kids. Now here she was, all grown-
up and ready to spend the night – and she didn't even have
to sneak in.

There was no solid gold inside, but it was every bit as
fantastic as she'd imagined: huge and elegant, with black
marble pillars and sparkling chandeliers. There was a

vast curved stairwell, and an impressive fountain in the shape of a water-nymph mid-foyer, surrounded by lush greenery.

Conscious that people were having to walk around her as she stood in the centre of the mosaic-tiled floor like an awestruck tourist, Maria collected her room pass from reception and took the super-silent lift up to the fifth floor.

Her room was cheap and basic, but it had everything she needed, so she was quite happy: generous-sized bed, TV, phone, coffee- and tea-making facilities. The tiny bathroom was spotless, with the usual toiletries, fluffy white towels, and dressing gown with the hotel's logo embroidered onto the lapel.

Drawing the blind up to check the view, Maria saw that there was an abandoned factory opposite, every window of which was smashed, making it look desolate and spooky. Pretty dismal, but she wasn't planning to sit here gazing out, so she didn't care.

Further down the road, the bus station had been rebuilt, and the Piccadilly Gardens had had a long-overdue sprucing-up.

That 'little oasis in the heart of the city' had been nothing but a squalid haunt for tramps and prostitutes when she'd lived here, the never-working fountain a repository for empty cider bottles and soggy condoms. Now it looked clean and cheerful, and there were several young mothers chatting happily on the benches while their toddlers played among the flowers so it was obviously safer, too.

Yawning when a wave of exhaustion swept over her, Maria checked the time to see if she dared risk a nap. But there was only an hour to go before her meeting, so she made herself a strong coffee instead. Then, opening the window wide, she turned the TV up loud and chain-smoked to keep herself awake.

★   ★   ★

In his office some time later, Nigel Grayson sat back in his chair with a sigh and ran a long-fingered hand through his hair – which, to his despair, was already receding at the tender age of twenty-six.

He usually blamed his mother for stressing the hair out of his head. But it wasn't her fault that his hands were clammy and his heart racing today.

It was Maria Price who had him all a-fluster.

To say that he had been surprised when she walked in was an understatement; he'd been shocked. And not just because she was so slim and pretty, with long honey-blonde hair and the bluest, most beautiful eyes he'd ever seen. Nigel was astonished that she was a *woman* at all, and not the fragile little orphan girl he'd been expecting – the waif in a shabby dress whom he had envisaged whenever his uncle had talked about her at family dinners over the years.

The Cinderella story had fascinated Nigel, and, since taking his uncle's place in the firm following the great man's death a few months ago, he'd been counting off the days until he got to meet Maria and hand over the keys to her kingdom.

That day had finally arrived, but things were hardly going to plan. Maria was having a hard time believing what he was telling her. And, more than that, it actually seemed as if she didn't *want* it to be true – and Nigel didn't understand that at all.

'I'm sorry,' he said when he had told her everything he knew. 'But there's really nothing more to add. I appreciate that this has come as a bit of a shock, but Miss Davidson's instructions were quite precise: if she were still alive when you reached the age of twenty-one, you were to be given access to a trust fund. But if she had passed on – which she *has* – then you would inherit in full. That's it.'

'And you're absolutely *sure* you've got the right person?'

Maria asked – again. 'It's a common enough name. There must be *thousands* of Maria Prices in England.'

'I'm sure there are,' Nigel agreed, wondering why she seemed so set on talking herself out of a fortune. 'But I am positive that you are the right one.'

Still unconvinced, Maria folded her arms. 'No offence, but you *are* a proper solicitor, aren't you? Only you look a bit young to me. Are you sure you're not a trainee making a cock-up?'

'I'm definitely *not* a trainee,' Nigel assured her, his cheeks flaming now. 'And there is *no* mistake.'

Reaching for the thick folder that was sitting between them on the desk, he flipped it open and rifled through it. Finding what he was looking for, he cleared his throat and read it out.

' "Maria Ann Price. Born at St Mary's Hospital, Manchester, 16 August 1985. Father unknown. Mother, Maureen Ann Price. Born 3 April 1965 – deceased 12 September 1996. Previous address: 535 Brook House, Merrydown Estate, Manchester. Present address: Flat 8, 23 Jackson Lane, Teignmouth, Devon." ' He glanced up, one eyebrow raised. 'Those *are* your details, I take it?'

'Yes, but that doesn't prove anything,' Maria muttered, disconcerted by the accuracy of the information.

Where the hell had they got it all from? Somebody had obviously done their homework – and that wasn't just creepy, it was a downright invasion of privacy.

And a downright lie.

Her father had died when she was still in the womb, and he hadn't had any family. Her mum had told her all about it, and why *would* she have if it wasn't true? She'd loved Maria, and would *never* have deliberately left her alone in the world if she'd known there was someone out there who could take care of her.

'Look, I *know* this woman wasn't my aunt,' she said adamantly. 'She couldn't have been. I didn't *have* any family apart from my mum, and she's been dead for years.'

'Miss Davidson was aware of that.'

'That doesn't prove anything. And neither does all that stuff you read out. Anyone could have found that out, considering it was all over the papers. Everyone in Manchester must have seen it. Oh, Christ . . .' Trailing off, Maria frowned as it occurred to her that she might just have hit on something. 'That's not what happened, is it? She didn't read about me being orphaned and get obsessed with me, like some kind of *weirdo*? Oh, my God! That's so *sick*!'

'I really don't think that was the case,' Nigel said, his pale eyebrows puckering with dismay at the venom in Maria's voice. 'My uncle knew Miss Davidson for many years and considered her both intelligent and astute. But he wouldn't have hesitated to caution her if he'd thought she was deluding herself – about this, or anything else.'

Giving him a cynical look, Maria said, 'Okay, let's pretend it's true, and this so-called brother of hers *was* my father. Why didn't he come forward when my mum died, then?'

'I, er, believe he was already deceased by then,' Nigel told her.

'What about *her*, then?' Maria flapped a dismissive hand at the folder. 'If she was so keen to include me in her freaky little family, why didn't *she* take me in instead of letting me rot in care?'

'I really couldn't begin to speculate on the whys and where-fores,' Nigel admitted, shifting uncomfortably in his seat. 'I only know the documented facts. Anything my uncle might have learned from their off-the-record conversations went with him to the grave, I'm afraid.'

'How convenient.' Giving a snort of contempt, Maria shook her head, biting her lip to contain the anger. It didn't work. 'Why did you make me come all this way?' she demanded. 'It's cost me a *fortune*, and for *what* . . . ? I'm sure there's nothing you've said that couldn't have been said over the phone. Then I could have told you it's a load of rubbish, and saved us *both* the bother.'

Sitting forward, Nigel rested his elbows on the desk, barely able to meet Maria's gaze. He couldn't blame her for being furious, and he couldn't deny what she'd said, because she was right – about the phone, at least. But he'd been so desperate to meet her that he'd made her come to the office – proving what a shamefully unprofessional creature he truly was. His uncle would be turning in his grave, wondering why he'd ever thought Nigel fit to fill his shoes.

'Would it help if I got you copies of some of the paper-work?' he asked. 'You could take it back to your hotel and go over it at leisure. Then we could meet up again in the morning when you've had a chance to—'

'No!' Maria interrupted waspishly, folding her arms and crossing her legs – a tight, simultaneous action that displayed how tautly her nerves were stretched. 'I want to sort it out *now*. Isn't there somebody else I can talk to – someone who actually knows what's going on?' She stared at him expectantly, the muscles jumping in her cheeks as she clenched her teeth. She knew she was being a bitch, but she couldn't help it. She was tired and frustrated.

'I'd be happy to refer you to one of the partners, but I doubt they'd have anything significant to add, because . . . well, they don't actually know as much as I do.' Pausing, Nigel gave a sheepish shrug. 'You were one of my uncle's favourite topics at family dinners, you see. He used to give us updates whenever your aunt received reports, and—'

'*Excuse* me?' Maria cut in incredulously. 'What do you mean, *reports*?'

Wincing when his leg gave an involuntary jerk and his

bony knee smashed into the underside of the desk, Nigel gritted his teeth. 'I, er, believe they related to your schooling and general home life.'

Squinting at him, her face deathly pale, Maria said, 'Are you telling me that my social workers knew about this?'

'As far as I'm aware, *no*body knew,' Nigel assured her.

'That can't be true,' Maria argued. 'Who provided these so-called reports, then?'

'A private detective.' Nigel dropped his gaze when she glared at him in disbelief. Rooting through the folder again, he took out a sheet of letterheaded paper. 'Here we are . . . Holt & Shaw Detective Agency, Longford Street, Levenshulme. I haven't actually spoken to them personally, but I don't think anybody was privy to the information they gathered, other than Miss Davidson – and ourselves, of course.'

'Oh, well, that's all *right*, then!' Maria's eyes were sparking with indignation. 'Let's see if I've got this straight . . . She *paid* some creep to follow me around and write reports about my personal business, but *you* don't think she was a weirdo?'

'I don't think you were followed, as such,' Nigel bleated lamely. 'I believe it was more of a yearly update sort of thing – exam results, and leisure activities, and what have you.'

'*Private* things!' Maria spat. 'Christ, this is unbelievable! How *dare* she stick her nose into my life like that!'

Nigel was at a loss as to what to say next. He'd had it so clear in his head before she'd arrived: he would fill her in on the details; she would be ecstatically happy. Hallelujah! Ring the bells, send in the clowns . . .

What he hadn't anticipated was anger and awkward questions. He hadn't prepared for that at all. But it was no wonder she had questioned his professional status. If *he* was listening to this, *he*'d be wondering what he was playing at, too. Any idiot could read a file and relay the facts. But Maria wanted *reasons*, and as he had never actually met Elsie Davidson he was sadly lacking in that department.

'Look, I'm truly sorry I can't tell you what you want to know,' he said apologetically. 'But apart from the little I picked up from my uncle, I only know the bare facts. And I'd rather not waste any more of your time until I've looked them over in more detail. And maybe I could speak to the detective.'

'And you'd feel better about wasting my time then, would you?'

'No, I didn't mean . . . I just . . .' Trailing off, Nigel flapped his hands in a gesture of defeat. 'If you'd just give me tonight, Miss Price?'

Seeing the distress in his nut-brown eyes, Maria felt a twinge of regret for snapping at him. He had the look of the underdog about him – and that was something she recognised all too well from her time in care. None of this was his fault, and it was unfair of her to take her frustrations out on him. If anyone was to blame, it was the crazy old bitch who had popped up from the grave with this mad tale of long-lost fathers and rich spinster aunts.

Sighing heavily, she ran a hand over her tired eyes.

'Are you all right?' Nigel asked hesitantly, wary of having his head bitten off again. She'd taken this so much harder than he'd expected, and she didn't look at all well. She was pale, and her hands were shaking.

Looking up, Maria forced herself to give him a weary smile. 'I'm fine. I'm just a bit tired, that's all. And I've got a headache.'

'Oh, I'm sorry.' Nigel immediately felt guilty. 'I should have thought . . . Can I get you a coffee? Or a sandwich, perhaps? There's an excellent deli a few doors down if you'd like me to send out for something.'

Shaking her head, Maria reached for her handbag. 'No.

I'd best just go back to the hotel and lie down before it turns into a migraine. I'll take you up on that offer of some copies of the paperwork, though – if that's still all right?'

'Absolutely,' Nigel assured her. 'You'll have to bear with me, though. I, er, think the secretaries might have already left for the day, and I'm not very good with machinery.'

'No rush,' Maria told him politely – hoping that he didn't take her too literally. If she didn't get out of here soon, she'd throw up.

Scooping up the folder, Nigel rushed out, glad of a chance to escape and compose himself: he'd been acting like an idiotic tongue-tied schoolboy since she'd arrived.

Selecting several pieces, he slotted them into the copier and keyed in the settings – keeping his fingers crossed that it didn't eat the originals or spew everything back out.

Going back to his office a few minutes later, he was smiling as he handed the still-warm copies to Maria.

'That should be enough to be going on with,' he said, making his way around the desk. 'There was a letter addressed to you, so I've slipped that in there, too.'

'Thanks.' Smiling tiredly, Maria folded everything and put it in her bag.

'If you'd like to go and see the house while you're here, just let me know,' Nigel said, joining his hands together on the desk. 'I can't release the keys to you until everything's legally transferred into your name, I'm afraid, but I'd be more than happy to show you around in the meantime.'

Maria rubbed at her temples as the ache turned into a sickening throb.

This was crazy.

Miss Elsie Leonora *Davidson* was crazy.

She must have been *some* kind of nutter, to hear about a poor little orphan girl and delude herself into believing that they were related.

And she must have believed it to leave her house to a girl she had never met, but whose life she had apparently followed so closely. And not just any old house, but the one she had spent the entire sixty-five years of her life in, it seemed.

'Do you know the Didsbury area?' Nigel was asking.

'Not really, no.' Shaking herself out of her thoughts, Maria sat up straighter. 'It was too posh for us lot. We tended to stick to Moss Side or town if we fancied a wander. Not that we ever went *too* far – we were a bit young for roaming back then. And our parents liked to know where we were, in case we were getting into mischief. But there you go . . .' Trailing off, aware that she was waffling, she gave a tight smile.

Gazing at her, Nigel sighed wistfully. She was so beautiful, and not nearly as brittle as she'd seemed at first. And when she smiled, there was a softness about her that reached right inside you and stroked your heart.

Maria stood up. 'Right, well, I'll get going. Thanks for your help. And I'm sorry if I was rude, but this has all been a bit weird.'

'It must have been quite a shock,' Nigel agreed, rushing to open the door for her. '*I'*m sorry I didn't handle it with more sensitivity, but I just assumed you'd be thrilled.'

'*Hardly!*' Maria snorted. 'Try completely pissed off.' Giving him a wry smile, she walked past him into the reception area. 'What a *crazy* day,' she said wearily, slipping her jacket on. 'I can't get my head around this woman thinking she was my aunt for all that time without telling anyone. It's *weird.*'

'She probably thought she was doing the right thing,' Nigel suggested. 'People of that generation tend not to view things in quite the same way as the rest of us. But at least she tried to put it right in the end. That must be some comfort.'

'Not really.' Maria shrugged dismissively. 'Anyway, I'll give you a ring when I've looked this stuff over and we can set up another meeting before I go home.'

'When *are* you going?' Nigel asked, casually, as if it were just a matter of business interest.

'Tomorrow afternoon – and I can't wait.' Maria peered out through the street door. It was dusky outside, and people were walking faster – wearing their coats now instead of carrying them. Maria zipped her jacket up in readiness for the cold.

Nigel struggled to mask his disappointment. He'd hoped there would be time for a few more meetings while she was in town – lunch, or dinner, maybe. But who was he kidding?

Making an effort to pull himself together, he said, 'I'll be here from eight-thirty in the morning, so just come in whenever you're ready. I've nothing on that can't be rejigged.'

'Thanks.' Smiling, Maria hooked her bag over her shoulder and held out her hand.

Nigel felt the heat rise to his cheeks when he shook it. Her skin was so soft, but her grip was firm. It was a heady combination and he was overwhelmed by a desire to kiss her hand.

Dropping it before he did something stupid and really embarrassed himself, he reached into his pocket and pulled out a business card.

'Why don't you take this?' he babbled, thrusting it into her hand. 'It's got my mobile number on it, so if you get a sudden urge to go and see the house before tomorrow, you can give me a call. I don't live too far out of town. I could be back within the hour.'

'I sincerely doubt I'll get the urge,' Maria assured him, slipping the card into her bag.

★   ★   ★

Watching from the window when Maria had gone, Nigel sighed. His shoulders slumped. He'd been so excited about meeting her, anticipating it as if he were reuniting with a long-lost friend. But in reality, she was *not* a friend, she was a client. A beautiful, *sexy* client, but a client nonetheless. And not even *that* for too much longer, he shouldn't wonder, for he had no doubt that she'd transfer her affairs to another solicitor as soon as she got home.

'Who's the honey?'

'Christ!' Jumping when Adam Miller crept up behind him and clapped a hand down on his shoulder, Nigel's forehead bounced off the glass. 'You bloody idiot!' he complained. 'You frightened the life out of me. I could have gone right through!'

'Never mind your big head,' Adam said dismissively. 'Who was she?'

'Cinderella,' Nigel murmured, gazing wistfully out again. Maria had disappeared from view.

'You *what*?' Drawing his head back, Adam gave a bemused smile. 'As in glass slippers and wicked stepmothers?'

Realising how ridiculous he must sound, Nigel grinned to cover his embarrassment. 'As in rags to riches, you plonker. Even *you* must know that one.'

'Haven't got a clue what you're talking about,' Adam teased. 'Must say, though, I never had you down as the fairy-tale type. Just goes to show, eh?'

'Very funny. Look, you remember Miss Davidson?'

'Your Uncle Ted's girlfriend? Yeah, what about her?'

'She was *not* his girlfriend, she was his client. And I wish you wouldn't speak about him like that. It's incredibly disrespectful.'

'Easy, tiger, it was a joke,' Adam said, chuckling softly. 'Remember them? Funny words – people laugh.'

Aware that he was overreacting, Nigel sighed. 'Sorry. No

excuse, I know, but I've been waiting to meet the niece for *years*, and today I finally get the chance, and what do I do? Totally balls it up, like the—'

'Whoa there!' Adam's eyebrows had risen sharply. 'Back up a step . . . The honey was Miss Davidson's *niece*?'

'Yep. Last living relative.'

'*Really*? So, she inherits—'

'The lot,' Nigel finished for him. 'Lock, stock, and three-storey house in Didsbury.'

'Wow,' Adam exclaimed enviously. '*Lucky* little honey.'

'Try telling *her* that,' Nigel countered mournfully.

'What's she planning to do with it all?' Adam asked, checking his reflection in the window behind Nigel now.

Well used to his colleague's vanity, Nigel moved aside. 'No idea,' he said, shrugging as he leaned back against the ledge. 'We didn't get that far, but it's my guess that she'll sell up. She's already said she can't wait to go home tomorrow.'

'And where's that?'

'Devon.' Another heartfelt sigh.

'That's a long way to come for a meeting,' Adam said, tucking his shirt in. 'Why bother if she's going straight back?'

Shrugging, Nigel reached down and plucked invisible lint off his trouser leg, too ashamed to admit that he had given her the impression that she *had* to come.

'So, what's she doing while she's here?' Adam asked. 'Has she got friends in town?'

'No. She's staying at the Britannia.'

'Can't be bad. Still, I suppose she can afford it with an inheritance like that.'

'Not until the papers are signed and everything's transferred,' Nigel said. 'Mind you, I doubt she'll want to touch it even then. She doesn't seem too keen on claiming it. But you can hardly blame her, I suppose.'

Adam gave him a questioning look. 'Why on Earth would

anybody object to inheriting that kind of money? She'd have to be stupid to turn it down. And from the little I saw of her, I wouldn't have thought she was that. Gorgeous, yeah. But not stupid.'

'Actually, this is the first she's heard of it,' Nigel said tersely.

Adam was displaying a bit too much interest for his liking and, given his track record, Nigel wouldn't put it past him to be hanging around when Maria came in tomorrow. She'd take one look at his handsome face and perfect smile, and it would be all over bar the panting. Pathetic, he knew, but he *was* a man, not just a solicitor.

'How could she not know her aunt was planning to leave her a fortune?' Adam wanted to know. 'That doesn't make sense.'

'She didn't know she *had* an aunt,' Nigel explained grudgingly. 'Her mum died when she was a kid and no one knew she had any living family, so she was shipped off to Devon. Miss Davidson managed to track her down and keep tabs on her, but she didn't tell anybody. Consequently, the niece got the shock of her life when I brought her in and told her she'd had an aunt all along.'

'Poor kid,' Adam murmured thoughtfully. 'I bet she's gutted she didn't find out earlier.'

'She's not *gutted*,' Nigel corrected him. 'She's *furious* that Miss Davidson didn't even try to contact her.'

Pursing his lips, Adam nodded. 'I can see her point. It's one thing finding out by accident after the fact, but knowing it was deliberately kept from you, that would be a bit of a slap in the face. Still . . .' He shrugged. 'You can't miss what you've never had, can you?'

'I suppose not,' Nigel agreed, sighing.

'Oh, don't worry, man,' Adam said. 'I'm sure she'll be fine when she gets her head around it – you'll see.'

'I wouldn't bet on it,' Nigel murmured. 'She's had a pretty

rough time of it, and I reckon it's going to take her a while to get used to handling this kind of money. She'll need financial guidance.'

'Which is where *you* come in, I take it?' Adam gave a knowing grin. He could read Nigel's face like the back of his hand – every expression, from mad to sad to horny; and this latest client had got his juices flowing. Not that Adam blamed him. He'd only caught a glimpse of her from his office when Nigel had led her through reception, but it was enough to know that she was an absolute babe.

'Actually, I doubt I'll still be involved after tomorrow,' Nigel told him glumly. 'I've given her some paperwork to go over, but I've got a feeling that our next meeting will be the last I see of her.'

'Oh, well, it obviously wasn't meant to be.'

'Yeah, I know,' Nigel agreed. 'Still, it's my own fault. I shouldn't even be thinking like this.'

'Because she's a client, and it's against the rules?' Adam teased.

'Exactly!'

Easing his cuff back, Nigel checked the time, surprised to see that it was past seven already. He'd spent far longer with Maria Price than he'd realised. No wonder she'd been so desperate to escape. It was high time he got out of here himself.

'Fancy a drink?' he asked.

'Best not,' Adam said, grinning as he added, 'I'm supposed to be meeting someone, and I'm already late.'

'Go on, then.' Nigel sighed good-naturedly. 'Don't let me keep you.'

'Don't worry, I won't.' Winking, Adam went to his office and snatched his jacket off the back of the chair. Slipping it on, he strolled out again. 'See you tomorrow. Try not to have *too* much fun.'

'Chance would be a fine thing,' Nigel muttered morosely.

Watching through the window as Adam sauntered out, Nigel winced when he collided with a pretty young woman who was walking past. Reaching out to steady her, Adam said something that she obviously found amusing, eliciting a coy smile from her. Giving one of his own cocky beauties in return, he went on his way. The woman did, too, but she couldn't resist sneaking a quick look back.

'Smooth bugger,' Nigel muttered when Adam gave a casual wave over his shoulder as if he'd been expecting it.

He couldn't imagine how fantastic it must be to have women falling all over themselves to go out with him, like they did with Adam – and he doubted that he'd ever find out. Adam exuded a self-confidence Nigel could only dream of, and he was so damn handsome it was criminal. If his morning-after-the-night-before stories were true – and Nigel had no reason to doubt them – women couldn't keep their hands off him. Every time he turned around there was another one thrusting her breasts at him, smiling, flirting, teasing, giggling . . . Nigel would die for a piece of that, but you either had it or you didn't. And while Adam did, Nigel most definitely didn't.

The phone on his desk began to ring. Hoping wildly that it was Maria Price calling to say she had changed her mind and *would* like him to take her to see the house, he locked the street door and rushed back to his office to answer it.

He was disappointed to hear his mother's voice.

'Oh, I *am* glad I caught you, Nigel. I was afraid you'd already left.'

'No, I'm still here,' he replied wearily. 'What's wrong?'

'Aunt Beryl's coming to stay,' she informed him, her tone its usual blend of complaint and resignation as she added, 'As if I didn't have enough to contend with. Anyway, I'm going to need you to pick up a few things on your way home, so get a pen and make a list, would you? And do hurry, Nigel. I've a lot to do before I can call the night my own.'

Closing his eyes, Nigel dropped his head into his hand. How he longed to be able to say '*Sorry, Mother, but I'm afraid you'll have to do it yourself, because I'm busy tonight – with my* girl*friend*.' But there was no point even *thinking* it, never mind saying it. She'd never believe it.

Sighing heavily, he flipped his desk pad open.

'Go on, then . . . What do you need?'

4

Maria called Beth when she got back to the hotel and gave her a quick rundown of what had happened. Keeping it brief because she was too exhausted to answer any of Beth's questions, she promised she would call back when she had gone over everything and was able to think straight.

Switching the phone off, she climbed fully clothed into bed, burying her head in the comforting coolness of the pillow.

Waking a couple of hours later, she felt much better. There was still a faint shadow of an ache behind her eyes, but her head was a lot clearer.

Taking a shower, Maria towel-dried her hair and changed into fresh clothes, then ordered a chicken sandwich and a bottle of Budweiser from room service. Settling on the bed with the tray when it arrived, she sipped the beer and picked at the food as she went over the paperwork.

Most of it concerned the house, and the rest related to various stocks and shares, and bonds, but it was all too complicated to get her head around right now. The money itself was being held in a special account set up by the solicitors as executors of the will. Nigel had told her that it would be released to her in cheque form once it had been to probate – whatever *that* meant.

Maria didn't have a clue about Probate, Land Registry, or Inheritance Tax, if truth were told. If she wasn't so proud she could have asked the solicitor to explain. But she'd gone into the meeting acting all worldly-wise and intelligent, and hadn't wanted him to see how ignorant she really was.

Giving up on it now, she reached for the letter, which was in a sealed white envelope addressed to *Miss M. A. Davidson-Price.*

Maria felt peculiar just looking at it; not only because it was from a woman who was now dead, but because of the addition of the name *Davidson.*

That name meant less than nothing to her, and she resented having it forced on her like that. It was like waking up after a party to discover that somebody has tattooed you in your sleep. You didn't ask for it, you don't *want* it, but now that it's there you can't get rid of it without leaving a scar.

She wished she was the kind of person who could shrug off the doubts and grab the prize with both hands – who *wouldn't* love to get their hands on a house and money for nothing? But it just wasn't in her. And, despite all the facts that Elsie Davidson had gathered about her, and her obvious belief that Maria *was* the niece she had never met, Maria *still* thought it was a mistake.

But mistake or not, the letter *was* addressed to her, so she figured that she might as well see what it had to say. Who knew . . . She might succeed where the solicitors and the detective had failed, and find a clue about who the *real* heiress was.

The letter was written in fine, spidery, old-lady hand, slanted classically to the right, with defined capitals and tight, elegant loops.

It was dated February, and Elsie Davidson had died in March, so Maria guessed she'd probably known she was dying when she wrote it. Talk about getting the last word! She'd known that she could say whatever she liked, and nobody would ever be able to dispute it, because she'd be dead by the time it was read.

Pouring herself another glass of beer, Maria settled back against the pillows to read the letter.

Elsie claimed that her brother Derek had been courting Maria's mum Maureen for a year when Maureen told him she was pregnant, and that he was the father. He immediately offered to marry her, braving the disapproval of his family who had warned him that she wasn't quite as innocent as she made herself out to be. They weren't happy about the age gap either, he being thirty-four, she just twenty. They thought that Maureen had got herself pregnant to trap Derek so that she could get her hands on the family money. But, instead of grovelling in gratitude for having hooked him, as they'd expected, Maureen not only turned him down, she added insult to injury by running away with another man – *obviously* a better financial prospect.

Determined to be a part of his child's life, Derek searched for Maureen, asking if anybody had seen her or heard from her – but no one admitted it if they had. When he suffered a fatal heart attack two years later – Maureen's fault *again*, apparently, because she had caused the stress which had led to it – Elsie continued the search. But not for the same reasons, for she admitted that she'd had no interest in the child at that time, her sole aim being to find Maureen and make her suffer like Derek had. She, too, got nowhere.

The breakthrough came when Elsie, alone and ageing and spending an increasing amount of time in bed with just the TV for company, saw a report of Maureen's death on the local news. Her thoughts turned to Maria, who was not just Derek's long-lost daughter now but Elsie's only remaining relative – the only one to whom she could leave the house and money. Aware that the social services were unlikely to tell her anything because she had no proof that she was related to Maria, she hired the private detective to track her down and keep tabs on her.

Concluding the letter, Elsie said that she hoped Maria would love The Grange as dearly as her father's family had. And that she would use the money to build a secure life for herself and any future children. The Davidsons would live on through her now – in blood if not in name.

Maria was drained by the time she finished reading, and she didn't believe a word of it. Or, rather, she didn't *want* to, because that was like saying she believed that her mum had lied to her, deliberately denying her the chance to know who her father was. And she couldn't accept *that* any more than she could accept that her mother was the heartless, unfaithful gold-digger Elsie had made her out to be.

That didn't tally with the woman Maria remembered – the quiet, pretty woman who had loved her and worked hard to build a good home for her, *never* letting a man come between them like the rest of the single mums on the estate who had let any old Tom, Dick or Harry move in, regardless of the cost to their kids.

Her mum had always said that her father had died before she was born. But if that wasn't true, then Maria couldn't say she blamed her for not wanting to have anything to do with the Davidsons. *She* would have run a mile rather than live under the disapproving glare of people who obviously thought themselves superior to her, and who expected gratitude for doing the right thing. And she *certainly* wouldn't subject her child to it.

She found it a bit weird that it didn't seem to have occurred to the Davidsons that Derek might *not* be the father. If Maureen *had* run away with another man, as Elsie claimed, wouldn't it be logical to assume that she had been having an affair all along, and that the baby might be the other man's?

The Davidsons might have believed that their genes were

so powerful that no other man's sperm could possibly compete. Or it was a lie that Maureen had ever been unfaithful, and Elsie had said it out of spite for Maureen having had the audacity to turn Derek's proposal down. Unable to find her to exact revenge in life, she'd plumped for the beyond-the-grave kind instead – planting seeds of doubt in Maria's mind, hoping that they would poison her heart and obliterate her happy memories of her mother.

Well, tough! It hadn't worked. Maria loved her mother as much as ever – and despised Elsie as much as she undoubtedly would have if they'd met.

'Cheers, Elsie,' she sneered, raising her glass in a toast to the letter as if it were the woman herself. 'I *will* take your house, but I'm not going to live there – and I will *never* call myself by your name. So say goodbye to your empire, 'cos it belongs to the *Prices* now!'

Tossing the letter aside, she downed her drink and reached for the bottle. She felt a lot better now – as if she'd redressed some of the wrongs that had been done to her mother.

There was no beer left.

She contemplated ordering another bottle from room service, but decided against it. She wasn't rich yet, and they probably charged double just for fetching it up on a tray. She'd just have to go and mix with the hoi polloi in the bar instead – which would have *disgusted* a lady like Elsie. But, oh, well . . .

Stashing the papers in her case, Maria slid it under the bed and stretched to relieve the tension in her neck. Catching sight of herself in the mirror, she grimaced. The past few days had certainly taken their toll on her complexion; she looked pale and drawn, and ten years older than she actually was.

Reaching for her make-up bag, she did a quick repair job, then headed out to the bar.

★   ★   ★

Joel Parry had been sitting in a corner booth for two solid hours with a shit-load of coke in his pocket, and he was pissed off *big* time. The Gallagher brothers had sent him to do a drop-off, but their guy hadn't shown, and now he couldn't reach them to ask what they wanted him to do because they weren't answering their phones.

Fan-fucking-*tastic*!

It was packed to the rafters in the bar, and loud as hell – everyone shouting to be heard above the booming 1970s soul-funk music being piped in from the nightclub in the basement below. Joel felt conspicuous with all the couples and groups around him. Smiley happy people, all dressed up for a Friday night out, and he was on his Jack – like the prick the Gallaghers obviously thought he was.

Well, he'd give their guy another half-hour, then he was gone – and the brothers could kiss the gear goodbye.

Until tomorrow morning.

Much as he wanted to tell them to piss off and quit using him as an errand boy, there was no way he could afford to make enemies of them. He still needed them to give him lay-ons while he was building his money up again.

If he ever found out who had mugged him, skinning him of all his money and gear and leaving him up to his eyeballs in debt, he would *kill* them. But at least the bastards had missed his face when they'd dragged him down that alley and kicked him from one end to the other like a football. His looks gave him the edge over the average dealer. Nobody ever questioned the smooth-talking handsome guy in the suit; they just took it for granted that his gear was clean and his prices fair. So, yeah, he might be skint, but he'd soon be back on top where he belonged.

For now, though, he was Nobby No One – gofer to the fucking Gallaghers.

Swallowing the last of his drink, Joel pushed his way to

the bar and slammed the glass down on the counter. He felt like being mean to someone, and the spotty little dick of a barman was it.

Looking around for his prey, he narrowed his eyes when he spotted a girl with long blonde hair sitting on a tall stool on the far side of the bar, staring into her glass as if she was oblivious to the din going on all around her.

He scanned the people standing behind her, sure that her man must be somewhere near by. Only a fool would let such a stunningly gorgeous woman loose in a bar on a Friday night in Manchester – with so many predatory men on the prowl. Surprisingly, she seemed to be completely alone.

Joel decided to take his chances with her. It wasn't like he had anything better to do with what was left of his lousy night. And she was one hell of a looker.

Forgetting all about the coke burning a hole in his pocket as his dick took control of his brain, he edged his way around the room. Lurching through a group of men who were too busy chatting about football to bother kicking off at him, he fell into her as if he'd been pushed.

'Sorry,' he said when she glanced up. 'It's a bit crowded in here tonight. Didn't hurt you, did I?'

'No, I'm okay,' Maria murmured, peering around confusedly as if she'd just woken up. She was sure there hadn't been this many people here when she came in. And why were they making so much noise? Didn't they know there were people trying to sleep in the rooms above?

'A man could die of thirst waiting for this idiot,' Joel commented, blowing off wearily. 'What do you reckon to my chances before last orders?'

'Sorry?' Maria frowned at him. 'Are you talking to me?'

'Hey, don't worry about it.' He gave her a slow smile. 'I have that effect on people. No, I was just moaning about him.' He nodded towards the barman who had miraculously reappeared and was frantically trying to keep up with customer demand on the other side of the bar. 'I don't suppose you're ready for another?' He cast a hopeful glance at her glass.

'I, er . . . no.' She shook her head, irritated by his presumption that she was looking for company. 'Thanks, but I'm just going to finish this and go up to my room.'

Eyes twinkling with amusement, Joel said, 'Hey, don't take this the wrong way, but that *wasn't* a come-on. I just thought you'd stand a better chance of attracting his attention than me. He seems more interested in the girls than the guys.'

'Oh, right.' Maria dipped her face to hide a blush. Great! She'd made a total fool of herself in under a minute. That *had* to be a record.

'Is it a deal, then?'

'Sorry?' Glancing up, Maria saw that he had his head tipped to the side, waiting for an answer to a question she hadn't heard. The alcohol was obviously affecting her hearing. It was time to get out of there.

'I said, is it a deal?' he repeated, smiling amusedly. 'You call the barman over – I buy the drinks.'

'Oh, I see,' Maria murmured. 'Well, no, not really. I mean, *yes*, I'll call him, if you think it'll make a difference. But I don't want a drink. I think I've had more than enough already.' This last bit was to herself, but Joel pounced on it.

'They don't sound like the words of a beautiful young woman having a fun night out.' Resting his elbow on the bar, Joel gave her his sincerest *I'm listening* look. 'Can I take it you're *not* having fun?'

Annoyed with herself, because she was obviously wearing her thoughts on her face for all the world to see, Maria said, 'I'm just a bit tired, that's all. And it's too noisy in here.' Flustered by the directness of his gaze as he peered into her eyes, she touched her forehead. 'I've, er, had a terrible headache all day, and I don't want to risk it coming back.'

'So, it's not the thought of having a drink with me that's scaring you away, then?' Joel said softly. 'Good, because there's no need to worry. I don't bite. Hell, I don't even bark – *most* of the time. Look . . . no leash.' He pulled his collar aside to reveal his neck.

'Okay, I believe you.' Maria smiled.

'That's better.' Joel rested his chin on his hand. 'So, about the barman . . . are you going to call him over, or do I have to die of dehydration?'

'I'll try. But don't blame me if he ignores me. He looks pretty busy.'

'And you look pretty gorgeous,' Joel purred. 'He'd have to be blind not to notice you.'

Biting her lip when he gave her one of the sexiest smiles she'd ever seen, Maria raised an arm to call the barman over. He came almost immediately, an eager look on his sweat-shiny face.

'What can I get you?'

'You can get *us* two Silver Mines, my friend,' Joel said, turning his head so that Maria couldn't see his face and fixing the younger man with a *back off* stare that was completely at odds with the friendly smile on his lips. 'I take it you know how to make them, don't you –' he peered at the other man's name badge '– *Rex*?'

Unnerved by the threat in Joel's ice-blue eyes, Rex nodded. 'Yeah, sure . . . Coming right up, sir.'

Maria smiled questioningly when Joel turned back to her. 'What just happened? I'm sure I said I didn't want a drink.'

'So you did,' he conceded, winking at her. 'But I figured if I went ahead and ordered, you'd be too polite to refuse. Surely you'll share *one* drink with me? That's not too much to ask, is it?'

Laughing softly, Maria shook her head. 'Okay, fine, I'll stay for one. But then I'm *going.*'

Grinning slyly, Joel took out his cigarettes and offered one to her – surreptitiously checking her ring finger when she leaned in closer for a light. It was bare. Great! Gorgeous *and* unmarried. All she needed to make her the perfect woman was money – and she must have *some* to be staying at a place like this.

Their drinks came in long ice-misted glasses. Handing one to Maria, Joel watched her face as she tasted it.

'What do you think?'

'It's lovely,' she said, nodding her approval. 'Thanks.'

'No, thank *you*. I was worried I might have lost my touch.'

'Sorry?' Drawing her head back, Maria gave him a quizzical look.

'Matching people to their perfect drinks,' he explained, cupping his hands and shaking them. 'Used to be a barman – once upon a *long* long time ago.'

'Ah, I see.' Maria took another sip of the darkly sweet drink. 'Well, you've definitely got this right.'

And she wasn't lying. The drink was delicious: rich and smooth, and deceptively intoxicating. She could already feel it working its way through her body, creating a pleasant tingling sensation in her arms and legs. But then, she *had* already polished off a bottle of beer in her room, and a couple of rum and cokes down here.

'Yeah, I was at the top of the game in my time,' Joel told her, shrugging modestly. 'I've moved on a bit since then, but there's nothing quite like the atmosphere of a good bar in full swing. Lights, music, happy punters.' Sighing wistfully, he pursed his lips. 'Wouldn't go back to it, though. It's much better being your own boss – hours to suit, no one to answer to but yourself.'

'Must be great,' Maria agreed, her gaze falling to his mouth.

His lips were a lovely shape – really sort of *kissable*. And he had lovely straight white teeth, and a lovely nose ... Lovely *everything*, in fact, with dark-blond hair, twinkling blue eyes, and a great-looking body. And he didn't seem remotely vain or arrogant, not like all the other good-looking guys she knew.

'It's Joel, by the way.'

Snapping out of her trance at the sound of his voice, Maria felt the heat rise to her cheeks when she realised she'd been staring at him. Taking the hand he was holding out, she gasped when a tingle of electricity snaked up her arm.

Careful, girl. You're more tipsy than you think.

'Maria,' she told him breathlessly. 'Sorry, I was miles away.'

'Somewhere nice, I hope,' Joel teased, holding on to her hand for several long moments. 'You know, I get the feeling we've met before.'

'Oh, I doubt it.' Maria slid her hand free before he felt her racing pulse and guessed the effect he was having on her. 'I don't actually live in Manchester. I *did*, but I left when I was younger. So I really don't think you could have seen me before.'

'Maybe not,' he conceded. 'But I *would* like to see you again. What are you doing tomorrow?'

'Going home.' Smiling at his disappointed expression, she took another drink, then bit her lip and rested her cheek on her hand. 'Out of interest,' she said, emboldened by the alcohol. 'Is *this* a come-on?'

'Might be.' Joel mirrored her position. 'So where's home?'

'Devon.' *Another* drink. 'I've a bit of business to take care of in the morning, then I'm gone.'

'Talk about bad timing. I was hoping I could persuade you to come out to dinner tomorrow.'

'Sorry.'

'So, this important business ... No chance of rescheduling?'

'None. Believe me, if I had a choice I wouldn't even *be* here.'

'And we'd never have met,' Joel said, aware that their voices were getting ever more sultry as their faces got closer.

'I suppose not,' Maria conceded, thinking it might have been better for her if they *hadn't*. How was she ever going to get to sleep tonight with the memory of those sexy eyes boring into her?

Reminded of sleep, she sat up a little straighter. 'Actually, I, er, really should be thinking about going. I've got an early start tomorrow.'

Joel narrowed his eyes as blue-grey cigarette smoke danced on the air between them. He'd been pissed off about coming here on a wild-goose chase, but meeting this babe had more than made up for it, and he didn't want to let the night end here – not now he was feeling so damn horny. She really was a very beautiful girl.

Reaching for her hand, sending a thrill skittering down her spine, he said, 'You're not really going to go and leave me by myself, are you? We'll probably never see each other again, so why not spend a bit of time together? We could find a decent club – have a dance, bit of dinner.'

'I don't know,' Maria said uncertainly, slipping her hand free yet again and reaching for her glass.

She was tipsy, but not so much that she could throw caution to the wind and leave the safety of the hotel with this man – no matter how gorgeous he was. She was enjoying his company, but that didn't mean she wanted to take it any further – and that was exactly what he would expect if she agreed to go out with him at this time of night, she was sure.

Watching as the doubts flitted across her eyes, Joel smoothly changed tack.

'*Or* . . . we could stay here, have a few more drinks and *talk*.' Gazing at her with puppy-dog eyes, making himself look even more adorable,' he added softly, 'And I'd *really* appreciate it if you said yes to that. I may *look* like a party animal, but I'm actually just a knackered old businessman with one too many meetings under his belt.'

Laughing softly, Maria felt the tension drift away. Not only a to-die-for hunk, but considerate, too.

'Okay, I'll stay for another drink. But only if you're sure I'm not keeping you from anything?'

'Nothing whatsoever,' Joel assured her. 'I'm free for the rest of the night. Ready for another?'

'Mmmm.' Finishing her drink, Maria handed the glass to him. 'What is that?' she asked, licking the sticky sweetness from her lips.

'A secret.' Winking, Joel called the barman over and ordered two doubles of the same. Then, turning back to Maria, he said, 'So, how long have you been modelling?'

'Excuse me?' Drawing her head back, she pursed her lips amusedly.

'Modelling,' he said again, looking her over slowly and whistling softly through his teeth. 'Catwalk . . . Body like that, it's *got* to be catwalk.'

'I don't *think* so.'

'What – not catwalk?'

'Not a *model.*'

'Really?' Joel raised a surprised eyebrow. 'You must be an actress, then.'

'Nope.'

'Maybe I *am* losing my touch. But I never give in without a fight.' Folding his arms, Joel tapped a fingernail against his teeth and stared at her for an age. Then, snapping his fingers, he said, 'Singer!'

'Definitely *not!*' Maria laughed. 'I've got a terrible voice.'

'For *real*?'

'For real.'

Joel pursed his kissable lips. 'Hmmm. I thought that's where I might have seen you before – in a studio, or at a gig, or something. But if you say you're not, then I guess you're not.' He shrugged. 'Go on, then – put me out of my misery.'

'I'm a teacher,' Maria said, aware that she was beginning to slur her words.

'*Really?*' He looked impressed.

'Uh huh.' Nodding, she gave a modest shrug. ''S only art, but it's okay.'

'Hey, don't sell yourself short,' Joel reprimanded her. 'Teaching is a great career – for *teachers*. *You* should be modelling, though.'

The barman brought their fresh drinks. Seeing that he still looked nervous, Joel tossed him a wink and told him to keep the change.

'Ah, that was sweet.' Maria wrinkled her nose cutely.

'I remember what it's like struggling on minimum wage,' Joel said, handing a glass to her and raising his own. 'To beauty *and* brains.'

Smiling, Maria clinked her glass against his and took a long drink. It was stronger than the last one, but so *nice*.

'So, haven't you ever considered modelling?' Joel asked, still playing the flattery card.

'No, never.' Maria shook her head slowly. It was beginning to feel weird – heavy on the outside, light on the inside.

'You should. You can make serious money in that game – with the right guidance.'

'Sounds like you know all about it.'

'Kind of.' Joel shrugged casually. 'I'm more involved in the music industry, really. But I know people who know people, so if you ever *did* feel like getting into it . . .'

'I don't think so.' Maria was trying so hard to look cool and in control, but her lips kept smiling by themselves, and her arms felt floaty.

'It's got to be the cushiest job ever,' Joel persisted.

'Actually,' Maria said, speaking slowly because the words felt clumsy on her tongue, 'I don't *need* a job.'

Her eyes were glassy as she gazed at Joel – and all the more stunning for it, he thought – like sapphires on ice.

'Oh, yeah? Rich, are we?'

'You could say that,' Maria giggled. 'See, I have just found out that I have got a . . . *Oops!*' Catching herself, she threw a hand up to her mouth and giggled. 'Oh, no, no, no!' She wagged a finger in his face. 'I can't tell you about *that*. I don't even *know* you.'

'Course you do,' Joel purred, slipping a supportive arm around her waist as she began to sway on the stool. 'We're friends now. You can tell me anything . . .'

5

Waking to the rumble of an early-morning tram trundling by down below, Joel rubbed his eyes and looked around. As the room slowly came into focus in the half-light, he looked at Maria beside him and smiled. She looked so innocent with her eyes closed and her hair fanned out around her head.

Getting up, he padded through to the bathroom for a wash, then came back and got dressed without waking Maria. Taking a sheet of paper off the little pad on the table, he started to write a note, then changed his mind and screwed it up. They'd had a great night, but they were never going to see each other again, so why complicate things?

Slipping his jacket on, Joel had a quick mooch around, then let himself quietly out.

The blind was partially drawn when Maria woke up some time later; morning sunlight streamed across the bed in a glittery dust-speckled shaft. Remembering where she was, she whipped her head around. She didn't know if she was more relieved or offended to discover that she was alone.

She was certainly ashamed.

Burying her face in the pillow, she groaned when she smelled the dark, musky scent of aftershave on the cotton slip.

Oh, God! How could she have let him sweet-talk his way into her bed? How absolutely *stupid* was that? And *her* of all people. She had never had a one-night stand. A few short-term relationships, yes, but *never* a one-night throwaway shag. That was the kind of thing that slags did, and Maria had fought so hard not to land herself with *that* tag. Care kids got enough stick without giving the haters ammunition.

Oh, Joel had seen her coming, all right. Flatter her with a sexy grin, and get her pissed on a few fancy drinks, and . . . *Hey, presto! Wham, bam, thank you, mam!*

But no, that wasn't really fair. She'd wanted him as much as he'd wanted her by the time they'd left the bar last night. She'd been drunk, but not so much that she hadn't known – *almost* – exactly what she was doing.

Well, more fool her for reading more into it than was there, because it obviously hadn't meant a thing to him. The only consolation was that it had happened here and not back home, so there was no danger of anyone finding out how low she had sunk.

Tossing the quilt aside in a fit of self-disgust, Maria marched into the bathroom and scrubbed herself clean in the shower – *praying* that she hadn't picked up anything nasty from her sleazy encounter.

Stupid, stupid, STUPID!

Feeling a little more in control once she was dressed, she checked her purse. The money was still there, so at least he hadn't ripped her off. That would have been a total disaster. And she'd have had nobody to blame but herself.

Making herself a strong coffee, she called the mobile number on the card that the solicitor had given her. If she had been wavering before, she now knew *exactly* what she had to do.

'It's Maria Price,' she said when Nigel answered. 'Sorry for disturbing you so early, but I've changed my mind about seeing the house. Would it be possible to show me around?'

'Absolutely,' Nigel said without hesitation. 'When?'

'As soon as you can,' Maria said, frowning at the eagerness in his voice.

The only reason she wanted to see the house was to gauge its worth for herself before handing it over to an estate agent. She had no intention of granting Elsie's wish to keep a 'Davidson' in residence. And after disgracing herself last night, she had no intention of staying in Manchester one moment longer than she had to.

'I was just about to set off, as it happens,' Nigel said cheerily. 'Traffic permitting, I could pick you up in – say – half an hour?'

'Make it an hour so you don't have to rush,' she told him curtly. 'And you don't have to come for me. I've got the address. I'll catch a bus.'

Maria didn't want to offend him, but he obviously had an emotional attachment to this estate, so the more detached she stayed from him, the less guilty she would feel when she told him what she intended to do.

'Please let me pick you up,' Nigel said. 'I'm not being funny, Miss Price, but you *really* don't want to be taking a bus on that route at this time of the morning. I have it on good authority from one of the secretaries that it gets quite hairy when kids from rival schools come face to face.'

'Fine.' Maria conceded, sighing wearily. 'I'll be waiting outside in half an hour.'

Flipping his phone shut, Nigel slipped it into his pocket, frowning. Maria had sounded odd, and he hoped it was nothing he'd done. It *had* been awkward when she'd been leaving the office yesterday – when they'd shaken hands and he'd snatched his away like an idiot. But she'd been smiling when she left, so he doubted it was that.

What, then?

Taking his jacket off the stand, he pulled it on and reached into the pocket for his comb. Standing in front of the mirror he tidied his hair, easing it into place to disguise the thinning bits. His jaw clenched when his mother came out of the parlour behind him.

'Who were you talking to just now?' she asked – as if it was any of her business.

'A client.'

'A *client*?' She cast a disapproving glance at the dumpy old grandmother clock standing against the stair wall in its glossy walnut dress. 'At *this* time?'

'An *important* client,' he informed her coldly, heading for the door.

'Aren't you going to say goodbye to your aunt?' she called after him as he rushed out.

Shuddering, Nigel slammed the door and hurried down the steps, deactivating his car alarm as he went. Climbing into the driver's seat, he started the powerful engine and shot forward, spraying gravel up in a neat arc as he gunned towards the gates. Pausing there just long enough to fasten his seat belt, he roared out onto the lane and headed for the motorway with his jaw still angrily clenched.

Say goodbye to his aunt, indeed! He'd had more than enough of the two of them last night – quizzing him about his love life like interrogators in the goddam Gestapo! Hitler would have been *proud* to have them on side. They could strip the flesh off a suspect with just a look.

Well, he wasn't going through another night of that. If his aunt's enormous backside was still suffocating the Chesterfield when he got home tonight, he'd turn right around and head back into town to book himself into a hotel.

The Britannia, perhaps . . .

Well, why not? It *had* been rated 'Best in the North-West' three years running. And it wasn't as if he'd be doing it to be near Maria. That was just ridiculous. Anyway, she was leaving this afternoon. She wouldn't even *be* there.

How weird if he got the same room, though. Now that *would* be freaky. Like some sort of sign that they . . .

'Oh, pack it in, you bloody idiot!' Nigel scolded himself out loud. 'It isn't going to happen – not in a million years.'

And that was the sad truth, he knew, because a gorgeous young woman like Maria would never look twice at a gangly, too-tall, too-thin fool like him.

But if he had to be alone for the rest of his life, he'd rather *that* than go along with the ridiculous suggestion that his mother and aunt had come up with last night. Christ, he'd rather date *Adam* than put himself through the humiliation of joining a dating agency. But the way his mother and her sister had ambushed him with it, he wouldn't be surprised if they didn't already have an application form.

Shit!

If they *had* picked one up, Nigel wouldn't put it past them to fill it out in his name. But he dreaded to think what they'd say about him, given that neither of them had a clue who he really was, or what he wanted out of life.

He could just see it . . .

Q: *What kind of women would you be interested in meeting?*
A: *Any!*
Q: *Do you prefer: blondes, brunettes, or redheads?*
A: *Any!*
Q: *Age group: 18-30 31-45 46-60 61-90*
A: *ANYYYY!!!*

A chill hand grabbed his gut as it occured to him that if *he*'d thought about them filling the forms out, *they* might not be too far behind. Closing his eyes, he groaned.

BBBBBRRRRRAAAARRRPPPP . . .

Almost dying of fright at the volume and closeness of the horn blast, Nigel snapped his eyes open and almost *choked* when he saw that he was straying into the path of an articulated lorry.

Swerving wildly onto the hard shoulder, he came to a screeching stop, his heart beating so hard and fast that it felt as if it was making a break for freedom. Leaning his head back, he breathed slowly and evenly until it slowed to near normal.

Angry now, he brought his fist down on the steering wheel. Shit! He couldn't put it off any longer – he had to get away from his mother before she *killed* him.

He'd give Quay Moves a call when he got to the office – see if they could slot him in to view one of their Deansgate apartments this afternoon. He could certainly afford it, and it was high time he had a place of his own. And if his mother tried to guilt-trip him into changing his mind by crying about the mausoleum she called home being too big without him, he would suggest that she move her precious sister in!

Decided, he eased back into the traffic and headed into Manchester with a lighter heart.

6

Standing in the sunny quarry-tiled hallway forty minutes later, Nigel watched Maria's face as she turned in a slow circle, taking everything in. She loved it, he could tell. And if she loved it, she might just consider keeping it.

Not, he reminded himself sternly, that it made any difference to *him* if she did. But it would be nice to keep the tradition alive – him handling the affairs for the niece that his uncle had handled for the aunt.

'It's quite something, isn't it?' he said.

'Beautiful,' Maria agreed, her voice soft as she fought to stem the tide of emotions washing over her.

She hadn't expected to *feel* anything, but now that she was here, in the place where the family she had supposedly shared blood ties with had lived, she was feeling a little choked, wondering how different life might have been had she had the chance to come here when the Davidsons were alive.

But she knew who to thank for that, didn't she – her loving *aunt*, Elsie, who had claimed to be so interested in Maria that she went to the trouble of hiring a private detective to track her down, yet hadn't made the slightest attempt to rescue her from those awful care homes. She hadn't even bothered to contact Maria to let the girl know that she wasn't alone in the world – not even when Maria turned sixteen, and the authorities couldn't have stopped her. Elsie had chosen to leave it until she was *dead* – dangling the family carrot in front of Maria's eyes, then snatching it cruelly away, leaving the house and money as a consolation prize.

'It looks a little neglected, I know, but it's actually in superb condition structurally,' Nigel was telling her, oblivious to the fact that she was so deeply immersed in her own thoughts. 'Miss Davidson was very sensible about maintenance. She had annual inspections done, inside and out, and any problems were dealt with immediately.

'There's no double glazing,' he went on, sounding more like an estate agent now than a solicitor. 'But that's par for the course in this type of property, because original stained-glass and leaded windows are incredibly difficult to replace with anything approaching like quality. And I'm afraid the boiler system is fairly old, but that's easily remedied. It depends whether you want instant hot water or are prepared to plan ahead.'

Smiling politely as Nigel followed her around, prattling about the fixtures and fittings, Maria phased him out and explored the ground floor, soaking everything up and committing it to memory to tell Beth all about it when she got home.

Two reception rooms branched off on either side of the front door, both large, with tall, bay-fronted windows. There were dust sheets draped over the bulky furniture, and everything smelled musty and neglected. Wrinkling her nose, Maria made a mental note to have everything valued. If it was worth anything, it could get sold. If not, it would go on the bin wagon. The sooner the place was cleared out and aired, the better the prospect of a quick sale.

There was a dark dining room with yet more dust-sheeted furniture, and an enormous kitchen with a long marble-topped table, a deep butler sink, and a dusty black cooking range. The window looked out onto a vast jungle-like garden, and there was a glass-panelled door leading to a dead-plant-riddled conservatory.

Making her way upstairs, Maria was pleasantly surprised. In contrast to the gloom of the lower floor, the landing was warm and bright, thanks to the stained-glass windows at either end of the landing, which cast a lovely muted rainbow over the area.

Four bedrooms led off the landing, the smallest of which was bigger than Maria's whole flat. They all had built-in closets and fireplaces, and the master had a small en-suite bathroom.

In contrast, the family bathroom was huge, beautifully decorated in deeply glazed blue and green tiles, and had an ornate claw-footed bath suite. No shower, which was a shame, but it would be easy enough to install one.

If she were planning to stay – which she wasn't.

Back out on the landing, Nigel opened a door which Maria had assumed to be a cupboard. She was surprised to see that it concealed a narrow staircase.

'There are two attic rooms,' he said, waving her to go up ahead of him. 'They were servants' quarters originally, but I don't think they've been used for a very long time. Miss Davidson must have used them as a storage area, because there are lots of boxes of clothes and jewellery, and what have you. It all belongs to *you* now, of course,' he added, conscious of his voice booming in the uncarpeted space. 'I'm sure you'll have fun sorting through it.'

He smiled, getting a pained look in return from Maria. The last thing she wanted was to nose through Elsie Davidson's belongings. There was no telling *what* she might find.

Looking around thoughtfully, Nigel said, 'These could so easily be converted into studio flats if you decide that you don't want to live here. With a little investment, you could make a tidy income letting the house as separate units. We manage a similar property for a client who lives abroad. I could show you the books if you're interested.'

'I'll think about it,' Maria replied vaguely.

Nigel seemed genuine enough, but she had a sneaking suspicion that he would try to dissuade her or obstruct her if she told him that she wanted rid of the place – and she really couldn't be bothered with the hassle.

'Right, I think I've seen everything I need to see,' she said, making her way back down the stairs. 'When can I sign everything?'

A little thrown by the abrupt way she'd brought the tour to an end, Nigel clattered down the stairs behind her.

'I can have all the relevant forms ready by early this afternoon. If you'd like to come into the office at around two, it shouldn't take too long.'

Maria checked her watch. It was only ten, and her train wasn't until five.

'Two's fine,' she said. 'Shall we go?'

Letting her out, Nigel reset the alarm and locked the door – trying his damnedest not to notice how brilliantly the sunlight picked out the gold in her hair as she preceded him down the path to the car.

Gazing out of the car window as they set off, Maria contemplated the events of the last week. Everything she'd had planned for the future had been flipped on its head and turned inside out. She'd inherited a large amount of money, and an amazing house – a fact that was finally beginning to sink in now that she had actually seen it. But it was a bitter-sweet legacy, because the part that was missing was the family.

Jolted out of her thoughts when they took a sharp left, she felt the blood drain from her face when she realised where they were heading. Nigel had taken the back roads through Withington that morning, but he seemed to have opted for the less congested route back into town – directly past the Merrydown Estate.

Unprepared for re-entering the territory of her youth and facing the memories that might evoke, a sickly churning started up in her stomach. She wanted to yell at Nigel to change course, but she couldn't bring herself to say it for fear of making herself look hysterical. Then, suddenly, the dark outline of the flats loomed into view.

Maria stared straight ahead when they stopped at a red light alongside Jacob House – the outermost of the concrete giants that made up the estate. She could hear her breath rasping shallowly in her chest as the dark shadow of the past blanketed the car like a cold dead hand. In the life-flashing-before-you way of the drowning man, a thousand memories flitted across her mind's eye. She'd experienced the best and worst times of her life here, and her every action and reaction since had been a direct result of that.

But wasn't this the best opportunity she would ever have to face and conquer those demons? She would never have come back of her own accord, but now that fate had brought her here . . .

Holding her breath, Maria forced herself to turn and look at Jacob House, fully expecting a bolt of lightning to snake down and smash it into a million pieces, bringing the whole thing down around her head and burying her alive – just as it had so many times in her sweat-soaked nightmares.

Nothing happened.

The dull grey eyes of the old concrete man looked sadly back at her, his voice whispering '*Welcome home*' on the softly stirring breeze. It hit Maria in the chest with the force of a punch, bringing tears to her eyes.

'Stop!' she cried, when the lights turned to green and Nigel pulled away. 'Please . . . I need to get out.'

'What, *here*?' Whipping his head around, Nigel stared at her as if she'd gone mad. 'Do you know how *dangerous* it is?'

'Probably not as bad as it used to be,' she retorted, her chin jerking up defiantly as she struggled to unbuckle the seat belt.

'Don't be fooled by the clean-up,' Nigel warned, his gaze darting every which way as he reluctantly slowed down. 'It's only cosmetic. It's still the same people.'

'People like *me*, you mean?' Raising an eyebrow, Maria gave him a challenging look. 'I *was* born here, don't forget. And I'd probably still *be* here if my mum hadn't been killed.'

'Yes, of course,' Nigel blustered, pulling up to the kerb. 'I didn't mean to offend you. And I know that most of the people are basically decent, it's just that, well, I've, um, had a couple of unpleasant experiences around here. My last car was taken off me at knifepoint, you see . . .' Trailing off, he gave an embarrassed shrug, his scarlet cheeks making his hair look almost ginger.

Sensing that he would never have revealed such a painful and humiliating experience if he weren't genuinely concerned for her safety, Maria released her irritation in a loud sigh.

'I'm sure that was terrible,' she said kindly. 'And I appreciate your concern, but there's really no need to worry about me, Mr Grayson, because I haven't got anything on me that's worth taking.' Getting out, she smiled before closing the door. 'I'll be fine – honestly. I just need to walk around and see what's what.'

'Please be careful,' Nigel urged, lowering the window part-way. 'And it's, um, Nigel, by the way. No need for the formality.'

'Nigel it is, then.' Still smiling, Maria shoved her hands into her pockets and waited for him to move off.

No need for the formality, indeed! She'd never met a more starchy, stiff-necked man in her life.

Crossing over the road when he'd gone, she walked slowly down Backhouse Lane – or The Border as it had been known by the residents on the Merrydown and the Greenwood: the identical estates it separated.

The Greenwood had been levelled now, and a new estate had been built in its place, made up of rows of bland red-brick houses, with glossy black fences, puke-green doors, and tiny burglar-proof windows sporting council-issue nets. All very neat and tidy, but with zero atmosphere – as if character had been abandoned for the sake of uniformity.

The Merrydown hadn't been demolished yet, but that was obviously on the cards. Every flat was empty, and there was a real air of desolation and abandonment about the place with all the doors standing open and most of the windows smashed.

No dirty-faced kids yelling and screaming as they raced around with their stick-swords and bin-lid shields . . .

No teenagers loitering in the stairwells, loading too much weed into the spliffs they were learning to roll – badly . . .

No old-timers on the balconies, dancing drunkenly in the twilight to Lovers' Rock, sharing white rum and hazy memories with their homies from the Islands . . .

Maria felt the ghostly gaze of the past following her as she reached the end of The Border and continued on towards town. Everything had changed too much. There was nothing left to remind her of the years she had shared here with her mother but the pictures in her head.

Coming to the narrow pedestrian bridge straddling the dual carriageway up ahead, she leaned her elbows on the metal handrail and blinked rapidly to hold the stinging tears at bay. Crying wouldn't change anything. Time moved forward, never back, and there wasn't a thing you could do but accept that.

Sighing heavily, Maria looked glumly down at the traffic streaming past below. *This* was the reality of life, she decided. Forget all that mushy sentimental memory nonsense. None of that really meant anything. People came and went, lived and died, loved and hated. But at the end of the day, they were always alone. Life was just a relentless flow of strangers passing through the same space. Seconds, minutes, hours, days, years apart . . . On and on . . . Over and over . . . Never really connecting, or—

''Scuse me.'

Startled out of her thoughts, Maria turned around. There was an overweight woman standing behind her, one hand on the push-bar of a shopping-laden pram, the other gripping the hand of a dirty-faced little girl.

'I hope you ain't thinking of jumping?' she said, as if she wouldn't really give a toss either way.

'God, no!' Maria said quickly, shocked that anyone could *think* such a thing about her. 'I was just reminiscing.'

'Only if you *was* thinking of it,' the woman went on as if Maria hadn't even spoken, '*don't*. It ain't high enough to kill you, and none of these bastards round here would get you an ambulance.'

'I'm *not* going to jump,' Maria insisted.

'If you say so.' The woman obviously didn't believe her. 'Wanna move, then?'

'Sorry.' Squashing herself up against the railings, Maria gave an apologetic smile. 'Bit narrow, isn't it?'

Muttering something under her breath, the woman pushed her load past. A few steps on, she turned back and gestured with a nod at Maria's handbag which was hanging loosely over her shoulder, unzipped and clearly displaying the contents.

'Do yourself a favour and fasten that before someone knifes you for it,' she said, adding ominously, 'Fact, I'd piss off home before the gangs come out, if I was you. They'll clock you for an outsider straight off. You'll get mashed.'

'I'm not an outsider,' Maria replied, zipping up her bag. 'I was born here.'

'*You?*' the woman snorted, looking at Maria's clean clothes and nice hair. 'Come off it.'

'Honest,' Maria said, aware that she was roughening her tone of voice to bring herself down to the woman's level. 'It was years back, mind. I used to live over there.' She nodded towards the flats.

'On the Merrydown?'

'Yeah. Brook House.'

'Oh, yeah?' Narrowing her eyes, the woman pulled the pram back up the slope to her. 'Knew the Stokeses then, did you?'

'Linda and Frankie?' Amazing herself with the speed with which the names slid from her tongue, Maria smiled. 'God, yeah! Lin was my mate.'

'Was she, now?'

'Yeah . . . and their Frankie was my first boyfriend.' Pausing, Maria grimaced sheepishly. 'Well, not *really* my boyfriend, but I did have a major crush on him. All the girls did, but I used to pretend I was going out with him and warn them off. Do you know them?'

'Should do. I'm Lin.'

'You are *not!*' Maria squawked, bringing her hand up to her mouth and giving her old friend a surreptitious once-over.

They were the same age, but Lin looked closer to *forty*-one than twenty-one. She was fat and scruffy, with her dull brown hair scraped roughly back off her spotty forehead, and her thick legs were covered in scabs.

'I don't remember *you*,' Lin said, blatantly looking her over.

'Maria Price.'

'No shit?' Lin's face opened as recognition set in. 'Maria Price! Yeah, I remember you. Your mam got snuffed by that drunk driver outside the brewery. Shit, that was a while back . . . How long ago was that?'

'Ten years,' Maria said, not wanting to dwell on that particular episode. 'So, what happened to the gang? What's everyone doing?'

'Jeezus, where do I start?' Lin scratched her head and looked skyward, narrowing her eyes as she struggled to remember. 'Sue moved to Ardwick not long after you went. Then Cathy's mam and dad split up, so they moved to Gorton. Oh, and remember Janice? Well, she run off when she was fourteen, to live with some old bloke she'd been shagging.' Pausing, she shrugged. 'The rest of us are still around. We don't hang out all that much now, but this pair takes up most of me time.'

Pair?

Maria shot a glance into the pram. Having assumed that it belonged to the little girl, she was surprised to see a baby nestled among the budget packs of toilet rolls, Pot Noodles, and oversized cans of dog food.

'That's Ant'ny,' Lin told her proudly. 'Spit of his dad, which is a shame, but at least he's got my nose so he won't grow up a complete minger. This is Keely.' She yanked on the little girl's hand. 'Her dad was Jeff Tully from our class – remember him?'

Frowning as she tried to think, Maria had a sudden vision of a spotty kid with big ears. 'Yeah.' She smiled. 'How's he doing?'

'He's dead,' Lin informed her flatly. 'OD'd before she was born.'

'Christ, that's awful.'

'No, it ain't. He was a selfish smackhead bastard.'

Trying not to react when Keely's tongue snaked out to mop up a trail of snot that was dribbling out of her nose, Maria said, 'So, how old are they?'

'She's three, he's seven mumf,' Lin said, reaching for the baby's dummy which had fallen out of his mouth and stuffing it back in. Straightening up, she patted her pockets. 'Aw, shit, I've left my fags at home. You haven't got a spare one, have you?'

'Yeah, sure.' Unzipping her bag again, Maria took out her cigarettes and handed one over. Lighting one for herself, she wasn't surprised that her hands were shaking. This was so weird – like stepping out of a time machine to find that everything has changed except you.

'What happened to Vicky?' she asked. 'Is she still around?'

'Yeah, course.' Lin inhaled deeply. 'She moved up to Denton after she had her first kid, but she couldn't hack it so she come back. She's over on The Skids now.'

Maria was surprised to hear that – and not in a good way. The Skids was an older block of flats behind the park, where the glue sniffers used to congregate in the bin cupboards with their stinking plastic bags. The kids on the estate had avoided it like the plague, terrified of the sniffers going off on mad paranoid rants, laughing hysterically at whatever whacked-out hallucinations they were having. There had been a rumour going round just before Maria left that the boggle-eyed head cases had found an old man dead in one of the flats and made a barbecue out of him on the stairs. *Way* too crazy.

'I'd have thought they'd have knocked that down by now,' Maria said, giving a little shudder.

'Nah, it's still there.' Lin sneered. 'They offered *me* a flat there when me mam kicked me out, but I told them to stick it. I'd rather have slept rough – pregnant or not. I've got me own house now,' she informed Maria proudly.

'Really?' Maria said – as if she actually cared.

'Yeah, behind the church,' Lin said, leaning comfortably back against the railings and crossing her scabby legs. 'I'm waiting on a transfer at the minute, though, 'cos it might as well be made of fuckin' cardboard the way the roof leaks when it's raining. But at least I've got a garden. I'd *die* if I was stuck up the top of that block, like Vicky and her four.'

'*Four?*' Maria gasped. 'You're *joking*!'

'No, why? What's up with that?'

'Nothing. I'm just surprised, that's all.'

'I take it *you* haven't managed to get caught yet, then?'

'No!' Maria shook her head, only just managing to keep a look of sheer horror off her face.

'No fella,' Lin surmised, nodding sympathetically. 'Ah, well, don't worry. I'm sure your turn will come soon enough.' Finishing her cigarette, she flicked it over the railing and straightened up with a sigh. 'Oh, well . . . best get a move on. I'm dropping these round our Frank's so I can have a bit of time to myself. Can't have a piss in peace without one of 'em banging the loo door down these days.'

'Your Frankie's still around, then?' Maria asked, feigning nonchalance as a fluttery feeling stirred in her stomach.

She hadn't been lying when she'd said she'd had the biggest crush on him. Frankie Stokes had been cool, with his long hair, his dragon tattoo, and the flashy BMX bike he'd nicked off some lad at the park and resprayed silver. He'd been a proper bad boy, and all the girls had wanted to be his girlfriend.

But that was *then*, Maria reminded herself. If he'd changed as much as his sister had, he was probably big, fat, bald and toothless by now.

'He lives with his bird over the back of the school,' Lin said. 'They've got three little ones so they don't notice if I slip mine in. And they love their Uncle Frank – don't you, Keels?' Grinning, she gave the little girl a rough shake.

Tired eyes riveted on Maria, Keely nodded.

'He's dead good with them,' Lin went on proudly. 'Better dad to 'em than their proper ones were, anyhow. And he's belting round the house, an' all – always cleaning, and fixing stuff. The lazy bitch he's shacked up with don't deserve him. I keep telling him he needs someone like me, who's a bit more appreciative.'

'Uh huh,' Maria murmured, wondering if she'd somehow landed on Mars by mistake.

She'd grown up with these *breeders*, but she couldn't be more different from them if she tried. And it wasn't just that Lin sounded like she had the hots for her own brother that was making her uneasy, it was the thought of all the kids they had produced between them. She couldn't imagine having *one* child at this point in her life, never mind two, three or – God forbid! – *four*. Christ, she hadn't even had four serious boyfriends yet.

'So, are you gonna go and see her, or what?'

'Sorry?' Snapping out of her thoughts, Maria frowned. 'Oh, you mean Vicky? Well, yeah, I guess so.'

'Right, well, it's number thirty-seven,' Lin said. 'But don't tell her you saw me, yeah?'

'I won't,' Maria assured her, folding her arms. 'Say hello to your Frankie for me.'

'I will.' Lin looked her over again, storing up the details to pass on to her brother. 'Anyhow, I'd best go before he pisses off out. See you again sometime.'

'Yeah, bye,' Maria said, not wanting to delay her any further. Lin's carping tone was grating on her nerves, and the little girl staring at her like that was freaking her out. 'Take care,' she added, keeping her arms firmly crossed in case Lin expected a hug. 'It was nice seeing you.'

Waving until they had disappeared from view, Maria sighed with relief. She just thanked God that Lin hadn't asked for her number, because she definitely would have had to lie.

Checking the time, she was surprised to see that it was still only a quarter to eleven. It felt as if she'd been trapped with Lin for much, much longer than the twenty minutes or so that it had probably been.

She had plenty of time before she had to go and sign those papers, so it wouldn't be a problem to call in on Vicky for a quick visit. Trouble was, now that she had seen Lin, she wasn't sure she *wanted* to. If Vicky had turned out even *half* as rough, it would be horrible.

But could she really come all this way without at least saying hello? It had been a long time since they'd last seen each other, but they *had* been best mates.

And if it didn't work out – so what? She'd be going home in a few hours. She'd never have to see her again.

7

Vicky switched the iron off and stuffed the board into its slot between the cooker and the fridge. That was the only problem with this flat – lack of space. Apart from that, and the fact that the kids were rapidly outgrowing their shared bedrooms, she had no complaints.

Heaping the pressed clothes onto the couch ready to put away when she'd finished, she pushed her sleeves up and started on the washing-up. Almost immediately, a loud repetitive banging started up in the boys' bedroom down the hall. Tyrell was obviously awake and looking for mischief. Drying her hands, Vicky went to see what he was doing. He was only one, but *boy* could he cause havoc when he got started.

Tyrell was standing up in the cot with a huge toothy grin on his face, whacking his brother's Walkman against the wooden bars with a pudgy little hand. Luke had obviously left it on the window ledge again – more fool him. He'd been warned that Ty could reach it, but it looked like he was going to have to learn the hard way.

'Give me that, you little bugger,' Vicky said, rescuing the Walkman and putting it out of reach on top of the wardrobe. Getting another grin from Tyrell, she couldn't help but smile. He was going to be a real heartbreaker, this one. Scooping him up, she gave him a big noisy kiss.

'Bic bic!' he demanded, wrapping his arms around her neck.

'In a minute.' Hoisting him onto her hip, Vicky opened the wardrobe. 'Let's get you dressed first.'

The melodic *bing-bong* of the doorbell sounded loudly in the uncarpeted hallway behind them.

'Dada!' Tyrell kicked his legs excitedly.

'Not unless he's lost his keys again,' Vicky said, grabbing a T-shirt and a pair of jeans. 'Shall we go and see if silly Daddy's lost his keys?'

Smiling in anticipation of seeing her boyfriend when she opened the front door, Vicky's jaw dropped when she saw who it was.

'Oh my *God*! *Maria*! Where the hell did *you* spring from?'

Tears of relief sprang to Maria's eyes. She'd been so nervous coming up the stairs, worrying that Vicky wouldn't remember her. But Vicky not only recognised her, she seemed genuinely pleased to see her. And, unlike Lin, whom time had battered and abused, Vicky looked exactly the same as ever. Same thick black hair, pretty snub nose, and wide smile – just ten years more wisdom in her lovely hazel eyes.

'You look fantastic,' Maria said, meaning it.

'Gee, *thanks*!' Vicky retorted amusedly. 'But you don't have to sound *quite* so surprised.'

'I didn't mean it like *that*,' Maria countered quickly. 'It's just that when I heard you had four kids, I kind of presumed—'

'That I was a fat old slapper?' Vicky interrupted, rolling her eyes good-naturedly. 'Yeah, well, as you can see, I'm not. And neither are *you*,' she said, looking Maria over with approval. 'Check *you* out, girl! You're gorgeous.'

'Don't be daft,' Maria murmured, blushing.

'Aw, you know you're a babe,' Vicky teased, dismissing the modesty with a flap of her hand. 'God, I can't believe you're here. How did you find me?'

'I bumped into Lin,' Maria admitted guiltily. 'Only she sort of said not to mention that I'd seen her.'

'I *bet* she did,' Vicky grunted. 'I lent the cheeky bitch thirty quid a couple of weeks back and I haven't seen her since. But never mind. She'll be round soon enough when she needs me again – and see if I give her a *thing* till she's paid me back! Anyway, never mind her . . .' Another dismissive flap of the hand. 'Let me get a proper look at you.'

Stepping back, Vicky reached out with her free arm when Maria came in and hugged her. Leading her into the lounge, she put Tyrell into his playpen in the corner and scooped the clothes up off the couch.

'Sorry it's such a tip, but I was just getting started on the cleaning when trouble woke up. Not that it makes any difference. It doesn't matter how many times you put things away, the kids just bring it straight back out. Anyway, just give me a minute and I'll make a brew.'

Taking her jacket off, Maria laid it over the back of the couch and sat down. Looking around, she saw a mess of dolls and books and jigsaw pieces strewn around the floor, but the rest of the room was quite clean and tidy – which she found amusing, considering how messy Vicky's bedroom had always been when they were kids.

Spotting several framed photographs vying for space between some potted plants on a wall unit next to the playpen, she couldn't resist going over for a closer look. They were mostly shots of four children of various ages: two girls, and two boys – the youngest being the baby in the playpen. Apart from the older boy, who had blond hair and Vicky's hazel eyes, they all appeared to be mixed-race.

Jumping when something hit the back of her leg, Maria turned around and saw a little stuffed dog lying on the floor behind her. Tyrell was staring up at her, an expectant grin on his chubby face.

'Did *you* do that?' she asked, squatting down until their faces were level.

He had the biggest, blackest eyes she'd ever seen, with long glossy lashes that curled up almost to his eyebrows, and his hair was arranged in a series of silky-soft bump-plaits around his head.

Picking up the dog, she handed it back to him. 'Cheeky,' she said when he immediately threw it back at her. Holding it out to him again, she pulled it back when he reached for it, sending him into a fit of giggles.

Coming back, Vicky smiled at them as she went through to the small kitchen to fill the kettle.

'He likes you,' she called back. 'I could hear him laughing from the bedroom – and that's an honour, let me tell you, 'cos he can be a right stuck-up little so-and-so when he wants to be. I never knew a baby who could give out such wicked looks.'

'He's adorable.' Handing the dog to Tyrell, Maria stood up. 'You must be really proud.'

'I am.' Vicky smiled back over her shoulder. 'Tea okay?'

'Fine, thanks.' Maria came into the doorway and leaned against the frame. The kitchen was spotless, and really bright and homely. Nothing like her own dismal dump. 'Where are the others?' she asked, not wanting to think about home just now.

'School,' Vicky said, taking two cups out of the cupboard.

Maria raised an eyebrow. 'You must have started young if they're at school already.'

'I was fifteen – more fool me.' Squeezing past her, Vicky reached for one of the photos of all four kids together. 'That's my eldest, Luke,' she said, pointing at the blond boy. 'He's six, so he's full-time now. Siobhan's four, and Demi's three – they're both at nursery, but Vonny's going up to proper school next year. Tyrell's just turned one. He's at playgroup, but it's only a couple of times a week at the moment. I love him to bits,' she added quietly, as if not to offend him. 'But I can't *wait* till he's full-time like the rest.'

'I don't know how you do it,' Maria murmured respectfully. 'I'd crack up if I had *one*.'

'You just get on with it. Not much else you *can* do once they're there.' Shrugging, Vicky put the photo back and went to finish making the tea.

'I must admit I was surprised when I heard you had four,' Maria said. 'You always said you didn't want any.'

'I *didn't*,' Vicky confirmed with a wry smile.

'So how come you didn't take precautions?' Immediately the words were out of her mouth, Maria wanted to kick herself. 'I'm sorry,' she spluttered. 'That's none of my business.'

'I *was* on the pill,' Vicky told her, not seeming to mind. 'I'm one of the unlucky ones that it doesn't work on, only nobody bothered telling me that could happen until I got caught with Ty. They said I'd have to have my tubes tied to stop it happening again. That, or quit having sex – and, honey, there ain't *no* way I'm going without dick!' Giving a dirty chuckle, she handed a cup to Maria. 'So, I got myself done, and now I can shag my brains out whenever I want without worrying about getting caught. Wish I'd done it *years* ago.'

Maria smiled shyly. The girls back home talked about their boyfriends, but never about the sex part of it – and certainly not as bluntly as Vicky just had.

Going back into the living room, they sat together on the couch. Putting her cup down on the table, Vicky started looking for her cigarettes.

'So, what's been happening since they took you away?' she asked, slotting her hand down the side of the couch arm. 'We were so worried when we found out what had happened. No one could believe it. It was like – *shit*! Maria's *mum*? No way!'

'I couldn't believe it either,' Maria murmured, moving her leg so that Vicky could look under the cushion.

'My mum tried to adopt you, you know.'

'*What?*' Maria's eyebrows puckered together. 'Are you serious?'

'Oh, yeah.' Vicky nodded, swiping her hair back when it fell across her eyes. 'They told her to get stuffed, of course, but she was on the case for ages – which is kind of funny, considering what a shit job she did with me and our Davy. But it takes all sorts, doesn't it?'

Finding the cigarettes, she tossed one to Maria without bothering to ask if she still smoked. Lighting her own, she blew the smoke towards the open window – her concession to Tyrell being in the room.

'We wrote to you for a while,' Vicky went on, reaching for her drink now. 'My mum used to send the letters to that social worker woman who took you away that day. She said she passed them on, so when we didn't hear back from you we figured you'd decided to make a clean break of it. *I* was a bit pissed off, though, I must admit,' she added in an accusing tone. 'I could understand you dropping everyone else, but you could have kept in touch with *me*. We were supposed to be besties.'

'I didn't even know you'd written,' Maria said quietly. 'Nobody told me.'

And it was true. Her social worker had never mentioned it, not even when she'd had Maria transferred to Devon. She must have deliberately withheld the letters and cards, denying Maria the comfort they would have brought her at that terrible time. So much for wanting to help Maria. *She* had decided that Maria needed a clean break, but she hadn't thought to discuss it with her. That was so unfair.

'So, where did they take you after they sent me and our kid packing that day?' Vicky was asking.

Forcing the thoughts of betrayal to the back of her mind, Maria said, 'To a children's home in Stockport. They had to keep me close by while they checked if I had any family to send me to.'

'You didn't, though, did you?'

'No. Not that I knew of at the time.'

'So, you've been in Stockport all along?' Vicky frowned, wondering why it had taken her so long to get in touch if she'd been living so close.

Guessing what she was thinking, Maria shook her head. 'They only kept me there a few months, then they sent me to Devon. I'm still there, but I've got my own flat now.'

'*Devon?*' Vicky repeated enviously. 'All right for some. It's supposed to be really nice there, isn't it?'

'Gorgeous, depending which part you're in,' Maria told her. 'There's some rough bits, but it's all right where I am.'

'Do you live near the sea? Bet you get loads of gorgeous lads coming in on their holidays?'

'Not really, no. We're a couple of miles out of the proper tourist area, so we tend to get the older couples who want a bit of peace and quiet. But that suits me, 'cos it's awful on the next Bay in summer – gangs of idiots drinking and fighting.'

'Sounds better than pensioners mooching about dribbling ice cream all over themselves,' Vicky griped, pulling a face. 'What's the point of living at the seaside if you don't get any action?'

'It's really nice,' Maria insisted. 'The beach is at the end of my road, and there's always something going on in summer – surfing competitions, and sand parties, and stuff. My old school used to take us horse-riding on the dunes as well, which was brilliant, 'cos we had—'

'You *what?*' Vicky interrupted, her eyebrows puckering

with disbelief. 'You went horse-riding with school? You *are* joking?'

'No.' Smiling, Maria shook her head and sipped her tea.

'Bloody hell! It sounds like one of those poncey boarding-school books we used to read – all jolly hockey sticks and midnight feasts. And there was us feeling *sorry* for you! Shit, I wish *my* mum had died and they'd sent *me*—' Catching herself mid-sentence, Vicky's hand flew up to her mouth. 'Oh, Christ, I'm sorry. I didn't mean that.'

'It's all right,' Maria assured her. 'I'm pretty good at not letting it get to me. There's no point wishing for what you can't have, is there?'

'Suppose not,' Vicky agreed. Then, changing the subject: 'So, are you working, or dossing?'

'I'm a teacher,' Maria said, sipping her tea.

'No *way*!'

'Mmmm.' Nodding, Maria gave a modest shrug. 'It's only part-time at the local primary, but it's been all right. I'm thinking of taking a bit of time out now, though – to think about what I really want to do.'

'Oh, I see.' Vicky gave a knowing smirk. 'Found ourself a sugar daddy, have we?'

'No, I haven't!' Maria replied indignantly. 'I'd *never* go out with a man for money.'

'I *was* joking,' Vicky said, surprised by the strength of her reaction. She'd obviously hit a raw nerve.

'Sorry,' Maria muttered. 'But that's what growing up in care does to you. You get a bit defensive when everyone's always looking down on you, waiting for you to mess up. Girls are the worst – calling you a slag if you so much as *look* at a lad for too long.'

'Girls are like that whether you're in care or not,' Vicky reminded her calmly. 'But if you react like that every time they get bitchy you're just playing into their hands. You've got to learn to shrug it off as if you don't give a *toss* what they think.'

'I suppose so,' Maria murmured, thinking it was all right for *her* to talk when she didn't know what it felt like.

'You should have heard the shit *I* got when I got caught with Luke,' Vicky said, letting her know that she knew *exactly* how it felt. 'And not just off the other kids; my own mother called me all the little tarts under the sun! And then she said I'd best get myself a job, because there was no way she was keeping me *and* a baby – not when she'd just got rid of the one *she* was having with Keith.'

'*Keith?*' Maria gave her a quizzical look. 'What happened to Brian?'

'*That* dirty bastard,' Vicky sneered. 'She got rid of him after she caught him sneaking into my room with his dick in his hand. He was so busy trying to remember if I had a hole he hadn't tried yet, he didn't hear her coming home early from the pub. She caught him red-handed.'

'Oh, Christ, Vicky. I didn't realise it was *that* bad.'

'It *wasn't* when you were around. It was a while after you left that he got worse – around the time I got tits, as it happens.' Lighting another cigarette, Vicky blew the smoke out noisily and tossed the pack to Maria. 'First time he raped me, I told her, 'cos I knew if I kept quiet like I had about all the other stuff, he'd carry on and something really bad would happen. Know what the bitch did?' she said, her eyes glittering with an anger that would never completely die. 'She *battered* me.'

'No way!' Maria muttered numbly.

'Oh, yeah.' Vicky nodded. 'The sneaky bastard had got in there first, you see – told her I'd been flashing my tits at him. She actually thought I'd been trying to *seduce* him – can you believe that?' Shaking her head, she took another deep drag on the cigarette. 'I was just lucky she was too skint to get properly pissed the night she caught him, or I don't think she'd have believed she'd really seen it.'

Maria was furious that her friend had suffered like that. She'd known that Brian was a groper – that he'd touched Vicky up and forced *her* to touch *him*. But she'd never have guessed that he would progress to rape. She'd always thought of him as pathetic rather than sinister.

'What did your mum do?' she asked.

'Kicked the living *crap* out of him,' Vicky said with a vindictive chuckle. 'Dragged him out onto the landing by his hair and battered him senseless in front of all the neighbours. Christ, I'd always known she was hard, but even *I* was shocked. She's a maniac when she gets going.'

'I wish I'd been there to see that.'

'Me too – you'd have loved it. And me and our Davy got a few good kicks in, as well – payback for all the shit.'

'Good for you. So, what did the police do when you told them? I hope they sent him down?'

'Behave!' Vicky snorted, drawing her head back. 'We couldn't have the pigs in the house with all the bent gear we had stashed there. It would have been *us* getting nicked, not him.'

'Good point,' Maria conceded, smiling at the memory.

Vicky's house had been *the* place for stashing knock-off gear on the Merrydown. All the local lads had used it as a temporary drop-off for the car stereos, briefcases and wallets they'd just nicked. And their mothers brought the VCRs, CD players and TVs they'd ordered from the catalogue and reported as undelivered. But it was the local dealers who were Vicky's mum's most hush-hush 'clients' – dropping their mysterious packages off with threats of what would happen if anyone found out. It was the worst-kept secret on the estate, but Vicky's mum had accommodated anyone and everyone, hiding gear in the kids' wardrobes and under their beds for the price of some weed or a cut of the profits.

'All that stopped once Keith moved in,' Vicky said reflectively. 'Which was great, 'cos it was a real pain having dodgy knob-heads rooting round in the bedroom at all hours. The dealers wouldn't come near once they knew he was on the scene, 'cos he was a *proper* maniac. But he treated *us* all right.'

'So how come your mum got rid of his baby?'

''Cos he was schizophrenic and she was scared the kid would be the same. That's why she wanted *me* to get rid of mine. She was convinced it was going to be deformed, or mental, or something.'

Maria frowned. 'So Keith was *your* baby's dad, as well?'

'No, he bloody well wasn't!' Vicky squawked indignantly. 'Jeezus, Maria – what d'y' take me for?'

'I didn't mean it badly,' Maria said apologetically. 'It's just with Brian doing what he did, I didn't know if this Keith – *you* know.'

'No, he didn't,' Vicky informed her frostily. 'Luke's dad was a lad from a few doors down.'

'Not Jimmy Platt?' Maria gasped, remembering Skinny Jimmy all too well. The gang had voted him the ugliest divvy on the planet – and Frankie Stokes the one they all wanted to be their first. 'Please don't tell me you went with *him*?'

'Do I *look* desperate?' Vicky snorted. 'Christ, he'd have been worse than Keith!' Grimacing, she gave an exaggerated shudder. 'No, it was a lad called Carl Hanson who moved up here from Rochdale about a year after you'd gone. He was drop-dead gorgeous,' she admitted reluctantly. 'But the bastard didn't half know it. I still can't get over what an idiot I was for believing him when he said he loved me, but you fall for any crap when you're a kid, don't you? Soon as I told him I'd missed my period he turned into a complete wanker – called me a slag, and said it wasn't his. Our Davy kicked his head *right* in for that.'

'Little Davy?' Maria exclaimed. 'You're *joking*!'

'Not so little by then.' Vicky smiled fondly. 'He *shot* up after you left; you wouldn't recognise him now. He was only twelve when Carl did the dirty, but he was already bigger than him. And it did the job, 'cos I never saw the bastard again. His lying bitch of a mother tried telling us he'd gone to work on the oil rigs with his dad, but we found out he'd gone back to the Dale and shacked up with some old tart.'

'I hope you made him pay for the baby?' Maria said indignantly.

'I've never asked him for a *penny*, and I never will.' Vicky pursed her lips stubbornly. 'No one's *ever* going to say I owe them – not my mum, not the dole, and *certainly* not Carl Hanson!'

Suitably chastened, Maria gave a thin smile, and moved onto what she hoped was safer ground. 'What about the others? Do their dads help out?'

'*Dad*,' Vicky corrected her coolly. 'They're all by the same one. And *yes*, he does help, thanks. We're very happy together.'

'Sorry.' Maria winced. 'I just thought—'

'That I was a slag?' Vicky raised a challenging eyebrow. 'New one in at the front before the old one's out the back?'

'God, no!'

Picking up on the invisible wall of tension that was rising between his mum and her friend Tyrell started to grizzle. Sighing, Vicky stubbed her cigarette out and went to get him. Bringing him back to the couch, she pulled a changing mat out from under the coffee table and laid him down on it.

'Sorry for snapping,' she said, taking Tyrell's nappy off and pulling a wet-wipe out of the tub. 'But people seem to think we do nothing but lounge around popping babies and scrounging off the dole round here. And we're not all like that – as *you* should know. Your mum was claiming while she was working, but you wouldn't have thought badly of her for it, 'cos she was decent. Well, *so* are me and Leroy.' Glancing up, she gave Maria a cool look. 'Only *we* don't claim anything, because we *both* work.'

'Sorry,' Maria murmured guiltily. 'I really didn't mean to insult you.'

Sighing, Vicky shook her head. 'Forget it.'

Turning her attention back to the baby, she cleaned him up and put another nappy on him with the quick, economical movements of one who has done it many, many times. Then she cleared everything away and stood up.

'I've got to take him to playgroup in a minute,' she said, carrying the soiled nappy to the bin. 'You can come with me, if you want. Or you're welcome to stop here if you don't fancy it. I'll only be an hour.'

'Thanks, but I think I'd best get back to the hotel,' Maria said, checking the time. 'It's getting late.'

'Are you sure? Leroy should be home soon, and I know he'd like to meet you. I've told him enough about you.'

'No, honestly, I can't.' Reaching for her jacket, Maria slipped it on. 'I've still got loads to do. And I haven't even packed yet.'

Showing her out, Vicky felt a bit guilty. She'd been so pleased to see Maria, but they'd managed to rub each other up the wrong way in no time, and now it felt awkward – which was a shame, considering they'd been such good mates once.

'Look, I'm sorry we didn't get a chance to chill out and really catch up,' she said. 'But it's kind of hard to relax when you've got a head full of kids' schedules.'

'I understand that,' Maria said, zipping up her jacket. 'You should see how wound-up some of the mums at *my* school get. There's one that *never* picks her kid up on time. She acts like it's an after-school club, or something. And she's such a *bitch* if you say anything.'

'That's what having kids does to you,' Vicky said. 'I can be a *super*-bitch when I get going. Anyway, you'll have to let me know when you're coming back,' she said then. 'I'll get Leroy to babysit and we'll go out for a drink – just the two of us.'

'Sounds great,' Maria said, relieved that they were ending on a more positive note. 'But I won't make any definite plans right now, if you don't mind. I wouldn't want to arrange something and then let you down.'

'No pressure.' Shifting Tyrell onto her other hip, Vicky reached for the pen and pad on the telephone table. Scribbling her number down, she handed it to Maria. 'Just give me a ring when you get time. We'll take it from there.'

Closing the door when Maria had gone, Vicky sighed wearily. Far from being envious of her friend's great new life by the sea, she thought it a bit sad that Maria had changed so much. And it wasn't just the posher accent that marked how far removed she was from her roots, it was everything – from the nice, neat middle-class clothes, to the way she walked with her nose in the air, to the way she sat with her teacup on her knee, as if she was visiting a spinster aunt and had to be on her best behaviour or something.

Scolding herself for thinking like that, Vicky reminded herself that they hadn't seen each other for years, and that this was *her* territory, so Maria was bound to feel awkward. It would be different when Maria called from the comfort of her own surroundings. They would chat about everything and everybody, and soon be back to how they used to be.

And if not – oh, well . . . Vicky had better things to do than worry about the past.

* * *

Clattering down the stairs, Maria shoved the heavy door open and fell out into the fresh air. She felt guilty and sad all at once, but she only had herself to blame. She should have listened to her instincts and gone straight back to the hotel instead of waltzing into Vicky's life like Lady Muck – going on about horse-riding and beach parties, when Vicky was scraping by on a cleaner's wage with four kids to feed. It was a good job that she hadn't mentioned the inheritance – that really *would* have been like pouring salt into the wound.

Walking quickly out to the main road, Maria hailed a passing cab. She couldn't really afford it, but she'd stayed at Vicky's way longer than she should have and there was only an hour left before she was due at the solicitor's. Anyway, she didn't know if she could handle being stuck on a bus right now; she was starting to get another headache.

She couldn't *wait* till this was over and she could go home and get her life back on track. She just hoped Nigel Grayson didn't try to change her mind when she told him what she was planning, because she didn't know if she could stop herself being horrible to him right now.

8

Hearing the street door closing, Adam glanced up in time to see Nigel stride across reception with a less than happy expression on his face. Given that he'd just been holed up in his office with the gorgeous little rich girl for the best part of an hour, he should have been happy as Larry.

Wandering into the doorway, he leaned casually against the frame, watching as Nigel jabbed viciously at the buttons on the coffee machine.

'Let me guess,' he drawled, folding his arms. 'She knocked you back.'

'Don't be ridiculous,' Nigel snapped, wrenching the over-full cup out of the slot and wincing when hot liquid slopped onto the back of his hand. 'How many times do I have to tell you – she is a *client*.'

'If you say so.' Curious to know what had got Nigel so het up, Adam followed him into his office and sat down on the corner of the desk. 'So what was it?' he asked. 'Already got a boyfriend?'

'None of my business if she has.' Irritably waving at him to get off the desk, Nigel slumped down heavily in his chair.

'Something must have happened,' Adam persisted, straddling the visitor's chair, which still felt warm from Maria's bum. 'You look like you've got a right cob on.'

'Will you mind your own bloody business!' Nigel snapped.

'Oi!' Drawing his head back, Adam frowned. 'I'm only trying to help.'

Sighing heavily, Nigel flopped his head back and ran a hand over his eyes. 'Yeah, I know. Sorry. I've had a bloody awful afternoon.'

'What happened?' Adam folded his arms, eager to hear the latest instalment of the Cinderella saga.

'Everything was going well, then I did my usual wrecking-crew job,' Nigel said, joining his hands together behind his head. 'She was a bit off when she called this morning and asked me to take her to the house, but she was all right when we got there. Then, when I was bringing her back to town, I made the mistake of taking a short cut past the Merrydown Estate.'

'And?' Adam shrugged, unaware of the significance.

'*And*,' Nigel explained glumly, 'that's where she was born. Where she was living when her mum was killed.'

'Ah . . .'

'Yes, *ah*. Anyway, she wanted to get out of the car and take a walk around, and I acted like it was a subdivision of Hell, or something.'

'I see,' Adam said, chuckling. 'So, she wants to take a look at her old home, and you make out like she's trailer trash?'

'Okay! There's no need to rub it in.' Nigel shot him an irritated glance. 'Anyway, then she came in this afternoon to sign all the papers, and comes right out and asks how soon she can put the house on the market.'

'She wants to sell?'

'Uh huh,' Nigel nodded slowly. 'And it's odd, you know, because I really thought she liked the old place. She got that look in her eye when she was walking round – like she'd really connected with it.' Pausing, he sighed heavily. 'She was obviously just pricing it up.'

'I thought you were going to show her the accounts for the Evans place,' Adam said. 'She'd *have* to be impressed by them. She could earn a fortune if she had the same kind of set-up.'

'What do you think I've been telling her for the past hour?' Nigel said despondently. 'She's not interested. And, worse than that, she said she no longer requires my services. I'm dumped.'

Adam's frown deepened. 'And you're giving up that easily? Come on, man. Your uncle dealt with that estate for years. He loved it – *you* love it. Hell, *I* love it, and I haven't even seen it. You've got to persuade her to keep it with us.'

'Don't you think I would if I could?' Groaning, Nigel ran his hands through his hair. 'Oh, for Christ's sake, what's *wrong* with me? It's got absolutely *nothing* to do with me what she decides to do with her own house. She can put a flaming bomb under it and blow it to kingdom come if she feels like it!'

'It's not like you to get so tetchy,' Adam said, giving him a concerned look. 'Why don't you take a couple of steps back from all this and chill, man?'

'I can't *chill*!' Nigel retorted irritably. 'That's the bloody problem. I can't stop thinking about her. It's like I'm possessed, or something.'

'Right,' Adam said, slapping a hand down on the desk. 'So, what have you done about it? Have you said anything to *her*?'

'No, of course not,' Nigel retorted, feeling the heat rush to his cheeks. 'And I'm not *going* to,' he added firmly.

'Well, hallelujah!'

'What's that supposed to mean?'

'Look, I know I take the piss,' Adam said. 'But I actually think you're doing the right thing – and I respect you for sticking to your principles.'

'For what they're worth,' Nigel grunted.

'They're worth it to *you*,' Adam reminded him. 'Know what you need, mate? . . . One of your own kind.'

'Oh, yeah, right!' Nigel gave an unenthusiastic snort. 'Because there are so *many* good-looking *single* female solicitors in Manchester.'

'There's always next month's convention. They'll be flooding in from all over.'

'In their smart little power suits, with cast-iron shoulder pads and solid steel knickers.' Nigel shuddered. 'No, thanks.'

Shrugging, Adam said, 'So do what the rest of us do and get yourself down to a nightclub.'

'Don't think it's really my scene, somehow.'

'Dating agency, then?'

'Don't even *go* there!'

Reaching for his cooling coffee, Nigel drank it in one and wiped his mouth on the back of his hand. Sitting up straighter, he rolled his head on his neck, making a concerted effort to shake himself out of the doldrums.

'Look, don't worry about me. This stuff with Maria Price is just a minor glitch in an otherwise sensible life. I'll be back to normal in a day or two – you'll see.'

'If you say so.'

'I do. So, thanks for the pep talk, but I'm sure you've got better things to do.'

'I have, as it happens.' Adam rubbed at his jaw. 'I've got a date with the dentist in exactly ten minutes.'

'Not that same tooth again? I thought they'd fixed that?'

'So did I, but they obviously missed something,' Adam grumbled. 'Anyway, are you sure you'll be all right if I take off? Miles and Jimbo are out. You'll be on your own with what's-her-name on reception.'

'I'm sure that *Heather* and I will be fine,' Nigel assured him, smiling at Adam's inability to remember the receptionist's name. The poor girl obviously wasn't attractive enough to register in the little black book that was his mind. 'Just do yourself a favour and get them to pull the tooth this time, eh? You could have bought a car with the money they've had off you this year. I'd get a new one if I was you.'

'Car?'

'*Dentist.*'

'You're probably right,' Adam agreed. 'But what can I do?' He gave a mock-modest shrug. 'The hygienist loves me – and she's got this sucking action to *die* for.'

Shaking his head, Nigel said, 'Yeah, whatever.' Then, 'Will you be coming back when you're done?'

'Wasn't planning on it.' Adam rubbed his jaw again. 'Might be a bit out of it when they've zapped me. Why, what's up?'

'I'm looking round an apartment on the Locks,' Nigel told him. 'I was going to ask if you'd come along and give your opinion.'

'*You*'re looking at an apartment on the Locks?' Adam repeated slowly, visibly surprised. '*You*?'

'Yes, *me.*'

'Aw, *shit*, man,' Adam groaned. 'Do you know how *bad* I want one of those places? I'd *die* to get my foot through the door, but you can't even get a *viewing* without a platinum card.'

'Oh, well . . .' Nigel gave a modest shrug. 'So, do you think you'll be up to it? Only I'd really appreciate it if you could be there, because I'm not sure what I'm supposed to be looking out for.'

'Man, I have *got* to get myself qualified,' Adam moaned. 'Soon as I am, I'll be moving in next door to you – parking the Alfa next to your crappy old Saab,' he added, grinning now.

'Yeah, well, stop partying and get your head into the books and you might actually do it,' Nigel said, feeling really good about himself all of a sudden. Adam *envied* him – how great was that? 'And get yourself back here by five.'

★　★　★

Maria reached the station at four and used the extra hour to mooch about in the concourse shops, looking for a thank-you gift for Beth. Finding a gorgeous turquoise silk scarf in the sale at Knickerbox, she reached into her bag for her credit-card pouch.

There wasn't much left of the money Beth had lent her and she wanted to save that for a taxi back from the station when she got home, because she really didn't fancy walking all that way. Her card was pretty much maxed out, but there might be just enough left on it for this one last little purchase – fingers crossed.

Flipping the pouch open, Maria was confused to see that the sleeve was empty. Putting her bag down on the counter, she rifled through it like a madwoman, hoping that the card had somehow fallen out, even though she knew that it couldn't have.

Feeling sick as it hit home that it was gone, she gabbled that she'd changed her mind about the scarf and fled from the shop.

Rushing into a quiet corner, she took her phone out of her bag with shaking hands. She had to report the card missing, but who to? She didn't know the hotline number, and she didn't have enough credit on her phone to start ringing around at random. But if she waited till she got home whoever had stolen the card might have already run up a massive bill, ordering goods off the internet or over the phone. She couldn't afford to take the risk.

But never mind *who*ever had stolen it. It was perfectly obvious that it must have been Joel. He was the only one who'd had access to her bags. He must have gone through them when she was sleeping, then taken off like the proverbial thief in the night. And he'd even been devious enough to leave the cash alone, knowing that she would have discovered the theft a whole lot sooner if he'd totally cleaned her out – the sneaky bastard.

Phoning the police, Maria reported the card as *lost*. Well, there was no way she was admitting that she'd had a seedy one-night stand and been ripped off at the end of it. She still had *some* pride.

A policewoman took her details and said they would keep a record of the call for verification purposes, in case somebody found and used the card before Maria had had a chance to cancel it. She followed that with the warning that almost every store in Manchester had active CCTV these days – something that Maria would be 'wise to keep in mind'.

Maria knew fell well what the woman was saying: that she thought Maria was lying about losing the card, and was letting her know that she wouldn't get away with it if she intended to try and buy something and then claim that it wasn't her who'd made the purchase.

Now she felt guilty, as well as used and abused.

Walking to the cold, dark end of the platform, away from the other passengers, she sat on a bench and chain-smoked to hold the self-pitying tears at bay until the train pulled in.

She just couldn't believe she'd fallen for a con merchant. Everybody thought she was so streetwise, coming from a ghetto like Moss Side, but they'd kill themselves laughing if it ever got out just how *stupid* she really was.

But they wouldn't get the pleasure, because Maria had no intention of telling *anyone* about this – ever. Not even Beth.

Especially not Beth.

9

Maria moped about for days after she got home. She just couldn't stop thinking about Joel, and that made her mad, because she *knew* he'd ripped her off. But he'd been so gorgeous and seemed so nice that she just wanted to pretend that it wasn't true. That he had only left without saying goodbye because an emergency had come up.

She was overjoyed when she got a call from the bank a few days later, telling her that her card had been recovered in an electrical goods store in Manchester – from a *woman* who had been trying to buy an expensive sound system with it. The woman had escaped, so there would be no prosecution, but at least no harm had come of it.

It took Maria a while to figure out how a woman had got hold of her card, but she came to the conclusion that it must have been someone who worked at the hotel. Someone with access to a master pass, who had known that she was alone and that it was safe to rifle her room when they saw her going down to the bar that night. Someone who would have assumed that she had money, because she was staying there in the first place.

Well, she'd make damn sure she didn't leave herself open to anything like that again.

Happy now that she knew Joel wasn't the thief, the next few weeks flew by, and Maria spent the time planning what she would do with the money when it arrived. Now that she had got over the shock of the inheritance, she became excited at the prospect of being able to do whatever she wanted to do. It was the first time she'd ever had two pennies to rub together, and she intended to have the time of her life.

Beth got a bit twitchy when Maria quit her job and gave two months' notice on her flat. Beth thought Maria should wait until the money was safely in her account before doing something so rash. But Maria was on a roll, and nothing was going to get in her way.

Still trying to inject a bit of sense into the proceedings, Beth suggested that she buy a cheap, low-maintenance property in the older part of town, and invest the rest in a high-interest account. Maria could live there for a couple of years, using the accumulated interest from the account to modernise. Then, when it had appreciated in value, she could let it out, or sell it, and move somewhere more upmarket.

But Maria was having none of that. She was way too impatient to work her way up the property ladder. She wanted the instant *Wow!* factor.

Thinking like a millionaire, despite still not having a penny of the money in her hands, she set up a load of viewings in a seafront estate of new-builds in the next Bay, and dragged Beth along for the ride.

They had great fun, but by the time they had seen just about everything that was available, Maria had changed her mind. Nothing *felt* right, and the 'Designer Apartments' tag just didn't fit with the reality of what were, in actuality, little more than poky, flimsily built, odd-shaped flats. But it was the prices they were asking that really turned her off. They weren't going for too much less than she'd been told she could expect for The Grange when she sold it, and that was an enormous, solidly built old house. Scandalous.

'So, what are you ging to do?' Beth asked, concerned that Maria had burned her bridges by giving notice on the flat before finding somewhere else. At this rate, she'd be on the street with her landlord's foot up her backside.

'Don't worry about it,' Maria said, trying not to let Beth see how worried she was actually becoming, now that she'd realised that buying a house wasn't going to be quite as easy as she'd imagined. Not a decent one, anyway.

The cheque arrived five weeks later. It was for almost a quarter of a million, and Maria had to count the noughts several times because she couldn't get her head around it. Seeing it in black and white should have made it more real, but it actually had the opposite effect. Now it felt positively *un*real, as if the last few weeks had been a crazy, vivid dream. The alarm would go off in a minute, and she would wake up to find herself back at the dawn of her twenty-first birthday, as poverty-stricken as ever.

There was a polite letter from Nigel in the envelope, reminding her that as the house was now hers, it was her responsibility to make arrangements for selling, letting, or whatever she decided to do with it. He'd be more than happy to pass by and check that everything was okay while she was out of the area, if she liked, but now that he no longer repre-sented her, he strongly advised that she got another solicitor to look over the paperwork, because there were rates and taxes that needed to be kept on top of.

Maria was a little ashamed about the way she'd given him the brush-off at their last meeting. But everything had been crashing down on her head that day, and he'd got the short end of the stick when she'd called in at his office to sign the papers.

Already fed up about Joel, and bumping into scruffy Lin Stokes, followed by that awkward reunion with Vicky, she'd just wanted to get the hell out of there. But Nigel had annoyed her by trying to show her the accounts for that other house in the hopes of persuading her to reconsider selling, and she'd snapped, telling him that she wouldn't be needing his services any more – thank you very much!

But after all that, he was *still* offering to help her out in a non-professional capacity. Some people were just too nice for this world.

Beth came round a short while later. They were supposed to be going shopping, but when she saw the cheque she hustled Maria straight down to the bank to deposit it. Then Beth made her sit through a meeting with a financial adviser who plied them with coffee and biscuits and spoke to Maria as if they were old mates, telling her that she could do this, that, or the other with her new-found fortune.

Maria didn't listen to a word of it. She wasn't ready to start thinking about options, and shares, and investment schemes. And she *wasn't* impressed with the bank's sudden eagerness to accommodate her. They hadn't been so keen to help when she'd needed a tiny loan to tide her over the holidays before she got her job last year. They had made her feel like a beggar for daring to ask, and she'd been forced to eat Netto noodles for two solid weeks – in the dark, to avoid the landlord. Now she'd bet this sycophant would rush out to get her a Chinese takeaway if she asked him to – with all the trimmings.

'What are you *doing*?' Beth asked when they left the bank and Maria promptly dumped all the leaflets she'd been given into the bin. 'You *need* them. You weren't even listening in there, and I can't explain it all to you.'

'I don't want you to,' Maria assured her. 'I've got no intention of doing *any*thing *he* suggests, because it's bound to be in the bank's best interests, not mine.'

'Yeah, but you need to do *something* to make it work for you.'

'Don't worry about it.' Maria smiled. 'I've decided to get some impartial advice. Anyway, thanks for coming with me, but I hope you don't mind if I don't come shopping. I need to sort something out.'

'Like what?' Beth looked at the leaflets in the bin and shook her head.

'Just stuff,' Maria said evasively. 'I'll tell you later.'

'Go on, then.' Beth sighed. 'I'll come round when I've finished. Just do me one favour, though: promise you won't do anything stupid and blow all the money on rubbish before you get it sorted?'

'As if.' Maria scoffed.

Back at the flat, Maria was nervous as she waited for Nigel to answer the phone. He'd offered to keep an eye on the house, but that didn't mean he'd want to have anything else to do with her. In fact, the more she thought about it, the more likely it was that the offer of help had been lip service. That he'd only said it because he thought she would refuse.

She needn't have worried. Nigel was genuinely pleased to hear from her.

'How are you? Did you get the cheque? Oh, good. I was so worried it might not reach you. Not that it shouldn't have, given that it was sent by courier. But I hadn't heard anything, so I was just contemplating ringing the company to ask if it had got there all right.'

'It did,' Maria assured him, jumping in quickly when he took a break for breath. 'First thing this morning. Anyway, I just wanted to say thanks. And, er, to ask if you'd consider picking up where you left off.'

'Sorry, I'm not sure . . . ?' Nigel sounded confused.

'Being my solicitor,' Maria explained, sure that he would tell her to get lost. 'You said there were things I needed to sort out with the house – legal things. And I was hoping you'd agree to deal with it.'

'I'd be delighted,' Nigel said readily.

'Great.' Maria gave a sigh of relief. 'I'm afraid I still want to sell it, though. Will that be a problem?'

'No, that's your privilege entirely,' Nigel reassured her. 'I can't actually put it on the market for you, but I'll certainly liaise with an estate agent on your behalf. And advise you during the process, obviously.'

'Thanks. I appreciate that.'

'No problem. But you'll, er, probably have to come up here again at some point, I'm afraid, because there'll be more paperwork to sign. I have some on my desk as we speak, as it happens. I was planning to send it on so that you could take it to another solicitor, but if you're retaining my services, I suppose I should keep it until we can arrange a meeting.'

'How does next week sound?' Maria asked, following Beth's example and being decisive for once in her life.

Meeting arranged, she phoned the train-ticket office and booked two weekend returns – knowing that Beth wouldn't be able to refuse to go this time, especially not if it was already paid for. Then she booked a double room at the Britannia, although she had to battle with herself over that one.

It *was* a beautiful hotel, but it held bad memories for her now. Joel running out on her, for one; and the card-thief chambermaid. But, given how much she'd gushed about the place, Beth would want to know why she hadn't booked them in there. And what could she say? That she'd decided not to stay at the best hotel in town now that she could afford to really enjoy it . . . That she really fancied roughing it instead.

Biting the bullet, Maria booked the room and waited for Beth to come back from the shops.

10

Beth had never been to Manchester before, so she was on a total high when their train pulled into the station a week later. Maria was amused by her friend's excitement, but the city held no wonders for her now. This trip was purely to tie up the loose ends and get proper advice from Nigel about the money – nothing more, nothing less.

That was the intention, anyway.

Leaving Beth to unpack, Maria nipped across to Nigel's office to pick up the keys to the house. He was so welcoming that she found herself inviting him to dinner that evening – as a thank-you for agreeing to help her through the financial maze. That done, she went back for Beth and took her to see The Grange.

Beth's face was a picture when she got out of the taxi and walked up the path; her mouth was hanging open, and her wide eyes were darting every which way.

'Oh, my God, it's fantastic,' she said breathily. 'And it's *yours*. Can you believe it?'

'Not really,' Maria admitted, unlocking the door and rushing to turn the alarm off, using the number that Nigel had given her.

It still smelled musty inside, but at least it was dry – unlike her Teignmouth flat, which was getting damper by the day.

Having spent the last few weeks dreaming about moving out of that dump, she had no emotional attachment to it.

But at The Grange, she found that she was getting that same strange sense of belonging that she had felt the first time she came. And possibly even stronger, given that she was so relaxed with Beth along for company.

Walking into the centre of the hall, Beth did what Maria had done and turned in a slow circle, taking everything in. Her parents were fairly well-to-do and their house was quite large, but their place was modern and bland compared to this grand old place.

'You are *so* lucky,' she said, wandering from room to room. 'I would *die* to live somewhere like this. Why on Earth do you want to sell it?'

'Because it's in Manchester,' Maria reminded her, following her around. 'And I don't live here any more.'

'Yeah, but you *could*,' Beth said, as if it were the obvious thing to do. 'You've already packed in your job, and you'll be moving out of your flat as soon as you've found some-where else to live. What's so great about Tinny that it's got to be there?'

'Friends.'

'Oh, we'll come and see you,' Beth said, flapping her hand as if that were too ridiculous a reason to be taken seriously. 'Hell, I'll move *in* with you, if you want – as long as I get the master bedroom.'

'In your dreams,' Maria said, grinning. 'If I stay, that's mine.'

'You've always been a selfish cow,' Beth teased. 'Ugh!' she said then, her mouth arcing down in distaste when she lifted a corner of a dust sheet and saw the couch beneath. 'That's *hideous*.'

'Nigel reckons it's really valuable,' Maria told her primly. 'But don't panic – I'm not planning to keep it. There was a list of contents drawn up for the insurance, and it's all supposed to be worth a fair bit, so I'm thinking about putting it into an auction.'

'Mmmm,' Beth murmured thoughtfully, putting the sheet back in place and smoothing the edge down. 'They are family heirlooms, though. Don't you think you should keep something?'

'It wasn't *my* family, so what's the point?' Shrugging, Maria led her friend up the stairs. 'Anyway, I'm getting a flat, so there won't be any room for all this bulky rubbish.'

'I actually think you should hang fire on selling up,' Beth told her. 'There's something about this place that I can't quite put my finger on. It's like— Oh, my *God*, they're *gorgeous*!' Cutting herself off mid-sentence, she gaped at the stained-glass windows.

'Aren't they?' Maria smiled fondly. 'First time I came it was sunny outside, and I just loved the way the colours met in the middle and kind of bounced off each other, like a kaleidoscope.'

'*See*?' Spinning around, Beth pointed an accusing finger at her. 'You *can* feel it. I can see it in your eyes. And you should hear yourself talking about it. It's like you're really proud it's yours.'

'Well, I *am*,' Maria admitted, wondering where this was heading. 'Sort of. But it's not really *mine* in the true sense, is it?'

'Course it is.' Pursing her lips, Beth nodded. 'It likes you.'

'Don't be ridiculous,' Maria scoffed, folding her arms as a weird tingling sensation tickled her spine. 'How can a house *like* you?'

'Don't ask me.' Beth shrugged. 'I'm just going by what it's saying.'

'You're freaking me out now,' Maria said, tutting loudly and shoving her sleeve back to check her watch. 'Anyway, hurry up and look around. I want to hit the shops while we've still got time.'

★   ★   ★

In the Britannia bar later that afternoon, they sat at a table opposite the door, waiting for Nigel. Every now and then, Maria found her gaze drifting to the corner where she'd been sitting when she'd met Joel.

She'd thought about him a lot since that night – with anger and shame, at first. Then she'd felt relief when a woman was found with her credit card. But, desire aside, she still had to remind herself that Joel wasn't the charming gentleman he'd made himself out to be. He *had* taken off without saying goodbye, and that stung, because she'd thought there'd been a real spark between them. But he'd obviously thought differently, and if there was one thing she'd learned, it was that there was no point yearning after could-have-beens.

'Excuse me . . .' Beth said, waving a hand in front of her face. 'I *was* talking, you know.'

'Sorry, I wasn't listening,' Maria admitted.

'No kidding,' Beth said. Then she repeated in a bored tone: 'I asked why you're not willing to even *consider* keeping it.'

'Because there's no point.' Maria rolled her eyes. 'Can you shut up about the damned house now? You're doing my head in.'

'Not as much as *you*'re doing mine in, you cheeky cow!' Beth retorted good-naturedly. 'Stop pretending you didn't feel it, because I *know* you did. You liked *it*, and *it* liked *you*.'

'Will you quit with the weird stuff,' Maria moaned, folding her arms.

'All right,' Beth said, coming at her from a different angle. 'You don't need the money, so why not just keep hold of it for a bit? Stay there for a holiday, and think about what you really want to do with it.'

'I live by the sea,' Maria reminded her tersely. 'That's where normal people take holidays – not in grotty old cities like Manchester. Now, *please* shut up!'

Shaking her head, Beth sat back. She knew her friend well enough to know that she *had* made a connection with the house. But if she pushed too hard, Maria was likely to dig her heels in and take the first offer made on it – however low that might be. And that would be a shame, because if there was one thing Maria needed after the childhood she'd survived, it was to find somewhere that she really belonged. And, much as Maria was resisting it, Beth had a strong feeling that this house was it.

'Here's Nigel,' Maria said just then. 'Be nice.' Standing up, she waved him over.

Turning to look, Beth saw a tall, slim man with neat reddish-blond hair and a lovely open smile coming toward them.

'Sorry I kept you waiting,' he said, shaking Maria's hand. 'I got a bit held up.'

'You're not late,' Maria assured him. 'We've not been here all that long ourselves. Anyway, let me introduce you. Beth – Nigel. Nigel – Beth.'

'Hi.' Still sitting, Beth reached up to shake his hand.

'Pleased to meet you.' Nigel smiled shyly.

Maria hadn't said anything about having a friend with her. But Nigel wasn't put out by it. In fact, he was quite pleased, because he'd been concerned that he would blush and fumble his way through dinner, but a third person might take the pressure off. And it certainly wouldn't hurt his credibility if one of his associates were to come in and see him dining with not just one, but *two* beautiful women.

'Can I get you a drink?' Maria asked. 'Or would you rather go straight in to dinner?'

'I really don't mind,' Nigel said, shrugging self-consciously. 'Whichever you'd prefer is fine with me.'

Watching the exchange, a lopsided smile crept onto Beth's lips. Oh, yeah . . . So, he was just business, was he?

'What do you want to do, Beth?' Maria gave her a funny look, wondering what the smirk was about.

'I really don't mind,' Beth replied nonchalantly. 'You choose.'

Sensing that she was making fun of Nigel, Maria shot her a warning look as she reached down for her handbag. 'We'll go straight in, then, shall we? We can get a bottle of wine when we order.'

Beth amused herself during dinner by watching how raptly Nigel listened when Maria talked; and how he seemed to trip over his words when she held his gaze when *he* talked. But she was particularly amused by how Maria seemed completely oblivious to it.

She'd never met anyone as pretty as Maria who was so totally unaware of herself. And it wasn't just living in care that had stripped her of vanity, because Beth had met other care girls who were so self-obsessed it was criminal – and none of them were a patch on Maria.

It was a shame, because Nigel seemed like a genuinely nice man, but Beth knew that he stood a cat in hell's chance with Maria. Not because she'd think herself too good for him, but because she had a *type* that she fancied, and he wasn't it. She was incredibly insecure in many ways, shying away from commitment in order to protect herself from getting hurt. Consequently, she went for the typical hand-some, sexy, smooth-talking charmer types, who wouldn't put her at risk by giving more than she expected. Nice as Nigel was, he was far too polite and gentlemanly to spark a flame in Maria's heart.

'Well, that was interesting,' Beth teased when dinner was over and Maria had walked Nigel out to the pavement. 'No wonder he was so eager to help. He's got the raging hots for you.'

'Don't be ridiculous,' Maria scolded. 'His uncle dealt with

the estate for years, and he's known about me since he was young, that's all. Anyway, I don't know why I'm bothering telling you all this again. Just take it from me, he's a thoroughly professional man whose only interest is the house and the money.'

'Yeah, well, I wish I'd had a camera,' Beth persisted. 'If you'd *seen* the way he was looking at you.'

'Right, stop it!' Maria held up her hand. 'I've got to see him tomorrow to work out an investment plan. I can't do that if I'm watching him to see if he's watching me.'

'Isn't that a song?'

Shaking her head, Maria reached for her wine. 'You're such a bitch sometimes. There's no way you're staying at my house with an attitude like that.'

'Excuse me?' Beth narrowed her eyes.

'I know you think I don't listen,' Maria said, smiling slyly, 'but I like to mull things over in my own time before I make a decision. Anyway, I *have* been thinking, and I reckon it *might* be worth holding on to the house for a while. Nigel's still advising me to renovate it and let it out, but he says I should wait until I've had a return on my investments and use *that* instead of cutting into the original. He's going to talk me through it all tomorrow.'

'Wow, you really are serious, aren't you?' Beth said approvingly. 'So, what are you going to do with it in the meantime?'

'No idea.' Maria shrugged casually. 'But there's no point paying for another night here when that's going spare, is there? So I thought we might stay there tomorrow.'

'*Really?*'

'Fancy it?'

'Too right!' Beth squawked. 'But only if we share a room.'

'Don't tell me you're scared?' Maria gave a mocking smile.

'Er, didn't you *see* the old lady in the kitchen?' Beth drew her chin in.

'Shut up!' Maria half laughed. Then, frowning, she said, 'You're joking – right?'

'No. She was standing by the window when I was over by the door,' Beth said, grimacing as if recalling something terrible. 'And she was all sort of haggard and . . . Oh, hang on . . .' She slapped her forehead. 'That was *you*!'

'Oh, very funny,' Maria said, breathing a sigh of relief.

'No, but seriously,' Beth said, no longer teasing. 'I'm really glad you've changed your mind. You might absolutely hate it, but at least you'll have given it a shot.'

'And what if I love it?' Maria asked, finishing her drink.

'Move in.' Beth shrugged.

'On my own?'

'Why not? I'll come and stay in holiday times. And I'm sure the girls would jump at the chance of the odd weekend away.'

'And what about Australia?'

'Bugger that,' Beth said, pulling a face. 'To tell you the truth, I went off the idea ages ago.'

'You never said.' Maria frowned.

'Well, I didn't want to ruin it for you if you were dead set on it,' Beth admitted sheepishly. 'But I honestly don't want to go. Especially not since you quit the job and I went full-time. It's a big responsibility. Please don't be mad at me,' she said then. 'I'll still go if you want to, but I'd really rather not. I'd rather see you settled and making a fantastic life for yourself.'

Maria pursed her lips thoughtfully. This had started out as a *let's spend the night and see what happens*-type scenario, but she could actually feel herself being drawn in by the idea of moving back to Manchester. Her roots lay here, after all. And as Beth had pointed out, there was nothing so great about Teignmouth. She'd tried to make the best of her life there, but it had never really been anything but the place she'd been sent to when other people were still in control of her life – the place she'd been too lazy to leave when *she* was holding the reins.

But things were different now. She'd already quit her job and given notice on the flat. And if Beth really didn't want to go to Australia, there was absolutely no reason to hang about. She didn't even have to go back for her stuff if she didn't want to. Most of it was already packed; she could just give the keys to Beth and have her send it on.

The more she thought about it, the more she could actually see it happening. She just didn't like the thought of doing it alone.

'Will you move in with me if I decide to stay?' she asked.

'Oh, I'd love to, you know that,' Beth said regretfully. 'But I can't. My parents are—'

'Dying to get rid of you,' Maria cut in.

'They are *not*,' Beth protested. 'They love having me at home.'

'Rubbish!' Maria chuckled. 'You're a total drain. Anyway, I bet they can't *wait* for you to go, so they can run round naked, and have mad sex in the conservatory.'

'Don't be disgusting!' Beth pulled a face. 'Anyway, I'm not a drain. I pay rent.'

'Yeah, and they pay you an allowance.'

'Not now I'm full-time. I only get my clothes allowance.'

'It's all right, baby girl,' Maria said, laughing now. 'I think it's quite obvious that you're not ready to leave home yet.'

'I will come and stay, though,' Beth assured her. 'Every school holiday.'

'You'd better,' Maria said, smiling sadly now, because Beth was the one thing she *would* miss.

Finishing her drink, Beth put her glass down and peered

out through the door. The foyer was getting busy as people arrived for a night in the bar, where the music from the disco below was starting to filter through, sending a throbbing vibration up through their feet.

'Fancy a drink in there?' she asked.

'Not really.' Maria pulled a face. 'I'm shattered. I just want a cup of hot chocolate and an early night. Let's go and see if there's any old black and white films on telly.'

Drawing her head back, Beth gave her a horrified look. 'It's eight-thirty on a Friday night – my *first* night in Manchester, I might add. There is no *way* I'm going to bed yet. My name's Beth, not *Death*! And what was the point of buying that new dress if you just wanted to look at it hanging in the flaming wardrobe?'

'I'm joking,' Maria laughed, standing up. 'Come on, party girl . . . Let's go get ready.'

Dressed to the nines – Maria in the sky-blue suedette minidress and long grey boots she'd bought that afternoon, and Beth in a clinging white halter-neck top, tiny skirt with huge silver belt, and stiletto heels – they dropped into the hotel bar and asked Rex, the young barman, for the name of a decent club. Looking them over admiringly, he recommended a place called Scarletts, assuring them that the music was the best in town.

Scarletts was packed when they got there, the pounding bass vibrating up their legs as they dropped their jackets off in the cloakroom. Beth was almost dancing as they made their way to the bar, her head whipping from side to side, like a kid on her first trip to the fair.

Shouting to make herself heard, Maria said, 'What do you want to drink?'

'Vodka,' Beth yelled back, her teeth as Californian white

as her top in the flourescent light. 'This is fan*tas*tic. Look at all the gorgeous guys!'

'Probably with their girlfriends,' Maria said cynically, side-stepping two specimens who were weaving their way towards her with leering grins on their sweaty faces. 'Don't bother!' she snapped when one of the hopeful Casanovas paused and opened his mouth to speak. 'I'm a lesbian.'

Wondering why the man gave her a funny look, Beth said, 'What did you just say to him?'

'I told him you were my girlfriend,' Maria said, stepping up onto the foot-rail and yelling her order at the barmaid.

'Cheeky cow,' Beth gasped. 'I thought I told you it was over between us. You hardly ever take me out, and you *never* pay me any attention.'

'Shut up, you idiot,' Maria laughed, shoving a bottle of vodka-and-cranberry Blastback into her friend's hand. Once she'd got her change, she stepped down and pushed Beth away from the bar. 'Let's go dance.'

The dance floor was packed with girls in full pulling gear, dancing in small clusters and gazing flirtatiously out at the men congregating around the edges. Creating a bit of space for themselves, Maria and Beth whooped and cheered with the rest of the crowd when the DJ announced that it was Old Skool time and started playing all their favourite old beach-party tracks.

It was almost an hour before Old Skool gave way to R'n'B Breakdown. Wiping her sweaty brow, Beth shook her empty bottle.

'I need another drink.'

'Me, too,' Maria said, standing on tiptoe to peer around. 'And I need a wee. Did you see a sign for the ladies' when we came in?'

'I think it's over there.' Beth pointed back towards the bar.

'Show me,' Maria said. 'And hurry up, 'cos I don't think I can hold it.'

'Not wearing your Tenalady?' Beth shouted back loudly over her shoulder.

'Shut up,' Maria hissed when a couple of girls smirked at her. 'Here,' she said, thrusting some money into Beth's hand. 'You get the drinks. I won't be a minute.'

Lucky enough to find an empty cubicle, Maria went to the loo, then retouched her make-up and fluffed her damp hair before going out to rejoin Beth.

Frowning when she found that Beth was nowhere to be seen at the bar, she looked around for her. The frown deepened when she spotted her chatting to two men on a raised area overlooking the dance floor.

Turning around just then, Beth saw her and waved her over.

'That's Eddie, and his cousin, Carlton,' she said, stepping forward to meet Maria with a mischievous sparkle in her eye. 'They insisted on buying our drinks, so I'm just having a little chat. They want to know if we'll dance with them.'

'Aw, do we have to?' Maria moaned under her breath.

'Be nice,' Beth said through a smile. 'Eddie says he's been watching me since he came in. And Carlton's just come over from Kingston. And guess what? He fancies you.'

'Great,' Maria muttered, glancing at the men over Beth's shoulder.

Beth's admirer *was* good-looking, she had to admit, but she didn't like the look of his cousin. He was huge and muscular, with dark slit-like eyes, which made him look dangerous. But even if he *hadn't* looked like an extra from a bad gangsta movie, Maria wouldn't have been interested. She had no intention of wasting her night out getting to know someone she would never see again.

Not after last time.

Nodding politely when Beth introduced her to the men,

Maria lit a cigarette and used the smoke as a barrier between herself and the big guy.

'Me and Eddie are going for a dance,' Beth said after a moment. 'You'll be all right, won't you?'

'Yeah, fine,' Maria muttered, looking daggers at her as she trotted off with her man.

Folding her arms, she gave Spare Man a tight smile, frowning when he leaned his elbow on the rail and gazed right at her. She hoped he wasn't expecting her to dance with him, because there was no way. He was so big, he'd probably stand on her foot and break it.

'Y' all right?' he drawled in a heavy Jamaican accent.

'Fine, thanks.' Another tight smile.

'You're not from round here?' he said – *stating, not asking.*

'No,' Maria replied – *uninterested.*

'So, where, then?' *Persistent.*

'Why?' *Irritated.*

'Jus' mekkin conversation.' *Fuck you.*

Silence.

Coming back after her dance, Beth whispered excitedly to Maria, 'They're going to a *blues* in the Moss, and Eddie's asked if we want to go with them. What do you think?'

'No way,' Maria answered quietly. 'I'm not really comfortable with them.'

'Not because they're black?' Beth frowned.

'Don't be ridiculous,' Maria hissed, hoping the men hadn't heard. Fortunately, they were having a conversation of their own and didn't seem to be listening. 'I just don't want to go anywhere with them. They're strangers. It's not safe.'

'Eddie's not a stranger,' Beth said, glancing back at him with a smile. 'He's really nice.'

'He *is* a stranger,' Maria muttered under her breath. 'And we're not going anywhere with them. Do you even know what a blues is?'

'A party?'

'Yeah, but not the kind *you*'ve ever been to. And in Moss *Side.*' Snorting softly, Maria shook her head. 'Sorry, Beth, but I'm pulling rank on this one. There's no *way* we're going to Moss Side with those two. It's dangerous.'

Beth looked at her for a moment, then sighed. 'You're right,' she said, remembering that she was supposed to be the sensible one. 'I got caught up in the whole *gorgeous man fancies me instead of you* vibe. I'll just ask him if he minds staying here instead.'

'And then what?' Maria tipped her head to one side and gave her a pointed look. Beth wasn't a virgin, but she wasn't experienced in the ways of horny men by any stretch of the imagination. And Maria had the feeling that this one would come on hot and heavy when the mood took him; he was too good-looking and cocksure.

'Okay, so what we going to do?' Beth asked, biting her lip. 'We can't just run away.'

'Oh, can't we?' Maria said, gripping her arm. ''Scuse us,' she said to the men, pulling Beth away. 'We need the ladies'.'

'Don't be long,' Eddie called after them. 'We'll be waiting.'

'Well, you'll be waiting for ever,' Maria muttered, smiling widely.

'You're terrible,' Beth laughed when they were safely in the toilets. 'How are we going to get away now?'

'Easy, we'll sneak out in a minute and go round the other side. There's another bar over there. We'll get our drinks there and keep out of their way.'

'You're such a spoilsport,' Beth scolded. 'I really liked Eddie.'

'No, you didn't,' Maria scoffed. 'He looked like Rio Ferdinand on a bad day.'

'He did not!'

'Here, you're not talking about the cocky cousins, are you?' a girl who had just come in and was retouching her lipstick asked. 'One of them's really big?'

'Yeah, why?' Maria asked.

'They've just tried copping off with me and my mate,' the girl told her. 'I'd watch your drinks if I was you. I'm sure they tried to spike ours.'

'Oh, shit,' Beth said, looking at the bottle in her hand with horror. Then, shaking her head, she said, 'No, they couldn't have. They paid for it, but I took it straight off the barman.'

'I'm not taking any chances,' Maria said, snatching the bottle off her and tipping that and her own down the sink. 'You left it on the ledge when you went to dance, and I wasn't watching it. And let that be a lesson to you!' she scolded then.

'What do we do if they're still waiting for us?' Beth asked, nervous now.

'I don't think they are,' the lipstick girl told her. 'I came in after you, and they were just chatting up a couple of right tarts.'

'Bastards!' Beth squawked indignantly.

'That's men for you,' Maria said.

'Well, I hope they get the clap,' Beth snarled. 'I'm never going near another man again as long as I live!'

All the girls crowded around the mirrors retouching their pulling make-up laughed.

Making their way outside at the end of the night, still swaying to the ghost of the music ringing in their ears, Beth saw Eddie and Carlton walking out with the tarts. Sticking her fingers up at them, she stumbled out onto the pavement.

Groaning when the chill night air bit into her flesh, she leaned her head back and stroked the sweat off her goose-bumpy neck.

'Oh, that's nice.'

'You'll catch pneumonia,' Maria warned her with a giggle, rubbing at her arms as her teeth began to chatter. 'God, I'm starving,' she said when two girls teetered past sharing a bag of chips, the sweet scent of hot vinegar trailing in their wake.

'Me too,' Beth said, peering down the road in the direction the girls had come from. 'There must be a chippy down there. Shall we go and look for it?'

'Yeah, why not? Fancy sharing a fish?'

'How about a burger?' Beth suggested greedily, slipping her jacket around her shoulders as they set off. 'Double cheese with salad and relish. Or a pizza!' She inhaled deeply as her imagination took off. 'Seafood special with prawns and tuna.'

'Twelve-inch stuffed crust, with garlic bread and—' Stopping dead in her tracks, Maria's heart leaped into her throat and pushed out a little gasp.

A group of people were spilling out of another club a few feet ahead. And Joel was among them, looking every bit as devastatingly gorgeous as she remembered.

'What's up?' Beth asked, wondering why they'd stopped.

Pulling herself together, Maria shook her head. 'Nothing. Come on, let's go.'

Joel turned around at that exact moment, and their eyes met. Frowning, he tipped his head to one side and squinted at her. He knew he'd seen her before, but he wasn't immediately sure where from. Not that it mattered. She was an absolute babe.

Then he remembered.

The hotel . . . The credit card . . . *Ah* . . .

But she wasn't giving him evils, so maybe she hadn't associated him with the card. Anyway, it was Linda Carr who'd almost been caught with it, not him, so she shouldn't think it had anything to do with him.

And she did look incredible in her short, tight dress, with her hair all loose and shiny, her face flushed and glowing . . . Well worth another shot.

All of this took less than a second to flit through Joel's head, then he was smiling and walking towards her, preparing for another fine performance.

But what was her name again . . . ?

Oh, who cared?

'I thought it was you,' he said, reaching her and hugging her. 'God, you look good.'

Immediately flustered when she inhaled the scent of the aftershave she had smelled in her dreams so many times, Maria pulled herself out of the embrace.

'Hello, Joel.'

'You didn't forget, then?'

'No.'

Glad of the masking darkness, Maria cast a guilty glance in Beth's direction. Beth was sure to ask who he was and how she knew him. But after making Beth shake off the guy that *she* had fancied earlier because he was a stranger, how could Maria admit that she'd had a one-night stand with Joel last time she was here?

'So, how are you?' Joel was asking, looking her over with an appreciative gleam in his eye. 'You look fantastic.'

'I'm fine,' she said, wishing he'd stop looking at her like that. Beth would be sure to wonder what was going on.

'Aren't you going to introduce us, Maria?' Beth said just then, looking Joel over with interest.

'Er, yeah . . . Beth – Joel, Joel – Beth,' Maria said. 'We're old friends,' she blurted out then, hoping to God that Joel backed her up.

Eyes dancing with mischief, Joel said, 'Yeah, that's right. We go *way* back, don't we, *Maria*? So, why didn't you let me know you were coming to town?'

'I haven't got your number,' she said, frowning. Surely he couldn't have forgotten taking off without a word after their last encounter.

'Yes, you have. I wrote it down for you last time I saw you,' Joel said, sounding so sincere that Maria actually wondered if it was true and she had somehow forgotten. 'It wasn't *that* long ago. Don't tell me you lost it?'

Beth narrowed her eyes suspiciously. Oh, yeah? Maria hadn't mentioned anything about bumping into him last time she was here. And he wasn't the kind of man you would easily forget. So what was going on?

'I really don't think you did give it to me,' Maria said quietly.

Joel peered at her quizzically for a moment, then shrugged. 'My mistake. But never mind . . . I'll give it to you now. Got a pen?'

'No, sorry.'

'Store it in your phone,' Beth suggested, wondering why Maria was being so stand-offish. If she had an old friend who looked like him, she'd be dragging him back to the hotel for a nightcap.

'Yeah, do that,' Joel said. 'Then you've got no excuse not to call, have you?'

Having no reason to refuse if they were 'old friends', Maria tapped his number into her mobile.

A platinum blonde who was standing in the doorway of the club Joel had come out of chose that moment to make her presence known.

'*Joel* . . .' she called, her petulant voice slicing through the cold air like lemon juice through grease. 'I'm *waiting*!'

'Shit,' Joel muttered. 'Sorry about that. She's my, erm—'

'Girlfriend?' Beth ventured cynically, her opinion of him changing in an instant. If there was one thing she hated, it was players.

'Date,' Joel corrected her. '*First* date, actually,' he told Maria then. 'And *definitely* the last, because she's a nightmare. But I'll have to be polite till I've dropped her off. She's a friend of a friend.'

'I see.' Maria glanced at the girl.

Scowling back at her, the girl stuck one long slim leg out in an aggressive pose and folded her arms, enhancing her pneumatic tits.

'I think she wants you to hurry up,' Maria said amusedly.

'She can wait,' Joel said, sounding as if he'd rather cut off his own head than go to her. 'So, is this just another flying visit, or are you staying over?'

'Visit,' Maria said, mirroring his date's stance to show the silly bitch that she wasn't intimidated.

'*Joel!*' Silly Bitch snapped. 'The taxi.'

'All right, I'm coming!' he called back, not bothering to mask his irritation now. Leaning forward, he kissed Maria on the cheek. 'Speak to you soon, babe.' Turning to Beth then, he nodded. 'Nice meeting you.'

'Well, you certainly kept *him* quiet,' Beth said when he'd gone. 'How long have you known him? Was he your boyfriend when you were growing up, or something? How come you've never mentioned him?'

'How many questions are you going to ask?' Maria said, sighing as the taxi pulled away.

In the back, the blonde was doing that jerky-head thing that women do when they're having a good old nag. Then her hand went up in front of Joel's face in a *Save it!* gesture.

First date, my backside! Beth thought, snorting softly.

'I bet he two-timed you, didn't he?' she said knowingly. 'He looks the type.'

'He *wasn't* my boyfriend,' Maria said, trying not to let her disappointment show as they set off again. 'He's just someone I knew.'

'Mmmm,' Beth murmured, not sure whether she believed that or not. 'Well, he obviously wanted to get reacquainted, the way he was looking at you. How come you get all the gorgeous ones?'

'I wish you'd make your mind up!' Maria laughed. 'You were all for Rio Ferdinand when we were in the club.'

'Yeah, but he was a slag,' Beth reminded her primly. 'At least you *know* this one. Then again, *he*'s a slag as well, so you're best off out of it,' she added disapprovingly. Sighing, she gave an exaggerated shiver and quickened her pace. 'I think I'm sobering up.'

'Good – you won't eat as much,' Maria said, pulling a face when they turned the corner and bumped into the back of the queue snaking out of a tiny fish and chips shop. 'Do you want to wait, or should we go straight back?'

Sniffing the air, Beth said, 'Wait. It stinks of all the unhealthy kinds of fat, but you just *know* it'll be delicious. Are we being greedy, or are we sharing?'

'Sharing.' Maria covered a yawn with her hand.

Hugging her suddenly, Beth said, 'Thanks for today, babe. I've had the *best* time!'

'Me too,' Maria agreed. 'But it wouldn't have been the same without you, so thanks for coming.'

'That's what best mates are for,' Beth said, pushing her forward when the queue moved closer to the shop. 'That, and weeding out the good guys from the bad. So, next time you bump into any gorgeous old friends, make sure they're single. Then find out if they've got a brother!'

'So much for never going near men again,' Maria laughed.

11

Maria and Beth checked out of the hotel early the next morning and headed into town to buy cleaning gear, and a couple of cheap tracksuits to protect their clothes. Taking a cab to the house, they opened all the windows, pulled off the dust sheets, and set about dusting, polishing, brushing and mopping.

It was almost three-thirty before they stopped, and they had barely scratched the surface, because it was such a large house and there were hundreds of hidden corners where decades' worth of dust had gathered and become trapped.

Maria made a list of all the things she would need if she was going to move in – the most essential for tonight being bedding. They had found a well-stocked linen cupboard in the master bedroom, but there was no way either of them wanted to risk unleashing on the world the ancient dust-mite family that was living in it.

If the washing machine had been working, they would have shoved it all in there and left it to soak. But the machine appeared to have died of old age, along with the fridge, and the boiler system – which was the *make an appointment and wait your turn* type. There was none of this newfangled instant hot water business here. No shower, no double glazing, no working radiators – hardly any concession to modern life at all, in fact.

God only knew how Elsie Davidson had survived her twilight years. Maria and Beth could only assume that she had enjoyed the hardship – like the nuns in those old films, who only felt *worthy* when their paths were riddled with obstacles and pain.

Back in town, Maria went to Nigel's office for her meeting, and Beth headed off to the Arndale Centre.

It was Saturday afternoon, so the centre was jam-packed, people pushing and shoving and dodging their way around the aisles. But Beth didn't mind the crush. She loved how cosmopolitan and sophisticated it all was compared to Devon, and she made a point of going into every shop so that she could tell Leanne and Sharon all about it when she got home. They would be so jealous.

Lugging her bags into the solicitors' offices when she was finished, Beth went to the reception desk to let someone know she was there. But there was nobody around.

Putting the bags down, she tiptoed up to the office doors and read the names on the brass plates. Finding Nigel's, she peeped through the glass panel. He was sitting at the desk with Maria, their heads bowed over the paperwork spread out between them. Leaving them to it, she got a coffee from the machine and sat down to wait.

Gazing around, Beth was impressed by how plush every-thing was. The visitors' couches were expensive designer models in smoky-grey leather, with splayed chrome feet and low rolled backs; the pictures were edgy black and white aerial views of New York; and the carpet was thick and made good soundproofing. The business was obviously doing very well – which was a bit weird, she thought, having met Nigel and seen how humble and unassuming he was. She'd have expected him to be an arrogant *look at me*-type tosser if she'd seen his office before she met him.

Maria and Nigel came out a short while later. Seeing Beth sitting there, Nigel frowned.

'Sorry,' Beth said, feeling immediately guilty for having helped herself to a coffee. 'I probably should have knocked and asked if it was okay, but I didn't want to disturb you.'

'No, no, that's not a problem at all,' Nigel assured her. 'I'm annoyed with myself. I must have forgotten to lock the door. That's the policy when there's only one of us in the building – for security reasons. Anybody could walk in off the street otherwise. Not you, of course. I'm sure you weren't intending to do any harm.'

'Absolutely not,' Beth told him, smiling. Then, pursing her lips thoughtfully, she said, 'Maybe you should get yourself a Saturday receptionist if you're worried about it. Maria could do it for you,' she added slyly. 'She can type, she *loves* talking on the phone, and she'll probably be looking for a job before too long if she carries on spending the way she has been.'

'Thanks for that, *Oh great voice of my conscience*,' Maria drawled, shaking her head at Nigel.

'Did she tell you the good news?' Beth asked Nigel then. 'About her staying at the house?'

'Yes, she did. And I think it's wonderful. Seemed such a shame to let the old place go without giving it a chance.'

'Yeah, well, it might only be temporary,' Maria said, reaching down for some of the bags. 'Look at the state of this lot,' she complained to Nigel. 'And she reckons *I'm* spending a fortune. She was only supposed to be getting something for dinner!'

'Don't be so cheeky,' Beth protested. 'You should have seen the list she gave me, Nigel. If I'd followed it, I wouldn't have been able to move for bags.'

'Oh, don't tell me you've forgotten something?' Maria moaned.

'*See?*' Beth said accusingly.

Smiling, Nigel folded his arms. The girls were obviously

close, and their easy banter was a breath of fresh air in his world, where bitterness and sniping and people trying to screw money out of their nearest and dearest was the norm. He felt so jaded at times from dodging the human venom that he wondered how people ever made friends or fell in love.

Calling a taxi, Nigel helped them carry their things round to the road at the back of the building to wait for it.

Helping them load everything into the boot when the cab came, he said goodbye to Maria, then held out his hand to Beth. 'It was lovely meeting you. Have a good journey home tomorrow.'

'Thanks, I will,' Beth said, climbing into the back seat. 'And keep an eye on this one, or she'll run you ragged. She's a right slave-driver.'

'I'm sure I'll manage,' Nigel said, stepping back to close the door.

'Somebody fancies you,' Beth teased, smiling widely and waving at Nigel as they pulled away from the kerb.

'Pack it in!' Maria hissed.

Reaching Didsbury, Beth swivelled her head as they drove past a Chinese takeaway in a row of shops not too far from the house.

'Hey, we haven't eaten yet. Shall we drop this off and go back for something?'

'Let's just phone and get it delivered,' Maria said, yawning. 'I just want to get home.'

'Excuse me?' Beth turned and looked at her. 'Did I hear that right? Did you just call it *home*?'

Maria frowned. 'I suppose I did, yeah.'

'Ha!' Beth smiled smugly. 'Now tell me Auntie Beth doesn't know best!'

'All right, calm down,' Maria said. 'It's only a figure of speech.'

'No need to explain,' Beth said, holding up a hand. 'I was thinking much the same myself . . . Can't wait to get home and snuggle up under the lovely new duvet, watching telly in bed, and stuffing ourselves with sweet and sour chicken. Heaven! Do you think they deliver wine?'

'Probably not,' Maria said, taking her purse out to pay the driver when they pulled up at the gate. Handing him a tenner, she flapped her hand when he said he didn't have change. 'You can give us a hand getting the bags to the door if you feel bad about it.'

'You're going to work your way through that money in no time if you carry on like that,' Beth reprimanded her when they were inside. 'That was four quid you just gave him for carrying a pillow up the path!'

'Don't worry, I won't make a habit of splashing out,' Maria assured her, dragging the bags and herself up the stairs. 'As soon as I've got everything I need, it'll be save, save, save. And don't forget how much I'll make when I sell the furniture. I'll be loaded all over again.'

'Aw, please don't sell it all,' Beth moaned, coming up behind her. 'The nasty sofas can go – and the dining-room table, 'cos that's skanky. But the rest is gorgeous. And you definitely can't lose *this*.' Dropping her bags on the bedroom floor, she sat down on the big old bed and ran a hand over the carved walnut footboard.

'Fantastic, isn't it?' Maria said, flopping down beside her. 'So bouncy and soft.'

'Aw, don't jump around,' Beth begged, lying back and closing her eyes. 'I could just go to sleep right here and now.'

'Right, up!' Maria said, jumping to her feet. 'Come on, we can't afford to fall asleep. We've got a bed to make, and dinner to order.' Grabbing one of the bags, she tipped it out onto the bed, saying bossily, 'You call the takeaway while I shove the sheets on. Come on – chop chop!'

'Slave-driver,' Beth complained, dragging herself up. 'Where's the phone book?'

'I don't know.' Maria shrugged as she tore the wrapping from one of the sheets. 'Try in that cupboard under the phone.'

Looking to where she was pointing, Beth saw a low dark-wood cupboard against the far wall. Going to it, she pulled the door open, coughing when a cloud of dust billowed out.

'Aw, there's all kinds of crap in here,' she said, jumping when a large folder slid out and spewed a load of papers out at her feet. 'Oh, bloody hell!' she snapped, kneeling down. 'It'll take me a year to pick this lot up.'

'Oi, don't start reading it,' Maria said, shaking the sheet out and floating it out over the mattress. 'Just shove it back in and get on with looking for the phone book.'

'Oh, wow, you've got to see this,' Beth murmured, glancing up from the paper she was holding. 'It's a letter about you.'

'Saying what?' Dropping the sheet into place, Maria started tucking the edge under the mattress.

'Saying that you've been located to a social-services children's home in Devon.'

'Let's have a look.' Reaching for the letter, Maria read it quickly. It was weird to see herself referred to as *the subject*, as if she was part of some top-secret spy game.

Beth was busy rooting through the rest of the letters. 'Look at this one,' she said, holding another out. 'It's got a photo of Belmarsh paper-clipped to it.'

Taking it, Maria got a weird feeling in her stomach when she looked at the picture. Belmarsh Heights was the first home they had sent her to in Devon. It was a huge, flat-faced house, with slate-grey walls and tall windows. It had been a mental asylum once upon a time, and felt just as eerie and chillingly desperate on the inside as it looked on the outside. Maria had hated it there, and had been overjoyed when they'd moved her to the less stately but far more homely

King House on the rise overlooking Lyme Bay. That had been *heaven* by comparison, and she'd been more than happy to spend her remaining care-years there.

'Hey, this one's got *my* name in it!' Beth squawked indignantly. 'Listen to this . . . "Upon commencement of the 2002 session, it was apparent that Maria had dissociated herself from the girls with whom she had been mixing throughout the previous two sessions. She seems to have struck up a friendship with a close-knit, less troublesome group of girls, her main connection being to a Bethany Louise Murray."' Open-mouthed, Beth looked up. 'Jesus, who wrote this?'

'The private detective I told you about,' Maria murmured, sitting down on the edge of the bed. 'Feels freaky, doesn't it?'

'*Freaky?*' Beth repeated incredulously. 'It's . . .' Lost for a word to describe how she felt, she shrugged, then settled for, '*Creepy*. Were they following us about, or what? Did they see *everything* we did?'

'I don't think they went that far,' Maria said, hoping that she sounded reassuring, because Beth was probably feeling as bad as *she* had when Nigel had first told her.

It was a peculiar sensation to know that someone had been watching you go about your business – taking pictures and reporting all your movements to somebody else. It was how Maria imagined being stalked would feel, only without the fear, because it wasn't happening right now.

Shell-shocked, Beth shook her head slowly. 'God, Maria, these must be the reports she commissioned. She *paid* for this. And look at all the *photos*. There's one here of you at the library. And one of me, you and Sharon in the arcade. School one here – year ten, judging by your hair. And, oh, my God . . .' she exclaimed, looking up. 'You've *got* to see this.'

'What is it?' Maria asked, not sure that she wanted to know. This was horrible – like she had never had a private moment in her entire life.

Reaching for it, Maria felt the room close in around her head. The man in the picture was young and handsome, with a nice, gentle smile, and the exact same eyes as her own – same shape, same shade. And the likeness didn't end there. He had the same blond hair, the same slightly pointy chin and high cheekbones, and even the same tiny uneven bit under the nose.

'It's your dad, isn't it?' Beth said quietly. 'You look just like him. What's it say on the back?'

Turning it over, Maria inhaled sharply.

Derek, aged 19, Colwyn Bay.

So it was true. Derek Davidson really was her father. There was no mistaking it now.

Gazing into the smiling eyes, Maria thought he looked perfectly nice and normal, but her mother must have seen something more sinister in him to make her cut him out of her own and Maria's lives so completely.

But whatever it was, Maria would never know for sure. And she wasn't sure she even wanted to think about it. There was no point. Nothing could come of it. She wouldn't suddenly gain a family; she'd just lose what was left of her mum. And she wasn't willing to give up those memories for anything. They were the only real things she had ever had in her life.

'You all right?' Beth asked.

'Yeah, fine,' Maria said, nodding determinedly. 'Shove that back in with that lot and shut the door.' She flipped the photo to her. 'I can't deal with it just now.'

'What about the phone book?'

'Forget it.' Taking a cigarette out of her bag, Maria lit it with shaking hands. 'We'll walk, if you're still up to it – see if we can find an off-licence on the way. I need a drink.'

'Do you want me to go through this lot with you later?' Beth asked, closing the cupboard door and dusting her jeans off when she stood up. 'It'll probably take all night, but I don't mind.'

'No.' Maria shook her head adamantly. 'We're supposed to be snuggling up with a good film and a Chinese, not depressing ourselves with that crap. Anyway, you're going home tomorrow and I might not see you again for ages, so there's no way we're wasting our last night together. Help me finish this bed and let's get out of here. I'll go through that lot when I'm ready.'

Not.

12

Keith Gallagher was an overgrown lump of a man, with crude prison-art tattoos covering his flabby white flesh. He had bad teeth and mean little eyes. Joel despised him, but he was the brawn to his brother Lance's brain, and you didn't get one without the other.

Following him into the lounge of the scruffy semi he and Lance shared with their bad-tempered old git of a dad, Joel's eyes almost crossed at the rank stench of dogs and unwashed feet. It never ceased to amaze him that they could earn so much money but still live like untrained pigs.

Lance was the boss, despite being a good foot shorter and several stones lighter than Keith. They both caned far too much of their own merchandise for their own good, but while it had affected Keith to the extent that you could actually *see* the brain damage in his eyes, Lance was as sharp as ever.

Lance was perched on the edge of a white-leather recliner in front of an enormous plasma-screen TV when Joel walked in. He was playing a gory slash-'em-up video game on a state-of-the-art console.

'How'd it go?' he asked without taking his eyes off the action.

'Okay,' Joel said, wincing as the all-too-real-looking man on the screen brought a blood-dripping machete down through the head of a woman with enormous tits and glossy suck-dick lips. 'Jeezus, that's gross,' he muttered, sitting down on the settee.

'That's what *I* said,' Keith agreed, flopping down on a battered swivel chair and snatching a bottle of vodka off the table. 'What's the point of offing a decent-looking bird like that without waiting for her to get her kit off?'

'She ain't *real*, you dense twat,' Lance muttered irritably. 'She's fuckin' plasmatronic!'

'Nowt wrong with plastic tits,' Keith said, swigging his drink. 'I wouldn't kick that Jordan one off me dick, and she's got more stuffing in her jubblies than her on telly.'

Glancing at Joel, Lance rolled his eyes and shook his head. 'That's the dangerous thing about this advanced graphics shit – morons like him think they're watching a proper film. You watch – he'll be trying to find out where she lives so he can fuckin' stalk her.'

'Up yours!' Keith grunted, shoving a hand down his jeans to scratch his balls. 'I'm no fuckin' pervert.'

'So, what you got f' me?' Lance asked Joel, still staring at the screen, his wiry shoulders jerking with each hack his man executed.

Taking a folded wad of money out of his pocket, Joel leaned forward and put it on the small table beside Lance's chair.

'Two and a half gees. The bloke said he'd had a word with you about the rest.'

'Yeah, that's right,' Lance grunted, his brows joining above his nose as his man started whacking the woman with a brick. 'For fuck's sake *die*, you cunt!'

Joel frowned. If he were braver he'd question why Lance had sent him to do a pick-up without bothering to mention that he'd okayed the guy to only give half of the money. He'd spent nearly half an hour arguing the toss, almost getting into a fight over it.

But he couldn't afford to tell the Gallaghers to fuck off and do their own dirty work, because the mugging had left him in debt to them for three grand. He was paying it off at one-fifty a time, but he owed almost as much as he had at the start, what with the interest Lance shoved on, and he felt like it was never going to end. If he'd been dealing with Keith, it would have been forgotten by now. But Lance was a different kettle of fish. He could be off his face from morning to night, but his brain was like a calculator with a long-life memory. Joel just needed one shit-hot deal and he'd be laughing. But until then, he was stuck sucking up to the Chuckle Brothers.

Freezing when he heard a low growling beside him, he swivelled his eyes to the left and saw Lance's crazy Dobermann bitch, Dotty, with her teeth bared.

'Lance,' he whimpered. 'The dog . . .'

'Yo, bruv,' Keith sniggered. 'Looks like Dots is after summat to eat. Shall I tell her to *GO FOR IT!*' Yelling the last three words, he cackled like the madman he was when Dotty barked and lurched forward an inch.

Fortunately for Joel, she was waiting for her real master to give the word, and Lance was too engrossed in his game to be bothered joining in with Keith's malicious idea of fun.

'Get t' bed, Dotty!' he bellowed. 'And you grow the fuck up and pass him that gear before I wrap that fuckin' bottle round your head, you mental twat!'

Pulling a face, Keith got up and lumbered across to the sideboard in the back room. Snatching a bag from among a stack of trainer boxes on the top, he tossed it to Joel, growling at him under his breath – which unnerved Joel even more than Dotty had, because he had a feeling that Keith would do more damage if he decided to bite.

'There's two ounces there,' Lance said, sparking up a fat spliff and filling the room with a pungent cloud of skunk smoke. 'Drop one off with Hanson, and you have the other. Pay me nine ton by Friday next – and don't forget the one-five.'

'Right,' Joel said, despondently slipping the bag into his inside pocket.

'Fuck off, then,' Lance said, jerking his head doorward. 'And tell that cunt Hanson that the other shit's coming in next week, so he'd best give us a bell if he wants in.'

'That it?' Standing up, Joel cast a nervous glance around for Dotty. He was relieved to see that she was out of the way behind Keith's chair.

'What the fuck *else* d'y' want?' Lance snapped. 'A fuckin' marriage proposal? Piss off, you plank.'

Letting himself out, Joel inhaled the fresh air as if it was pure oxygen and set off in search of a cab. No way was he in the mood for trekking up to Longsight. He hated the place almost as much as he hated Lenny Hanson – and he resented Lance for sending him there like some kind of lackey.

His *safe* mobile rang just as he reached the taxi rank at the end of the road. The only person who had the number was Mack – his one remaining friend from back home.

He was immediately irritated. The only reason Mack ever rang these days was to tap Joel for money, but he'd had a couple of hundred just a few weeks back so he was out of luck if he was after more already. Joel was skint.

Sighing heavily, he answered the call.

'Where've you been?' Mack grunted without so much as a hello. 'I've been trying to reach you for the past half-hour.'

'I was in someone's gaff,' Joel told him patiently. 'Must have lost the signal. What's up?'

'I'm up your way,' Mack said. 'I need to see you.'

'You're *here*?' Joel said, surprised because he hadn't expected that. 'How come?'

'I'll tell you when I see you. I'm behind a boarded-up pub called The Fox and Hounds off the end of the M6. D'y' know it?'

'No, but I'll find it.'

'How long?'

'About half an hour,' Joel said, checking the time. 'I've just got to go and drop something off somewhere first. Hang tight.'

Tossing his mobile onto the passenger seat, Mack rolled himself a single-skinner and turned the radio on. Twiddling with the knob to find a station playing anything *but* the shite they called dance music, he settled back in his seat when he came across an old Scorpions track. Now, *that* was what you called music.

Seeing a movement at the upstairs window of one of the houses behind the overhanging trees a few minutes later, he sat forward and shielded his eyes to peer out of the bug-spattered windscreen. He hoped it wasn't some nosy resident spying on him. The last thing he needed was for some twitchy do-gooder to get suspicious and bell the police.

Mack couldn't believe his luck when he saw a woman standing at the window with her tits out, rubbing herself with a towel, her hair wet on her shoulders like she'd just got out of the bath.

His dick stirred in his pants.

Yeah, go on, baby, he leered. *You rub them nice big titties for Uncle Mack. Yeah . . . that's it . . . that's the way I like—*

No, don't do that! . . . Nooo! Aw, shit!

Sucking his teeth in disgust when the showgirl drew the curtains, he slumped back in his seat.

Great!

Now he had a stiffie, and there was nothing he could do about it but wait for it to droop. He'd never get it wanked off before Joel got here – he'd snorted too much wakey-wakey powder for the drive.

Doing his damnedest to ignore his throbbing cock, Mack glanced at the dashboard clock and tapped his fingers agitatedly on the steering wheel. His stomach was churning now. It was probably just the soldiers being called back to barracks, because he'd heard that unreleased spunk made you ill, but it could be a paranoia coming on. He hoped not. He'd rather have bollock-rot than head-fuck any day.

Come on, Jay . . . Come on . . .

Joel was the closest thing Mack had to a brother. They'd been mates since Joel was seven and the battered women's brigade had moved him and his mum, Diane, into the flat next door to Mack's. One of Diane's so-called 'sisters in crisis' must have had it in for her for looking like Marilyn Monroe, though, 'cos of all the places they *could* have sent her, they'd stuck her in the Gordons – one of the worst estates in the *world*.

Not that ten-year-old Mack had been complaining. He'd fancied the arse off Diane, and had taken her precious little boy under his wing as a means of getting near her. But he'd had his work cut out, because Joel had been a right pretty fucker, with blond curls, and baby-blue eyes with long black lashes. All the other kids went into attack mode when they saw him – like wild dogs with a wounded kitten. But Mack hadn't minded protecting him, because it earned him some wicked hugs off Diane – proper tits-in-face stuff.

Luvvly jubbly.

When they hit their teens, everyone thought Joel was an arse bandit because he dressed smart and talked like he was cleverer than the rest of them – which he probably was, in all honesty. But he liked pussy way too much to be a poof – Mack could vouch for that. And he'd had enough of his leftovers over the years to know. He'd only had to turn up at a club with him back then, and he was guaranteed a fuck.

Nowadays, he was lucky if his mam's auld drinking cronies gave him a gobble.

Flashing his lights when he saw the taxi pulling up out on the road, he rolled his eyes when Joel got out and shook his pants out to straighten the crease before strolling up to the car, like he had all day and next week, too.

'No way was I expecting to see you,' Joel greeted him, yanking the passenger door open and hopping in. 'How are you?'

'All right,' Mack grumbled, touching fists with him. 'Been better if you hadn't kept me waiting so fuckin' long, though.'

'It's only been half an hour,' Joel reminded him, pulling his cigarettes out. 'So, what's the crack?' he asked, lighting up. 'Let me guess . . . You're getting married, and you want me to be best man?'

'I need money,' Mack said without preamble. '*Urgent.*'

'How much?' Joel asked, frowning as the forced good humour evaporated. He'd guessed it was money, but it had to be a substantial amount for Mack to come all this way.

'A grand.'

'A *grand*?' Joel was shocked. It was usually a ton – two at the most. 'Christ, Mack. How come you need that much?'

Exhaling wearily, Mack shook his head. 'It's me ma. She's got herself in a right state. The collectors have been, and everything. You've got to help her out, man.' Turning his head, he looked Joel in the eye. 'She was good to you when you needed her.'

It was blackmail, and Joel resented it. True, Sue Macdonald *had* taken him in when his own mother had run away to Canada with her new boyfriend when Joel was just fifteen. But any loyalty he'd felt towards her had been seriously dented when, a year later, she stole all the money he'd been saving to go and look for his mum, blowing the lot on whisky and scratch cards.

He hadn't told Mack because he hadn't wanted to fall out with him over it, but he'd never made the mistake of trusting Sue again, and had moved out as soon as he got a chance.

So, no, he didn't *owe* her – and certainly not a grand.

'I haven't got that kind of money lying about,' he said, cracking the window to get a bit of air. It stank like a dentist's surgery in the car – the cold chemical smell that only a coke-head or a nurse can truly call their own. Mack must have necked a whole lot for it to be seeping out in his sweat and on his breath. And if he could afford that, he shouldn't be here begging for yet more fucking money.

'You know I wouldn't be asking if it wasn't life and death,' Mack persisted, not believing him. Joel *always* had money. 'Come on, man, we're supposed to be family.'

'I've worked my arse off this year, and made next to nothing,' Joel told him, wondering why it hadn't occurred to Mack to try getting a job to help his mother out. 'You know I lost everything when I got ripped off. I owe money out left, right and centre, and I'm behind with my rent, so I'm going to lose my flat before too long as well.' Sighing heavily, he flicked his cigarette ash out of the window. 'You should have rung before you came. You'd have saved yourself a trip.'

'Oh, well . . .' Mack slumped moodily back in his seat and picked at the skin on his lip until it bled. 'If you won't help, I suppose I'll just have to pull a job while I'm here.'

'Like what?' Joel asked warily, not liking the sound of this.

'Dunno.' Mack shrugged, licking the blood. 'Passed a nice quiet petrol station on the way here – tart on her own behind the counter. Might pay her a little visit on my way home.'

'Oh, Christ,' Joel muttered when Mack subconsciously moved his hand towards his groin. 'Don't do it, mate. I know you. You'll fuck it up and land yourself right in it.'

'Not got much choice, have I?' Mac replied, shrugging. 'Me ma took out a loan with Caldwell, then thought it was a great big fucking joke when she missed a payment – till he sent the collectors round and put the fear of God into her. Wouldn't mind, but she only borrowed a fucking ton; now she owes him more than she'll get off the social if she lives to be two hundred. He'll have her down the docks giving two-quid blow jobs when she's ninety to pay it off, if she ain't careful.'

'Shit,' Joel murmured.

'Yeah, shit.' Mack exhaled loudly. 'They're coming back in a week, and if I haven't got a grand to give 'em, she won't have two tits next time you see her. But, hey . . .' Flapping his hands in the air, he slapped them down on his thighs. 'It ain't your problem, so don't sweat it.'

Joel peered at him, trying to read his eyes. If this was a scam, Mack was getting better at it, because he looked dead serious.

'Why the hell did you let her take out a loan with Caldwell?' he asked. 'He's ruthless.'

'That a posh word for a cunt?' Mack snorted, sparking another fag. 'Truth is, I wasn't there. We'd had a row and I'd fucked off to Jeff's. She got a thirst on and went down Caldwell's. And you know what he's like – he don't care *who* he signs up, so long as he's got *someone* by the bollocks at the end of it. And that'd be me now, I suppose, 'cos there's no way my ma's ever gonna find that kind of money. Might be best if I just don't go back,' he added gloomily. 'Let him have the addled auld bitch.'

'You don't mean that,' Joel said quietly.

Turning his head slowly, Mack looked at him with a bleakness Joel had never seen in his eyes before.

'Yeah, I do. It'd solve everything, that. I wouldn't be able to go home again, but so what? You've done all right.'

'It's not that easy starting from scratch,' Joel said, hoping to dissuade him. 'Leaving all your mates and family behind. I've had to give everything up – real name included. You think that was easy? You've got no *idea* what I went through to get new papers. I live in constant fear of being found out by the authorities. You can't sign on, or get a passport, or—'

'I don't give a toss about all that, if that's what it takes to start again,' Mack said, warming to the theme. 'I've totally had it with that place. There's nothing but arseholes and shit gear up there no more. I'm gonna fuck it all off and move down here. It'd be just like old times – me and you, kicking arse and getting laid. And we'll work together,' he grinned, nudging Joel in the ribs now. 'I'll soon have you back on track, pal. I've always fancied myself as a weed merchant.'

'Sorry, mate, but it's just not possible,' Joel said, choosing his words carefully to avoid offending him. 'I'm on the verge of losing my place, like I said. And the dealing's dried up big time, 'cos everyone's growing their own these days. I'm actually thinking of getting a proper job in a hotel – so I can live in,' he added, letting Mack know in no uncertain terms that there would be no place for him. 'Anyway, your mam needs you. You can't just abandon her, can you?'

Shrugging, Joel gave a regretful smile, as if to say he would have done it if he could. But the truth was, there was no way in *hell* he was having Mack move in with him. Mack was an addict, and it didn't take a genius to see how bad his habit was these days; his nose looked set to cave in, and he'd been fidgeting the whole time they'd been sitting here, like his nerves were shorting out.

'Don't fret it,' Mack said. His voice took on a dark edge now as he added, 'You've enough of a job on taking care of yourself without worrying about me and me ma. Especially now Psycho's out.'

Joel's head shot around, the colour draining from his face.

'He's *out*? Are you sure?'

'Yup.' Mack nodded, a small glint of malice in his eyes as he reminded Joel exactly why he couldn't afford to refuse to help his old friend. 'I went down the Galley with Jeff last week, and Psycho's kid brother was in there – pissed as a cunt, celebrating him getting an early for good behaviour.'

'You didn't actually see Psycho, then?' Joel asked, hoping that it was just a rumour.

'Nah, just Little Jimmy-nae-mates,' Mack sneered. 'Eamon don't say nowt to no one, but you know what a loose-lipped twat Jimmy is. Two drinks, and he's telling the world how their Psycho's still the main man, and how no one had best fuck with him now he's out, 'cos he's mad as fuck and planning on pulling in his debts – with *interest*.'

'Meaning?'

'*Meaning*, he's planning a hit and wants cash in his pockets so he can piss off to Spain,' Mack said, giving Joel a pointed look. When Joel gazed blankly back at him, he said, 'In case you haven't figured it out yet, *you*'re the hit – for fucking him over on that deal.'

'I *didn't* fuck him over,' Joel muttered sickly, knowing full well that no one believed him – not even Mack, apparently. And definitely not Pat Muldoon, aka Psycho; so named because of the pleasure he got from slicing people up. He wasn't averse to the odd spot of shooting, either. Or head-stamping. Or torture. Or rape. He was the only man Joel had ever known who genuinely had no conscience.

How the *hell* he'd got himself an early release for good behaviour, Joel did not know. But if it was true, it was time to watch his back, because ten years was a long time for a lunatic like Psycho to fester in prison dreaming of revenge.

Joel had been a naive eighteen-year-old when Psycho took a shine to him. He'd been so flattered that the hardest man on the estate wanted him around that he'd jumped at the chance of clubbing together with him to buy a kilo of coke cheap off a dealer who was having to disappear for offing a copper.

Everyone had known that Psycho was using him for the money, but Joel had been clueless. He'd thought that his ship had well and truly come in – that they would make a killing on the coke, and *he* would be untouchable as Psycho's partner.

He'd been so wrapped up in the fantasy that he hadn't batted an eyelid when Psycho went off to do the deal without him. If all had gone to plan, Psycho would have scored and kept the lot – and sliced Joel's throat from ear to ear if he'd dared ask for *his* share. But someone had tipped the police off, and they'd crashed in on the deal like the SAS at a terrorists' tea party – beating the shit out of the cop-killer *and* Psycho, and confiscating the gear and the money.

Stitched up by the police – who had been trying to pin *anything* on him for a long time – Psycho got twenty-five years for his part in a murder he hadn't, for once, had anything to do with.

And Joel got the blame.

He wasn't the grass, but he was the perfect fall guy for whoever was, because everyone assumed that he had sussed that Psycho was ripping him off and had set him up out of spite.

Suddenly, everyone wanted Joel dead, but Mack had really come through for him. He'd gone to his flat and packed a bag of clothes and personal papers for him, then smuggled him off the estate in the boot of his car to the station, seeing him safely on to the first train out. And Joel had been so grateful that he'd been sending him money regularly ever since.

But Mack had changed a lot over the last few years, and Joel's gratitude had been stretched to the hilt. It wasn't just that Mack had a drug habit that he wouldn't admit to, or that he only ever got in touch when he wanted money. It was something about the order in which he'd done things today that was ringing alarm bells.

Mack had known for a full week that Psycho was out of nick. But instead of picking up the phone to warn Joel, he'd waited until he had time to drive all the way here, then tried to tap him for a grand – almost as if he knew that Joel wouldn't be around for too much longer, and wanted to get as much out of him as he could before the gravy train hit the buffers.

And it was particularly sinister that he hadn't even *mentioned* Psycho until Joel had said he couldn't give him the money. That should have been the first thing out of his mouth, not the afterthought, and Joel suspected that he might not have been going to tell him at all.

'Did Little Jimmy mention me?' he asked casually, hoping to gauge exactly what Mack knew in order to safeguard himself.

'Course he did,' Mack snorted, as if he was stupid for asking such an obvious question. 'But don't worry – I said you'd fucked off to Jersey.'

'*Jersey?*'

'Yeah, well, I'd been watching *Bergerac*, and it was the first thing that come to mind,' Mack said, shrugging irritably. 'Didn't want me to say you was here, did you?'

'Course not,' Joel said, ignoring what he took to be a veiled threat. 'That's not such a bad idea, though.'

'What's not?'

'Moving. Well, I can't stay here if Psycho's looking for me, can I? I need to disappear. Maybe not to Jersey, but somewhere far out.'

'Where?'

'No idea.' Joel shrugged, injecting as much sincerity into

his voice as possible as he added, 'But don't worry, wherever I end up, you'll be the first to know. About that money,' he said then, hoping to buy himself a bit of time. 'I'm not promising anything, but if you can give me a couple of days I'll see what I can do.'

'For real?' Mack peered at him, narrow-eyed.

'Yeah.' Smiling tightly, Joel nodded.

Joel's smile slipped the instant he'd waved Mack on his way. Legging it to the shopping centre down the road, he hopped into a cab and rushed back to the flat.

He had three days at the absolute most before Mack realised he wasn't getting any money and blew him up to Psycho. After that, it would only be a matter of hours before Psycho was kicking the door down – and he intended to be long gone by then.

Locking the door, Joel drew all the curtains and dragged his suitcases out of the wardrobe, packing everything with lightning speed. Preparation was the key to staying alive now.

Going into the kitchen when he was done, he dumped the ounce out on the kitchen ledge and cut it with bicarb and powdered baby laxative until he'd turned it into three. It was a greedy cut, but needs must – and all that. And if anyone complained, he'd be long gone – so, tough!

Splitting the coke into three piles, Joel prepared two into gram bags and left the remaining one intact on the off chance. That done, he set about calling his customers to let them know that he was going to be out of town for a while, and to come and get what they needed while they had a chance.

13

Watching from the platform as the train pulled out, Maria waved until she could no longer see Beth. The station felt cold and desolate when the engine roar had faded along with the tail lights into the dark distance. Now the silence was punctuated only by the breeze whispering up the tracks and the throaty gurgling of the pigeons settling in for the night on the iron roof girders.

Folding her arms as a feeling of abandonment settled on her, Maria walked quickly out to the taxi stand. She was glad that there was no queue, because she didn't think she could have stood among people just now without bursting into tears.

Back at the house, the sense of aloneness intensified when she closed the front door. It was too quiet without Beth's laughter and incessant chatter, and Maria felt awkward and self-conscious now – like a visitor waiting for the host to show up.

Closing the curtains, she turned lights on all around the house in an attempt to lighten the atmosphere. Making herself a coffee, she sat at the kitchen table with a cigarette in one hand and her phone in the other.

Feeling thoroughly sorry for herself, she contemplated calling Beth and begging her to get off the train at the next station and come back, but she couldn't bring herself to do it. Beth would only tell her to grow up and stop being so stupid.

She called Sharon instead, only to be told that Sharon and

Leanne had gone ice-skating with some girls they'd met from the next Bay.

Disappointed, Maria scrolled through the rest of the numbers in her phone book, alarmed to see how few belonged to people she actually considered a friend. There were lots of 'official' numbers: doctor, dentist, library, bank, etc. But few real friends.

Coming across Vicky's number, she bit her lip guiltily. It was ages since she'd seen her, and she hadn't called when she'd got home like she'd said she would. But Vicky would understand, she was sure.

Taking a chance, she dialled the number. After several rings, a man answered.

'She's not in,' he told her curtly when she asked for Vicky. 'Wanna leave a message?'

Disappointed, Maria said, 'Er, yeah, can you tell her that Maria Price rang? I'll try her again sometime.'

She frowned when the man said he'd pass it on and then abruptly hung up. She guessed it was Vicky's boyfriend, but he hadn't been very nice considering Vicky had said that she'd told him all about Maria and was sure he'd want to meet her. But then, maybe he was being funny with her because she'd let Vicky down.

There was no one left on the list now but Joel.

Just seeing his name on the screen sparked a little thrill of excitement in her, but she was reluctant to call him in case his bitchy girlfriend answered. Having seen her, she doubted the girl would believe that it was just a friendly catch-up call – which was all it was.

Honest.

But then, why *shouldn't* she call him? Maria thought defiantly. He'd given her the number in full view of the girl, so he obviously wasn't bothered about her knowing. And if *he* wasn't bothered, why should she be?

Taking the bull by the horns, she rang him.

'Er, hi, it's Maria,' she babbled when he answered, hoping to God that he didn't say *'Maria who?'* Not that he *should*, seeing as it was him who'd insisted she take his number. 'I just remembered that I said I'd call, and I was at a bit of a loose end, so I thought I'd give you a quick ring. I'm not disturbing you, am I?'

'Not at all,' Joel assured her. 'How are you?'

'Fine.' Maria felt shy now. 'You?'

'All the better for hearing your voice,' he said. 'I've been thinking about you, as it happens.'

'Really?'

'Yeah, I was wondering if you'd got home all right. Where was it you said you lived? Devon?'

'Actually, I'm still here. Things have sort of changed since I saw you, and I'm moving back for good. Well, for a while, anyway.'

'Really? That's great news.'

'Yeah, well, I thought I should give it a chance – see if it works out,' Maria said, feeling ridiculously nervous now. 'Anyway, I was thinking, now I'm back I should probably have my friends round. So, I was wondering . . . Well, if you're interested, would you like to come for dinner some time?'

'Are you kidding me?' Joel said without hesitation. 'I'd *love* to. When?'

'I, er, hadn't actually thought that far ahead,' Maria admitted, blushing deeply – glad that he wasn't there to see it. 'When's best for you?'

'Tonight,' Joel said with a smile in his voice. 'Unless that's too soon?'

'No, that's fine.' Maria tried not to sound too eager. 'Have you any preferences food-wise?'

'Anything – as long as it's hot and spicy.' Joel laughed softly. 'I'll bring the booze. Shall we say eight?'

★   ★   ★

Hanging up, Joel raised his eyes heavenward in a silent *Thank You*.

He'd shifted two full ounces in the last few hours, more than covering what he owed the Gallaghers. But he still needed to shift the rest as soon as possible, to get himself some money.

It would have been so easy to do a runner, but he'd considered it and decided against it within the space of a second. The Gallaghers would come after him, and the last thing he needed were yet *more* maniacal enemies hunting him down. Anyway, he'd much rather have them on his side if the worst came to the worst and Psycho *did* find him.

The one good thing that Joel had going for him was that he was smarter than Psycho. He just had to stay calm and alert to avoid making himself vulnerable to surprise attacks. He had a few days' grace, because Mack was too greedy to sell him out until he'd received the money – or realised that he wasn't going to get it. But now that Maria had thrown him this lifeline he could afford to relax a little.

Taking a shower in preparation for what he was sure would be a great night, he contemplated this latest piece of good luck. If he played Maria right – and he had a feeling it would be as easy as melting ice cream in the kettle – he might have found himself the perfect hideout until he'd planned his next move. And he'd be safe, because no one had the first clue that she even existed. How perfect was *that*!

Giving his reflection a wry grin as he dried himself off, Joel very much doubted that he'd have any problem charming his way into Maria's bed tonight. He wouldn't frighten her off by arriving for dinner with his suitcases in tow, though. If all went as planned, he'd come back for them in the morning. If not, he'd just have to go and stay with one of his other tarts instead.

But he didn't anticipate that happening, somehow.

★   ★   ★

Maria was cursing herself for inviting *anyone*, never mind *Joel*, to dinner. She didn't even have any food in the house. And even if she *had*, she couldn't have done anything with it, because she had no idea how to turn the bloody cooker on.

Stupid!

But, stupid or not, she had just over one hour to get it sorted, and herself ready.

Remembering the menu leaflet that Beth had picked up at the Chinese takeaway the night before, Maria ran upstairs to get it. She shouldn't really eat fast food two nights on the run, but this was an emergency. Crossing her fingers that Joel had meant what he said about liking hot food, she ordered spicy ribs, chilli chow mein, and chicken satay for two.

Boiling a kettle of water, she washed her hair, then rooted through her case for something decent to wear. None of it was very dinner date-ish, but she couldn't wear the blue dress again. Joel had already seen it, for one thing, and it was way too dressy for a takeaway in the kitchen.

Beth's top!

Rushing into the bathroom, Maria found the white Lycra halter top hanging over the towel rail where Beth had left it to dry after washing it the other night. Beth had been wearing her jacket by the time they'd bumped into Joel so, with any luck, he wouldn't remember seeing it.

Slipping it on, she teamed it with black jeans and strappy sandals and looked herself over in the free-standing bedroom mirror. She looked great – even if she *did* say so herself.

Taking her time to do her make-up, Maria sprayed herself with perfume, then made her way down the stairs just as the food was delivered.

Joel arrived a few minutes later – wine in one hand, Jack Daniel's in the other.

He was dead on time, which was amazing given that he'd

taken two cabs to shake off anybody who might be following
him: one from his flat to town, another from town to a
restaurant a few streets away from here where he'd stood
in the doorway as if waiting for a date until the cab pulled
away. Then he'd run the rest of the way.

Ludicrous lengths to go to, but he wasn't risking anything
with Psycho on the loose.

As soon as he saw Maria, Joel knew that he'd made the
right decision in coming. Not only had she made an effort
to look good – which told him that she definitely had the
hots for him – but the house was far better than he'd
expected: huge, safe, and reasonably secluded. And the area
reeked of old money, so there was less than zero chance of
him bumping into anyone he knew.

'You look incredible,' he told her, leaning down to kiss her
cheek. 'Really beautiful.'

'Thanks.' Blushing prettily, Maria flapped a hand towards
the kitchen. 'We're through here.'

Joel whistled softly through his teeth as he followed her
into the kitchen. Christ, she was fit!

And *rich* . . . And *single* . . .

God was truly on his side, for once.

The food was on the table, still in its foil trays.

'Smells great,' he said, taking his jacket off and hanging it
over the back of one of the two chairs at the table. 'Just us,
is it?'

'I, er, yeah.' Maria's blush deepened. 'Like I said, I hadn't
really planned anything. I was just sounding people out, and,
well, you were the first one I rang.'

'I'm honoured,' Joel said, giving her that sexy smile she
remembered so well. 'Got a corkscrew?'

'There should be one round here somewhere,' Maria said,
opening several drawers before she found it. Handing it to him,
she said, 'You're lucky. Beth only made me buy that last night.'

Going to the draining board while Joel removed the wine bottle's cork, she got the glasses that she and Beth had taken from the dining-room cabinet the night before.

'Crystal glasses and paper plates,' Joel said, chuckling softly. 'Odd combination, but it works for me.'

'Sorry,' Maria said, grimacing. 'I didn't really fancy using the old plates, but I haven't had a chance to go shopping for a new service yet. Me and Beth bought these when we were cleaning up. Oh, and I've got plastic cups as well, if you'd rather go totally downmarket.'

'The glasses are fine,' Joel said, pulling the cork with a dull *Thwok*! 'Bit bright in here, though,' he teased, shielding his eyes against the ceiling light. 'No candles?'

'I have, as it happens,' Maria said, taking a fat church candle out of the cupboard. 'It's a bit big, but Beth insisted on getting it – in case the electric went off in the middle of the night.'

'Very sensible,' Joel said, tipping the rice out onto the plates and standing the candle in the empty foil tray. Folding the edges artistically inwards, he lit it with a flourish. 'There you go . . . your very own solid silver candle-holding house-warming gift.'

Laughing softly, Maria sat down. 'Thanks. I'll keep it for ever.'

'Make sure you do,' Joel said, giving her a meaningful look as he switched off the overhead light. 'I'll expect you to bring it out every time I visit – even when you're sixty, and losing your marbles.'

'I will,' Maria murmured shyly, spooning satay onto the rice.

Pouring the wine, Joel handed a glass to her and peered into her eyes.

Falling headlong into his as they clinked glasses, Maria knew she was lost. It was crazy and impetuous and exciting, but she just wanted to feel his arms around her again, taste his lips on hers, run her hands through his hair, and smell him on her when she woke up in the morning.

This was the first time she had ever felt this way, and she wasn't sure how to handle it. Usually, she would be building the wall faster than she could blink right about now, but she just couldn't seem to lift the bricks this time.

'Shall we . . . ?' Joel picked up his fork.

'Oh, yes, of course,' Maria said, pulling herself together. 'Sorry . . . I hope it's not cold.'

'We'll just stick it in the microwave if it is.'

'I haven't actually got one,' Maria admitted. 'I've got a list of things I need, so I'll have one by next . . .' Stopping herself before she could come out and say '*Next time you're here*,' which would be *too* presumptuous, she gave a little shrug. 'I'll be getting one.'

Joel smiled to himself. This was working out better than he could have hoped. She was doing all the work for him. All he'd have to do would be close the deal, and he'd be home and dry.

'This is really nice,' he said, tasting the food. 'It reminds me of the first time I went to Amsterdam. I was on tour with some girl singer from the States.' Pausing, he frowned, as if trying to remember the name. Then, shrugging, he said, 'I think it was Maria, actually – small world, eh? She said it kind of different, though. Maria Clary – or something like that.'

'You don't mean Mariah *Carey*?' Maria asked, open-mouthed.

'Yeah, that's the one.' Joel flapped his hand dismissively. 'You tend to forget their names after a while, 'cos they're all so alike.'

Maria nearly choked on her food. He was so nonchalant about it, but she'd be having *kittens* if she was around stars as big as Mariah Carey.

'She was really demanding,' Joel went on with a chuckle. 'Great voice, but *boy* did she run you ragged. Soon as she was off stage, she wanted food. But she couldn't let you know what she wanted beforehand so you could have it waiting, you had to wait till she came off stage, then run out and try and find whatever she had a taste for. So, anyway, this night she wants chicken satay and egg fried rice, and she wants *me* to go for it. But it wasn't my job, and I was getting a bit pissed off with her by then, so I said, "No! Enough's enough! If you want food, you can damn well go and get it yourself!"'

'You *didn't?*'

'Too right,' Joel snorted softly. 'I wasn't her gofer. I told her – I said, I'm working *with* you, not *for* you. And if you don't like it, I'll leave, and you can try and find someone else to hold it all together for you. And you're not the only one who's hungry, I said. *I*'m starving, your *manager*'s starving, and your bloody bodyguards are wasting away.'

'So what did she say?' Maria asked, sure that he would say he'd been sacked on the spot.

'She said, "Sorry, babe",' Joel said, affecting an American female voice. '"I didn't realise I was being such a bitch. Give me a minute to get changed and we'll *all* go look for a place to eat. Ok*aaay?*"'

'So you went to a restaurant together? You and Mariah Carey?'

'Yeah – me and Mariah, and the rest of the crew.' Joel shrugged, getting into his stride now. 'It's par for the course with most of my clients, but some just need reminding that we're not their fans. Without us, they wouldn't be out there doing what they do. Most are great, though. Like the Gallagher brothers – I do a lot of work with them, and they're sound.'

'As in *Oasis?*' Maria was awestruck all over again.

'Yeah.' Nodding, Joel grinned. 'Nice lads, I know them well. They were one of my first, actually. Tour of Germany – retracing one of the Beatles' early tours.'

Listening raptly as Joel told her about that and other tours he'd organised, Maria picked at the food and took regular sips of wine. She found the melodic sound of his voice hypnotic, and his gorgeous eyes twinkling in the candlelight mesmerising. And his smile was so bright and warm that he made the large, cold kitchen seem really cosy and intimate.

She could hardly believe that a man with such a fascinating lifestyle would be interested in an unsophisticated girl like her. He had mixed with some of the most famous singers and musicians in the world, but she had done nothing, been nowhere. How could she possibly compete?

'It's sounds fantastic,' she said, when Joel stopped talking. 'You must really love it.'

'I do.' Resting his elbows on the table, Joel licked the spicy barbecue syrup off his fingers. 'You never know where you're going to be from one week to the next – or who with. But it's not all plain sailing, believe me.'

Laughing softly, he wiped his mouth on a napkin and reached for his drink. Maria had fallen hook, line and sinker for his favourite fictitious career. Now it was time to find out where she stood on the subject of his *real* occupation. Not that it mattered *what* she thought, it just saved all the hassle of having to lie if he felt like having a line or two. And all the better if she had one with him, because the sex would be out of this world.

'We all know about demanding *American* divas,' he said, reeling out his *tester* story. 'But our lot can be just as bad. Take this young boy band I was working with last year. Nice lads – really polite and cooperative. Then, a few days into the tour, their manager takes me to one side and asks if I know where they can get hold of any coke, 'cos the lads have run out. And I'm like, we're in *Germany*. Like I'm gonna know anyone *here*.'

'That's terrible,' Maria said, shaking her head with disapproval as she finished her wine. 'Fancy expecting you to do something illegal, just because they're famous.'

'Ah, well . . . that's celebrities for you,' Joel said casually.

Well, that told him. But he had to admit that he was surprised, considering she'd been born and raised on the borders of a major drugs ghetto like Moss Side. Still, much as her views clashed with his livelihood, there was something really naive about her that he found quite appealing. Finding a true innocent was almost as good as bagging yourself a virgin – and there weren't many of them about these days.

Finished with the food and wine, Joel opened the Jack Daniel's and poured two large shots. Handing Maria's to her, he leaned back in his chair and looked around.

'This is a great house.'

'It is, isn't it?' Maria agreed with a tinge of pride in her voice. 'I thought it was amazing when I first saw it, but it just gets better the more time I spend here.'

'So, you've definitely decided to move in?'

'I'm seriously considering it,' Maria said.

She didn't bother to mention that just a few hours ago she'd been so lonely that she'd been on the verge of running back home to her dingy old Teignmouth flat. Now, thanks to Joel's reassuring presence, she felt totally at ease.

And the booze was helping, too.

'There'll be a lot of work to do if I do stay,' she went on, 'but I'm getting good advice about the money, so it shouldn't kill me. And it's a good investment, even if I decide I want to move at a later date . . .' Tailing off when she realised that Joel was peering at her with sexy half-closed eyes and a lopsided smile, she gave a sheepish smile. 'Sorry. I'm going on, aren't I?'

'Not at all,' Joel assured her, downing his drink in one and refilling his glass. Holding the bottle up, he raised an eyebrow, waiting for her to empty her glass.

'Are you trying to get me drunk?' Maria asked, downing it and holding her glass out unsteadily.

'Might be,' he murmured. 'Is it working?'

'A bit *too* well,' she admitted, biting her lip because she could feel the smile trying to spread itself all over her face. She wanted to be sexy, not grinny.

'Going to show me around?' Joel asked after a moment, his voice soft and low.

'Yeah, sure.' Pushing her chair back, Maria stood up. 'Oops!' she giggled, stumbling against the table. 'Where do you want to start?'

'How about the bedroom?' Joel purred, going to her and pulling her into his arms.

Closing her eyes, Maria gave a tiny gasp of pleasure when his tongue grazed hers. Slipping her hands under his shirt, she scraped her fingernails slowly down his smooth back.

Moaning, Joel lifted her off her feet and carried her out through the hall and up the stairs.

'Which room?' he asked huskily.

Maria pointed the way, too breathless for words.

Falling onto the bed together, they kissed deeply and pulled at each other's clothes, desperate for the sensation of flesh on flesh.

Running his hands gently over her breasts when she was naked, Joel lowered his lips to her nipples, sucking one then the other until she was writhing beneath him. Trailing his tongue down over her smooth flat stomach, he gently pushed her legs apart and lapped at the juices glistening on the fine blonde hairs framing her sweet-tasting pussy, pushing ever deeper until she cried out, her back arching, her hands in his hair, holding him to her until the waves had subsided.

Easing himself into her with a gentle thrust, Joel pushed himself up onto his hands and gazed at Maria's face as she opened herself up to him. Her lips were swollen, her eyes glazed.

'You're so beautiful,' he murmured, thrusting harder and deeper. 'So . . . very . . . *beautiful* . . .'

Groaning as hot liquid gold tore through him, he gripped her hips in his hands and held her tight, his face a mask of agonised ecstasy as he exploded inside her.

'Christ, that was incredible,' he said when his breathing had slowed.

Maria didn't speak – she couldn't. Pressing her face into his shoulder, she clung on tight, struggling against a sudden urge to cry.

That had been wild and raw, yet intimate and tender, too. She had never experienced anything like it before – and doubted whether she ever would again.

If this was love, she was about to enter a whole new world.

14

'You did *what*?' Beth squawked, sitting bolt upright and switching the phone to her other ear. 'The one from the club with the snotty-bitch girlfriend?'

'Believe me, she is *not* his girlfriend,' Maria informed her primly. Lying back in her own bed, she stroked the pillow where Joel's head had been just a short while ago. 'Like he said the other night – he was only taking her out as a favour to a friend. He hasn't seen her since, and he *won't* be seeing her again. Or any other woman,' she added, laughing softly.

'Good luck with *that*,' Beth said sceptically. 'I'm not being funny, Maria, but he's probably got women throwing themselves at him left, right and centre. And men as good-looking as him don't tend to say no when it's being handed out on a plate.'

'Joel's different,' Maria said confidently. 'But it'll be easy enough to keep an eye on him while he's staying here, won't it?' she added with a sly chuckle.

'Do *what*?' Beth yelped. 'Christ, Maria, what the bloody hell's going on up there? I only left a few hours ago. Did you call him from the station while you were waving me off, or what?'

'No, I didn't,' Maria protested, dismayed that she was being so funny about it. 'I called him when I got home and asked him round for dinner. What's wrong with that?'

'Nothing – if that's all it *was*. Come on, Maria. It's one

thing having an old friend over for dinner and things going a bit too far. But moving him *in* . . . ? That's just crazy. You haven't seen him for years. And people change. You don't know the first thing about this man.'

'He's not moving in,' Maria corrected her irritably. 'He's just staying for a week or two until he finds a new flat, that's all. It's not *his* fault that his landlord gave him twenty-four hours' notice.'

'Nice and convenient, though, you've got to admit,' Beth countered scathingly. 'You just happen to call at the exact time he's heading out the door with his bags. You, with your big *empty* old house.'

'Actually, that's *exactly* what happened,' Maria said, miffed that Beth was trying to turn this into something it wasn't when she didn't even *know* Joel.

It was quite beside the point that Maria didn't really know him either. *Beth* didn't know that – and she could never find out if this was the way she was going to react.

'It was *me* who called *him*,' Maria reminded her. 'And he didn't even know about the house, so it's not like he thought, *Oh, I know, I'm being made homeless, I'll move in with Maria.* He didn't even tell me he was getting evicted till I asked what he was doing today, and he said he was going flat-hunting. When I invited him round last night, he just saw it as a chance to relax for a few hours before he had to start walking the streets.'

'Then he tripped over your bed and lost his way home?'

'What can I say?' Maria gave a little self-conscious laugh. 'He's drop-dead gorgeous – I couldn't help myself. To think I actually thought you'd be *pleased* for me,' she added with a sigh. 'Stupid, huh?'

'I can't help being protective,' Beth said quietly, feeling a bit guilty for taking the shine off Maria's obvious joy. 'You're my best mate. I don't want to see you hurt.'

'Yeah, well, I won't be, so there's no need to worry.' Maria softened her tone. 'Joel's really different from everyone I've ever been out with. And I know there's not been that many to compare him with but that just makes it better, because it feels really sort of *pure.*'

At her end, Beth pulled the phone away from her ear and stared at it incredulously. Maria had definitely lost the plot! Joel was certainly a looker, but he was a *player.* There was no way the blonde they'd seen him with that night hadn't been his girlfriend. Any fool could see they were a couple by the way she was having a go at him in the taxi. She must have got wise to him and dumped him.

Of *course*! That must be it!

He'd been living with the bitchy blonde, and she'd kicked him out – probably because he kept giving his number to other girls. Then, just in the nick of time, Maria calls to invite him round and *Bingo*! New girl – new place to stay.

'Are you still there?' Maria asked after several moments of silence.

'Yeah, I'm here,' Beth said, wondering how best to voice her suspicions. 'Look, you know this girlfriend of his—'

'He hasn't *got* one.'

'So *he* says.'

'And I believe him,' Maria replied tersely. 'Look, I invited him to dinner, we got drunk and ended up in bed – end of. Nothing suspicious. Nothing pre-planned. You just don't like him for some reason.'

'That's not true,' Beth protested. 'I don't even know him.'

'Exactly. So you've got no right to judge him.'

Beth sighed heavily. Maria was digging her heels in, and pushing the issue would make her do something rash – like marry the idiot, or something equally ridiculous.

Well, okay, maybe she wouldn't go quite *that* far. But Beth knew her well enough to know when to back off.

'Right, fine,' she said softly. 'I won't say another word about it.'

'Good.'

There was an awkward silence that lasted several long, long seconds. Then Maria said, 'Right, well, I'd best go. Want me to give you a ring later?'

'Yeah, do,' Beth replied with a soft chuckle. 'And I promise I'll have my nice head back on.'

Grateful that she was trying to lift the tension, Maria said, 'Thanks. And sorry I got so snotty. I just wanted to talk to you, 'cos I miss you like mad.'

'Me too,' Beth said. 'But I'll be back before you know it for that holiday, so don't go doing anything stupid without speaking to me about it first – okay?'

'Like what?'

Oh, I don't know . . .' Beth drawled. 'Tattoos, piercings – *wedding rings*.'

'As if!' Maria laughed. 'Right, I'm definitely going now. Joel should be back any minute, and we've got loads to do. I'm buying all the kitchen stuff today.'

'It's Sunday,' Beth reminded her. 'The shops will be shut.'

'I'm not in Tinny now,' Maria chuckled, happy again. 'Manchester *never* shuts. Joel's taking me to an electrical goods warehouse he knows about. He reckons we'll get loads of discount if we get everything in one go.'

'And are *we* paying for it?' Beth asked slyly.

If Maria's new man was only supposed to be staying for a week or two, shouldn't he be out looking for a place of his own instead of shopping for domestic appliances that he wouldn't even be using? He seemed to be shoving his attractive feet pretty far under the table.

'Don't be daft!' Maria gave an embarrassed little laugh. 'I wouldn't *dream* of asking him for money. It's my house, so it's my responsibility.'

'So what's the rush?' Beth asked reasonably. 'You don't even know if you're staying yet. Why not wait until you've made up your mind? Then at least you won't have wasted money on stuff you don't need.'

'Actually, I, er, *will* be staying,' Maria told her, quickly adding, 'Well, *you* said I should. You said the house was gorgeous, and there was nothing so great about Tinny.'

'Yes, I know,' Beth conceded. 'And I meant it. Just as long as it's what *you* want.' *And not something you've been manipulated into.* 'Just do me a favour,' she said then, 'and don't go overboard with the spending, or you'll find you've got nothing left and you won't have a clue where it's gone. Maybe you should give Nigel a ring? Tell him what you're planning, and get some advice.'

'No need,' Maria said breezily. 'I've talked it over with Joel and *he*'s helping me. Actually, just *having* him here is helping. I was a bit freaked out after you left, but I felt a lot better when he came round. And I know he'll be gone soon, but I think I'll be fine by then.'

'Oh, babe, I'm sorry,' Beth said guiltily. 'I didn't even think about how you'd feel on your own. I should have stayed a bit longer.'

'I'm all right,' Maria assured her. 'And I didn't say it to make you feel bad, so *don't*. Anyway, I'm going before we upset each other. I'll call you later and let you know what's happening.'

'Okay, but leave it till after three,' Beth said. 'I'm going to see my nan in a bit, then my dad's giving me a lift to pick your stuff up. He says you can store it in the garage till you're ready to pick it up, but I wouldn't leave it too long if I was you, or it'll get damp. I'll keep your clothes in my room so they don't get wrecked.'

Thanking her, Maria said, 'There's not much I'm taking, actually. But don't forget to take my birthday mobile down off the curtain rail. I didn't pack it 'cos I liked looking at it, but I'll never forgive myself if it gets left behind.'

Assuring her that she wouldn't forget, Beth said goodbye. Lying back against the pillows then, she mulled the conversation over, frowning thoughtfully.

It had been quite a shock to hear about Joel. Talk about a fast worker! If he really *had* been on the verge of eviction, he must have thought it was Christmas come early when poor lonely Maria invited him to stay in her big old mansion.

Beth didn't quite believe the story about the landlord, though. She was sure it was illegal to evict people at such short notice; and a whole blockful . . . ? She couldn't see it, somehow. Anyway, it was way too convenient, and she thought *her* version about his girlfriend kicking him out was probably much closer to the truth.

But, cynical theories aside, at least Maria had someone to keep her company for a week or two until she had settled into her new home. And if *she* was happy, then Beth should be, too. And she *could* be totally wrong about Joel. He might be a perfectly nice man, who had genuinely only gone along for an innocent dinner with an old friend and had ended it realising just how beautiful and lovely she was – no ulterior motives whatsoever.

Highly unlikely, but time would tell.

Maria had just finished getting dressed when she heard the key in the door. She ran down the stairs just as Joel lugged two heavy-looking cases and several plastic bags into the hall.

'I didn't hear a car. Don't tell me you walked with that lot?'

'No, I got a cab, but I needed to go to the shop, so I got it to drop me round the corner.' Dropping the bags, Joel kicked the door shut. 'But, never mind that . . . come here.'

Taking Maria in his arms, he held her to him for a while, then kissed her hair and eased her away.

'Enough, or you'll get me started, and we'll never get anything done.'

'Want me to help you unpack?' Maria offered, thrilled by the easy intimacy between them.

'Best not,' Joel said, checking his watch. 'It's half-nine already, and I'm afraid I haven't got quite as much time as I'd have liked to help you choose your stuff. I've got to be free by two to see the flat.'

'The flat?'

'Oh, sorry, yeah. I meant to tell you when I got here, but you distracted me. One of my neighbours knocked when I was getting my stuff, to tell me there's a vacant flat in the place she's moving to. Long story short, she knows the letting agent, so she rang him and put in a word for me, and he's asked me to go and see it at two. If it's okay, I thought I might as well move straight in. Is it all right if I leave the bags here till I've seen it, though?'

'Yeah, sure,' Maria said disappointedly.

She'd thought they would have a *bit* of time together before he moved on. Now it felt like the prize had been snatched from her grasp. And not only that, she was actually a bit miffed about this neighbour of his setting him up for a flat near her own.

'That's very nice of your neighbour,' she said, trying not to let the twinge of jealousy show in her voice. She'd bet this woman *friend* hadn't gone to those lengths for any of the other neighbours. 'You must know her quite well if she's prepared to put herself out for you like that?'

'Oh, yeah, she's a lovely girl.' Smiling, Joel lit two cigarettes and handed one to Maria. 'And her new flat's right next door to the vacant one, apparently, which is cool, because it's nice to have someone you know nearby, so you can pop in for a chat, or a drink.'

'Where is it?' Maria asked, trying to sound interested rather than irritated.

'Salford,' Joel said, shrugging. 'Wouldn't be my *first* choice, but it's better than nothing. Anyway, are you ready to get started?'

'Suppose so,' Maria said, taking her jacket down from the peg with a sigh.

Walking around White Warehouse a short while later, Maria couldn't summon the enthusiasm to do more than glance at the huge array of fridge-freezers, cookers and washing machines. Everything was as cheap as Joel had promised, and ordinarily she'd have been jumping for joy, but she had more pressing things on her mind just now.

Like, how much she'd enjoyed waking up next to Joel this morning – and how much she would miss him tomorrow.

God, if she didn't know better, she'd swear she was falling in love – and that frightened her as much as it thrilled her. If Joel could see what was going on in her head right now, he'd think she was some kind of psychotic stalker and run a mile. One night, and she's already declaring undying love and affection. Help!

'Seen anything you fancy?' Joel asked, glancing pointedly at his watch. 'Apart from me, obviously,' he added with a grin.

Smiling sadly. Maria shook her head. 'Not really. Have you?'

'Yeah, there's a brilliant fridge over there – one of those big American jobs: brushed steel, double doors, ice-maker. I'd get it for the flat, but I doubt I'll be able to fit anything bigger than a worktop cooler in there. Still, I'll only be using it as a base until I find somewhere better, so I'll bide my time on buying stuff. But it would look great in *your* kitchen. Come and have a look – see what you think.'

Reaching out as Joel began to walk away, Maria touched his arm. She didn't want to frighten him off, but she just wasn't ready to lose him quite so soon. Especially not to let him go and move in next door to a woman who probably had the hots for him. He didn't know Maria as well as he obviously knew Little Miss Helpful, and she didn't want to risk them getting even closer until she had established her own foothold in his emotions.

'About that flat,' she said nervously. 'I've been thinking, and . . . well, if you really don't want to move to Salford, you could always stay with me until you've found somewhere better.'

'No, I couldn't.' Joel smiled gratefully. 'Thanks for the offer, but you've been away from Manchester too long if you think decent flats come along every day. It might be months before I find something else.'

'That doesn't matter,' she assured him, throwing caution to the wind. 'Honestly. You could stay as long as you liked. Can't say I haven't got the room, can I?'

'Really?' Joel looked down at her with narrowed eyes as if he was actually considering it. Then, shaking his head, he said, 'No, I couldn't impose on you like that. I wouldn't want to risk ruining what we've got. But thanks, anyway.'

Biting her lip when he hugged her, Maria laid her head on his chest, saying quietly, '*Have* we got something?'

Raising her chin with a finger, Joel peered sincerely into her eyes. 'Do you really need to ask?' he said, his voice so soft that it curled around her heart. 'I've felt something with you these last few hours that I never thought I'd feel with anyone.' Pausing when a tear slid from her eye, he wiped it away with the tip of his finger. 'Hey, what's this?'

'Nothing.' Embarrassed, Maria shook her head and looked down. 'Sorry, I didn't mean to do that.'

Holding her to him until she had composed herself, Joel smiled inwardly. He'd taken a gamble and it had paid off. And he didn't feel too bad about it, because he wasn't outright using her – he actually did like her. Quite a lot, as it happened. She was sweet, kind, smart *and* sexy. And all in nice manageable amounts. If she'd been too sweet, she'd become sickly really fast. Too kind, he'd start looking on her like an aunt. Too smart, she'd have to go. Too sexy . . . Well, no, sack that. You *couldn't* be too sexy.

'Come on, gorgeous,' he said after a minute, taking her hand. 'Let's go find what you need to make that house of yours a home. Oh, and if you meant what you said, by the way, then, yeah – I'd love to stay until I find somewhere decent. I just hope you meant what you said about not caring if it took a while, though, because this could drag out. If you think I've been there too long, just say you want me out and I'm gone.'

Maria felt like a princess as they walked hand in hand through the store. Beth would be less than impressed, but Maria didn't really care what anybody thought right now. This *felt* right, and that was all that mattered. And whatever came of it – whether it developed into something serious or not – right now she was happy just to know that there would be more nights like last night, and more mornings like this morning.

After choosing and ordering all of the kitchen equipment, Maria and Joel headed into town and spent the next few hours in the Arndale Centre, splashing out on clothes, shoes, towels, dinner service, TV, DVD player, hi-fi . . .

Staying in town to have dinner at a great little Italian restaurant that Joel had been meaning to try out, they didn't get back to the house until seven, by which time Maria was exhausted.

Helping her to lug the bags up to the bedroom, Joel said, 'You unpack, and I'll make coffee. And if you tell me where the immersion switch is, I'll put the water on so you can have a bath.'

'Put it on now and it might just about be ready by morning, if I'm lucky.' Maria smiled, then laughed when it turned into a yawn. 'God, you'd never guess that a little thing like spending would take so much out of you,' she quipped, sitting down heavily on the bed. 'Good job I've been poor for so long, or I'd probably be dead by now. No wonder Beth told me to be careful.' Yawning again, she blinked as tears filled her eyes. 'Wow, I haven't felt this wiped in years.'

'What was that about Beth?' Joel asked, looking through the bags for the jeans and jumper that she'd insisted on buying for him.

'Oh, nothing really,' Maria said, standing up. 'I rang her this morning to let her know I was all right, and when I told her we were going shopping she warned me to go easy.' Hanging her jacket in the wardrobe, she smiled fondly. 'She's so protective, she swears I can't cope without her to watch over me. She's convinced I'm going to blow it all and have nothing to show for it.'

'You're way too smart for that,' Joel said, ripping the plastic wrapping off the sweater and shaking it out. 'She can't know you very well if she thinks you're that stupid.'

'She probably knows me *too* well,' Maria laughed.

'I don't buy that,' Joel said, pursing his lips and narrowing his eyes playfully. 'I haven't known you for long, but I can see how intelligent you are. And funny, and sexy . . .' Moving towards her, he put his arms around her, cupping her bum in his hands. 'And did I say sexy?'

'Yeah, you did,' she grinned, looping her arms around his neck. 'But you can say it again, if you like. I don't mind.'

Joel's mobile began to ring.

'God! That scared me!' Maria laughed, putting a hand on her chest. 'It's *loud*.'

'Must have turned it up by mistake.' Joel patted his pockets. 'Damn! Where *is* it?'

'Hurry up.' Maria pushed him away. 'I'll be deaf in a minute.'

Finding the phone, Joel pulled it out and looked at the name on the screen. It was Jippi Hinari – a freaky Japanese artist with a voracious appetite for coke and with money to burn.

'Yo,' he said, nodding when Maria picked up the towels and mouthed that she was going to the bathroom. 'Long time no see, man. How's it going?'

'I wanna see you – like *now*, dude!' Jippi announced dramatically. 'I've just got off the plane. I've been exhibiting in the goddam *States*, and I haven't had a decent high in like three goddam months! Release me from these chains of sobriety, per-*lease*!'

'Where are you?'

'In a big fat smelly man's cab on my way to the hotel,' Jippi answered loudly – no doubt the driver was listening. 'I'm like *dying*, guy.'

'How much you after?' Joel asked quietly, wishing Jippi would learn to be a bit more discreet.

'Whatever you've *got*,' Jippi said, as if it were a stupid question. 'Better be good, though.'

'It's fine, don't worry about it,' Joel said, grimacing about the greedy cutting he'd done. But Jippi mightn't notice if he'd been without it for that long.

'Best had be, or I'll ass-fuck you,' Jippi threatened, laughing uproariously. 'My favourite place at ten,' he said then, pleasing Joel that he didn't come out with the name of the bar he was referring to.

Agreeing to meet him there, Joel hung up.

'Everything all right?' Maria asked, coming back in, wiping her hands on a towel.

'Fine,' Joel said, putting the phone back in his pocket. 'That was a client. I've got to nip out and see him for a drink later on, to talk over some gigs he's planning. Shouldn't take more than a couple of hours. You'll be all right, won't you?'

'Yeah, course.' Maria smiled, pleased that he was okaying it with her even though she would never have dreamed of interfering. This was work, not pleasure.

Stretching, Joel rolled his head on his neck. 'I could do without this tonight,' he said tiredly. 'I reckon I'll take a break after this. In fact, I might even suggest that my guy gets himself another organiser for this one. He's a great bloke to work with, but I think I'd rather spend a bit of time with my new lady.'

'You can't turn work down for *me*,' Maria said guiltily.

'It won't kill me to lose one job,' Joel assured her, pulling her to him and kissing her neck. 'I'll see how I feel when I see him. But if it's going to take me away for too long, I'm definitely not doing it. I might find another flat in a couple of weeks, and you might decide you want to go back to Devon.'

'No, I won't,' Maria said quickly. 'I'm definitely staying. I even told Beth this morning.'

'Oh, yeah? I bet she didn't take that too well, if she doesn't think you can cope without her.'

'She couldn't really object, seeing as it was her idea for me to move in here in the first place,' Maria said, sitting down on the bed and leaning back against the pillow. 'She was more concerned about *you* staying here, actually.'

'How so?' Frowning, Joel lit two cigarettes and passed one to her.

'Oh, nothing, really,' Maria shrugged, smiling fondly. 'She's just being a mother hen – doesn't want the nasty man to take advantage of me.'

'Is that what *you* think?' Joel asked, a serious look on his face now as he sat down. 'Because there's no *way* I'd do that to you. I'd rather leave right now than stay for one minute longer than I was welcome.'

'Of course I don't think that,' Maria assured him, wishing

she hadn't said anything. 'And neither does Beth. She's always been protective of me. It isn't personal.'

'Yeah, well, I hope not,' Joel murmured. 'Anyway, I'll be looking for somewhere as soon as. I wouldn't want to come between you and your friend.'

'You won't,' Maria insisted. 'And I don't want you to move straight out. You're absolutely *not* putting me out and, like I said before, there's no point taking something unless it's perfect. And, to be honest, I don't really *care* what Beth thinks, because I know she's wrong. Anyway, she hasn't got a clue what you're like, so she's got no right to an opinion.'

'Just so long as you don't fall out with her over me,' Joel said, reaching out and stroking her leg. 'You're so beautiful. It's no wonder she doesn't want me to get too close to you. She must have spent years watching from the sidelines while guys fell in love with you.'

'Not really,' Maria said, blushing, because he wasn't *too* far from the truth. 'I admit there were more lads after me than her, but she had her fair share. She's a really lovely girl.'

'I'm sure she is,' Joel agreed. 'But she's not a patch on you, and that's got to affect the way she deals with you having relationships.'

'What do you mean?' Maria frowned confusedly.

'You're too sweet,' Joel said knowingly. Then, holding up his hands, he said, 'But I'm biased, so I shouldn't be saying any of this. And I'm sure she wouldn't begrudge you having fun. But even if she did,' he added, with a sly half-smile, 'I'm sorry, but she'll just have to get used to me being around, because even when I've found a new place, I've got no intention of losing you. Don't mind, do you?'

'No.' Biting her lip, Maria smiled shyly. She didn't really think Beth was jealous, but if she was – tough! Men as gorgeous, and considerate, and lovely as Joel didn't come along too often, and there was no way she was letting him go. Anyway, she'd be lucky to see Beth from one month to the next now that they were living so far apart.

Getting up, Joel leaned down and kissed her. 'Better make that coffee, then get ready to go, I suppose. I'll sort my cases out when I get back if it's not too late. I shouldn't think it'll take long, but Rod does tend to get a bit chatty.'

'Rod?' Maria's eyebrows rose. 'You don't mean Rod *Stewart*?' When Joel grinned and shrugged, she said, 'Oh, my God! I *love* him. What's he like?'

'A right one,' Joel chuckled amusedly. 'You wouldn't believe the lengths he goes to for privacy. Knowing him, he'll be dressed up as a Japanese transvestite, or something crazy like that when I meet him. He does it all the time.'

'Why?' Maria was intrigued – thrilled to be getting inside info on such a major star.

'Because now and then he likes to be anonymous in a crowd,' Joel explained. 'He gets recognised everywhere he goes, and sometimes he just wants to cut loose and do his own thing. And it works. I mean, he comes into Manchester every couple of months, or so, to have meetings and visit his girlfriend. But you never hear about it, do you?'

'No.' Maria frowned thoughtfully. 'But isn't he married?'

Nodding slowly, Joel gave her a pointed look. 'Why do you think he goes to such pains to fool the press? But you never heard that from me – okay?'

'I wouldn't dream of telling anyone,' Maria assured him. 'But I'll never look at him the same again – the dirty dog.'

'Yeah, well . . .' Joel shrugged. 'You'd be surprised what celebrities get up to. That's why they insist on secrecy. *I'm* cool, because they know me, but if I tried taking *you* along, they'd be gone before I had a chance to say hello, and word would spread that I couldn't be trusted. My career would be over like that!' He clicked his fingers sharply.

'I can imagine,' Maria said, masking her disappointment.

'But don't worry – I won't be bugging you to take me to work with you.'

'Shame I can't,' Joel said regretfully. 'If they met you, they'd soon realise you're nothing like the little slappers who try to get to them via people like me and the managers – skirts up to their armpits, tops down to the navel. It's embarrassing.'

'Sounds it,' Maria said, shaking her head. 'I could never do something like that.'

'If it's any consolation, you're not missing anything,' Joel said, winking. 'Between you and me, most stars are complete tossers.'

Taking Maria's keys so that he could let himself back in without disturbing her, Joel kissed her goodbye, promising to be as fast as he could.

Pausing at the gate to light a cigarette, he peered out along the dark street before setting off to make sure there was no one about, and no suspicious shadows lurking in the bushes. Seeing nothing, he shook his head. There was no reason to be paranoid round here. It was way too upmarket for your average class of scally to be hanging about. And a car full of Glaswegian hard men would stand out like a sore thumb.

Reminded of Psycho, he decided to give Mack a ring to see how the land lay that end.

'It's me,' he said when Mack answered. 'Any news?'

'I can't talk right now,' Mack said evasively. 'Ring back later and I'll see if I can sort you out, yeah?'

'You all right?' Joel asked, knowing that it was a stupid question, because Mack obviously didn't want to talk just now.

'I'll get back to you,' Mack said, still trying to sound casual. 'All right, *Chris*?'

Joel heard the fear in Mack's voice and it made his blood run cold. And he'd called him Chris, so there was obviously somebody there who was connected to Psycho. Mack was trying to protect Joel and that made him feel guilty for ever having doubted his loyalty.

'Look, I know you can't talk,' he said quietly and quickly. 'But don't worry about that money for Caldwell, 'cos I'm going to send you the lot first thing tomorrow – okay? Just give me a ring as soon as you can and let me know you're all right.'

'Will you quit fucking *bugging* me, you smack-head bastard,' Mack snapped back at him. 'I've told you I'm fucking busy. And I ain't got nothi—'

Joel frowned when the phone went suddenly quiet. 'You still there, Mack?' he ventured tentatively. '*Mack?*'

'Well, well . . . If it isn't Kyle Johnson. Nice of you to get in touch after all this time, you fucking little *grass*.'

Joel almost choked when Psycho's voice hissed down his ear.

'Oh, I get it,' Psycho said softly. 'You'll talk to *this* fuck-wad, but you don't wanna talk to me? Well, I can't say I blame you. Even *I'd* think twice about talking to the bloke I'd stitched up like a cunt – 'specially if the bloke was gonna rip my fucking heart out and eat it! You hearing me, Kyle? You getting the picture, pretty lad? Still not talking, eh? . . . Well, let's see if this helps. Keep listening, you fuckin' little arse bandit – keep listening . . .'

Joel covered his mouth with a hand to stop himself yelling out when a blood-curdling scream ripped down his ear, followed by agonised sobbing.

'Hear that?' Psycho was back on the line. 'That was me ripping your mate's front teeth out with *pliers*. Imagine the fuckin' pain of that, eh? Isn't half fuckin' bleeding, an' all – all over his mammy's saggy auld tits. Which is kind of dis-respectful, if you ask me, but you know what these half-breeds are like.'

Laughing coldly, Psycho took a deep, audible drag on a cigarette.

'Oh, I didnae tell you his mam was here, did I?' he went on in a conversational tone. 'Yeah, auld Sue's here – lying on the floor with her cunt all ripped up, 'cos I've just fucked the arse off her!'

Another drag on the fag, designed to draw the tension out – and it worked, because Joel could barely breathe now.

'Not my usual type, as you know,' Psycho went on, as politely as if they were two old mates discussing the weather. 'But this pal of yours needed teaching a proper lesson, 'cos he had this mad idea that I should *pay* him to give you up. How fucking *crazy* is that, eh? Oh, 'scuse me a minute, Kyle . . . he's trying to get away. Won't be a sec.'

Stumbling into the shadows of a darkened shop doorway, Joel retched at the muffled sounds of kicking and punching, followed by yet more screams.

'Fuck me – he's got a gob on him,' Psycho yelled, sounding as if he was having the time of his life as the screams went on and on in the background. 'All that fuss over one little bollock! Anyone would think I'd cut his cock off. That's *next*, you tosser!'

Laughing, he came back on the phone.

'What's he like, eh? Right mardy arse – crying over one little nadge. Fuck knows what he's gonna be like when I make him shag his old lady.'

'I'll tell you where he is!' Mack cried out in the background. '*Please* . . . I'll tell you! *PLEEEASE* . . .'

'Hoo-*eee*!' Psycho chuckled. 'Hear that, Kylie? Your mate's gonna tell me where you are. So, I guess I'll be seeing you soon, eh, pretty lad! Hope you're ready for me?' His voice changed now, taking on a chilling edge as he said, 'I've been waiting a *long* time to catch up with *you*, Johnson. You are one walking fuckin' dead man!'

The phone went dead in Joel's hand and he stared at it in horror, wanting to throw it away – smash it, and rid himself of the disease of fear that it had poured into him through his ear. His hands and legs were shaking wildly – *everything* was.

Those screams had been truly awful, and he dreaded to think what Psycho had done to cause them. He couldn't blame Mack for giving him up. If Joel had been the one on the receiving end of what he'd just heard, he'd have happily sacrificed the Virgin Mary *and* Baby Jesus.

Setting off at a run, hoping that the cold air would clear the images from his head, Joel reached town in record time and leaned against a wall to catch his breath.

The run *had* helped; he was thinking a bit straighter now. Terrible as it had been hearing Mack being tortured like that, at least he knew exactly where he stood now: Psycho wanted him dead, and, armed with whatever information Mack gave him, he would be on his way here. But if Psycho set off right this minute and drove like the wind it would still take him a good few hours, so Joel still had time to do what had to be done and get back to Maria's.

He just thanked God that he hadn't told Mack – or anyone, in fact – about her. So that was one trail Psycho could never pick up on, no matter whom he tortured or threatened.

The one spark of hope in this particularly dark and dangerous abyss was that Psycho wouldn't stick around for too long once he realised that Joel had escaped. Knowing him, Joel reckoned that he would come to the conclusion that Joel had pissed off to Spain, or somewhere like that – like anyone with half a brain *would* if they had a murderous bastard like Psycho hunting them down.

A little calmer now, Joel pushed himself away from the wall and walked the rest of the way to the bar to meet Jippi. Being philosophical, he knew there was no point dwelling on what he'd heard on the phone. He couldn't change whatever Psycho had done. If Mack was still alive, he'd recover. If he wasn't . . . well, at least Ronnie Caldwell wouldn't be able to get to him.

Either way, Joel's life was safe – for now.

Going into the Cuba Café, Joel spotted Jippi immediately. Always out to shock, he looked truly bizarre tonight with his sky-blue contact lenses, scarlet Afro wig, black Lycra dress and stilettos.

Jumping up when he spotted Joel, Jippi waved theatrically. 'Baby, baby . . . come to momma!'

Frowning when all eyes swivelled his way, Joel dipped his head and rushed across the room to join Jippi at his table in the far corner.

'Sit down, for fuck's sake,' he hissed. 'Everyone's looking.'

'Don't be mean, or I'll have to spank you,' Jippi scolded, slapping Joel's hand flirtatiously. Drawing his head back then, he gave him a penetrating look. 'You look *weird*, guy. I hope you're not going to mess with my head, 'cos I'm *way* too fucked-up for that. I only just got off the motherfucking plane!'

'I know, you told me,' Joel said, wiping sweat from his brow. 'And no, of course I'm not going to mess with you. This isn't about you. I'm just having a bit of woman trouble, that's all.'

'Oh, change to *boys*, dear,' Jippi advised blithely, with a dismissive flap of a long elegant hand. 'They don't *want* you to respect them in the morning, and they've got much bigger mouths for sucking cock.' Opening his own mouth wide, he flicked out his tongue.

Flinching back when he saw that the tip had been split to make it snakelike, Joel shuddered. 'Christ, Jippi . . . No offence, man, but that is *way* too whacked-out.'

'You know, I really should paint you,' Jippi said, changing the subject with lightning speed and slapping his hand down on Joel's thigh – far too close to his groin for comfort. 'How about it? You get naked and roll around in paint, and I get on top of you and move you into different positions on the paper. Oh, it'll be *such* great fun. I'll exhibit you in Paris and make you famous. I'll call it *Cock on Coke* . . . Or maybe just, *Cock on* Cock! What do you think?'

'Er, no, I don't think so,' Joel said nervously. If Jippi was half the *woman* he wished he was, Joel would be in Heaven. But Jippi actually scared him, he was so full on.

'Oh, you'd be such a boring shag,' Jippi said disapprovingly. 'And that's a real shame, because you are so damn *hot* to look at. But, hey ho – maybe *one* day I'll get you to loosen up. So . . .' Another dismissive flap of the hand. 'You've got the coke?'

'Yeah, I've got it,' Joel said, lowering his voice in the hope that Jippi would do likewise. Talk about broadcasting to the nation.

'Let me see.' Jippi held out a hand.

Taking a sample wrap out of his pocket, Joel handed it to him under the table.

Chuckling softly, Jippi opened it up on his lap. Sucking his little finger suggestively while gazing into Joel's eyes, he dipped it into the powder, then pulled his skirt up and rubbed it onto his Prince Alberted dick.

'Christ,' Joel gulped. 'Put it away, man. If anyone sees you, they'll think I'm shagging you.'

'Bet you wish you were now that you've seen Big Daddy-O,' Jippi teased, bringing the finger up and licking it. 'Want some?'

'No,' Joel said in a manly tone. 'Never touch it when I'm working.'

'Cock, or coke?'

'Both.'

Laughing loudly, Jippi pulled the skirt back down. 'You kill me, you homophobic little hottie! Go on, then . . . I'll take it. What you got?'

'An O,' Joel said, breathing a sigh of relief.

'How much?' Jippi reached for his handbag and pulled out a thick wad of cash.

'One and a half,' Joel said, doing a double take. The handbag looked like a baby alligator.

'Like it?' Jippi held it up proudly. 'I got it off a *foul* little swamp-man in the Everglades. My friend Lilli put a zip in it for me, and I walked straight through Customs with it over my shoulder. *Fab*ulous, isn't it?'

Joel grimaced. He'd seen stuff made out of skin before, but never with the face still attached. That made it particularly gross.

'I thought it was illegal,' he said.

'And this *isn't*?' Jippi laughed, dangling the coke bag in the air – almost giving Joel a heart attack.

'Put it away!'

'You're *way* too straight, guy,' Jippi teased, slipping the coke into his bag. 'You should come and spend a week in my Paris loft. I'll blow your *mind*.'

'I won't say I'm not flattered,' Joel said, winking as he pocketed the money. 'But it's not my scene.'

'I'm patient.' Jippi smiled slyly. 'But think about letting me immortalise you in paint in the meantime. Those looks won't last for ever, you know.'

'We'll see.' Joel held out his hand. 'Have fun while you're in town, but I've got to go, man. Give me a ring when you want another meet. But leave it a couple of weeks if you can. I'm going to be out of action for a while.'

'Yeah, well, I'll be busy for a while myself,' Jippi said, lighting a long, thin spliff. 'I sold up in the States, so I'll have to get a whole new set together. But soon as I'm back on track, I'm getting a place here and having parties. And you know what that means, don't you? . . . Lots of fuck-head starlets flashing the cash and snorting their little tushies off. You want in on that, don't you?'

'Too right.' Joel grinned. 'Just give me a bell and I'll be there.'

Hailing a cab down the road from the bar, Joel had the driver take him to Rusholme and wait around the corner while he ran round to pay the Gallaghers what he owed and tell them he was taking a short break. Jumping back in the taxi then, he had it drop him in Didsbury, a few streets from Maria's house. Feeling safer by the second, he trotted the rest of the way and let himself in. Then, locking up with a satisfied sigh, he made his way up the stairs.

Maria had fallen asleep watching TV. Kissing her, Joel smiled when she opened her eyes.

'Sorry, babe . . . didn't mean to wake you.'

'It's all right,' she said softly, rubbing at her eyes. 'How did it go?'

'Fine.' Taking his clothes off, Joel draped them over the back of the bedside chair. 'Rod wanted me to go to France for a week to check out a venue, but I told him I was busy.'

'You shouldn't have done that for me,' Maria said guiltily.

Climbing into bed beside her, Joel pulled her into his arms. 'I told you I want to spend some uninterrupted time with you, and that's more important to me right now – okay?'

'Okay,' Maria murmured, moaning softly when he started to kiss her.

15

The Volvo looked like a low-rider as it rolled slowly along the rain-slicked street. But it was the weight of the five men crammed into it that made it sit so close to the ground: Fletch and Psycho's kid brother Jimmy up front; Psycho and his other brother Eamon in back with Gerry the Genius – all built like brick shithouses from pumping iron in prison gyms.

It was dark and windy out, the trees spitting bits of branch at the car as it passed. Swerving when a bin bag billowed up like a black ghost and smeared itself across the windscreen, Fletch cursed and flipped the wipers on to shift it.

'Hurry the fuck up,' he barked irritably at Jimmy who was peering out at the house numbers. 'This is the third time round. We get clocked, I'll do ye in, pal!'

'There,' Jimmy said, pointing to a small block of flats, the door of which was partially shielded by a row of bushes that ran alongside the path to the pavement.

'Halle-fuckin'-*lujah*!' Psycho grunted. 'Park up down that lane we passed back there, Fletch. We'll walk back round in ones – meet up at the door.'

'How we getting in?' Gerry asked in a pissed-off voice.

They had set out on a high after getting Mack to cough up the address. But Gerry's mood had dipped two hours back, when they'd pulled in for a piss and a cuppa at a Little Chef and Jimmy had nicked his place, leaving him squashed between Psycho and Eamon in the back.

'With your magic wee fingers,' Psycho said, pulling on a

pair of gloves and flexing his fingers to loosen the leather. 'Straight in – straight out. Fast and furious. Everyone got their gloves and masks?'

They all confirmed that they had what they needed.

'He'll be long gone by now, if he's got any sense,' Fletch muttered, wired from all the driving.

'Maybe not,' Gerry said thoughtfully. 'It's only been a few hours since Psycho worded him up. That's not long to pack ten years' worth of shite. And he'd have to be thorough, because he cannae afford t' be leaving anything behind that we could trace him by. We might catch him at it.'

'Yeah, well, if we don't we'll just have to talk to his neighbours,' Eamon said, testing his flick knife out on the back of Fletch's headrest.

'Fuck off with that before ye stick me with it,' Fletch complained, switching the car lights off and turning along the dark little lane they'd spotted on the way in.

'Quit griping,' Eamon laughed. 'Anyone'd think it was *your* motor, y' possessive cunt, ye. It's nicked – get over it.'

'I don't give a flying twat about the motor,' Fletch snarled. 'It's me fuckin' head I'm worried about. It's bald enough without you scalping me.'

'Save it for when we find the fucker and get him out on the moors,' Psycho said when Eamon started making Red Indian whooping noises. 'You can make as much racket as you want once we're out in the open,' he went on, grinning evilly. 'Just so long as I can still hear the grass screaming like a little pussy cunt.'

Rolling to a stop beneath a flapping tin canopy at the side of a derelict cottage that was more or less hidden by overgrown hedges, Fletch cut the engine and everyone got out, stretching and stamping to get the feeling back in their limbs.

Trudging back up the lane on foot, they headed for the

back of the flats in single file, blending easily into the shadows in their dark clothes.

There were no lights at any of the windows, and the rear security door was locked, but that wasn't a problem for Gerry the Genius, who more than made up in electrical know-how what he lacked in humour. After a couple of minutes of messing with the circuitry, the door popped open.

'*Voilà!*' he whispered, stepping aside to let Fletch go in ahead of him.

Taking a hammer out of his pocket, Fletch slipped one of his leather gloves over the head and gave the wall-mounted communal light a quick smack, plunging the hallway into gloom.

'Jimmy, get your mask on. You can stop down here and watch the door,' Psycho hissed when they were all in and the door was locked behind them.

'What the fuck is *that*?' Fletch hissed when Jimmy pulled his mask on.

'The fucking Scream,' Jimmy snarled. 'What's it look like?'

'Like a fucking dickhead.'

'Fucking idiot,' Psycho said, shaking his head. 'I telt ye to get someone famous.'

'Yeah, well The Scream *is* famous. He was in a film with that Courtney shag-Cox.'

'Just stay out of sight, and bell us if anything happens,' Psycho hissed. 'Rest of ye, up here.' He jerked his head for the others to follow him up the stairs.

Careful not to make any noise, Fletch took out each of the lights along the way.

Gathering around Joel's door on the third floor, Psycho put an ear to the wood and listened. Silence. Glancing furtively around, he motioned Gerry forward with a flick of his hand.

Taking his collection of lock-picks out of his pocket, Gerry did the deed, and they were in.

Spreading out, using torches so as not to alert anyone of their presence, they checked all the rooms. There was nobody here, but there was plenty of stuff lying around: TV, hi-fi, fully made-up bed, kitchen equipment. There were bits and pieces of food in the cupboards, and milk and wine in the fridge. But no clothes in the drawers or wardrobe, and not a scrap of paper anywhere – no letters, address books or scribbled phone numbers. Nothing.

'He's definitely done one,' Eamon said disappointedly.

'*Twat*,' Psycho spat, flicking his blade out and angrily slashing at the couch. 'That should have been his fucking throat!'

'Have you thought this might not be his place?' Gerry said, frowning at the mess Psycho had made of the sofa. 'Mack could have been lying.'

'Was he *fuck*,' Psycho snarled. 'Would *you* fucking lie if I was cutting *your* cock off? I don't fucking think so. Anyhow, you can smell the cunt. All that poncey fucking perfume he likes. It's his gaff, all right.'

'Let's go wake some neighbours,' Fletch said, taking the wine out of the fridge and rooting through the drawers for something to open it. Settling on a screwdriver, he rammed the cork into the bottle and took a swig before handing the bottle to Psycho.

Taking a long drink, Psycho wiped his mouth and passed the bottle to his brother.

'Right, there's another two flats on this floor,' he said. 'Me and Fletch'll take the left; Eamon and Gerry take the right. First sign of a screamer, cut their fucking throats. And mask up as soon as you're through the door, 'cos we don't want no one giving our descriptions out. I'm not going down for that cunt again.'

'Might be an idea to ditch the accents,' Gerry said, affecting a perfect Liverpudlian twang. 'Summat like this, yeah?'

'Fuckin' mental.' Psycho grinned approvingly. 'Anyone else do any?'

'Why aye, man,' Fletch piped up.

'What's that supposed to be?' Eamon sneered.

'Geordie.'

'Behave, y' mad fucker!' Eamon snorted out a laugh. 'Y' sound like a fuckin' kangaroo.'

'All right, so I'll be a fucking Aussie,' Fletch said moodily. 'Least I'm making an effort. What can *you* do, y' cunt?'

'Keep me fucking gob shut,' Eamon said, still chuckling.

'Best idea you've ever had, our kid!' Psycho grinned again. Pulling his mobile out of his pocket when it vibrated against his thigh, he flipped it open. 'What?'

'Lass and two lads on their way up,' Jimmy whispered. 'Student types – pissed as cunts. Deffo on their way to the third, 'cos she's griping about all the stairs.'

Flipping the phone shut, Psycho told the others what was happening, then went to the door and eased it open a fraction so that he could see out into the hallway.

The giggling threesome came around the corner a few minutes later and tripped along to the door at the furthest end of the hall, effectively trapping themselves.

'Mask up,' Psycho said, pulling his Richard Nixon mask over his face.

Fletch was Reagan, Eamon was Marlon Brando, and Gerry was Prince Charles.

Satisfied, Psycho flicked his blade out again and waved for the others to follow him.

'Take it easy, aye?' Gerry cautioned, seeing the glint in Psycho's eyes.

Turning on him, Psycho jabbed the knife at his throat. '*Don't* fucking tell me what to do, you gimpy fucking twat! I had enough of that shit in the pen, and I ain't taking it off you!'

'I'm just saying,' Gerry replied calmly. 'You don't want to go straight back there, do you? Just don't do anything stupid.'

'I *never* do stupid,' Psycho hissed. 'Mad, and fucking bad, yeah . . . but not *stupid*. Now keep your fucking mouth shut, Prince fuckin' Dumbo, or you'll be walking back with two broken fucking legs – got it?'

Backing off, Gerry held his hands up. Psycho was too hyped up to be reasonable. God only knew what would happen if he didn't get the answers he wanted off the neighbours. All Gerry could do was make sure their traces were covered afterwards.

Creeping up on the unsuspecting trio just as one of the lads opened the door, Psycho grabbed the girl by the hair and laid the blade against her throat.

'Inside, all of you, and no fucking noise or you're all dead,' he hissed in a weird mad-Irishman-type voice.

The small flat shrank to matchbox capacity with Psycho's lot and the students crammed into the front room. Shoving the terrified hostages down onto the couch, Psycho shone the torch into their faces. They looked like startled rabbits: pupils the size of saucers in shock-wide eyes.

'We're looking for your neighbour,' Eamon said in a thick imitation of Gerry's perfectly affected scouse. 'Ponce called Kyle.'

'I don't know who you're t-talking about,' the lad with the keys stuttered, the fear rich in his voice. 'There's no one called Kyle in this block.'

'Don't fucking lie to me,' Psycho said threateningly. 'We've just been in his gaff.'

'I swear to *God*!' the lad squealed, flinching back when Psycho balled his fists. 'I've lived here for three years. I swear there's no one called Kyle.'

'Flat in the middle,' Gerry said, trying to prompt the lad to save him a savaging.

'That's Joel's flat,' the lad said. 'But he's gone.'

'What's this Joel look like?' Fletch asked.

'Blond, good-looking,' the lad said, his voice shaking wildly. 'Not too big.'

'Sounds like him,' Eamon said, turning to Psycho. 'Still a fucking ponce.'

'Where did he go?' Psycho asked the lad.

'I don't know,' he whined. 'He never said.'

'You,' Psycho grunted at the girl. 'He telling the truth, or what?'

'Yes,' she squeaked, shrinking back into the cushions.

'How d'y' know?' Fletch demanded. '*You* know this *Joel* an' all, do you?'

'Yeah,' she admitted, swallowing noisily. 'I live on the other s-side of him. We – we knew him to s-say hello, but that's all.' Bursting into tears then, she said, 'Please don't hurt us. We don't know where he's gone, I swear it. He just said he was going away for a while.'

'I take it youse knew him well enough to say more than hello, then?' Eamon cut in. 'So, what else did he tell you?'

'Nothing,' the first lad answered shakily. 'Honest. None of us really knew him. He comes and goes a lot. We don't even know his last name.'

Psycho narrowed his eyes, putting the pieces together. The first lad and the girl lived in the flats on either side of Kyle – or *Joel*, as he was apparently calling himself nowadays. And they weren't too far off being the same age as the grassing cunt, so, chances were they knew more about him than they were letting on.

'Who does he come and go with?' he demanded, leaning over the girl and running the blade slowly down between her tits. 'Mates? Bird? Where does he go, who does he visit?'

'We don't *know*,' the girl sobbed, her eyes riveted to the

knife. 'Honest. We only ever talked to him when we wanted a bit of gear.'

'What kind of gear?' Gerry asked.

'Coke.'

Gerry and Psycho exchanged a look. Mack had said that Joel was dealing grass, but if he'd progressed to powders, chances were that he was using it himself and wouldn't want to stray too far from his supplier. On the other hand, he was such a vain, smart-arsed bastard, he was probably selling without using and would have had a stash of money set aside to get himself well out of the country.

'You,' Psycho shone the torch at the so-far-silent one of the lads. 'What do you know?'

'Fuck all,' the lad grunted, full of whisky and bravado. 'I don't live here, and I don't know who you're talking about, so fuck you.'

'Do what?' Psycho drawled, his voice deceptively low.

'I said, *fuck . . . you*,' the lad repeated, too drunk to pick up on the danger. 'You've got what you wanted. They don't *know anything*.' He said it slowly, as if talking to an idiot.

'Oh, I *know* you didn't just talk down to me,' Psycho hissed.

'He didn't mean it,' the girl yelped. 'Please – don't hurt him.'

'You shut your fucking whinging,' Psycho told her nastily, somehow managing to maintain the weird accent. 'I'll deal with you when I've had a word with rude boy.' Reaching down, he gripped the lad by the throat.

'Get the fuck off me, you piece of shit,' the lad spat, gripping Psycho's powerful wrist and glaring into his eyes which were just visible through the slits in Nixon's eyes.

'Watch them,' Psycho told his crew, yanking the lad to his feet and propelling him out of the room with a hand over his mouth now to stop him shouting. Almost carrying him into the bedroom, he kicked the door shut.

'What's he going to do to him?' the girl sobbed, nearly hysterical now.

'Teach him some manners,' Fletch told her sneeringly. 'And if I was you, I'd start talking before he decides you're holding out on him.'

'Yeah, she looks his type, innit,' Eamon said, laughing crudely. 'And he'll have the right horn once he's finished in there. Hope you're on the pill, love?'

'No, please, don't!' she squealed, clutching at her friend's arm. 'I'm a virgin!'

'Fan-fuckin'-tastic!' Eamon leered, unzipping his pants and grabbing her by the hair. 'You can get your gob round this while you're waiting for your first fuck. Call it a dress rehearsal.'

'Wait!' Gerry said, sensing that everything was about to get out of hand. 'Use this.' Pulling a condom from his pocket, he handed it over, purposefully not looking at the girl whose face had collapsed into a terrified mess of tears as she realised what was about to happen to her.

'Fuck, she was a struggler!' Eamon laughed when they were all back in the car fifteen minutes later. Pulling his mask off, he ran his hands through his hair. 'I don't know how I contained myself, I really don't. You know that feeling you get when you've got your dick right down their throats, and you've got your hands round their necks, squeezing and squeezing, like a big fat wank, and you could just snuff 'em right there and then.'

'Good job you had Gerry boy to keep you under manners, then,' Psycho chuckled, rolling his mask off and sticking it in his pocket. 'Tell you what, though, I fucking hate them johnnys myself. They don't make 'em big enough no more. I've got a right friction burn on me tadge.'

'Did the little laddie greet?' Eamon asked sarcastically, sniggering as Fletch eased the car out onto the road.

'More than the real pussy did,' Psycho scoffed. 'Never

heard nowt like it. *Mwah! Mwah!* Had to stuff a sock in its gob to shut it up. Right tight fucking arsehole he had on him, an' all – but not no more. He'll be wearing Pampers for a fair wee while!' Throwing his head back, he laughed loudly and slapped his palm against Eamon's.

'Wish ye'd let me come,' Jimmy complained, ducking to avoid them hitting him. 'I hate watching fucking doors.'

'Learn to be more sensible, and I'll consider it,' Psycho told him, as if he himself was a reasonable sort of person. 'There's one thing fucking people up, but y've got to know when to strike and when to hold back.'

'Says the fucking beast of Govan!' Eamon laughed, safe in the knowledge that he was his brother's right-hand man, and could get away with ribbing him in a way none of the others – big as they were – would dare.

'I ain't no beast,' Psycho growled, banging his fists on his chest. 'I'm a fucking *werewolf*!'

'Yeah, well, don't start howling till we're on the motorway,' Fletch warned, peering alertly out to make sure there were no police cars around. 'We need tae get back and torch this fucker before the three back there get found.'

'Best burn all these clothes, as well,' Gerry said quietly.

'Don't think I'm running round naked on the estate with you lot up ma fucking arse,' Psycho jeered. 'One of you can stop off and get us all some gear to put on.'

Looking back worriedly, Gerry said, 'You'd best put your foot down as soon as you hit the straight, Fletch. The pigs are gonna be out in force when they find them three.'

'Chill out,' Psycho told him, grinning. 'They'll be looking for fucking Paddies and Scousers!'

'You don't think them lot fell for the fake accents, do you?' Fletch said doubtfully. 'I wouldnae have.'

'I don't give a toss whether they did or didn't,' Psycho said, his mood darkening as if a cloud had passed over his head as they reached the motorway. 'There's nothing to link us to it, and them three know what'll happen if they say anything, so I doubt they're gonna be stupid enough to start spilling to the pigs. All it means is we'll have to leave it a bit longer before we come back.'

'Probably nae point *coming* back,' Gerry said, cracking the window an inch and lighting a spliff. 'Kyle's probably left the country by now – if he's got any sense.'

'Yeah, well, he'll have to come back sooner or later,' Psycho snarled. 'And when he does, I'll be waiting for the fucker. There's nae fucking way I'm dropping this one. *Nae* fucking way!'

PART THREE

16

Joel's feet were itching big time. Maria was a lovely girl, and the house was great, but he needed to get out for a bit before he suffocated.

They'd been holed up together for six long weeks, spending full days in bed, surfacing only to eat, or to walk hand in hand to the local shops for fresh booze supplies. This was the longest time that Joel had ever spent indoors – certainly the longest he'd ever been with a woman.

But, sweet and generous and accommodating as Maria was, he needed variety to keep him stimulated. He was starting to feel like an old married man – and that was *guaranteed* to make him run for the hills. And he didn't want to do that; not when he had it so cushy, with Maria refusing to take a penny off him for rent, bills or food. If things carried on like this, he'd be raking it in when he started working again.

Life couldn't be more perfect – in *that* respect. But Joel knew himself too well. If he didn't get a bit of time to himself soon, he'd do something stupid – like rip her off and do a runner, or something. And he didn't want to do that, because he had much more to gain in the long run by staying.

He'd done a lot of thinking while he'd been hiding out, and he knew it was time to get back to work. But one thing he was sure of – there was no *way* he was going back to selling piddling grams. It would be too time-consuming now that he couldn't let his punters know where he was living. Before, he could just sit back and let them call round to the flat for it. Now, he'd have to do all the legwork, and that meant putting himself about. And he didn't want to do that. Not while he didn't know what Psycho was up to.

He'd heard about the rapes and beatings at the flats from a punter who lived nearby, who'd called just after it happened to make sure he was okay. Joel knew full well who was responsible, even though the victims had told the police that they couldn't remember anything, insisting that they had all been too drunk and high to know who had attacked them.

With nothing to go on but a vague sighting of five men driving slowly up and down the road in the early hours of that morning, in what the witness described as an American-looking car, the police had appealed for anyone else with information to come forward. They needed a lead as to the make of the car – also where it might have come from, and where it had gone.

Joel could have told them exactly who to look for, but there was no way he was getting involved. Then Psycho really *would* have a reason to kill him.

He hadn't known the neighbours well, but they had scored off him a few times and they were nice enough. But while he felt bad that they had suffered such a horrible attack because of him, at least they were alive – which was more than they might have expected after a visit from Psycho. And he was greatly relieved that they hadn't been able to tell the mad bastard anything.

Psycho wouldn't write him off, Joel knew that, but he doubted they'd come back for a while now that they'd done what they'd done. Psycho would have put the frighteners on the poor sods to keep them quiet, but he wouldn't risk showing his face until he was sure that they had heeded the warning and hadn't grassed him up.

But that didn't mean Joel was safe. He wouldn't put it past Psycho to have left someone behind to watch out for him.

Which was why he'd nipped into the local hair salon on one of their walks the other day and had his hair clipped right down and dyed black, along with the goatee he'd grown while he'd been hiding out.

He looked like a completely different person. *Unrecognisable*, Maria had said, which was exactly what he'd wanted. She loved it, and he had to admit it didn't look half bad. If anything, it made him even more handsome than before, because it enhanced the blue of his eyes and gave definition to his cheekbones and jaw.

He was a handsome fucker – even if he did say so himself. But what was the point of looking good if he was stuck in the house with just one adoring woman to feed his ego?

But a new door was about to open, so he needn't have worried.

Lying in bed with Maria one morning, Joel got exactly the call he needed to get him up and running again.

'Yo, dude! Your voice just gave me the *biggest* hard-on!' Jippi gushed when Joel answered the phone. 'Hope you're back in town, my hot little friend, because *I* am, and guess what? I'm *staying*! *Yaay*! I've bought myself the *best* penthouse you've ever seen, and I've just finished getting my new exhibition stuff together, so I'm having the party of part-*ays* to launch it. So *you* get your cute little assikins round here at nine – and bring all the shit you can get your hands on, 'cos there's a whole *load* of greedy little stars coming, and we are all *gagging* for some decent gear. It's been *deadsville* without you, guy!'

'I don't know,' Joel said hesitantly, glancing at Maria. 'I'm not sure I can get away.'

'Is it a job?' Maria whispered. 'Go,' she urged when he nodded.

Joel chewed his lip thoughtfully. He *should* go. This was exactly the opportunity he'd been waiting for. But it sounded

as if he'd need a couple of ounces at least, and he didn't
have the money to buy that much up front. And there was
no way he was getting into debt with the Gallaghers again.

'Come on, Joey Joey Joey,' Jippi groaned. 'Stop holding
out on me. I'm a desperate little girl.'

'All right, I'll be there,' Joel said decisively.

'Yes!' Jippi whooped. 'But don't bother wearing shorts, my
super sexy boy, 'cos I'll be sending everyone home early so
me and you can finish the party alone.'

'See you at nine,' Joel said with a note of amusement in
his voice.

'You're with someone, aren't you?' Jippi said perceptively.
'Who is it? Better not be a dick donor or I'll spank you, you
naughty thing. You know I've got to be your first.'

'I'll see you at *nine*,' Joel said again, more firmly. Chuckling
softly, he disconnected.

'Who was it?' Maria asked, curious to know who had
tempted him out of his self-imposed semi-retirement.

She'd been so happy to have him here, and more than a
little flattered that he had fobbed off all the clients who had
been ringing since he came to stay. But she'd been feeling
guilty, too; afraid that she was destroying the business he
had built up by keeping him all to herself.

'Gareth Gates,' Joel said, blurting out the first name that
came to mind – though God only knew why *that* one had
been in there in the first place. 'I need the loo.' Pushing the
quilt back, he strolled naked to the bathroom.

'I didn't know he was still around,' Maria called after him.
'Has he got a new record coming out?'

'Suppose he must have,' Joel said evasively. 'I'll find out
when I get there.'

Frowning, he shook his dick, then ran water into the sink
to have a wash. He'd best start checking out his facts if he
was going to pull the wool over Maria's eyes. She read all

the showbiz-gossip magazines, and it would be easy for her to trip him up if he said he was meeting someone who she knew to be out of circulation, or even out of the country.

Maria was up when he went back to the bedroom, plumping the pillows and laying them neatly on top of the smoothed out quilt. She'd make someone a great little wife, he thought fondly. Always cleaning and tidying. Never refusing him anything.

With that last thought in mind, he said, 'I've, er, got a bit of a favour to ask.'

Turning to him, Maria smiled questioningly. 'What's that?'

'Say no if you don't want to,' he said, sitting down on the chair and patting his lap.

'Don't want to what?' she asked, sitting on his knee and gazing adoringly into his eyes. Whatever it was, she'd already decided he could have it.

'I'm going to need a bit of cash to get myself back on track with the tours,' Joel said, frowning up at her sheepishly. 'I wouldn't ask, but I've left it a bit longer than I should have, and I'm going to have to kind of start from scratch – checking out venues, and schmoozing managers, and what have you. Trouble is, I've left myself a bit short.'

'Oh, I'm sorry.' Maria's face fell. 'That's my fault for keeping you away from work, isn't it? I didn't realise.'

'Of course it's not your fault,' Joel assured her. 'I've loved spending time with you. But the music business is fickle. People forget fast. And there are so many egos to stroke, it's not even funny. But it has to be done. It doesn't take much, though, thank God – a few meals, a few bottles of champagne.'

'How much do you need?' Maria said without hesitation.

'I really hate to ask,' Joel said again. 'But two grand would do for now. I'll get it back to you as soon as I'm earning again. You never know, I might even get it back to you tonight.'

'There's no need,' Maria said, getting up and looking around for her bag. 'Will a cheque be all right?'

Smiling apologetically, Joel said, 'It would be better in cash, if you could manage it. If it's too much hassle, forget it. I'll just take Gareth for a kebab and a pint. He's young – he'll cope.'

'Don't be daft. Just let me get washed and dressed and I'll go to the bank.' Blowing him a kiss, Maria headed for the bathroom.

Joel was dressed when she came back, sitting on the chair with a cigarette in his hand.

'I know it's a lot,' he said, watching her as she pulled her jeans on. 'But I'll get it back as soon as I can.'

'I don't think two grand is going to make much of a dent in my inheritance, do you?' she said, laughing softly as she pulled her jumper over her head. 'And you don't have to pay me back,' she went on, sitting on the dressing-table stool to brush her hair and slip her trainers on. 'The amount of interest I'm earning, it'll be back in my account in no time.'

Joel shook his head. 'No, babe. Thanks for the offer, but I can't take your money.'

'I want you to have it,' she insisted, blushing slightly as she added, 'You're my boyfriend, and we're living together. What's mine is yours.'

'I'll pay you back,' Joel said firmly.

'Not listening,' Maria chirped, grabbing her bag and her jacket and heading out the door with her fingers in her ears.

Handing the money to him when she got home from the bank, Maria reached up to kiss him.

'There, and I *don't* want it back, because you've more than earned it putting up with me. Anyway, I owe you for making you turn down so many jobs. So, no arguments – okay?'

'You're too kind for your own good,' Joel scolded softly.

Smiling when he hugged her, Maria bit her lip to stop herself blurting out that she would gladly give him the shirt off her back if he needed it, never mind a couple of lousy grand.

They had shared an idyllic few weeks, and she hoped he felt the same way about her as she felt about him. But they hadn't gone so far as to say those three little words to each other yet, and she didn't want to scare him by being the first to take the plunge.

'Right, well, I'd best get going,' Joel said, easing her away and checking his watch. 'I've got to sort out a couple of things for tonight.' Taking his jacket out of the wardrobe, he pulled it on and leaned down to kiss her. 'See you in a bit. And thanks again for this.' He patted his pocket where the money was safely stashed away.

It was a bright day outside, but the wind was biting, and Joel's fingers stung as he lit his cigarette. Turning his collar up, he kept his head down and his eyes peeled as he made his way to the main road.

He was going to see Lance Gallagher – to score, and to find out if he'd heard of any strange Scots hanging about. Lance had eyes and ears all over the city. It was the reason he'd never been busted. The first whiff of anything that could potentially threaten his empire, and he was on it in a flash. And he was a dangerous man to cross, with his collection of firearms and swords, and his army of meat-heads.

Hailing a cab when he hit Palatine Road, Joel told the driver to take him to Rusholme. Then he sat back in his seat and thought about how to use Lance to his advantage.

'Long time no see,' Lance said when Keith brought Joel into the lounge.

As usual, he was in front of the TV playing a video game. For a change, he actually paused it and turned to give Joel his attention.

Joel was pleased. He'd paid his debt to the Gallaghers in full after that last deal, and now he was buying with cash, so he was back to being a punter instead of an errand boy.

'So, what you been up to, Jay boy?' Lance asked, lighting a spliff and leaning back in his chair.

'Not much,' Joel said, looking around nervously as he sat down on the couch. The dogs were outside; he could hear them barking in the back garden. 'I had a bit of trouble, so I had to lie low for a while.'

'What kind of trouble?' Lance asked, passing the spliff to him. 'You know we do protection – for a price.'

'Yeah, I know,' Joel said, wondering if Lance would be so quick to offer his services if he heard Psycho's version of events. No one wanted to be associated with a grass – true or not. 'It was just some Scottish crew putting the heavies on.'

'Meaning?' Lance peered at him narrow-eyed.

Sighing, as if he really didn't want to have to involve anyone in his troubles, Joel said, 'I suppose you heard about the three kids getting attacked back at my old place?'

'Yeah, I heard some,' Lance said, shrugging. 'Raped and battered, or some shit like that.'

'Yeah, well, it was the Scottish crew who did it.' Joel sucked deeply on the spliff and passed it back.

'And what's that got to do with you?'

Joel exhaled loudly. 'They were looking for me.'

'Why?'

'Because they were trying to make me give up the name of my supplier.'

'Meaning me?' Lance said darkly.

'Well, yeah.' Joel shrugged apologetically. 'That's why I took off. 'Cos there was no way I was dropping you in it.'

Frowning so hard that a deep line split his forehead smack down the middle, Lance said, 'So, how did they get to you in the first place?'

'I used to know them,' Joel admitted. 'Well, kind of. I grew up in Scotland, and they were the local hard men.'

'Oh, so they fancy themselves a bit, do they?'

'And then some,' Joel muttered. 'Anyhow, they heard I'd moved here and started dealing, and they thought they'd come and muscle in on it. They took me for a *ride*; tried to put the frighteners on to make me give them your name.'

'You fucking *what*?' Keith cut in, making Joel jump because he'd forgotten the lump was in the room. 'You'd best not have fuckin' said owt, or you're dead meat!'

'Course I didn't,' Joel protested. 'D'y' think I'm stupid?'

'Well, you fuckin' look it with your hair like that. You look like a right soft wanker.'

'Pull your friggin' neck in, you,' Lance snarled, flinging the TV remote at Keith.

He ducked and it smashed into the wall behind him, spewing batteries onto the floor.

'Aw, look what you done now,' he complained. 'I won't be able to turn the telly over now.'

'I'll stick your bleedin' head in it so you can watch every fuckin' channel at once if you don't fuck off and button it,' Lance warned, his eyes flashing a clear warning. 'We was talking, case you hadn't noticed.'

'All right, I'm fuckin' going,' Keith retorted sulkily, bending down with a loud grunt to scoop up the batteries.

'Right, tell me the rest,' Lance said, his attention back on Joel. 'And don't leave nothing out, 'cos I'll mash you the fuck up if something goes down and I'm not prepared.'

'They wanted your name and address,' Joel told him quietly, 'and info on how you operate – where you stash your gear, how much you keep around at any one time. And they wanted to know what kind of back-up you've got – weapons, how many men you've got behind you, that kind of thing.'

'And you told them what?'

'I gave them a false name and address,' Joel said, ticking the lies off on his fingers. 'Said I had no idea where you kept your gear, no idea the amounts you shift, and that as far as I know, you're armed to the teeth, with an army of hundreds.'

'Well, you got that right.' Lance grinned evilly. 'You ain't got a clue who I've got behind me, Jay boy, you ain't got a fuckin' clue. See them Triads . . . ?' Raising an eyebrow, he jutted his jaw forward and nodded slowly. 'That goes out of this room, though, and Keith's right – you're dead meat.'

'Christ, Lance, I'd never breathe a word of anything you told me – you know that. Why do you think I went on the run? There was no way I was hanging around when they found out I'd fed them a dummy. I knew they'd come after me – and they did. They just happened to get the poor bastards in the flat next door instead.'

'So why didn't you tell me right away?' Lance asked, killing the spliff and immediately lighting a straight. 'Didn't you think I might want to *know* some fuckers were looking for me?'

'I knew they wouldn't find you,' Joel said simply. 'No one knows I get my gear off you. With me out of the way, they had nothing. So, they took it out on the kids and did one.'

'How d'y' know they've done one?'

'I *guarantee* they wouldn't have hung around to get nicked for rape,' Joel said. 'They're all fresh off long stretches. There's no way they'll want to go back inside. They'll definitely be after me next time they come back, though – to do me in for protecting you.'

Mulling all this over, Lance sat in his smoke cloud, nodding slowly to himself. After a while he looked up and peered at Joel with a deadly serious light in his eye.

'So, what's their purpose? Just to rip me off?'

'They want to take over the Manchester powder scene,' Joel said, swallowing nervously as the lies and the atmosphere became heavier. 'They reckon if they take you out they'll be on top, and me and all the other dealers will have to score off them.'

Nodding again, Lance said, 'Right, here's the deal . . . I'm not going looking for these pussy tartan twats, 'cos I can't be arsed. They want me, they'll have to find me. But I'm telling you now, they walk on my turf, they'll be getting carried off it in body bags. As for you,' he went on, 'I ever find out you gave me up, it'll be *me* doing you in, not them. But I'm giving you the benefit of the doubt, for now. So, if I was you, I'd keep my head down and get on with life. If this crew turns up and I get wind of them, I'll deal with it. But you'd best *pray* you ain't involved, because I *will* take you out. You got me?'

'Absolutely. But trust me, man, there's no way I'd give you up – not for them, not for anyone.'

'Glad to hear it,' Lance said. 'And, just for the record, what the fuck *have* you done to your hair? You look like Colin fucking Farrell gone wrong.'

Joel was shaking when he left the Gallaghers – as much from relief as fear. It was a huge risk involving them in this business with Psycho, but it looked like it had paid off. If the two crews clashed, Lance wouldn't give Psycho's lot a chance to tell them why they were really after Joel. He'd just go at them all guns blazing – literally.

Joel felt as if a ten-year heavy weight had dropped off his back. But he still had to be careful. If Psycho caught up with him in the meantime, he was still deader than dead.

Hailing another cab, he had it take him back to Maria's. He had two and a half ounces tucked in his pocket – all fully paid for. All he had to do now was find a way to get Maria out of the house for an hour so he could cut it and bag it. He'd make an absolute *bomb* if he shifted it all at Jippi's party tonight, and with Maria refusing to take her money back, he'd have enough to buy double this next time.

17

Jippi's new place was incredible. It was right at the top of a revamped Victorian office block, directly overlooking the trendy wine bars lining Deansgate.

It was the penthouse, so Jippi had his own elevator which took you right to his fortified front door. It had a foolproof security system, in that it could only be accessed once you'd got past the doorman, then it could only be activated by Jippi with his electronic pass-key, or by him keying the password into a pad inside the apartment to allow guests to travel up. It was a fortress, designed to keep unauthorised people and unwanted visitors out.

Coming out at the penthouse floor, Joel looked around, one eyebrow raised. The space between the elevator and the apartment door was bigger and better than his old flat had been, with parquet flooring, subtle ceiling lights and, standing by the window, an amazing wrought-iron statue of a woman with a frail young boy tucked under her muscular arm, as if she were an Amazon who had captured him and was carrying him home for some rough sex.

It had to be one of Jippi's creations, Joel guessed, heading for the door. He'd probably modelled the woman on his perception of himself in drag. God only knew who the boy was supposed to be, though – he just hoped it wasn't him.

Oh, Christ . . . what if there was no party tonight? There was no noise coming through the door. What if the invitation had been a ploy of Jippi's to get him alone?

Hesitating before he knocked, Joel jumped when the lift doors swished shut behind him and he heard it whoosh quietly down. Shit! Now he really was trapped.

The flat door opened and heavy dance music flooded the hallway. Jippi followed it out in a silver minidress, and the most natural-looking fake tits that Joel had ever seen. His long shapely legs were clad in sheer black silk hold-ups and impossibly high stilettos. He'd ditched the Afro and opted for a waist-length electric-blue wig, with matching contacts. And his make-up was professional-model quality.

He looked incredible, and if Joel were a different kind of man he might actually have been tempted to overlook the fact that a dick lay between those exquisite legs.

But he wasn't, and that would never happen in a million years.

'*There* you are!' Jippi yelled delightedly, grabbing Joel and kissing him on both cheeks. 'I thought you'd got lost. I sent the lift back down because I thought you'd missed it. You'd better *hope* no smelly hoboes jump in and come gatecrashing!'

'Sorry, I thought I was too early when I didn't hear anything,' Joel said, glad when he saw people milling about inside.

'*Heavy* soundproofing, isn't it?' Jippi grinned. Then, walking around Joel, he looked him over and clapped a hand to his mouth. 'Oh, my God! I *love* this hair. And the beard is so fucking hot!'

'Glad you approve,' Joel said, smiling.

'Don't get me started,' Jippi teased, linking his arm and pulling him inside. 'Come and meet the peasants – they're climbing the walls. Hope you've got lots of pop?'

'Five O's,' Joel said, sure that Jippi would be shocked that he'd brought so much.

Jippi sucked air in through his teeth. 'Oooh . . . hope that's enough. But you can go and get more if we need it, yeah?'

'I suppose so,' Joel said, surprised but thrilled. Shit! If he got rid of everything and they still wanted more, he'd be loaded by the time he went home.

'Everyone, this is my boyfriend, Joel,' Jippi announced, dragging Joel into the party. 'He's mine, so no funny business, or I'll be spanking lots of tush tonight!'

Embarrassed, Joel nodded at the other guests and accepted a drink from a waiter who was circulating with a tray loaded with glasses of champagne. He did a double take when the waiter moved on. The boy was completely bare-arsed, the backside cut clean out of his skintight black leather pants. Looking around, Joel saw that all the waiters were dressed the same, and the waitresses were topless.

'Let me show you around,' Jippi said, still holding on to his arm. 'Then you can set up shop in the kitchen. Do you need scales? There's a flat-top set on the ledge – feel free to use them. Anyway, this is the living room . . .'

It was a vast space, with a real wood floor and raw brick walls. Numerous canvases of Jippi's weird, colourful artwork lined the longest wall, his latest theme being of naked half-humans in orgiastic poses. Striking images but a bit disturbing, too, Joel thought, wondering what kind of collector would buy this type of stuff. It wouldn't sit too happily with more conventional collectables, but Jippi was up and coming, so he was obviously selling well.

The windows went from one side to the other, a complete wall of glass through which Joel could see not just the bustling bars on Deansgate down below but the whole of the beautiful old cathedral and the rest of the surrounding city-centre buildings.

There were several weirdly shaped chairs, and one ultra-long couch onto which numerous outrageously dressed friends of Jippi's were crammed. More sprawled around on floor cushions, each trying to out-funk the others: bigger heels, higher hair, more piercings. *Anything* to make them stand out in the crowd. But they had taken it to such extremes that it had backfired, because it was Joel in his *normal* suit who stood out.

'Come and look at my tart's boudoir,' Jippi said now, dragging him off through a set of double doors into the bedroom.

This room had the same full wall of windows, but the rest of the walls were covered in satin drapes of deep purples and reds. The bed was on a raised platform in the centre, encircled by candles.

'You want to lie down?' Jippi asked, grinning.

'Er, no, thanks,' Joel said, backing out. 'Show me the kitchen so I can get rid of this and enjoy myself.'

The kitchen was at the rear of the living room, separated by a low glass partition wall that was actually an aquarium full of floaty exotic fish. The units and work surfaces were all made out of ultra-modern beaten steel.

'*COKE!*' Jippi yelled above the music.

Rolling his eyes at the sheer indiscretion of the man, Joel nervously backed himself into the furthest corner and laid his coke out on the ledge. Suddenly everybody was around him, and he felt like he was backstage at a freaky fashion show. There were oddities of both sexes, some whose gender was indistinguishable, and several faces that Joel recognised from various TV offerings.

'Just give them what they want,' Jippi told him magnanimously. 'I'll settle up with you later.'

Growing in confidence once he realised that there wasn't a single straight among the guests who could blow him up to the drug squad, Joel started chopping and allotting.

In just under two hours, he was clean out, and the party had stepped up several hundred notches – the clothes coming off as the volume of the music went up.

High as kites, and free of inhibitions, the guests took inspiration from the paintings and an orgy started up in the bedroom, the double door thrown open for all to join in, or just watch.

And Jippi was right in the centre of the action.

He'd lost his dress now but had kept the wig and was striding around in a basque and suspenders, like a director on a film set, barking instructions and giving naked buttocks playful slaps with a thin leather whip.

Keeping well clear, Joel did a couple of lines and went out onto the balcony to look down at the people drinking at the tables outside the wine bars. The music was pumping out behind him, and he tapped out the beat on the handrail and threw his head back, relishing the chill breeze on his face after the heat of the sexual inferno inside.

'Cool gaff, isn't it?' A female voice sounded in his ear.

Turning his head, Joel saw a girl whose face he vaguely recognised. It took him a moment to think where from, then it came to him: she was one of the stars of a soap that Maria watched.

He didn't generally watch TV, but being holed up in bed with Maria for so long he was quite the expert on her favourite soaps now – one of which was *Picture Perfect*, set in a run-down cinema in Salford. The girl played Pippa, a gobby usherette who was having a fling with the popcorn boy. She was always at odds with the manager, who also fancied her but was about a thousand years too old.

'I wanted one of these flats,' the girl was saying now, holding onto the rail and leaning her head right back – as if doing the end scene from *Titanic*, Joel thought. 'But you should see how much they cost.'

'Expensive, huh?' Joel couldn't think of anything else to say.

'Try *über* expensive,' the girl snorted. 'I'd have to start selling my body to pay the rent.' Turning to peer directly at him now, she bit her lip. 'Reckon I'd make enough?'

'I'm sure you would,' Joel said, flicking a glance at her body. She was very slim, with a tiny scarf of a dress that hung in folds, barely skimming her nipples which were pointing up at him stiffly in the cold air.

'What do you do?' she asked, leaning her elbows on the rail, so that her tiny skirt rode even higher up her slim thighs. 'Apart from selling coke, that is. Model?'

Smiling, Joel shook his head. It was the first time he'd had his own line used on him, and he found it quite amusing.

'Music,' he told her evasively. 'But never mind me. Tell me about you.'

'Don't you know who I am?' she asked, her perfectly shaped eyebrows arching. Then, giggling, she said, 'Shit! I never thought I'd hear myself coming out with that one! *Don't you know who I am!*' she repeated in a snobby voice. 'What a wanker!'

'I think I've seen you somewhere,' Joel said, playing it cool. Now that he'd finally got his foot through the door of the world he'd been pretending to be in for so long, he had no intention of blowing it. 'Do you go clubbing in town?'

'Yeah, but that's not where you've seen me,' the girl said, too young to be modest about her success. 'I'm a soap star.'

'I see,' Joel said, smiling, because he'd hardly describe her as a star. She was good, but not *that* good.

'Yeah, I'm in *Picture Perfect*,' she went on, trying to be cool about it, but not quite managing as the pride shone through in her voice. 'You must have seen it? It's like the biggest thing since *EastEnders*. Can't really compare it to *Corrie*, 'cos that's been going on so long and they're all old now. But ours is *great*, 'cos we're all young and gorgeous – bit like *Hollyoaks* with better scripts.'

'Uh huh,' Joel murmured, sipping his drink.

'Don't tell me you haven't seen it?' she said, squinting up at him as if she *totally* didn't believe that was possible.

'Can't say I have,' he told her casually. 'Sorry. What's it about?'

'Oh, it's like *so* funny,' she gushed. 'We're all supposed to be working at this run-down cinema in Salford, and it goes into like everyone's personal lives. So, I play this girl called Pippa, and I'm like the usherette, and like everyone really fancies me, but I'm having a fling with the popcorn boy. Which is so cool, 'cos he is *lush!*' Pausing for breath, she sighed wistfully, then flapped her hand. 'No point going there, though, 'cos he's as bent as the guy whose party this is. But I always stick my tongue in his mouth when we've got to do kissing scenes, and he gets like *so* uptight.'

'Naughty girl,' Joel chuckled, liking her for her vivacity.

Pursing her lips flirtatiously, she said, 'So, are you really his boyfriend?'

'Who – Jippi?' Joel said, frowning incredulously. '*Please!* Don't tell me you thought I was gay?'

Giggling, she said, 'Thank God for that. I was starting to get worried. Seems like everyone who's good-looking in this place is into arse. Or tits, if it's a girl. There's so many lesbians in there, I was scared I was going to go home with a girlfriend.'

'Not into it, huh?' Joel teased.

'Wouldn't say never.' She shrugged. 'But only if there was a really fit bloke in the middle. What about you?'

'Only if I *was* the fit bloke in the middle,' Joel said smoothly, giving her the sexy eye. She was getting to him now, and he was getting an urge to . . .

'Hey, I wonder if that's the balcony outside the bedroom,' the girl said, heading for a sloping metal partition separating the balcony they were on from the next. Holding on to it, she cocked her leg to climb across, sending her skirt right up around her hips and revealing her perfect bum.

'Don't!' Joel called, worried that she would fall. 'It's dangerous.'

'Dangerous is good,' she laughed excitedly. 'Come on – you'll miss all the fun.' Hopping down on the other side, she shielded her eyes with both hands and pressed her face up against the glass. 'Oh, my God!' she giggled, waving him to come over. 'You have *got* to see this! It's like so horny! Everyone's fucking everyone!'

'Come back over,' Joel hissed. 'They'll see you.'

'Like they *care*!' she scoffed. 'Christ, I'm getting wet.'

'Come here and show me,' Joel said softly, feeling the hard-on straining to get free.

Still giggling, she climbed back over and fell into his arms. 'You've *got* to do me like *now*,' she whispered, looping her arms around his neck.

Pushing her into the corner, Joel unzipped himself and lifted her so that her back was against the slim section of wall at the side of the glass. Holding her legs around his waist, he thrust his dick into the warm wetness and hammered into her, thrilled by the cold air on his thighs, and by the sensation of being visible from all sides.

'Oh, Christ, yeah . . .' she moaned. 'Yeah . . . yeah . . .'

Putting a hand over her mouth as she started to cry out, the coke and alcohol making her forget where she was, Joel gritted his teeth and came in a burst of silver lights.

'Oh, wow!' she gasped, holding on to him with her legs. 'That was like amazing! What's your name?'

'Joel,' he told her breathily. 'You?'

'Honey,' she said. 'It's Julia, really, but Honey's better for showbiz.'

'Nice to meet you,' Joel said, chuckling now that his breathing was slowing to normal. 'Gives a whole new meaning to the "Do you come here often?" line, doesn't it?'

Giving a tinkling little laugh, Honey disentangled her legs and slid down till her feet touched the floor.

'Guess you're definitely not that guy's boyfriend, then,' she said, reaching into a tiny handbag that Joel hadn't noticed and which was looped around her waist. 'Smoke?' She took out a pack of cigarettes.

Taking one, Joel pulled his lighter out and sparked it for her.

'Thanks.' She inhaled deeply. 'You'll have to start watching my show now,' she said, smiling up at him flirtatiously. 'And when you see me, you can say, "I shagged her."'

Joel snorted softly. He could just see himself saying *that* in front of Maria.

He shook his head amusedly. How the hell had that just happened? No way had he expected it. But he didn't feel quite as guilty as he'd thought he would. Maria was a sweetheart, but she was the serious kind. And that was a shame, because she was gorgeous, and lovely, and funny.

But, oh well . . .

'Do you come to many of his parties?' Honey was asking, gesturing back through the window.

'Oh, yeah, all the time,' Joel lied, shrugging nonchalantly. 'You?'

'This is my first,' Honey admitted. 'My agent got me the invite. He only did it 'cos he wants to get in my knickers, but he couldn't get here 'cos his wife caught him phoning me and told him he couldn't come. But it's not my problem – so, tough!'

'So you'd have shagged him instead of me, would you?' Joel asked with a smirk.

'No way!' Honey blurted out. 'He's got to be *forty* if he's a day! I only said I'd come 'cos I wanted to meet Jippi Wotsisface. He's like mega-cool.'

'He's all right,' Joel said, amused that she was so star-struck, for all her bragging.

He didn't actually see Jippi as a star. He'd met him a couple of years back by accident – literally. They'd both been involved in fights and ended up in A&E. Jippi was still an unknown back then, and had only been in town to promote his first exhibition. Scared of being infected by the motley crew of Saturday-night drunks and tramps, he'd made a beeline for Joel, and Joel had amused himself by feeding him the music-biz line. Then, when Jippi had asked him outright if he knew where to get hold of any drugs, he'd taken him outside and sold him a gram – sure that no one as weird as Jippi could possibly be connected to the police. He'd been supplying him ever since – whenever Jippi was in town, that was. But now that he'd bought this place, it looked like he was going to be around for a while. Which was great news for Joel, because there were bound to be more parties.

'I go to loads of do's,' Honey was saying now. 'TV stuff, mainly. Nothing like this. I'll have to take you to one some-time. I know loads of soap stars who like a bit of coke. You'd do all right out of it.'

'I don't get much free time,' Joel said, still playing it cool. 'But you can take my number if you want, then you can ring me if you need anything.'

Taking her phone out of the bag, Honey tapped his number in.

'Thanks for that,' she said. 'It's way cool knowing a big dealer. I'll be like Miss *Thang* when I go back on set.'

'Er, best keep it to yourself,' Joel said, nervous that she would blurt it out to all and sundry and get him busted.

'Oh, yeah! Course! Like I'm really gonna give it out to everyone! If they want anything, they can ask me, and I'll ring you. You never know, we might just meet up on another balcony sometime. That'd be cool, wouldn't it?'

'Way cool,' he said, mimicking her.

It was almost six in the morning before Joel got back to the house. Sober now, having hopped out of the taxi a half-mile away to let the air clear his head, he had a quick shower, then joined Maria in bed.

Stirring when she felt him beside her, Maria rolled over and opened her eyes.

'Hi,' she said, her voice husky with sleep. 'How did it go?'

'Great,' Joel said, trying to remember who he was supposed to have been with. Oh, yeah – Gareth Gates. 'You were, um, right, by the way. He's not doing much at the minute, but he's contemplating getting started again, so he wanted to run through all the possibilities. That's why it took so long. His manager was there, and we ended up at his hotel, chatting in his room.'

'Glad it went well,' Maria murmured happily, snuggling up to him.

Putting his arm around her, Joel stared up at the ceiling in the semi-light coming through the curtains and smiled as she drifted back to sleep with her sweet-smelling hair fanned out across his chest.

He had almost six grand in his pocket, a load of new clients, and a good idea of the kind of lifestyle he wanted to aim for. As long as Maria didn't get wind of what he was doing and carried on supporting him, life was definitely on the up.

Be great to get an apartment like Jippi's, though. But he'd never be able to rustle up that kind of money. If Maria were to sell this place, though, he was pretty sure they'd be able to afford it.

Definitely something to think about for the future . . .

That, and a car, so that he didn't have to keep wasting money on cabs.

18

The next six months flew by, and Maria was in a state of constant bliss. She and Joel had settled into a comfortable routine: him going out to meet with his high-flying clients, her staying home to keep house.

She was more than happy to potter about until he came home, making everything nice for him. When he had free time and they were both here, they were just as loved-up as it was possible to be, so her efforts were more than worth it. In fact, the only thing that could have made her any happier would have been if Joel were to propose. She would say yes in a heartbeat, but it hadn't come to that – yet.

Being in love was an alien feeling for Maria. After the pain of losing her mum and being sent away from her home and her friends, she had built a protective wall around her heart, afraid of letting anyone get too close in case they too were taken from her. Apart from Beth and, to a lesser degree, Sharon and Leanne, she had never allowed herself to really care about anybody.

Her previous boyfriends had been mystified by her coolness, and the speed with which they found themselves dropped if they tried to take the relationship to a deeper emotional level. She had never imagined she would *ever* let the barriers down enough to fall totally and hopelessly in love, but Joel had slipped into her heart as if he had been there from the start. He was *the one*.

She'd had plenty of time to think about this when Joel was

away, and she'd realised that her life had been a series of events leading to where she was at present. If her mum hadn't died, Elsie Davidson would never have seen the news report and hired the private detective to track Maria down. Then Maria wouldn't have inherited this house, and would probably still be living on the Merrydown – or wherever the council had relocated them to now that it had been demolished. And if she was still there, chances were she'd have been as broke as the rest of her old friends, and couldn't have even dreamed of staying at the Britannia. And then she wouldn't have met Joel.

Neither of them had known the importance of that first meeting, but fate hadn't allowed the initial misunderstandings to keep them apart. It had pushed them back together on her very next visit to Manchester. And the rest, as they say, was history.

Joel was in London at the moment. He'd driven down yesterday to meet with the manager of a new boy band he was organising a tour of universities for, and he was due back later this afternoon.

Before he got back, though, Beth would have arrived for her first visit since Maria had moved back to Manchester. And that gave them a few hours alone, to catch up and gossip.

Maria kept rushing to the window now, in between polishing and dusting, to see if the taxi was here yet. She'd just finished vacuuming the lounge when she heard the squeal of brakes as the taxi came to a stop at the gate. Taking a last look around, she ran to the door.

Paying the fare, Beth waited for her change, then gathered her things together as the driver walked around to take her case out of the boot.

She'd called Maria before she caught the train this

morning, and had been relieved to hear that Joel wouldn't be here till later. The one aspect of this trip that she'd been dreading was the Joel overload. She got it every time they talked: *Joel said . . . Joel did . . . Joel thinks . . .*

The one thing she *hadn't* heard was that Joel had finally found a flat.

It was perfectly obvious that he had moved in, and Beth didn't know why Maria was hiding it from her. It wasn't like she could *do* anything about it – apart from tell her friend that she was being stupid, maybe. Or that, in her – admittedly limited – experience, men like Joel Parry didn't do the faithful-boyfriend thing. But they were only words, and Maria was more than capable of not listening when she didn't like what she was hearing.

Getting out of the taxi now, a huge smile crept across Beth's face when she saw Maria standing in the porch – looking even more gorgeous than usual, the bitch!

'Gonna stand there all day and leave me to carry my own bags?' she called out.

'Lazy as ever!' Maria shouted back and grinned, running to help her.

'I was only joking,' Beth said, hugging her. 'You look amazing. Poncing about in mansions obviously suits you.'

'Not quite a mansion,' Maria said, taking Beth's case from the driver. 'But I've got my eye on a nice little castle down the road, so I shouldn't think I'll be here too much longer.'

'You *are* joking?' Beth said uncertainly.

'Course I am,' Maria laughed, stepping aside to let her go in.

Putting her bags down, Beth tugged her gloves off and hugged Maria again. 'I've missed you so much. It's not been the same without you.'

'Don't – you'll make me cry,' Maria said, sniffing and

laughing. 'I miss you too. And how are the girls? Did Sharon get the birthday card?'

'Yeah. She said to say thanks, it was lovely. And they're both dead busy, or they'd have come with me.'

Taking her coat off now, Beth looked around with surprise.

'Wow! I can't believe how different it looks in here,' she said, stroking the textured wallpaper. 'It looks amazing. And it's so *warm*. Oh, I *love* that rug . . . And where did you get that mirror? It's fantastic!'

'Isn't it?' Maria said proudly. 'I got it at this incredible shop Joel found in Ancoats. All the Man United players get their furniture there when they get flats in town, apparently. So it's quite expensive, but well worth it. Anyway, come and look at this.' Pulling her into the front room, she waved her hand with a flourish. 'Da da!'

'The dreary old couches are gone,' Beth said, casting an approving eye over the new cream suite. 'About time, too! Did you sell them?'

'Yep. And I didn't have to do a thing, because Joel sorted it all out for me,' Maria gushed. 'He's so good, Beth. I haven't had to worry about anything since he came to stay. He's been looking after my accounts as well, making sure the investments are working for me.'

'What about Nigel?' Beth asked with a flicker of concern.

'He's still my solicitor,' Maria said, flapping her hand as if that were unimportant. 'He's there if I need him, but he shouldn't have to be bothered with the money side of things. That was just a favour he was doing me. But Joel's got a really good head for figures, so I trust him. And he's been great with all the work I've had done on the house, too – making sure it all gets done properly, and that no one's ripping me off.'

'Uh huh,' Beth murmured lightly. 'I take it he still hasn't managed to find a flat, then?'

A flicker of a frown flitted across Maria's brow. Beth asked that question every time they talked. And Maria's answer was always the same: 'It's not that easy finding anything decent in Manchester.'

And she said it again now, even though she knew it was wearing thin.

She wanted to come straight out and tell Beth that Joel had moved in. But then Beth would be bound to say something derogatory, and she'd have to tell her to mind her own business, and they'd end up falling out. And she didn't want that.

She didn't know why Beth was so suspicious of Joel. She'd only met him once and didn't know the first thing about him apart from what Maria had told her – and every word of that had been good. But Beth was always so unresponsive when his name was mentioned, like she thought he was some kind of con merchant, or something. Now that she was here for the weekend, Maria was hoping she would get to know him properly and see how lovely he really was.

'Come and see the kitchen,' she said now, dragging Beth down the hall. 'I know I've told you about it a hundred times, but it looks so much better than it sounds. I *love* it. I spend all my time in here.'

'Nice fridge,' Beth said, opening it up to take a look. 'And you've even got proper food in it – I'm impressed.'

'Gorgeous, isn't it?' Maria beamed. 'Joel chose it.'

Why doesn't that surprise me? Beth thought, closing the door and wiping her hands on her skirt.

'You've got it really nice,' she said when she'd looked at everything. 'And it feels lovely and homely. I told you the house liked you.'

'Yeah, well, I like it, too,' Maria said, sighing contentedly. 'Anyway, come upstairs and see your room. I found some gorgeous bedding in your favourite colour, so you'll love that. And there's a portable TV, in case you can't sleep.'

'No en-suite?' Beth teased, reminding her that she had said she would get one put in.

'Sorry.' Maria gave her a sheepish smile. 'Joel said—'

'I was joking,' Beth held up a hand to stop her. She didn't want to hear any more Joelisms. She'd only been here two minutes, and she hadn't even seen him yet, but she was already fed up with him.

'Joel's on his way back from London,' Maria said, un-zipping Beth's case to see what she'd brought with her. 'He drove up yesterday to meet the manager of some boy band he's organising a tour for. He's so busy, the poor thing. Always travelling up and down the place.'

'Oh, well, at least he's still working,' Beth said, not bothering to mention that Maria had already told her all this.

'Yeah, course.' Maria nodded. 'He takes the odd day off here and there, but he'd never quit – and I wouldn't ask him to. He's so lucky, meeting all those stars.'

'You met any yet?' Beth asked casually.

'No, but I don't mind. It's business, at the end of the day. Joel's friendly with them, but he's got to be professional about it. Anyway, most celebrities are wary of the public getting in on the behind-the-scenes stuff, because they're always scared someone's going to sell stories about them.'

'I see,' Beth murmured, thinking, *Great excuse . . . Leave the girlfriend at home and go and party with the stars.*

'God, that's nice,' Maria said, pulling a floaty green top out of the case.

'Have it,' Beth said, flapping her hand. 'I'll just root through your stuff later. Still got that nice blue dress you bought last time I was here?'

'There's *no* way you're getting your hands on that,' Maria

told her, smiling coyly. 'Joel *loves* that dress. He says it reminds him of when he fell in lust with me.'

Mentally sticking a finger down her throat, Beth unpacked her clothes and hung them in the wardrobe.

'Right, what have you got planned for tonight?' she asked, rubbing her hands together when everything was done. 'Nightclub? Pictures? Restaurant? All of the above?'

'Er, none, actually.' Maria wrinkled her nose sheepishly. 'Sorry, babe, I know it sounds awful when we haven't seen each other for so long, but Joel could be back any time, and he'll be knackered, so I was thinking we could have a nice night in. I've got dinner all planned: steak and garlic mushrooms – just how you like it. And we've got *stacks* of DVDs, so we can just slob out and watch films and drink wine.'

'Sounds great,' Beth said, smiling tightly.

'Aw, I know you're disappointed,' Maria said apologetically. 'But I'll make it up to you tomorrow when I take you to the Trafford Centre. You'll *love* that. You thought the Arndale was big, just *wait* till you see the size of this place. Then we'll go out tomorrow night. Joel wants to go to some new club he's found in Alderley Edge, but we can go back to Scarletts, if you'd rather.'

'Gee, I can hardly wait,' Beth muttered.

This was going to be a whole barrel of fun if Joel was the hub around which they were going to revolve this weekend – *not*. Maria was simpering over him *now*, so what the hell was she going to be like when Miracle Man was here in person? Beth felt like she was on the set of *The Stepford Wives*, or something. She was going to need help to survive this weekend.

Taking her cigarettes out of her bag, she looked around with a frown.

'I don't see an ashtray . . . *Please* don't say I've got to go into the garden to smoke. My mum's driving me crazy with that.'

'No, of course not,' Maria said, nipping into her own room and bringing an ashtray back. 'I didn't know you were smoking again.'

'Yeah, well, I needed it after you buggered off and left me at the mercy of those bratty kids,' Beth said, lighting two and handing one to her.

'*See!*' Maria exclaimed with glee. 'I *told* you they were dwarf demons disguised as kids! Why do you think I quit so fast?'

''Cos you turned into a rich bitch and didn't need the money any more,' Beth said wryly. 'Anyway, shut up about school or I might just slit my wrists. Where d'y' keep the wine in this place?'

'It's one o'clock in the afternoon,' Maria laughed, sure that Beth was messing about.

She wasn't.

'It's Saturday, and you're not taking me out, so we might as well have *some* fun,' she said. 'I'll show you the pictures of the art gallery I've set up in the school hall, and you can show me all the weird stuff you found in the attic.'

'Oh, yeah, I forgot about that,' Maria said, grinning as she jumped up to go and get the wine. 'Wait till you see the rings. They're just incredible. Joel says . . .'

Sticking her fingers in her ears, Beth did a silent *La La La* as she followed Maria back down the stairs.

Sitting at the kitchen table, they spent the next hour drinking wine, looking at Beth's photos, reminiscing about the old days, and chatting about what Maria had been doing.

Catching Beth rolling her eyes when she was telling her a story about one of Joel's clients, Maria frowned.

'Am I boring you?'

Smiling sheepishly, Beth said, 'A bit. Sorry, Maz, but I came to see *you*, not to talk about Joel all day.'

'You don't like him, do you?' Maria asked quietly, hoping that Beth would deny it and they could get on with the weekend in peace.

'I don't really know him,' Beth replied evasively. 'What do your other friends think of him?' Sitting back, she peered at Maria over the rim of her glass.

Swallowing the last of her drink, Maria got up and went to the fridge for another bottle.

'I haven't actually seen anyone since I got back,' she admitted, bringing it back to the table and reaching for the corkscrew.

'No one?' Beth frowned. 'I thought you said you'd got back in touch with your friend Vicky.'

'I did ring her,' Maria murmured, feeling as if she was on trial now. 'But she wasn't in. Her boyfriend said he'd tell her to ring me, but she didn't.'

'That was the first *night*,' Beth said, remembering how offended Maria had been by the guy's brusqueness when she related the story to her. 'It's been six months. You mean you haven't rung her since then?'

'What's the point?' Maria shrugged, pouring wine into their glasses. 'She obviously doesn't want to keep in touch.'

'You don't know that. What if her boyfriend forgot to pass the message on?'

'It doesn't really matter. I'm not sure I want to go back to all that, anyway.'

'All what?' Beth persisted. '*Friends*?'

'*Old* friends,' Maria corrected her. 'I don't know them any more. We've got nothing in common.'

Beth gave her a funny look. 'Oh, right . . . So, if I can't get any more time off work and don't manage to come up for another year, you won't want to know me?'

'Don't be daft,' Maria tutted. 'You're different. We've known each other for years.'

'Yeah, and you knew Vicky for years.'

'Yes, well, she's not the type of—' Stopping herself, Maria shrugged. 'I just don't want to go back to all that. It reminds me of my mum.'

Still frowning, Beth chewed this over. Maria had been about to say that her old friend wasn't the type of person she wanted as a friend any more. But since when did she get so snobby? That wasn't like her at all.

'Haven't you made any friends round here?' she asked then.

'Not really.' Maria shifted uncomfortably in her chair. 'I have a laugh with the hairdresser round the corner, but she's a lot older than me, so I can't see us being friends.'

'Your hairdresser's *supposed* to have a laugh with you,' Beth told her quietly. 'That's what you pay them for. I'm talking about proper friends – the kind you have round for coffee. What about your neighbours? You've been here six months, but I can't honestly say I've ever heard you talking about them. Please tell me I'm wrong.'

'Why are you going on at me?' Maria said defensively. 'What's the big deal if I talk to the neighbours or not? They're all too snobby, if you must know.'

'You mean they don't think you're their type of person?' Beth threw her own words back at her, one eyebrow neatly arched.

'I'm not a snob,' Maria protested, realising what Beth was getting at. 'If I don't choose to keep in touch with people I used to know, that's my business.'

'What about Joel?' Beth countered smoothly. 'He's someone you used to know, but you're certainly keeping in touch with him.'

Maria felt the heat rise to her cheeks. Beth was making a point, not exposing the lie, but it felt just as bad.

'He's totally different,' she murmured, looking around for

her cigarettes so that she didn't have to meet Beth's gaze. 'If you saw the way the others lived, you'd understand.'

Beth was afraid she understood all too well. Maria thought she was better than her old friends because they lived in council flats and she owned this great big old house.

Sitting in uncomfortable silence for the next few minutes, the girls smoked their cigarettes and drank their wine. Then Maria sighed wearily.

'Why are we arguing?' she asked, her voice pained. 'We were having a laugh till you started having a go at me about Joel.'

Beth could have said it had gone sour because Joel was *all* Maria wanted to talk about. That they'd only been having a great time because they'd merely skimmed the surface of everything else. That Maria had only been happy to see her because she hadn't talked to *anyone* in six months but Joel and the hairdresser. That she seemed to have isolated herself and turned into one of those sad little under-the-thumb housewives that they had always vowed they would never become – spending more time worrying which fragrance of washing powder smelled best fresh off the line than what to do with her talents and intelligence.

Beth *could* have said all of that. Instead, she shrugged and gave her friend a weary smile.

'Too much wine, I guess. You know what a belligerent cow I am when I drink.'

'Yeah, I remember,' Maria said, with a sad smile of her own. 'Not usually with me, though.'

'Yeah, well, I've got a lot on my plate at the moment,' Beth said. 'Sorry. I didn't mean to be horrible.' Swallowing her wine, she reached for the bottle.

'Are you sure you should?' Maria laughed. 'I don't want you getting even more drunk and gobby.'

'*Moi?*' Beth said, looking shocked. 'As if!'

★   ★   ★

Peeling his eyes open when he felt a warm, wet sensation on his dick, Joel raised his head and looked down. Oh, it was *her* – the girl from the party. Rita something-or-other.

Yawning, he peered at the clock on the bedside table. Three-thirty. No *way* had he been sleeping all day. What the hell had he been drinking last night? If he didn't know better, he'd swear he'd been spiked.

A gnawing feeling of irritation gripped Joel's stomach as the girl's head bobbed up and down, up and down, and he found himself fighting the urge to grab her hair and wrench her off him. He'd rather have no blow job than a bad blow job, but she'd obviously been taking lessons from one of those ill-informed glossy mags, and was going for it good style: *Nibble delicately on the tip, then lick the shaft and squeeze, all the while gently cupping the balls.*

What was wrong with just *sucking*, for fuck's sake?

Nope . . . this wasn't working. He was stone dead from the inside out. Nice girl – from what he could remember – but she just wasn't doing it for him.

'Sorry, babe,' he said, easing himself out of her mouth – trying not to show the revulsion he felt when his limp dick flopped wetly onto his thigh.

Ugh!

'It's not *your* fault,' he assured her. 'You're fantastic. But I've, er, got things to do, and I didn't realise how late it was.'

'It's all right,' the girl said, getting up. Her lips were swollen from her efforts, her eyes clouded with disappointment.

Watching as she walked into the bathroom, Joel frowned. He vaguely remembered being introduced to her last night, but he was sure she hadn't looked as young as she did right now. She had a slightly boyish shape to her bum and hips, and she walked like a sulky little girl. But then, she probably *was* sulking after that brush-off. Poor cow had been trying so hard.

Coming back, she tossed a towel to him. Thanking her, he wiped himself and sat on the edge of the mattress to pull his pants on.

Still naked, the girl sat on a straight-backed chair and reached for a half-spliff that was lying among the dimps in the ashtray. Lighting it, she drew her feet up onto the seat and rested her chin on her knees to watch him.

'Am I going to see you again?' she asked, giving Joel a full-on view of puffy red pussy lips, complete with a shockingly dick-like clit.

Blanching, Joel averted his gaze. Shit! He hadn't noticed *that* last night. No wonder she had boyish hips – she probably *was* a boy. He had to stop getting so out of his head. It was going to be the death of him.

'Er, no, I don't think so,' he said. 'I had a great time, but I don't think it's very fair, me getting this for free after charging you for the gear.' Frowning then, he glanced up at her. 'You *did* buy some off me, didn't you?'

'Yeah, I took a twenty bag,' she said. 'But I don't mind paying,' she added quickly, a spark of hope in her voice. If that was his only problem . . .

'Nah, it wouldn't feel right.' Joel smiled apologetically. 'You're a lovely girl, Rita, but—'

'Anita.'

'*Anita.* Sorry. You're a lovely girl, but you deserve better than that. I wouldn't want to be accused of taking advantage.' Getting up, Joel pulled his shirt on and buttoned it up. 'Any boy would be proud to have you as his girl.'

'I'm not a *girl.*' Anita interrupted, pouting now. 'I'm a woman. I thought you would have realised that after last night.'

'Oh, I do, believe me. But you still deserve better.' Joel took the spliff from her fingers and took a drag before handing it back. 'I've, er, got a wife and six kids waiting for me at home.'

'You're *married*?' Anita drew her knees up a little higher, covering her pointy little tits. 'You never said.'

'*Not* the kind of thing you advertise when you meet someone you really like,' Joel said, gazing at her regretfully. 'Believe me, if I wasn't, you'd be the perfect . . .' Pausing, he inhaled deeply. Then he said, 'No, that's not fair. Nothing can happen, so there's no point saying I'd like it to.'

Anita frowned. He really was gorgeous, and she really wanted to see him again. But *six kids* . . . ?

'I'd best get off, then,' Joel said, pulling his jacket on. 'You've got my number, so just give me a ring if you want another score, okay?'

'Yeah, fine.' Anita reached for her dressing gown. Folding her arms when she'd pulled it on and fastened the belt, she pursed her lips thoughtfully as if she wanted to say something.

'I'll see myself out,' Joel said, wanting to escape before she came out with something *meaningful*.

'Look, I know you're hooked up,' Anita blurted out. 'But I don't mind if you fancy coming round for a shag now and then – no strings.'

'Thanks, babe.' Joel kissed her softly on the cheek. 'I'll keep it in mind.'

Patting his pocket to check that the money was still there, he winked at her and let himself out of the flat.

Lighting a cigarette as he trotted down the stairs, he reached into his pocket for the car keys. Maria had insisted on buying the second-hand Beemer after he started working again – to save on cab fares. He didn't think she'd even driven it yet, but she didn't seem bothered, so why should he worry? She was happy, as long as he took her shopping. And that was a small price to pay for the extra freedom the car afforded him.

Walking outside, he stopped in his tracks when he didn't see the car. Rushing down the path to the pavement, he scratched his head and looked up and down the street. The car was nowhere to be seen. For one horrible moment he thought it had been stolen, and everything crashed down on his head. He'd have to report it to the police, and they would tell Maria. And what excuse could he give for being in Manchester when he was supposed to be in London?

Shit!

He had a sudden flashback of getting out of a cab with Rita-Anita last night. That was right . . . He'd been so pissed that he could barely walk, and Jippi had made him leave the car in the residents' car park. Great!

Calling a cab, he leaned against a tree at the kerb and smoked until it arrived. Dashing head down to the under-ground guards' booth when he got there, he persuaded them to let him in. Retrieving the car, he drove out with his head still down – to avoid having Jippi see him and delay him with nonsense. He was a great guy, but he was way too in-your-face for daytime consumption, and Joel was feeling too rough to deal with him just now.

It was his own fault that he felt like this, though, because he'd been getting a little too much of a liking for the coke lately. But he wasn't stupid enough to let it get out of hand, so it wasn't too much of a problem. His profits were suffering a bit, but he was having a good time, so he couldn't really complain. Apart from when he mixed it with alcohol, like last night, and ended up feeling rough as shit.

He just wanted to get home and fall into a steaming hot bath, then into bed with Maria. Except that her bloody friend would probably be there by now. Oh, well, it would give him a chance to sleep this off while they gossiped.

'That you, Joel?' Maria called from the kitchen when she heard the front door closing. 'We're in the kitchen.'

'I'll be with you in a minute,' he called back. 'I'm just going to jump in the shower. It was a bummer of a drive. Got stuck in traffic on the M1.'

'Beth's here,' Maria said, coming into the hall to give him a kiss. 'Just come and say hello before you go up – please?'

Relenting when he saw a spark of desperation in her eyes, Joel said, 'Okay, but no hugs.' Putting his hands on her hips, he eased her away. 'Sorry, sweetheart, but I've been stuck in the car for hours. I *reek* of sweat.'

'You smell fine to me,' Maria murmured, sniffing his lapel. 'Smells more perfumy than sweaty.' Drawing her head back, she narrowed her eyes and gave him a mock-accusing look. 'Anything you want to tell me?'

'Oh, like what . . . ?' Joel said wryly. 'Like I've just jumped out of another woman's bed and come straight home to you?'

Maria laughed and gave him a soft slap. 'Yeah, right. And I've been having it off with the boiler man while you've been gone.'

'Not the big fat one with the builder's arse?' Joel grimaced. 'I thought you had better taste than that!'

'When you've quite finished,' she scolded playfully, 'my friend is waiting to say hello. So, move it . . .' She pushed him into the kitchen.

As soon as Joel saw Beth, he remembered why he didn't like her. She had a sharpness in her eyes that screamed of suspicion and distrust – of him. He'd only ever seen her that once, but she'd had that same look in her eye then – like she could see right through him.

And he wasn't imagining it, because Maria had told him that Beth was forever advising her to do this, that or the other with her money. Safeguarding herself, she called it, but he suspected that she thought he was trying to rip Maria off. It was the other way around, in his opinion. Beth wanted to keep Maria and her money all to herself – to be her only friend, so that she'd be first in line if Maria met an untimely death. The bitch was probably kicking herself for leaving Maria alone that fateful night, giving her the space to get involved with Joel. But if she thought she could waltz in here and oust him now, then she was sadly mistaken. He wasn't going anywhere.

'Hi, Beth,' he said now, stepping into the kitchen and offering her his hand with a pleasant smile on his face. 'Nice to see you again.'

'You, too,' she said, shaking his hand with a tight smile on her lips.

Snotty bitch. Sitting there like she belonged and he didn't.

'You're looking really good,' Joel said, giving her the lopsided grin. 'Had your hair done?'

'It's a bit shorter, yeah,' Beth responded coolly. He could try flattery if he wanted to, but it wouldn't work.

'Don't mind if I nip straight up, do you?' he said then, refusing to let his feelings show on his face. 'Long drive . . .'

'Yeah, I heard,' she said, still crocodiling. 'No problem. Take as long as you like. We're quite cosy.'

Oh, I bet you are, he thought nastily. *But don't get too damn cosy, lady, 'cos if you don't play nice you won't be coming back anytime soon.*

'I know you don't really know him,' Maria whispered when he'd gone, 'but you'll love him when you do. He's really, really nice.'

'Mmmm,' Beth murmured, lifting her glass to her mouth so that she didn't have to answer.

'Maria . . .' Joel shouted a short while later. 'Can you come here a minute?'

Maria was on her feet in an instant.

'Won't be a sec,' she told Beth, rushing out.

Shaking her head, Beth refilled her glass. She shouldn't really, but she needed it to stop herself from screaming with frustration. Joel had done that on purpose – to let her know that he had Maria exactly where he wanted her. *He snaps his fingers – she comes running. What a man!*

He was too smooth by far, but his smile didn't fool her. There was no warmth in it. It was the smile of a man who knew what he wanted and wouldn't let anyone get in his way.

The old Maria would never have fallen for it. She'd been sassy and funny, but most of all independent, with plans, and dreams, and ambitions. Beth had sensed from their phone calls that Maria had changed, but it was only today, talking to her face to face, that she'd realised how much. She seemed genuinely content to languish in this house, cooking and cleaning and waiting for her master to return. The whole set-up felt wrong – and Joel definitely wasn't right for Maria.

'He wanted me to wash his back,' Maria explained when she came back a few minutes later, her face flushed from a passionate kiss.

'Weren't his arms long enough?' Beth asked with the tiniest hint of sarcasm.

'I don't mind doing it,' Maria said, wondering why Beth was being funny again. Joel hadn't said anything wrong to her. He'd been really nice, in fact.

'No, I'm sure you don't.' Beth sighed. 'Drink?'

Joel yawned and fidgeted his way through two DVDs. He'd felt the shift in the atmosphere when he came down from the shower and knew that something must have happened. He hoped it was nothing to do with him. That would be awful.

Not.

'I'm really sorry, ladies,' he said when the credits rolled at the end of the second film. 'But I'm dead on my feet. Got to go and hit the sack.'

'Oh, right,' Maria said, casting a glance at Beth. 'I'll just, er . . .'

'Take your time,' Joel insisted, getting up. 'You've not seen each other for ages – don't let me interrupt.'

'No, you're all right,' Beth said, yawning exaggeratedly. 'I'm pretty knackered myself.'

She wasn't, but it was obvious that Maria would rather go up with lover boy than sit up chatting to her. Anyway, she didn't really feel like being nice for the sake of keeping the peace. She'd been doing that all day, and it was crippling her to keep her mouth shut. She just wanted to shake Maria, and ask where the real Maria was hiding. And as for that smug bastard . . .

'Sure I'm not driving you out?' Joel asked, smiling at her as if everything was just fine.

'No, I just want to go to bed,' Beth said, trying not to look at him.

Up in their room when they'd said their goodnights, Joel laid his clothes over the back of the chair and climbed into bed. Putting his hands behind his head, he watched as Maria unhooked her bra. She really did have the nicest tits. Bigger, rounder and more womanly than Rita-Anita Dickclit's. Sometimes, he didn't know why he bothered shagging half the girls he did when he had Maria to come home to. But he just couldn't see the point of depriving himself if it was available. And it definitely wasn't hurting Maria. She had no clue.

'Your friend really doesn't like me, does she?' he said when she got in beside him.

'What makes you say that?' she asked, snuggling up to him when he held his arm out for her. 'She hasn't said anything, has she?'

'Not to me,' Joel said softly. 'But I know she says stuff to you.'

'Not really,' Maria murmured, closing her eyes guiltily.

'Well, she's got *something* against me, 'cos she can barely look me in the eye,' Joel said, sighing as if it really pained him. 'But you can't say I haven't tried. I left you alone so you could talk, and I even offered to come to bed alone – much as I didn't *want* to,' he added, dropping a kiss onto the top of her head. 'She's just so uptight with me.'

'She'll be fine,' Maria assured him, playing with the little thatch of fine hairs on his chest. 'Wait till we take her to the Trafford Centre. She loves shopping. We'll buy her something nice – that should cheer her up.'

'I don't want to *buy* her friendship,' Joel said, as if that were a terrible idea. 'I just want her to give me a fair try. That's not so much to ask, is it?'

'So, you don't think it's a good idea to treat her?'

'Do you want my honest opinion?' Joel said, waiting for her to nod before continuing. 'No, I really don't. I know she was your best friend, but things have changed in your life, and I think you're in danger of turning this into a friendship based on guilt.'

'What do you mean, guilt?' Maria asked uncertainly. She didn't *think* she felt guilty, but Joel was so sharp that he might have picked up on something she had missed.

'I could be totally wrong,' Joel said, as if he really didn't want to say anything negative. 'But I think you feel guilty that she's come to visit you and I'm here.'

'No, I don't,' Maria told him quickly. 'Honestly – I love you being here.'

'I'm probably saying it wrong,' Joel sighed. 'Maybe it's just that you know subconsciously that she wanted you to herself, and you feel guilty because you're putting your own feelings first.'

'Oh, God, do you think I'm being selfish?'

'Not at all. You *should* put yourself first. You only get one shot at life, and as they say – this ain't no dress rehearsal.' Pausing, Joel gave her a gentle hug. 'Hate to say this, babe, because I really don't want to get between you, but if anyone's being selfish, it's Beth. If it was the other way round, and you knew how much heartache she'd had in her life, wouldn't you be happy for her that she was finally making a life for herself? Tell me if I'm out of order, but I think she liked it better when you were totally dependent on her. Does that make any sense?'

Maria was chewing her lip. She didn't want to admit it, but he might actually have a point. Beth *had* always been happiest when it had been just the two of them. They'd hung out with the girls back home, but it had always been her and Beth as one half of the group, and Sharon and Leanne as the other. But you couldn't carry on like that for ever. There came a point when you had to allow somebody else into your life, or you'd never fall in love, get married, have children. Friends were supposed to slot themselves in around that, not in the middle of it, or *instead* of it.

'Oh, look, ignore me,' Joel said when she stayed silent. 'I shouldn't have said anything. Your friendship's got nothing to do with me. How about I don't come with you tomorrow? Then you can just go back to the way it used to be.'

'No, I don't want that,' Maria said, looking up at him now. 'It's great that she's here, but I've got a life with you now, and I don't want that to change. If Beth's got a problem, she'll have to deal with it, or . . .' Pausing, she shrugged. 'Well, it's none of her business, is it? And, like you said, she should be happy for me.'

'Are you happy?' Joel asked, stroking her hair back from her face. 'Really happy?'

'Deliriously,' Maria murmured. 'What about you?'

'Me?' Joel said, tipping her chin up to kiss her. 'I'm the luckiest man alive.'

★   ★   ★

The rest of the weekend was overshadowed by the underlying tension between not just Joel and Beth, but between Beth and Maria. They had a miserable day shopping, followed by a less than enjoyable night at Scarletts.

When Monday dawned, Maria and Beth shared a quiet breakfast together, then Beth went up to her room to pack her things. Everything had changed, and she was too weary to carry on fighting it. With Joel in the picture there was no point. Maria had handed herself to him lock, stock and barrel, and there was nothing left of her for anyone else.

Coming down with her bags when she'd finished, Beth shook her head when Maria offered to drive her to the train station.

'I've already ordered a cab,' she said, pulling her coat on. 'It should be here any minute. You stay and get things back to normal.'

'I'm really sorry you didn't have a good time,' Maria said regretfully. 'I wish we could start again.'

'You already have,' Beth told her sadly. 'And I hope you'll be happy. Just do me one favour, and make sure you don't forget that there's a world outside this door – and you've as much right as *anyone* to enjoy it. You might not think it now, but you need friends to talk to. I'm always at the other end of the phone, but you need girls to go out and have fun with. Promise you'll get in touch with Vicky, at least.'

'Oh, please don't let's get into this again,' Maria said, folding her arms. 'I'm really, really happy with things the way they are. Don't make me feel bad.'

'I'm not trying to,' Beth assured her, 'I'm trying to make you feel *good*, because you deserve that after everything you've been through.'

Outside, a car horn sounded.

'That'll be the taxi,' Beth said, putting her bags down and giving Maria a hug. 'Take care, babe.'

'I'll miss you,' Maria said tearfully. 'Come back as soon as you get another break. We'll do something different, I promise.'

'Let's see how it goes,' Beth said.

Saying goodbye, they both knew it would be a long time before they saw each other again – if ever.

19

Life fell easily back into its routine once Joel and Maria had the house back to themselves. Maria and Beth talked a few times on the phone, but their conversations were awkward now that Maria couldn't talk about Joel. He was her life, so she really didn't have too much else to tell Beth, and the calls inevitably dried up. Which was sad, but also a relief – for them both.

Maria did take one piece of Beth's advice, though. Realising how boring *Beth* had obviously found her, she feared that Joel would soon get fed up of having a girlfriend whose only topic of conversation was what she'd done to the house while he was away, or what she was cooking for dinner. So she started to go out, to the library, and the museum, and the art gallery. And Joel seemed happy enough to listen to her prattling on about it when he was home, so she figured it must be working.

And, eventually, she contacted Vicky and arranged to meet up with her in town for coffee.

'I'm so glad you called,' Vicky said when they had carried their cups to the table. 'Leroy's hopeless at passing messages on. It was weeks after you called that he remembered, but he'd lost your number by then, so I couldn't call you back.'

'It's all right,' Maria said. 'I've been kind of busy anyway. I've moved back for good now, so I've been getting the house right.'

'And?' Vicky said, smirking knowingly.

'And what?' Maria asked, trying not to blush.

'And who are you shagging?' As blunt as ever, Vicky came right out with it. 'Don't tell me you're not seeing anyone, 'cos you've got that look about you.'

'Yeah, I'm seeing someone,' Maria said cautiously. Given how negative Beth had been, she was reluctant to talk about Joel.

'Spill,' Vicky said, sounding genuinely interested.

'Well, his name's Joel,' Maria said, trying not to smile at the mere mention of his name. 'He's twenty-eight. Tallish, blond, good-looking. Well, gorgeous, actually. He's just . . .' She flapped her hands. 'Gorgeous.'

'Check you, all loved-up.' Vicky chuckled. 'Hope he treats you right?'

'God, yeah!' Maria nodded emphatically. 'He's really affectionate. Always hugging me and telling me how lovely I am.'

'And you've been seeing him how long?'

'Nearly a year. It's gone really fast, but it still feels really new.'

'Well, make the most of it while it lasts,' Vicky said, sighing wistfully. 'And don't rush into having kids, whatever you do. Me and Lee have been together a long time, and I love him to bits, but all the mushy stuff stops once you start smelling of nappies and baby puke.'

'I'm not even thinking of having kids,' Maria assured her. 'Not for a *long* time.'

'Yeah, well, learn by my mistakes, and get some super-thick condoms next time you pick up your pill,' Vicky advised her grimly. 'But enough of that . . . When do I get to meet this sex god of yours?'

Maria picked up her coffee and gave a little shrug. 'I don't really know. He's really busy.'

'Doing what?'

'Working. He's a tour organiser – for singers and bands.'

'Local stuff?' Vicky asked. 'Only Leroy might know him, 'cos him and his crew do a bit of MC-ing at some clubs in town. What's his name? I'll ask Lee if he knows him.'

'Joel Parry,' Maria told her. 'But I doubt he knows him if he only works in town. Joel works mainly with big names.'

'For real?' Vicky said, really interested now. 'Like who?

'Oh, loads,' Maria told her, trying not to sound too name-droppy. 'The last one was Seal. He was with him for a couple of nights last week. Before that it was Oasis. And he's worked with Phil Collins, and Mariah Carey. Oh, and Britney.'

'Piss off!' Vicky gasped. 'That's fantastic. Shit, bring him round and introduce him to Lee. He could do with meeting some proper stars. You never know, he might get a deal out of it. He should. He's brilliant at it. Wait till I tell him.'

Maria frowned, wondering how to get out of this. She shouldn't have said anything. Now Vicky thought that Maria could help her boyfriend, but she really couldn't.

'It's not really like that,' she admitted after a moment. 'Joel can't take anyone with him when he goes to meetings or on tour. It's work; he can't even take me.'

'What, never?' Vicky asked, not sure whether she was being fobbed off.

'Never,' Maria affirmed, sighing softly. 'I've never met any of them. I can't even go to the gigs in case they realise I'm connected to Joel. They're just really paranoid about people selling stories to the press.'

'You poor thing,' Vicky said, shaking her head. 'So near, yet so far. Leroy will be gutted when I tell him. But, oh, well . . .' Pausing to light a cigarette, she slid the pack across the table to Maria. 'So what do you do when he's working? Have you found yourself a job yet?'

'No, I'm pretty much at home most of the time,' Maria said, wondering why she suddenly felt like a failure. 'But I'm planning to start painting again. Just for myself, though. I'm not good enough to sell. It was all right for teaching, but I didn't really like that.'

'Don't you go out to any clubs or pubs?' Vicky asked, thinking that Maria must be leading a very lonely life.

'I haven't really had time,' Maria said. 'Anyway, I don't know too many people yet, so it's not that easy. My friend came to stay a while back, and we went to a place called Scarletts in town.'

'Oh yeah?' Vicky smiled. 'That's one of the gigs Lee's been doing on a Thursday night. 'Nice, isn't it?'

'Yeah, I've been a couple of times now,' Maria said. 'It was loads better the first time, but the last time was pretty boring, really.'

'Was it a Sunday?' Vicky asked. 'Thought so,' she said when Maria nodded. 'That's grab-a-granny night. You'll have to come with me and Lee sometime – you'll have loads more fun. I'm going this Thursday, as it happens. Do you fancy it?'

'I'll have to see what Joel's doing,' Maria told her, not wanting to commit herself to something she might have to cancel. 'But I wouldn't mind. What's MC-ing, though?'

Laughing, Vicky explained about the nights that Leroy and his crew hosted, where MCs and rappers could get up on stage and take the mike to free-style over the DJ's mixes.

'It's really kind of underground,' she said. 'But they do all sorts – hip-hop, garage, rap, Bashment . . . It's mental, but it's *well* wicked.'

'Sounds it,' Maria said, getting caught up in her friend's excitement.

'Give me a ring when you've had a word with your fella, and we'll arrange it,' Vicky said. 'Then you can meet Leroy – at last. And when you do, you can bollock the dozy sod for not passing your message on.'

★   ★   ★

Joel was less than impressed when Maria told him later that afternoon.

'I don't want you to go,' he said, gazing at her seriously. 'I'm not being funny, Maria, but I know what those things are like. Something always kicks off.'

'Vicky didn't say anything about trouble,' Maria said. 'Are you sure it's the same thing? You might be getting it mixed up with something else.'

'I'm not,' Joel assured her. 'Believe me, I've been to loads of those nights. They're full of black guys.'

'Leroy's black,' Maria told him. 'I've not met him yet, but Vicky's been with him for ages, so he must be all right. Anyway, I had loads of black friends when I was growing up.'

'I'm not being racist, if that's what you're thinking,' Joel said quickly. 'It's the *kind* of men that get involved in this kind of thing that I'm talking about. There's always drugs and guns around, and there's too much gang stuff going on. It's not safe. I really don't want you to get caught up in the middle of some rival crew war. Bullets don't know who they're being aimed at.'

'Ooh, stop it, you're scaring me now.' Maria shuddered.

'Good, because I'm being serious. I don't want to lose you.'

Joel's eyes were so full of concern when he gazed at her that Maria felt herself melting, and knew that she would not be going to the club with Vicky that Thursday night – or any other. Joel knew far more about this kind of thing than she did, so she'd be stupid to ignore his advice. He was only trying to protect her, and that was an incredible feeling when you've had to fend for yourself for most of your life.

'I'll ring her and tell her I can't go,' she said, smiling when he squeezed her hand. 'But what excuse should I give? I can't say it's because of the gangs. She might think *I'm* being racist.'

'Just say you've changed your mind,' Joel said, shrugging lightly. 'She can't say anything about that, can she?'

'She might try and persuade me.'

'Yeah, but you're stronger than that. When you don't want to do something, you just say no – simple.'

Having neatly turned it around, so that Maria now believed that she didn't want to go, Joel sat with her while she called Vicky.

'See how easy that was,' he said when she came off the phone, having told Vicky that she'd been thinking about it and really didn't fancy it.

'I feel terrible,' Maria said glumly. 'I'm sure she thinks I'm really up myself.'

'Ah, but we know you're not, don't we?' Joel said, pulling her to her feet and walking her backwards until she touched the wall. Easing her skirt up and her panties down, he kissed her neck as he unzipped himself. 'There's not enough room up there for both of us.'

Kissing Maria goodbye a few hours later, Joel threw his bag into the boot of the car and, blowing her another kiss as she waved him off from the porch, reversed out of the drive and headed off to London for a weekend-long meet with a new boy band called SouthSyde.

He was *actually* going to an after-show party at the Palace Theatre with Honey, the soap starlet, then back to her flat for a private party. She and a few of her co-stars from *Picture Perfect*, and various stars from some of the other soaps, had taken part in a one-off Abba tribute concert for charity. She'd invited him to the show itself, but he'd never been an Abba fan so he'd said he would meet her when it was all over. In reality, he'd had no intention of sitting with Joe and Joanna Public in the audience. He was only interested in mixing with the celebrities.

Honey was all right, but she was a very young eighteen, so she could be a bit childish at times and that grated on him. But she had opened another door for him and, being a proper coke fiend, the sex was always good, so he was happy enough to carry on seeing her until something better came along. And she'd promised there would be some big names there tonight, so Joel was feeling fairly positive.

Thanks to Honey and Jippi, he was making a bit of a name for himself in the so-called inner circle of Manchester celebrities. He had so many new clients that he'd managed to distance himself from most of his old punters, which was great. But he still didn't have nearly enough money to dump Maria. And, anyway, he saw no reason why he should. In many ways, she was the perfect girlfriend – always available, never demanding, and generous to a fault. And he did genuinely care for her, so what more did he actually need?

Joel just wished she'd sell the house so that he could set himself up in an apartment like Jippi's – an apartment befitting his new status. But it would be a long time before Maria was willing to do that, because she still seemed to be in the honeymoon stage with it. But that wouldn't last for ever, he was sure, so he just had to stay tuned for the right moment to suggest a change – and keep a watchful eye on who she took advice from in the meantime.

Beth was out of the picture now, but Maria's friend Vicky inviting her to that gig had been too much. Those gigs *were* quite dangerous, so that hadn't been a total lie, but that wasn't Joel's main objection to Maria going along. It was the thought of her mixing with guys he might have done business with. Not many of them knew his full name, but it wouldn't take too long to suss it out if she started yakking about him. And she was so crazy about him that she wouldn't be able to stop herself.

Still, she'd given in without a fight when Joel had objected, so that had ended well. Any other girl would have known he was talking rubbish and told him to piss off, but Maria didn't know Manchester as well as they did so she'd bowed to his greater knowledge. It was more a marker of her insecurity than his persuasion technique that made her acquiesce so easily, though. She was forever asking his advice, which he found a bit odd, given how self-sufficient she'd been when they first met. Dropping the barriers had obviously pushed her too far the other way, into total dependence.

But Joel wasn't complaining. It was nice to know that something in his life was entirely his. And that's how he intended to keep it.

Honey was waiting at the stage door. Waving as he drove past, Joel held up a finger, indicating that he would be one minute. Parking up in the multi-storey around the corner, he checked that he hadn't forgotten his pre-bagged deals, then strolled around to meet her.

He could smell the booze from several feet away, so the party was obviously in full swing already. Good. There was nothing worse than that first awkward hour when everybody was being polite and uptight.

'It was *brill*!' Honey squealed, rushing up to him and linking arms with him. 'There were just like so *many* massive stars in the audience, and they've all been coming over to congratulate me.'

'Great,' Joel said, a tad disappointed to hear that he'd have been among the stars for a good couple of hours already if it hadn't been for his pride.

'You should have seen me,' Honey gushed, skipping with excitement as she dragged him inside. 'I was really good. I sang "Waterloo" with that girl who used to be Sam in *EastEnders*, then I did "Mamma Mia" with Shelley from *Corrie*, and we had a right laugh.'

'Oh, yeah?' Joel said, smiling as if he was really proud. 'She's here, is she?'

'Yeah, but don't mention drugs to her whatever you do. There's no way she's into all that, she's way too nice.'

'I won't say a word,' Joel assured her.

'Give me mine now,' Honey whispered as they neared the backstage area. 'I'll go and have a line in the bog. Wait for me outside. When we go in, don't tell *anyone* what you're doing here. I've already sounded out everyone I know, so I'll sort them out when we're inside. Oh, and don't forget we're not together, or I'll get the sack. My producer warned me to stay single and out of trouble, 'cos they're toying with the idea of setting me up in a lezzy fling with the hot-dog girl, and they don't want the public to know it's not true.'

'It's cool,' Joel said, smiling wryly. 'So, shall I be your cousin again? Or how about your dad, this time?'

'No way do you look old enough for that,' Honey giggled, taking the little bag from him. 'You can be my agent if you want – I've just sacked mine.'

'Why? What's happened?'

'He's a greedy knob,' Honey sneered. 'He waited till he knew I was getting a new contract, then told me he's whacking an extra five per cent on his commission. But he didn't have anything to do with me getting a new contract, 'cos the producer had already told me my part was safe for another year. And he didn't even have to negotiate my pay rise, 'cos we all got one, so there's no way I'm paying more for him doing less.'

'Quite right,' Joel agreed, coming to a stop at the toilet door.

'Apart from that,' Honey said, turning to face him, 'his wife caught us having a shag on his office couch, so she's kind of banned him from representing me. Don't mind, do you, babe?' She tipped her head to one side and gave him a repentant-little-girl look. 'I was just feeling a bit horny.'

'None of my business.' Joel shrugged. 'I'm only your cousin.'

Taking a quick look around to make sure nobody was watching, Honey reached out and gave his dick a squeeze.

'Will you mind later, when you're *not* my cousin? 'Cos if you think you will, I'd best take my punishment right now.'

'Just get your arse in there and do what you're doing, so we can go party,' Joel chuckled, pushing her through the door.

'Wait for me,' she told him bossily, disappearing with her goodie bag.

The party was being held on the stage itself, and Joel couldn't believe how many faces he recognised. Shelley and Rosie from *Coronation Street* were mere feet away from him, helping themselves to food from the buffet table. Just past them, Sonia from *EastEnders* was chatting to two fit blonde girls he vaguely recognised from *Hollyoaks*. And he swivelled his head to ogle when the old Sam from *EastEnders* sashayed past wearing a tiny skirt and a sexy smile. His heart skipped a beat when he caught a glimpse of Patsy Kensit over by the front of the stage. Standing on tiptoe to get a better look, he nearly died when he saw who she was talking to.

'Have you seen who's over there?' he said when Honey came back with the drink she'd got him. 'Patsy Kensit and Liam Gallagher!'

'Yeah, I know,' she said, her eyes bright with coke and excitement. 'I said hello to her before, but she was a bit off with me. I don't think she watches our show, so she probably didn't recognise me. I haven't spoken to him yet, but I'm deffo gonna grab him before he goes. If he heard me singing, he might want me to do a duet with him.'

In your dreams, Joel thought.

'Great idea,' he said. 'Who knows where you'll end up? You might get a record deal.'

'Shut *up*!' Honey squealed, jumping up and down. 'Shit! Now I'm horny again. Fancy nipping out the back for a quickie?'

Joel's eyebrows rose. *What – and risk some of these people getting away before he'd had a chance to mingle . . . ?*

'Er, no, not just yet,' he said. 'I've only just got here. Anyway, we're going back to yours straight after, so why not save it? And we're not supposed to be *together*, remember. What if someone saw us?'

'Okay,' she agreed, giggling as she added in a whisper, 'I'll just go and rub my pussy up on the corner of the buffet table – it's the perfect height.'

'Knock yourself out,' Joel said, grinning. 'So long as you save something for later.'

'Do I ever run out of it?' she teased.

'Not so far,' he said, sipping his drink. 'Anyway, weren't you supposed to be sorting your mates out?'

'So I was!' Honey said, biting her lip. 'You be all right on your own? Where you gonna be? I'll come and find you when I've taken orders.'

'I'll be around,' Joel said, nodding at a young black lad he recognised from a band he'd see on *Top of the Pops*. 'Go on . . . Don't worry about me. I'm a big boy now.'

'You said it,' she quipped, giving him another sneaky feel before going off in search of her fellow coke-heads.

20

Maria was trying to watch TV, but she couldn't concentrate. Seeing Vicky again today, she'd actually begun to feel a bit more like her old self, and she'd liked that. Being with Beth was different, because she hadn't approved of Joel and that couldn't work. But Vicky hadn't said a word against Joel, not even when Maria said he couldn't help her boyfriend, which made life a lot easier.

Despite what Joel had said, Maria actually *had* wanted to go to that gig with Vicky. She couldn't now, because she'd promised him she wouldn't, but it didn't make her feel any better about the way she'd told Vicky. She wanted to explain, to make sure that Vicky didn't get the wrong idea and give up on her.

Taking a deep breath, she picked up the phone.

'Hello again,' Vicky said, sounding happy. 'To what do I owe the honour of two calls in one day?'

'I just wanted to explain about before,' Maria said. 'Just so you didn't think I was being funny.'

'I didn't.' Vicky sounded amused now. 'It's not everyone's cup of tea, I know that.'

'Yeah, but I shouldn't have said I wanted to go in the first place. I feel like I messed you about.'

'Will you shut up!' Vicky was actually laughing now. 'Christ, girl, you're not my *wife*. If you don't want to go somewhere, don't go – simple.'

'Thanks,' Maria said gratefully. 'I was just worried that you'd think I was being funny.'

'You seriously need to chill,' Vicky said more softly. 'I don't know what's going on in your head these days, but you were really on edge when I saw you earlier. Then you sounded weird when you rang, like you had a gun to your head or something. And now you're worrying about nothing. Just relax, will you?'

'Sorry.'

'And stop apologising. Listen, what are you doing tonight?'

'Nothing, really. Joel's working, so I'm just watching TV.'

'Why don't you come round here for a bit?' Vicky suggested. 'Leroy's playing snooker with his mates, so I'm just chilling on my own. Kids are all in bed.'

'It's pretty late,' Maria said, glancing at her watch.

'Is it hell,' Vicky countered. 'This is early for me. My time doesn't start till I get the kids out of the way. And I don't have to get up for school in the morning, so I'll be up for hours yet. Are you expecting your man back soon?'

'No, he's away for the weekend.'

'So what's stopping you? Get a cab and get your arse round here, girl.'

'I don't know,' Maria said uncertainly.

'There you go again,' Vicky sighed. 'Just do as you're told for once in your life. I'm hanging up now . . . *Bye . . .*'

The phone went dead in Maria's hand. Looking at it, she couldn't help but smile. Vicky and Beth were so alike when it came to speaking their minds – which was probably what had drawn her to Beth in the first place. But where Beth had that small-town mentality that stopped her from going too far, Vicky didn't give a toss. If it was in her head, she thought nothing of opening her mouth and letting it out. And Maria had missed that.

She contemplated giving Joel a ring to ask what he thought, then gave herself a mental slap. Was she really that pathetic that she couldn't make a simple decision like going to visit her friend without getting his approval first? He must be getting so fed up with her; she'd better watch she didn't turn him right off her. Anyway, he was working, so she *couldn't* call him.

Getting herself ready, Maria phoned a cab.

It was scary getting out of the cab in the dark when she reached The Skids. Paying the driver, she ran to the door, wrenched it open and clattered up the stairs as if the ghosts of the speed-freaks with their weird eyes and cackling laughs were chasing her.

Knocking quietly on Vicky's door, Maria looked around nervously as she waited for her friend to answer. She hoped to God nothing had happened since they'd spoken; that Vicky hadn't got all her kids up and gone out somewhere. She didn't think she could face having to go back down the stairs and out into the dark.

Opening the door, Vicky smiled. 'I knew you'd come. You always hated not getting the last word.'

'No, I didn't,' Maria said, following her in.

'Did.'

'Did *not.*'

'*See!*' Vicky laughed, showing her into the lounge.

Maria thought that it looked different with the curtains drawn and the lamps lit; really warm and cosy. And quite funky, too, with its leather couches and beechwood furniture. There was a sleek, expensive-looking stereo system on a unit beside the TV, purring out studio-quality Whitney Houston.

'I didn't realise how nice it was in here,' she said, sitting down on the couch.

'It's all right,' Vicky said, going into the kitchen for another glass. Bringing it back, she sat down and poured a large brandy and Coke and handed it to Maria, saying, 'Take your jacket off, for God's sake. And your shoes. Come on, girl, get comfy.'

With the help of the brandy, they were soon chatting and laughing about the old days, but without the tension that had been there on Maria's first visit.

Before they knew it, it was midnight. Leaning back to look down the hall when she heard the sound of a key slotting into the lock, Vicky said, 'Hiya, babe. Good night?'

'Yeah, it was cool. I won a couple of ton on the tables. I got you a weed while I was there.'

The good-looking black guy Maria recognised from the photos on the wall unit walked in and tossed a small plastic bag to Vicky. Seeing Maria, he nodded and smiled. 'Y'all right?'

'This is Leroy,' Vicky said, the light in her eyes clearly showing how much she loved him. 'Lee, this is Maria – my friend from—'

'Yeah, I know, you've only told me about a thousand times,' he cut in. 'Nice to meet you at last, Maria.'

'Oi! Don't be giving her the Mr Nice Guy act,' Vicky scolded him playfully. 'She's got a bone to pick with you – haven't you, Maria?'

Blushing, Maria shook her head.

'Yeah, she has,' Vicky said. ''Cos she spoke to you ages ago, and you said you'd tell me, but you didn't. So, what've you got to say for yourself?'

'Humblest apologies,' Leroy drawled, flashing a pure white grin as he gave Maria a penitent bow. 'Mind like a fishnet stocking, I'm afraid.'

'It's all right,' Maria said, liking his easy manner.

Down the hall, the toilet flushed.

'Oh, no,' Vicky moaned. 'One of the kids must have heard you coming in.'

'Nah, it's your big 'un,' Leroy said, heading for the kitchen.

'Met up with him down the snooker hall, so he said he'd come back for a blow. Skin up while you're doing nothing.'

Just then another man came in. He was tall, and very broad in a rugby-player kind of way, with really dark hair and an incredibly handsome face. Staring at him, Maria couldn't believe that the last time she had seen him he'd been smaller than her, with a scruffy old bike and dirty legs. *Boy*, he'd changed.

'Look who's here,' Vicky was saying to him, giving him a teasing smile.

Looking at Maria, he nodded hello. His eyes, which were the exact same hazel shade as Vicky's, showed a vague recollection.

'Hi, Davy,' Maria said, tipping her head to one side. 'Don't you remember me?'

Realisation dawned.

'Christ, Maria!' he said, his voice so deep compared to the last time she'd heard him speak that it gave her a start. 'Wow! When did you get here?'

'A couple of hours ago,' she said, feeling a little tearful all of a sudden. Smiling and blinking rapidly to hold the emotion at bay, she said, 'I can't believe how much you've changed.'

'Told you,' Vicky said, pride rich in her voice. 'He's a babe, isn't he?'

'Shut up,' Davy murmured, his eyebrows puckering together with embarrassment.

'You look really well,' Maria said. 'What are you doing with yourself?'

'He manages the Asda in the precinct,' Vicky told her before Davy had a chance to open his mouth.

'Really?' Maria said approvingly. 'You're not even twenty yet, are you?'

'Just turned,' he said, shrugging shyly.

'Never guess it to look at him, would you?' Vicky said. 'He's so responsible, it's sickening. Got a gorgeous flat, as well,' she said then, giving Maria a conspiratorial look. 'His girlfriend's a *model* – fancies herself as a bit of an interior designer. But we won't talk about that, will we, *David*?'

Maria smiled bemusedly. Vicky was obviously making fun of him, but Davy didn't look too impressed.

'Me and Nicola don't get on,' Vicky explained quietly. 'We've got what you'd call a clash of personalities – I've got one, she hasn't,' she added in a whisper.

'Leave her alone,' Davy moaned, sitting down on the other chair. 'She's okay. You've just got to give yourself time to get to know her.'

'No, thanks,' Vicky murmured coolly. 'I already gave her more time than she deserved, and she's *still* a stuck-up madam. And I wish she'd stop calling you David, 'cos it really gets on my tits. It's like she's trying to posh you up – and you don't need that. You're lovely as you are.'

'All right, stop moaning,' Davy said, as if he'd heard it all before. 'You're boring Maria.'

'I'm fine,' Maria assured him, amused that scruffy little Davy had turned into such a hunk and landed himself a social-climbing model girlfriend.

Coming back in just then, Leroy tossed a can of beer to Davy.

'Bit of a reunion going on here?' he said, opening his own can and flopping down onto a chair with one leg sprawled over the arm. 'Must be kinda weird.'

'It *is*,' Maria agreed, still looking at Davy. 'You were nine last time I saw you.'

'And madly in love with *you*,' Vicky cut in, grinning slyly. 'Remember how he used to follow you around?'

'All right, that's enough,' Davy said, ripping the tab off

his can. 'So, what have you been doing with yourself, Maria? Married? Kids?'

'Neither.' Maria shook her head. 'I went to uni, then had a job teaching art for a while. But I'm living back here now.'

'Yeah, Vicky was saying. Not planning to pick up the teaching again?'

'No!' she said adamantly. 'I'm not sure what I want to do yet. I'm just lazing about at the moment, getting to grips with the house.'

'Bought somewhere already?'

'No – actually, I inherited it from an aunt.'

'Really?' Vicky drew her head back. 'I didn't know you had one.'

'Neither did I,' Maria told her, sighing. 'It's a long story, but, briefly, I got a letter from a solicitor on my twenty-first, saying I was the sole beneficiary of some woman's will. When I came up to sort it out, it turned out to be my father's sister. Apparently, my mum left my dad when she was pregnant and they didn't hear from her again. Then, when she was killed, this aunt saw it on the news and got a private detective to track me down.'

'Did she apply for custody?' Vicky asked, lighting the spliff that she'd rolled.

'No, she just got the detectives to send yearly reports. Then she died, and I inherited everything.'

'Oh, so you're loaded, are you?' Vicky asked without a trace of envy or rancour.

'A bit.' Maria gave a modest shrug. 'Doesn't really feel like anything, though. I'm just getting used to owning the house. And I suppose the money's a bonus, because I can pay the bills without worrying. I've got a fair bit invested, and that's doing all right, but I'm not sitting on it watching it, so I forget about it half the time.'

'Well, forget some of it *this* way whenever you feel like it,' Vicky laughed, offering her the spliff.

Shaking her head, Maria said, 'Do you need some? I'd be happy to—'

'No, I was only joking,' Vicky assured her, leaning forward to pass the smoke to Leroy. 'You know what they say about lending money to friends and family – *don't*!'

'Oh, right, so you won't be asking to borrow off me again, then?' Davy said good-naturedly.

'Don't even go there,' Vicky said, dipping a finger in her glass and flicking it at him. 'You're forgetting who brought you up when mam was shagging her way round the pubs, mate! If it wasn't for me, you wouldn't be bossing all those girls around in your shop, you'd be collecting trolleys in the car park!'

'Don't start, you two,' Leroy said wearily. 'You've got a guest, in case you've forgotten.'

'Maria's not a guest,' Vicky scoffed. 'She's my bestie.' Turning to Maria then, she said, 'Remind me to show you where the kettle is before you go, by the way, 'cos if you think I'm running round after you every time you come, you've got another think coming.'

Maria took a cab home at two. Saying goodbye to Davy and Leroy, she hugged Vicky at the door and thanked her for a great night, and promised to give her a call and arrange a night out – just the two of them.

A few streets from the house, the taxi passed a car with several men inside it driving slowly along. Maria gazed at them disinterestedly, wondering if they were looking for a party somewhere. But she soon forgot about them when they were out of sight.

Paying the driver when they reached the gate, she walked briskly up the path and opened the door. Locking up after herself, she shrugged out of her jacket, relishing the heat after the cold outside. Getting the heating system updated had been one of her better investments in the house by far – that and the new super-shower. That was blissful.

Heading straight to the kitchen, Maria made herself a cup of hot chocolate and carried it up to the bedroom, looking forward to getting into her pyjamas. She never wore them when Joel was home, but when she was alone she loved the feel of the soft satin against her skin.

Going to the bedroom window to draw the curtains, she spotted the same car that she'd just seen driving slowly by, only now it was cruising along at the far end of the road. She knew it was the same one because it looked odd, being so low to the ground. Curious now, because this definitely wasn't the kind of area for late-night parties, she watched to see where it went. But it didn't stop, so when it disappeared around the corner after a moment Maria drew the curtains and got ready for bed.

'This is Francine,' Honey said, dragging a sulky-looking girl with long dark hair over to Joel as the party began to wind down. 'She's bi.'

'By what?' Joel asked distractedly. He'd just had an amazing chat with Liam Gallagher about football, of all things, and he was still mulling it over.

'Bisexual,' Honey said, rolling her eyes. 'Remember the sandwich? Well, she's the brown bread, I'm the white – and *you* can be the beef filling.'

'What *are* you talking about?' Frowning, Joel looked down at her eager young face.

'Do you want to fuck us both, or not?' Francine said bluntly, giving him a sultry look. 'Make your mind up, 'cos I've got loads of possibilities lined up if you don't.'

'Please say yes,' Honey pleaded, gripping his arm and

jumping on the spot. 'I need to rehearse. I've already let her finger me down in the orchestra pit, but I need us to get like proper naked to see if I can pull it off.'

Joel felt his dick stirring to life. They were such a contrasting pair – Honey so light and fluffy, Francine so dark and moody.

And Liam had gone now, so there was no chance of another chat.

'Okay,' he said, checking out Francine's large, still-firm tits. 'But don't fight over me, ladies. I'm more than enough for both of you.'

21

Maria saw the same car again the next day. It was parked up opposite the shops when she walked round to the bus stop.

Sitting down on the narrow plastic bench in the tiny Perspex shelter, she deliberately looked in the direction the bus would be coming from, not wanting the men in the car to think that she was being nosy. But her curiosity was definitely roused now, because they certainly couldn't still be looking for a party.

Still, it really was none of her business.

She'd arranged to meet up with Nigel while Joel was away. Maria didn't like to go to meetings when he was home, because he liked her to stay with him when he had a rare bit of free time. But if she was honest, the real reason she didn't like to consult with Nigel when Joel was around was because she didn't want it to seem as if the financial advice Joel had given her wasn't good enough. He was such a sensitive soul in some ways, and she didn't want to insult him: she'd come to rely on him pretty heavily since he'd been living with her.

But she didn't feel too guilty about today's meeting because they wouldn't be discussing the money, as such. Nigel was going to talk her through the maintenance programme for the house that Elsie Davidson had adhered to for so many years. It was overdue, apparently, and Nigel was strongly advising her to consider contacting the firm who usually dealt with it soon, or to think about contracting somebody else to do the work before it adversely affected the insurance.

Maria could have passed it over to Joel, she supposed, but she didn't want to lump this onto him when he'd already taken so many burdens off her shoulders. It was time she stopped being so needy and sorted her own problems out.

Anyway, business aside, it would be nice to catch up with Nigel and see how he was getting on in his apartment. He'd been so excited about it last time she spoke to him, declaring it the best decision he'd ever made. And it seemed he was right, because he'd certainly come out of his shell since he'd resolved to live independently. He was far more confident these days, and seemed much more at ease in his own skin than the blushing, apologetic man she had first met had been.

Stepping forward when the bus came into view, Maria caught sight of one of the men in the car looking straight at her. It gave her a bit of a start, but she quickly shrugged it off. She obviously wasn't getting out as much as she should if she'd forgotten about men and their roving eyes. It wasn't personal, they just couldn't seem to help themselves. He probably had a perfectly lovely wife and kids waiting for him at home. Then again, maybe not, if all he had to do with his time was kerb-crawl with his mates for nights on end.

Boarding the bus, she walked to the back and sat down. Glancing back when the bus had pulled off, she felt a thrill of fear when she saw the car turning around in the road and falling in behind the two cars that were behind the bus. Facing forward again, she clutched at her handbag, wondering if they were following her.

But no – that was too ridiculous for words. Just because she'd *looked* at the man? What was he going to go? Beat her up for being nosy? Ask her for a date?

Turning the corner when they reached the Princess Parkway junction, Maria dared to take a peek out of the corner of her eye. She almost cried out when she saw that the car was still there, the man in the front passenger seat staring straight up at her.

What should she do? Call the police and tell them to meet her at the other end? *Because . . . ?*

She had no proof that she was being followed. No reason to believe she was in danger. The police would tell her she was overreacting, and they'd be right.

Maria was so nervous by the time they reached the terminus at Piccadilly that she didn't even look back to see if the car was still there. Jumping off the bus, she rushed through the milling shoppers, desperate for the safety of Nigel's cool quiet offices. Making a mad dash down Market Street, she yanked the smoked-glass door open – only to bump straight into Nigel as he came out to meet her.

'Whoa!' he said, smiling brightly as he reached out to steady her. 'Where's the fire?'

Panting hard, Maria shook her head and pushed him back inside.

Concerned now as she stood with her back against the wall catching her breath, Nigel said, 'What's happened? You haven't been mugged, have you? Oh, God! I knew I should have picked you up. It's awful round here on a Saturday – so many gangs looking for victims. Are you hurt?'

'I'm all right,' Maria managed at last. 'Really . . . I was just a bit spooked.'

'By what?' Nigel asked, leading her to the couch and sitting her down while he went to fetch her a coffee.

Feeling a bit stupid now that she was here and no madmen had come busting in behind her, Maria rolled her eyes and gave a small self-effacing smile.

'My overactive imagination, apparently,' she said, thanking

him for the coffee. 'I thought I was being followed. But nothing's happened, so I obviously invented it.'

'Want to come into my office and tell me about it?' Nigel asked kindly, noticing that Maria's gaze was straying towards the doors. She was obviously scared that somebody was out there, despite her words to the contrary. 'You might feel more comfortable in there. I need to lock up, though,' he said then, standing up and taking the keys out of his pocket. 'Don't mind, do you? Only it's the policy outside of office hours.'

'No, of course I don't mind,' Maria said, frowning now. 'But I didn't realise you weren't usually open at the weekend. This isn't the first time we've had meetings on a Saturday. Don't tell me you only come in for me?'

'I honestly don't mind,' Nigel assured her, locking the street door and giving the handle a tug so she could see it was secure.

'Oh, no, I feel terrible now,' Maria said, following him to his office. 'I honestly thought you worked Saturdays, but gave the receptionist the day off.'

'Will you quit beating yourself up?' Nigel told her firmly. 'I live about two minutes away from here. I could actually walk here faster than I can drive – if I wasn't such a lazy caraholic. But, all that aside, I really don't mind, because I can always find things to do. The minute I open my door, things jump out at me, screaming for attention. Better dealing with it when I know I won't be disturbed by phone calls, don't you think?'

'Better if you stayed home and relaxed, like you're supposed to,' Maria said, giving him a meaningful look.

'I happen to find *work* quite relaxing,' Nigel said, taking his seat. 'I know that makes me something of an oddity, but it's a habit I developed a long time ago. Believe me, if you knew my mother, you'd understand. Anyway . . . shall we get this over with?'

★　★　★

They finished within an hour, with Maria agreeing that she would retain the same maintenance firm, and Nigel agreeing to arrange things.

'Well, that was pretty straightforward,' Nigel said, putting the file away. 'Anything else you'd like to discuss while you're here?'

'No, everything else is fine,' Maria told him, not wanting to get into the investment stuff because she was sure she had put his nose out of joint when she'd told him she didn't need him to look after that for her. 'Fancy going for a sandwich, or something? It's almost lunchtime, and it's the least I can do for bringing you to work on your day off.'

Nigel pursed his lips thoughtfully, wondering if he dared make the suggestion that had just sprung into his mind.

'If you've something else to do, don't worry about it,' Maria said, sensing his hesitation. 'I won't be offended.'

'No, it's not that,' Nigel said, feeling nervous now. 'I was just wondering if you'd like to come to see the apartment? Please say no if you don't want to, but I've told you so much about the place, and . . . well, I'd love your opinion. And I can rustle up a chicken salad if you'd like to stay for lunch.'

'Are you sure?' Maria asked. 'I don't want to put you to any trouble.'

'It's no trouble at all,' he assured her, smiling shyly. 'To be honest, I could do with your advice.'

'Oh?'

'I'm, er, not too good at the old fixtures-and-fittings lark,' Nigel said, shrugging sheepishly. 'I love the place, but I'm finding the kitchen a little restrictive, so I thought I'd invest in a new unit. I was hoping you'd be able to give me some suggestions.'

'Me being a *woman*, and all that?' Maria teased.

'Not at all,' Nigel said quickly. 'I just think you've probably got a better eye for style. You only have to look at my clothes to know I'm somewhat lacking in that department.'

'Rubbish,' Maria scoffed. 'There's nothing wrong with your dress sense. Although I can't really imagine you out of a suit. You don't really look the jeans type.'

'I'm not,' Nigel admitted, amazed that they were having such a casual conversation about *him* and he wasn't blushing. 'I prefer trousers, actually.'

'So does Joel,' Maria said, smiling as she pictured him in her mind's eye in her favourite slate-grey pair. They made his bum look super-firm and sexy. 'Anyway,' she said, shaking herself out of her reverie, 'I'd love to come for lunch.'

'Right, well, shall we go, then?' Nigel said, pulling his jacket on and opening the door for her – a little deflated now that he'd been reminded of her boyfriend.

He had only actually met the man once, but he could perfectly well see the effect that he'd had on Maria over the year, because she was far less independent in her approach to things, always wanting to talk things over with him before making a decision. Nigel had kept his fingers crossed that it would fizzle out. But he'd had to accept that Maria and this Joel were a serious 'couple' when she'd rung to tell him that she'd be looking after her own investments, and would only need Nigel to deal with legal matters in future.

It was obvious that she'd done that at Joel's behest, because she'd been perfectly happy with Nigel's involvement until then. That made him more than a little suspicious about her new boyfriend's motives. But he was in no position to argue or voice his unfounded doubts, because she was entitled to take advice from whoever she chose.

Maria's calls had lessened to almost none over the next six months, and Nigel had been a little concerned about her. But it would have been unprofessional to call merely to ask how she was doing. And, of course, he didn't want to be seen to be treading on another man's territory.

He'd been so pleased when he realised that Maria had overlooked the date of the annual maintenance check, because that had given him a legitimate excuse to see her. And he was glad that he had, because it had reassured him. And, better yet, he'd enlisted her help in sprucing up his apartment.

Adam had offered to give him some tips, but it had never come to anything because Adam was far too busy bedding anything that moved – and pretending to study for his bar exams. Nigel had all but given up hope of him ever sorting himself out where that was concerned. But, if he was honest, Adam was the real reason he didn't mind meeting Maria on a Saturday. He actually *preferred* it, because there was no chance of Adam coming into work when he didn't have to.

Not that Maria would be interested now that she had her very own superhero in Joel. But once she saw Adam, she wouldn't be able to resist checking him out when she came to the office, because he was too damn good-looking to ignore.

But, oh, well . . . As his father used to say whenever events overtook him: *you can build the walls high and wide, but they'll never hold a determined tide.* If Maria and Adam were destined to meet, they would meet no matter *what* Nigel did to prevent it.

'This is fantastic,' Maria said when they arrived at the apartment. 'I love open-plan; it feels so spacious and light. And your furniture's absolutely fine,' she said, casting an eye around the room.

The floor was polished beechwood, and there was a long Scandinavian-style sofa, a low glass coffee table, and a wall unit in which one or two quirky ornaments were stylishly displayed on each of its shelves. The plasma-screen TV and stereo unit were built into one wall, the speakers suspended from the ceiling. Two enormous paintings of what looked like naked women – although they were so modernistic it was hard to tell – graced the walls, one above a diamond-shaped glass-fronted fire, which was also built in. The other directly faced the ceiling-to-floor windows, outside which was a balcony. The artwork added much-needed colour and vivacity to what would otherwise have been quite a bland backdrop.

'It's perfect,' Maria said, nodding approvingly. 'Honestly, I wouldn't change a thing.'

'Really?' Nigel said uncertainly. 'You don't think it's a bit *minimalist?*'

'That's fashionable,' Maria told him, going to the window and looking out. 'Wow, you can see most of Manchester from here. Is that the Granada studios?'

'Yes, and the V&A Hotel behind it.' Coming over, Nigel unlocked the door and slid it open. Standing out on the balcony, he pointed out where everything was. 'Deansgate's over there. Hulme and Moss Side over that way, and Chorlton to the right. The M62's back down that way, and town's directly over there. Your house is somewhere over that side.'

'Amazing,' Maria murmured, gazing around. 'It's really freaky, seeing it all laid out like this. A bit like being in a helicopter, hovering over everything.'

'Never thought of it quite like that.' Nigel smiled, knowing that from now on that was what he would think whenever he sat out here with his wine in the evening. Going back inside after a moment, he said, 'Can I get you a drink?'

'Yeah, coffee would be great.' Maria followed him in. 'Want me to make it while you do the salad?'

'No, I'm fine. But you can come and sit in the kitchen if you like.'

Watching as he moved deftly around the small but perfectly

adequate kitchen, Maria was amazed how at ease he was with himself here.

'Living alone suits you,' she said. 'You seem to have everything exactly how you need it. Really economical and functional.'

'That's half the problem,' Nigel admitted, keeping his back turned while he prepared the food. 'I tend to think that if *I* like it, there must be something wrong with it – something a bit lacking. But obviously I wouldn't know what it is, so there's no way I can remedy it.'

Recognising something of her own lack of confidence in his words, Maria felt a twinge of sadness for him. They couldn't have had more different childhoods – his rich, hers poor – yet they had quite a lot in common, it seemed.

From the little that he'd told her, Maria knew that Nigel was an only child who had been surrounded by critical adults who demanded complete obedience at all times. Then they'd expected him to be a fully fledged 'man' when it came to him making his way in the working world.

Maria, on the other hand, had enjoyed a wonderfully loving childhood – until her mum had died. After that, she'd been nothing but a statistic; she'd been expected to abide by the myriad rules and regulations laid down by the various care workers whose job it had been to raise her. No love, just *care*. And most of *that* had been particularly *un*caring.

It was incredibly difficult to survive that with any sense of self-worth, and any child of the system would be forever seeking affection and approval. Which was probably why, once she'd allowed her carefully built barriers down, Maria had been so grateful for Joel's love that she'd reverted to a state of girly dependence.

Nigel was a successful solicitor with a partnership in an established, well-respected firm, who owned a fantastic apartment in a really sought-after location. Yet he still needed to be told that he'd done a good job in choosing his own furniture.

Tragic.

Sitting out on the balcony to eat their food, they chatted for a while. Then Maria said that she'd best head off home. Nigel offered to drive her, but she said she'd rather call a cab.

'I've already taken up enough of your time today,' she said.

'It was my pleasure,' he assured her. 'I've had a lovely time.'

'Me, too,' she said. 'I'll repay the favour sometime – have you round for dinner. You and Joel will get on like a house on fire.'

'I'm sure we will,' Nigel agreed, actually doubting it very much.

Walking Maria down to the pavement to wait for the cab, Nigel told her that he would give her a ring when he'd arranged for the maintenance company to come round – to make sure that it was an acceptable time for her.

'It'll be fine whenever,' she said. 'I'm usually in. And if I'm not, I'm never too far away that I can't jump in a cab and get back within ten minutes.'

'I'll check first,' Nigel said. Then, folding his arms, he said, 'Didn't you mention that you'd bought a car recently? Only, with you taking the bus in today and a cab home now . . .'

'Joel's using it,' she explained. 'He's been in London for the weekend, so it seemed daft for him to take the train when I'd probably be inside for most of the time.'

'Ah, I see,' Nigel murmured. 'Sounds like he's very busy.'

'Oh, he is. He's out more than he's in, these days. But I can't complain. At least he's making his mark on the world.'

Without contributing a thing to the house, no doubt, Nigel thought perceptively. He'd seen enough of the accounts when he was still advising Maria financially to know that every payment had been made from her account alone. If that were still the case, then this man of hers had landed square on his feet.

But it was really none of his business.

'Take care,' Nigel said when the taxi came. 'And give me a ring if you see that car again. I know you've put it down to paranoia, but you were very upset when you reached the office and I'd hate to think of you sitting on your own like that. I could come over and wait with you until Joel gets back.'

'I'll be absolutely fine,' Maria told him confidently.

Despite telling Nigel that she was fine, Maria felt nervous as the taxi neared her house. Looking every which way for the car, she was relieved when she didn't see it.

Letting herself in, she hung her jacket up and slipped her shoes off, then made herself a coffee and carried it through to the lounge. She had nothing to do now but wait until Joel came home tomorrow, so she switched the TV on and channel-hopped for a while. But nothing held her interest.

Bored, she poured herself a glass of wine and carried it up to the attic. There were still some boxes up there that she hadn't gone through, and she thought she might as well do it now while Joel was away.

The attic was dusty and quiet – like a crypt, she thought. Which wasn't too far from the truth, she realised. It was the one part of the house that she still thought of as Elsie Davidson's, because it was so full of the dead woman's life.

Maria had been meaning to deal with the last boxes for months, but had never got around to it – scared that she might find more weird stuff about her dad.

She'd been freaked-out after that first night here with Beth, when they'd found the private detective's reports. But it was the photo of Derek bearing such a strong resemblance to

Maria herself which had really shattered her. That was proof absolute that her mother had lied to her, and Maria hadn't been willing to deal with it. Not then, not now. In fact, she doubted whether she would ever look at any of that stuff again. And she wasn't willing to give up her good memories for any reason. So she stored the evidence of betrayal away in the furthest recesses of her mind, and stashed the paper-work and photos with the rest of the dead stuff in the attic where she didn't have to see it.

Maria spent a good couple of hours rummaging through the other boxes now, but there was nothing of any particular interest in them; mainly clothes and books. The first few boxes had been much more exciting, particularly the one with the porcelain dolls in their ancient lace dresses, and the one stacked with jewellery boxes, full of old-lady-type glittery necklaces, bracelets, and rings.

Joel had been with her when she'd found those, and he'd said that the dolls were probably worth something to a collector, but that most of the jewellery was paste. He said he knew someone who specialised in old jewellery who would buy it all off her if she didn't want it. Feeling no emotional attachment to it, she kept one strand of black pearls, an emerald and ruby ring that she thought was particularly decorative, and an enormous oblong diamond solitaire – which she was convinced was real, and Beth had agreed. The rest she gave to Joel to offload on the dealer, pleased when he came home with the two hundred pounds he'd managed to push the man to. They went out that night and splashed the lot on a meal and a club. A short time later, Joel had taken the dolls to an antiques fair on one of his trips to London, coming home with two hundred and fifty that time – which again went towards a good night out.

There was nothing so interesting in this search, and Maria was even more bored than when she'd started when she gave up and resealed the boxes. She'd call one of those house-clearance places and have them take the lot. At least then the whole of the house would be hers.

Going down the stairs, she set the bath running, then went into the bedroom. Flipping the TV on for background noise, she stepped up on the stool to reach for a towel from the top of the linen closet. Catching a flash of blue out of the corner of her eye, she almost toppled over with shock when she looked out of the window and saw the same car as before driving slowly by.

The man who had been staring at her from the passenger side earlier was now in the back, staring up at the houses.

Giving a tiny yelp of terror when he looked straight up at her window, Maria clapped a hand across her mouth. He couldn't possibly see her through the nets, but she felt as if he had looked straight at her. And she was sure that he had spoken to whoever else was in the car with him – probably telling them that he'd seen her.

Her heart began to beat a furious tattoo in her chest and throat. They *were* looking for her, she just knew it.

Stepping shakily down off the stool when the car went by, she closed the curtains, then immediately reopened them. If they came straight back round, they'd know that the curtains had been moved. They'd know she was in. *Alone.*

But what if they already knew? What if they had followed her back here? She'd been so sure that she'd lost them when she got to town today, but what if they'd still been watching her – waiting to catch her on her own?

Oh, God!

What it . . . what if . . .

'Stop it!' Maria scolded herself sharply.

Sitting down on the bed, she chewed her nails and thought it out.

If they had followed her home, then they would know

where she lived and wouldn't need to scan the houses. So, chances were that they were just doing the rounds on the off chance of seeing her. But why? What had she done to attract their attention?

Her heart gave a painful lurch in her chest as a news report from last year flashed into her mind, about three people being raped and beaten at a flat on the other side of town. All the police had said was that several large men had been seen . . .

Driving slowly up and down the victims' road some time before the attack . . .

Oh, my, God! I'm going to get raped!

Panicking now, Maria slid down to the floor and crawled to the phone. Picking up the receiver, she held it shakily in her hand, the dial tone buzzing loudly in her ear.

'Police, please . . .' she whispered when the operator answered.

22

'I shouldn't think you've anything to worry about.'

Sergeant Paul Dalton sat down at the other end of the couch from Maria, his kind eyes showing that he understood the fear and wasn't dismissing her concerns.

'PC Corcoran checked all your doors and windows, and they seem quite secure. He thinks you'd be wise to have your cellar door fitted with a new lock at some time in the near future, but it looks okay for now.'

'Thanks,' Maria said gratefully, shivering despite the heat in the lounge. 'I feel really stupid now.'

'No need,' Dalton assured her. 'Better safe than sorry. Anyway, if you see the car again, give us another call and we'll have a squad car check it out – see what the men are up to. If it's any consolation, the majority of these things usually have a perfectly innocent explanation. They're probably looking for a party, or something.'

'No.' Maria shook her head. 'That's what I thought when I saw them yesterday. But it can't be that, or they wouldn't have still been out there this morning. Or now. Parties don't last that long.'

'It could be any number of things,' Dalton told her calmly. 'Rest assured we'll be looking into it, so there's really no need to worry. As you said, they were looking at all the houses, not just yours in particular. When we see them, we'll give them a pull. If they were planning anything, that's guaranteed to put them off.'

'You won't tell them who rang you?' Maria's eyes were dark with fear.

'Of course not.' Smiling now, Dalton wrote something in his pad, then ripped the page out and handed it to her. 'This is an incident number. If anything happens, give the operator this number and ask for me.'

'Do you think it *is* those men you're looking for?' Maria asked, folding the paper and slipping it into her pocket.

'Highly unlikely,' Dalton said. Then, 'Look, is there anyone who could come and stay with you until your boyfriend gets home? Mum and dad live nearby?'

'No.' Maria shook her head.

'Friends, then?'

Blushing, Maria shook her head again. Nigel had offered to come and sit with her, but she had an instinctive feeling that Joel would be less than impressed to find that a man had stayed the night. Vicky was the only other person she knew, but she couldn't drag her away from Leroy and the kids.

'Anywhere you could go and stay, then?' Dalton persisted. She was genuinely scared, and he didn't want to leave her until he was satisfied that she was going to be all right.

Sighing heavily, Maria said, 'No, I don't really want to bother anyone. Anyway, like you said, this is probably nothing. I always did have an overactive imagination.'

As soon as she said it, she wished she hadn't. It wasn't true, for one thing – she had always been a realist. And now, if anything *did* happen, they probably wouldn't believe her. She could just see the report: *Neurotic; self-confessed exaggerator. Ignore wild claims of break-ins, mad rapists beating down the door, axe murderers, or other . . .*

Dalton stood up. 'I'm sure you'll be fine, but I'd try to think of somebody to keep you company – just for peace of mind's sake. We'll have a patrol car drive round on the hour, so you'll be quite safe. And don't hesitate to call in the meantime.'

Showing the two policemen out, Maria locked the door and put the chain on. Crazily, she actually felt *more* nervous now, because they had been *too* considerate – as if they knew something she didn't.

Scolding herself again for being ridiculous, she put the alarm on and ran upstairs. Locking herself in the bedroom, she kept the light off for a few minutes so that she could peer out along the quiet road. Squinting, she scanned every hedge, every bush, every driveway – anywhere someone could possibly be hiding. There didn't seem to be anybody about.

One of the neighbours came out of his drive with a large Alsatian dog on a leash. Watching as they strolled towards the fields at the rear of the houses at the far end of the road, Maria saw the dog sniffing at every gateway it passed. If there was anybody hiding, it would bark, or react in some way, she thought, relaxing a little when it trotted happily past each one.

Closing the curtains, she switched the lamp on and changed into her PJs. Climbing into bed, she used the remote to turn the TV back on, lowering the volume so that she would hear any noises.

Maria couldn't settle. As the night dragged by, every sound outside seemed to be magnified a thousandfold. Hearing a car, she switched the lamp off and peered through a crack in the curtains. It was a police car. As it passed by her gate, moving at a walking pace, she saw that one of the two men inside had a torch in his hand, and he was shining it up the path, checking the porch and the bushes.

Going back to bed, she pulled the quilt up around her shivering shoulders. This was the worst night of her life – barring when her mum had died. She no longer felt safe in the house. Now it felt like a huge box, and she was locked inside, and somebody could come along at any time, tear the lid off, and squash her like a bug.

Maria wanted to ring Joel, to tell him to come home. But she couldn't. He was in London, and it would take him four hours of solid driving to get back. And what could he do, anyway? Come and hold her hand, like the big baby she was being?

No, she had to learn to stop freaking out about every little thing and stand on her own two feet.

Across town, Joel was lying on his back, with Honey under his left arm and Francine under his right. They'd had the mother of parties since coming back from the theatre on Friday night. Francine was a session singer, but she'd obviously been picking up more than singing tips from her late-night studio sessions because she was a very dirty girl – and even more of a coke fiend than Honey was turning into.

After two full nights and a day in bed, Joel was utterly wiped and his dick was begging for mercy, so he was more than a little relieved that Francine had finally zonked out.

Honey was still horny, and she had her arm across his chest, playing with Francine's pierced nipples.

'Don't think you'll have any problem convincing anyone that it's true when you start doing your gay scenes,' Joel said, chuckling softly. 'If I didn't know better, I'd swear you were a lesbian.'

'I might be,' Honey said thoughtfully. 'I'll have to try it a few more times and see how I feel. But I don't want to be one of those butchy ones, with a crew-cut and Doc Martens. I think I'll be a lippy lessy. D'y' reckon there's many gorgeous gay girls in Manchester? I don't want to commit myself to it then run out of options.'

'I'm sure there's loads,' Joel said, amused by her logic. Her youth really shone through sometimes. Unlike Francine, who probably wasn't too much more than twenty but had the air of a debauched older woman about her.

'Is that your phone ringing?' Honey said, lifting her head and looking around. 'It's not mine, 'cos I've got our theme tune on that. And Francine's got herself singing – poser that she is.'

'Sounds like mine,' Joel said, easing himself out of the sandwich to look for his jacket. 'Shit,' he muttered when he saw the display on the bedside clock. 'It's five in the morning. Who the hell's calling me at this time?'

It was Lance Gallagher.

'Just checking up on you, Jay boy,' he said. 'Heard a whisper that some Scottish guys have been hanging about looking a bit dodgy.'

'When?' Joel said quietly, sliding the glass door open and stepping out onto the tiny balcony. The wind gusting up through the railings snatched at his dick and slapped it against his thigh.

'Earlier tonight,' Lance said. 'One of my blokes clocked them in Brannigan's. No one else has seen them since, though, and I've had eyes out looking. But there's no sweat as far as I'm concerned, 'cos we're well and truly ready for the cunts if they turn up here. Thought I'd best word you up, though, 'cos I don't wanna be losing my best customer, do I? Probably best if you keep out of sight while I sniff about, yeah?'

'Yeah, I will. And thanks for the warning, man,' Joel said, his teeth chattering wildly.

Honey had her face buried between Francine's legs when he came back in. Looking up, she wiped her mouth on the back of her hand. 'Trouble?'

'Er, no, nothing to worry about,' he said, picking his clothes up off the floor and sitting down on the edge of the bed.

'Must be urgent if this hasn't given you a stonker,' Francine drawled sleepily, pushing Honey's head back down. 'Any normal man would be riding that lovely little arse of hers like a stallion right about now.'

'It's just family stuff,' Joel lied, pulling his pants on.

Sex was the *last* thing on his mind with Psycho back in town. It had been almost a year since his erstwhile neighbours had been assaulted and he'd genuinely thought the gang had given up on him. But then, maybe they had. Maybe it wasn't them that Lance's bloke had seen. They weren't the only Scottish guys that had ever visited Manchester.

But whether it was them or not, he couldn't afford to ignore the warning.

'I'll give you a ring,' Honey called as he made his way to the door. 'Let you know if I'm still into dick, or I just need a score.'

'Do that,' he called back distractedly.

Collar up, head down, Joel ran to the side road where he'd left the car. Glad to see that it was still there, he hopped in and set off for home, keeping his eyes peeled in case he was being followed.

23

The chain was on when Joel got home, and the alarm went into its delayed beeping because the door had been cracked open. Maria *never* put the chain on. He couldn't remember how many times he'd told her to, but she wouldn't – in case he came home in the middle of the night and couldn't wake her to let him in. So why now?

A surge of panic welled up in his throat.

Oh, God, no . . . please don't let Psycho have got to her.

'Maria!' he yelled, banging his fist on the wood. 'MARIA!'

Running into the garden, fighting his way through the shrubs, he grabbed a handful of stones and tossed them up at the bedroom window.

'*MARIIAAA . . .*'

Maria had fallen into a fitful sleep. Waking with a start when she heard Joel's voice, she jumped when something hard hit the window. Rolling off the bed when Joel called her name again, she lurched across to the window. The sun was just beginning to rise, and the light made her squint. She just about made Joel out, standing in the garden below with an anguished look on his face.

The alarm went off now, its clanging bells sending shock waves through her. Rushing downstairs, she tapped in the number to deactivate it, then tugged the chain off the door. Pulling it open, she stumbled over the step and fell into Joel's arms.

'Oh, thank God you're all right!' he said, holding her tight.

'How did you know?' she asked, clinging to him. 'Did the police contact you? I don't remember giving them your number, but I must have. I was so freaked out when they came, I don't know *what* I said.'

'The *police*?' Joel eased her back and frowned down at her. 'Why were the police here?'

'Don't you know?' Maria gazed up at him confusedly. 'I called them last night, because of the men in the car.'

'What men?' Joel asked. Then, glancing quickly around, he took her arm and pulled her inside. 'Right, tell me what's going on,' he said, sitting her down at the kitchen table while he filled the kettle.

Maria explained about the car that she'd seen when she came back from Vicky's the other night, and how she'd seen the same one again the next morning.

'I got so scared when it started following the bus,' she said, her hands shaking as she lit two cigarettes and passed one to him. 'I ran to the solicitor's, but no one came after me so I thought I must have imagined it. I didn't see it again when I was coming home, but a couple of hours later I was getting a towel out of the cupboard and I saw it driving past. The man in the back was the same one that had been looking at me at the bus stop, and he looked right up at the bedroom window. All I could think about were those people who got attacked last year, so I called the police.'

'And what did they say?' Joel brought the coffees back to the table and sat down.

'That it was probably nothing.' Maria shrugged. 'They were really good, though. They could see I was scared, so they checked all the doors and windows. Then the sergeant said he'd send a patrol car round. I saw it going past after I locked myself in the bedroom, so that was all right, and I heard it a couple more times before I fell asleep.'

'Christ, why didn't you ring me? You should have let me know.'

'You were too far away to do anything about it. Anyway, I didn't want to disturb you. How did it go, by the way?'

'What?' Joel frowned, wondering what she was talking about. 'Oh, SouthSyde. Yeah, fine. But never mind that. This is more important. Did anything else happen?'

'Not that I know of,' Maria said, embarrassed because she'd obviously made it sound as if her life had been in danger, and now Joel was worried. 'I fell asleep, and you woke me up just now. How come you were so freaked out when I came to the door if you didn't know what had happened?'

'Instinct, I guess,' Joel lied. 'With the chain being on, I thought . . . Well, I don't know what I thought. You don't usually use it, that's all. Then the way you ran down.'

'Like an idiot.' She smiled self-effacingly.

'You had a shock.' Joel patted her hand. 'So, about these men . . . Did you get a good look at them?'

'Only the one who was staring at me. They all looked pretty big, though, because they were really squashed up in the back.'

'No descriptions?'

'Now you sound like the police,' Maria laughed. 'And as I told them – no. Just that they were all big, with short hair. Oh, and the one who looked at me had a broken nose, like a boxer, or something. And I think he had a scar here.' She traced a line from her right eyebrow to her cheekbone.

Joel felt the blood leave his face. She had just described Psycho to a T. Somebody must have told him that Joel was living round here. But who? He hadn't told a soul. And no one knew about Maria, so how had Psycho connected her to him?

Unless somebody had seen them together walking to the shops.

Yeah, that must be it . . . Somebody had seen *them*, but not where they went, which was why Psycho was driving around. And if the same person had described Maria, Psycho would have recognised her as soon as he saw her at the bus stop. There weren't too many natural blondes with model-girl looks and figure around here. He'd probably guessed that it was her and followed her in the hope that she would lead him to Joel.

Shit!

'What's wrong?' Maria asked, seeing the panic in his eyes. 'Joel – what's the matter? You don't know them, do you?'

Looking back at her, Joel chewed his lip. He needed to get away from the house before they came back for him. But where could he go? He didn't have enough money to start again some-where else. He'd been partying too hard lately – eating into his profits as fast as he made them.

'Joel, will you please tell me what's going on?' Maria persisted, scared now.

'I can't,' Joel said after a moment. Sighing deeply, he looked at her and shook his head. 'I'm really sorry, sweetheart, but this is too heavy. I've got to go.'

'Where?' Maria followed when he got up and walked out of the room. 'How long for? Joel, talk to me.'

'It's complicated,' he said, striding into the bedroom and taking one of his cases out of the wardrobe. 'Take it from me, you don't want to get involved. You're better off without me at the moment. It's too dangerous.'

'Whatever it is, I'm already involved,' Maria told him, feeling desperate when he started packing his clothes. 'It's me they were following, don't forget. And if you know why, then I think you owe it to me to tell me. What if they come back while you're away? What am I going to do – fight them off by myself?'

Looking at her, Joel felt a twinge of guilt. He hadn't thought of that, and she was right. This was nothing to do with her, and it wasn't fair to leave her to suffer what Mack and the neighbours had already suffered because of him. She didn't deserve that, and he'd never be able to live with himself if something happened to her. He did actually care about her – in his own way. As much as a man who didn't trust women could, anyway. What he felt for Maria was probably the closest he'd ever come to loving anybody.

And then there was the money. It would make life a damn sight easier if he stayed in touch with *that*.

Sitting down, he ran his hands through his hair, then reached for her and pulled her down beside him.

'All right, I'm going to tell you the truth,' he said, gazing seriously into her eyes. 'If you don't want to be with me when you've heard what I've got to say, then I'll totally understand, and I'll get out of your life. I genuinely hope you *do* still want to be with me, but either way I'll have to get out of here.'

'What is it?' Maria asked quietly, afraid that she was about to hear something really awful – like he'd been seeing someone else, and the woman's husband had found out and was coming after him, or something.

Joel decided that the truth probably *was* his best option – with a little adjustment as to his part in the matter, of course.

'These men that you've seen,' he said, choosing his words carefully. 'I *do* know them; they're from where I grew up. Thing is, one of them was involved in some really dodgy stuff and he tried to bring me in on it. I was only young, but I knew better than to get associated with people like that, so I said I didn't want to know. Anyway, in brief, he ended up getting into trouble with the police, and everyone thought I'd grassed him up. He went to prison, and I had to leave the area, because everybody was gunning for me. I came to Manchester so nobody could find me, but I kept in touch with one old friend, and a while back he told me this other guy was out and looking for revenge. That's why I had my hair cut and grew the beard – so they wouldn't recognise me.'

'Is that why you had to leave your flat?' Maria asked perceptively.

'God, no. You don't think that's why I came here, do you? You and me, we're nothing to do with all that.'

'So, what now?'

'I've got to get out of here,' Joel said, shrugging. 'I really don't want to leave you – I hope you know that. But I've got no choice. These men are dangerous.'

'So, where are we going?'

'*We?*' Joel looked at her questioningly. 'You mean you still want to be with me?'

'Course I do,' she murmured. 'What did you think I'd do?'

'I don't really know,' Joel admitted. 'I thought you loved it here.'

Maria wrinkled her nose. 'I kind of did,' she said, looking around. 'But last night I realised that it's not the house that makes me feel safe – it's you. I think I'd go crazy if you weren't here.' Biting her lip now as her heart began to beat faster, she dipped her gaze and said, 'It's *you* I love, not the house.' It was the first time she had ever said the words – to anyone. And she could feel the blood rushing to her cheeks.

Reaching out, Joel gently tilted her head towards him and gazed into her eyes. 'Did you mean that?'

'Yes,' she whispered. 'I really did.'

'Well, it's mutual,' he told her softly. 'I've loved you for a long time. And I've wanted to say it so many times, but it never felt right. This house . . . all this.' He waved his hand. 'It's yours, not ours. And your friend was so suspicious of me when I first came, like she thought I was only after you for your money, or something. I couldn't come out and tell you I loved you after that. You might have thought that was *why* I'd said it.'

Maria felt tears stinging the back of her eyes. 'I never knew you felt like that.'

'Yeah, well, now you do.' Joel smiled wistfully. 'And so do I – and I couldn't be more happy about it. But right now, we really need to get moving. You definitely want to come with me?'

'Definitely.' Maria nodded adamantly. There was no way she was staying here without him. Wherever he wanted to go, she would be right beside him.

'Great.' Leaning towards her, Joel kissed her. Then, getting up, he started packing. 'Use my other case.' He nodded towards the wardrobe. 'Just take what you need for now. We'll sort the rest out when we know what we're doing.'

'Where are we going?'

'Probably best if we book into a hotel in your name for the time being,' Joel said, checking that there was nothing stuck at the back of his document drawer. 'We can decide what to do from there.' Turning to look at her then, he said, 'But I would like to discuss selling up here and starting again. If we're in this for the long haul – and I guess we are, given that we feel the same way about each other – then we need a place that's *ours*.'

'Whatever you want,' Maria said, smiling happily.

They were on the verge of something special here, and she had no intention of letting anything get in the way – especially not a house. Great as the old place was, she'd meant what she said. Without Joel, it meant nothing.

They decided not to go to the Britannia. Being in the town centre, there was too much risk of somebody who knew Joel dropping in and seeing him. So they booked in at the Lowry Hotel in Salford's thriving regeneration zone instead.

Leaving Maria to settle in to the room, Joel nipped out for a pack of cigarettes. Down in the foyer, he went into a quiet corner and phoned Lance Gallagher.

'It's me,' he said when Lance answered. 'Re your call last night, it's a positive on the Scots. They've been seen several times by a friend of mine, driving round near where I've been staying.'

'Which is where?'

'Didsbury.'

'How many bodies?'

'Five, as far as I know.'

'Armed?'

'Most likely, yeah.'

'You out the way?'

'Yeah, I'm safe.'

'Right, leave it with me. Give us a ring in a couple of days if I haven't been in touch, see what's happening.'

'Will do. And thanks, Lance.'

'I'm not doing this for you,' Lance grunted. 'I ain't having no fucker prowling round looking for me and getting away with it. Laters.'

Feeling a huge sense of relief, Joel got his cigarettes from the machine and went back to the room. If Psycho was still hanging about, he wouldn't be for long once Lance picked up his trail. And even if it didn't end in Psycho being dead, at least he'd have got the warning, and wouldn't be back again in a hurry. Mad as he was, when he realised what he was up against, he'd figure it wasn't worth the hassle. Not when he was so far off his own territory, with no troops to call in as back-up.

'Everything all right?' Maria asked when he came back smiling.

'Couldn't be better,' he said, taking her in his arms and walking her backwards towards the bed. Pushing her down, he fell on top of her. 'How's about we try out the soundproofing in this room?'

'How?' she asked, gasping when she felt his hardness pressing against her.

'If we get any complaints about the noise, we'll know it's no good,' Joel murmured huskily, pulling Maria's skirt up around her hips.

24

'I know he's round here somewhere,' Psycho spat, staring out into the dark as Fletch reversed the car out from under the tin canopy at the side of the derelict cottage where they'd parked the night they'd broken into Joel's old flat – and where they'd been sleeping for the past two nights.

Easing out onto the road, they set off in the direction of Didsbury.

'That bloke wasn't sure it was definitely him he'd seen,' Gerry reminded him. 'He did *tell* you that.'

'Shut your yowling gob-hole,' Psycho warned him, giving him a less than playful slap across the back of his head.

'Aw, come on, man, this is crazy,' Gerry responded edgily. 'Enough is enough. I want to go home.'

'*Mwah* . . . M-fuckin'-*wah*!' Psycho jeered. 'Don't let me stop ye, y' mardy fuckin' cunt, ye. Go on – fuck off out the fuckin' car and walk back to your mammy!'

'I want to go an' all,' Fletch said tersely.

This was getting too much. They'd spent three solid days driving up and down, round and round. But, apart from the blonde that Psycho – in his dubious wisdom – had decided was the one that the bloke they'd pulled in the pub had seen the grass with, there had been nothing. Fletch was sick of sleeping sat upright with the driving wheel cutting into his thighs; sick of the stench of the other guys. And Psycho was totally living up to his name at the moment – he'd lost it big time.

'What are *you* saying?' Psycho glared at Eamon and Jimmy.

Jimmy kept his mouth shut and rubbed at a spot of condensation on the window. He was trapped in back with his big mean brothers – close enough for a real smacking, not just a slap.

Eamon shrugged apologetically. 'Does seem like we're wasting our time, bro. I reckon Kyle fucked off last time he knew we were coming. He knows you, big man . . . He knows you won't drop it, so there's no way he'd have risked coming back. I reckon we'd have more chance of finding him if we took a trip to Tenerife. And it'd be a sight more fun than this shite.'

'Aye, too right,' Fletch agreed. 'Think about it, Psycho, man. All them wee lassies with their tits out in the sun.'

'Get fuckin' driving,' Psycho said coldly. 'One last time round.'

'Then we go, yeah?' Gerry asked flatly.

'I'll let you know when I'm ready for the off, pal.'

'Fetch that bag out from under the sink,' Lance told Keith, strolling into the kitchen. 'I've belled a few of the guys, and they're gonna meet us by the pub on Palatine.'

'We gonna kill 'em?' Keith wanted to know, struggling to get down on one knee without getting chinned by his own gut.

'Only if we have to,' Lance answered distractedly, peering down at the buckle on the side of his bulletproof vest. 'I hate this fucking thing,' he snarled, getting angry with it now.

'I can't fit into mine no more,' Keith grumbled, tugging the heavy sports bag out from its hiding place.

'Yeah, well, you'd best get your fat bastard self on a diet.'

'Piss off! I hardly eat nowt as it is. I should be a fucking anorexic by now.'

Giving him a scornful look, Lance gave up on the last

buckle and sat down at the kitchen table. Tipping a wrap of coke out onto the small mirror, he chopped it deftly into two long fat lines and snorted one up his left nostril, the other up the right. Sniffing hard to keep it all in, he held his head back.

'*That*'s what I'm fucking talking about!' he said when it hit.

'Where's mine?' Keith moaned, seeing him mop the traces up with his finger.

'Up your arse, second shelf,' Lance jeered. Taking another wrap out of his pocket when Keith's face fell, he tossed it to him. 'Here, you whining git.'

Snorting his straight from the wrap, Keith licked the traces off his nose. 'I'm coming with youse, ain't I?'

'If you want, but you'd best stop in the car till we know if they're packing,' Lance said, stalking across the kitchen to the bag and taking several guns out. 'Don't want you getting shot if you ain't got your vest on.'

Weighing each of the weapons in his hand to see which felt right, he settled on a slim-line black semi-automatic and slid the magazine out to check that it was fully loaded. Choosing another as a back-up, he checked it and slipped it into his pocket.

'Hurry up and get ready,' Lance said then, checking the time. 'We're meeting up in twenty.'

'Wait till I've got me trainers on.' Keith waddled out into the hall. 'Think we'd best tell the old man where we're going?' he called back over his shoulder.

'Nah, we'll be back before the old fuck's sober enough to figure out what we said,' Lance called back, pulling a large padded black jacket on over his body armour. If they got a tug from the pigs and they clocked the bulletproof, he'd get nicked for sure.

★　　★　　★

The black 4x4 flashed its lights when Lance drove into the pitch-dark car park at the rear of the pub. Parking up at the opposite end, Lance and Keith got out. Locking the doors, they ran across to the 4x4 and hopped in – Lance up front, Keith in back.

Three local faces were already inside: Cody Willis driving, Henry Lord and Tommy Davis in back. Cody had done a few jobs with Lance before, and knew what was expected of him. Henry and Tommy were in Cody's crew and had been worded up.

'How much?' Cody asked as soon as Lance was settled.

'A gee apiece,' Lance told him. 'I'll up it to three if we have to do a body dump.'

'Cool.' Cody nodded. 'Youse two all right with that?'

'Sound.' Henry cracked his knuckles like a sledgehammer on concrete in the back.

'Great, yeah,' Tommy said quietly, already spending the money in his head. Little Tommy's fifth birthday – new bike; Mrs Tommy's new tits – maybe not, but he'd get her some more of them push-up bras she liked while she was waiting.

A huge man, Cody was a retired football hooligan who'd run his own army called The Manc Maniacs in the 1970s and 1980s. They had travelled the length and breadth of the country in highly organised groups, meeting up at the motorway services along the way to plan their attacks on the rival fans. As big as the Chelsea Headhunters in their day, the Maniacs had terrorised many a rival firm into taking flight and missing the match. And Cody had a rock-solid head from all the nuttings he'd dealt out in those first mad adrenalin-fuelled surges before the knives and knuckledusters had come out.

Retired from the matches since his face got too well known to get past the police cordons, Cody had set up his own

wholesale business. He didn't need the money that Lance
was going to pay him for tonight's job, but violence was
something you were born with: age didn't diminish the thirst,
it just stole the opportunities to quench it.

'How's it going?' he asked Lance now, starting the engine
and easing out of the car park.

'All right,' Lance said, already peering out of the window
as they rolled off the pavement, itching to get game-on. ''Cept
for these tartan twats trying to muscle in. I've got a load of
guys on standby, depending what we find when we catch up
with 'em, but I'm not anticipating needing no one else. You
and me go far enough back to do the deed, eh, Codes?'

'We do that,' Cody agreed, sounding like the cool calm
businessman he was in his day-to-day life, despite the excitement building in his gut. 'So, we looking to take them out,
or scare 'em off?'

'Think just a scare for now,' Lance said. 'You know me –
I'm a fair man. If they don't want to heed the warning, then
we go after them – simple. You tooled?'

'Don't worry about it.' Cody smiled mysteriously.

'Fuck, this is gonna be good,' Lance declared jubilantly.
'Been a while since anyone dared step this far out of line
round here.'

'So, how d'y' hear about this takeover coup?' Cody asked.

'Just whispers,' Lance told him. 'That's why I don't want
to go in too heavy to start off with – give them the benefit
of the doubt, and all that.'

'For real?'

'Fuck off! I want the cunts off my land, man!'

'So, you ain't gonna bother talking to 'em to see what the
crack is?'

'Cody, my friend, I don't *do* talk,' Lance sneered, his face
feral in the lights from the impressive dash. 'The only talking
I'll do is warning them to get the fuck off my turf and not

come back if they know what's good for 'em. After that it'll be bye-bye, you kilty fuckers!'

'What car we looking for?' Henry asked from the back.

'Shit! I forgot to ask,' Lance admitted.

'Only asking, 'cos we just passed a car packed with heavies back there.'

'Where?' Cody growled, slamming the brakes on.

'Back there, down the side road two back.'

Turning the car around in the middle of the road, Cody gunned it in the direction Henry had pointed.

'Keep it cool,' Lance said, getting a crystal-clear head on. 'Tail 'em till they're in a less inhabited bit, then block them off. Everyone got a piece?' Nodding when the two in the back said yes, he said, 'Surprise is the key. Fast, accurate, no fuck-ups. And keep your eyes wide, 'cos there's a good chance they're tooled.'

'I think we're being followed,' Fletch said, eyeing the 4x4 in his rear-view.

Turning his head to look, Psycho squinted to make out the outlines in front, then shook his head.

'Nah. It's nothing.'

'This is a quiet street, so why's it been following us all the way up it?' Fletch persisted.

'They probably fucking live up here, you paranoid cunt,' Psycho jeered. 'We're not in fucking Govan now, you know. People actually *buy* them poncey wheels up here.'

'Yeah, well, I don't like it,' Fletch muttered, still eyeing it. Swerving sharply, he took a left into a dark uninhabited cul-de-sac.

The 4x4 came right in behind them with a powerful roar and cut sideways across the back of them, blocking them in.

'Look what you done now, y' clever cunt!' Psycho yelled, raising a foot and kicking the back of Fletch's seat.

'Quit it, man!' Eamon yelled, struggling for room to get at the gun in his pocket.

It was too late. Four balaclavaed men hopped out of the 4x4 and surrounded them, guns pointing at every window.

'Wind it fucking down!' Lance barked, rapping his gun on the driver's-side window. 'All of 'em!'

'What you want us to do now?' Fletch hissed at Psycho.

'Do as he fucking says,' Psycho snarled, his eyes fixed on the eyes he could just about make out through the slits in the mouth-man's bally.

'I hear you been looking for me?' Lance said when the windows were down and he had a captive audience.

'I havnae got a fucking clue who ye are, pal,' Psycho spat, still glaring.

'I take it you're the head honcho,' Lance jeered, giving an upward flick of the gun. 'Lean closer, my friend. I want to word you up about how these things go down in my town.'

'And what are you?' Psycho retorted in a low, mean voice. 'Wyatt fucking Earp?'

'Listen, you Scotch twat,' Lance said, equally low and mean. 'I ain't gonna stand here chatting all night, so I'll just say what I've got to say, and if you're a good boy, you can go.'

'Don't threaten me, you sheep-shagging cunt,' Psycho spat furiously. 'I don't think you know who you're messing with, pal.'

'Do I look like I'm fucking shaking?' Lance sneered.

He fired a round off into a tree behind them, then immediately turned the gun back on the car. The bullet made a dull *thwok* as it embedded itself in the bark.

'Oh, for fuck's sake,' Eamon said, flinching back from the window. 'All right, pal, quit pointing it. We don't know who the fuck ye are, and we havnae been looking for ye, so just back off, aye? We'll be on our way.'

'Sensible man,' Lance said. 'And we'll follow youse to the

motorway to make sure, eh?' he went on, as if giving direc-
tions to a stranger. 'Know the way? Or do we have to spell
it out?'

'I know the way,' Fletch said, nervously eyeing Tommy's gun.

In the back, Jimmy had shrunk to half his size and had
his eyes squeezed shut so that he didn't have to look into
the muzzle of Henry's piece.

Gerry was sitting stock-still in front, his hands palm down
on his thighs to show that he wasn't about to reach for a
weapon. Cody was impressed by his calmness under the
circumstances. He'd have made a great Maniac.

'Y' still havnae told us who ye are, pal,' Psycho said coolly.

'Your worst nightmare, that's who,' Lance said with a nasty
laugh. 'And that, my friend, is all you need to know. 'Cos
you're in my town now, and I want you out – *capiche?*'

'Aye, we got you, pal,' Eamon said.

'How about Honcho?' Lance pointed the gun straight at
the spot between Psycho's eyes. 'You got me – *pal?*'

'He's got you,' Eamon said, giving Psycho a dig with his
elbow. 'Eh, bro?'

'Aye,' Psycho said reluctantly. 'Me, too.'

'See us?' Lance said, staring straight at Psycho. 'We've got
a bigger car, bigger guns, and a much bigger fucking chance
of walking out of this alive. So don't be no heroes, eh, lads?
Just turn this shit-heap around, get the fuck out of here, and
don't let me hear about you coming back again or I won't
be so reasonable – all right?'

'Aye, right,' Eamon said. 'Nae problem.'

Psycho was livid as they headed onto the motorway. The 4x4
stopped at the entrance to the slip road and sat watching so
there was no way they could turn back.

'Take the next slip road,' he growled at Fletch. 'We're going
after the cunts.'

'No way!' Fletch retorted adamantly. 'We're nae ready for that lot. I'm going back hame to get ma heed together.'

'Do as you're fuckin' told!' Psycho roared, kicking out again.

'Quit it!' Eamon yelled at him. 'We'll come back another time, but we're *nae ready*! You might want to die the night, but we're nae going with ye! And quit rocking the fucking car before you have the police after us, eh?'

'I'm coming fucking back!' Psycho declared. 'Kyle's gonna get what's fucking coming to him, then I'm gonna track those cunts down!'

'Aye, man, aye,' Eamon said placatingly. 'And we'll all be with ye. But not now, eh?'

Up front, Gerry shook his head. Psycho was turning into a loose cannon. Even with four guns on him, he was still mouthing off. He was going to get them all killed if he carried on like that.

'Pussy fucking cunts!' Lance sneered as Cody reversed and turned to head back into Manchester.

'You did good.' Cody grinned. 'Head fuckin' Honcho!'

'Wyatt fucking *Earp*!' Henry snorted amusedly.

'Just call me Sheriff Fuck-Off-Outta-My-Town!' Lance laughed. 'They won't be back in a hurry.'

'I wouldn't bank on it,' Cody said, still chuckling. 'See the evils the dude in the back was giving out?'

'Didn't get him nowhere but on the road fucking out, did it?' Lance jeered, reaching into his pocket for the money. Turning, he handed a wad each to the two men in back.

'What about me?' Keith moaned.

'You didn't fucking do nowt!' Lance reminded him. 'Anyhow, why am I gonna pay you, you mental toss-pot? You own half of it. You'd be paying your fucking self.'

'I still don't see why they should get it and not me,' Keith grumbled. 'They didn't do nothing, either. Just stood there pointing guns, like they was playing cowboys and fucking Indians.'

'That's all I wanted them to do,' Lance explained, rolling his eyes at Cody. 'He don't get it, does he?'

'Aw, he's all right, aren't you, Keith?' Cody said, craning his neck to look at him in the rear-view. 'You want to go to Blackpool?'

'Yeah!' Keith grinned. 'To see the lap dancers?'

'Stop teasing the idiot,' Lance scolded Cody. 'He'll be sulking all fucking night now.'

'Fuck off, then, if youse don't wanna take me,' Keith said, guessing that they were going to drop him off and go without him. 'I'll get me dad to come with me.'

Laughing out loud, Lance shook his head. 'I love the cunt like a brother, but he ain't half deformed.'

'I *am* your brother,' Keith muttered grumpily, folding his arms over his gut. 'Me da said me mam was lying about that.'

Joel eased his arm out from under Maria's head when he heard his phone ringing. Easing the quilt back, he padded across the room to get it out of his jacket pocket.

'Yo,' he said quietly, taking it into the bathroom.

'We're cool,' Lance said, sounding manic, like he'd been having a fair old bit of fun.

'You found them?' Joel's heart was beating hard in his chest. 'What happened? What did they say?'

'Exactly what I expected,' Lance snorted, sucking deep on a spliff and blowing it down Joel's ear via the phone. 'But they wasn't going to admit that they knew who I was, were they? Clever cunts played innocent all the way.'

'Did they mention me?'

'Did they, fuck. They was after me, not you. But they got a bit more of me than they bargained for, so I don't think they'll be making that mistake again. Anyhow, just thought I'd let you know the heat was off.'

'So, where are they now?'

'On their way home, with a word to the wise that they'd best not let me catch wind of them mooching about in my town again.'

'And you think they've really gone?'

'Oh, I know they have, Jay boy. I escorted them to the motorway personally, saw them on their merry old way.'

'Shit, man, you don't know how glad I am to hear that.'

'Yeah, well, you can relax now, can't you?' Lance said, with another deep suck. 'When you coming round for your next lot?'

'Next couple of days,' Joel said, exhaling slowly to still his pounding heart.

'Good, 'cos I need to shift a lot of gear now to get back what I've just shelled out to my guys. Don't leave it too long.'

'Who were you talking to?' Maria asked sleepily when Joel went back into the bedroom.

'A mate,' Joel told her evasively. 'Sorry, I didn't want to wake you.'

'Have you heard something?'

Joel wondered if he should tell her that he'd had the all-clear, then decided not to. If she knew, she might want to go back to the house. But now that he was on the verge of getting the apartment he so desperately wanted, there was no way he was going back to that.

'No, nothing. Seems they're still driving round by the house. My guy's seen them a few times already. But don't you worry about it. Get some sleep, and tomorrow we'll start planning our escape from there. That's what you still want, isn't it?'

'As long as I'm with you,' Maria murmured, snuggling up to him. 'That's all I care about.'

25

Joel was up bright and early. Coming out of the bathroom, he smiled when he saw that Maria was awake.

'Morning, beautiful,' he said, leaning down to kiss her.

'You're all wet,' she complained, wiping a drip of water off her cheek.

'Shower,' he told her, rooting through his case for deodorant.

'Are we going somewhere?' she asked, sitting up and brushing her hair back from her face.

'*I* am.' Joel sprayed himself with Lynx. 'I want *you* to stay here where it's safe. I'm just going to nip back to the house, see if anything's happened. Anything you want me to pick up while I'm there?'

'Not just now,' she said, not able to think of anything she desperately needed. 'You will be careful, won't you?'

'Course I will.' He pulled a jumper over his head. 'Got your mobile switched on?'

'Oh, that's something you can get.' Maria reached for her handbag. 'The charger. It's next to the socket on my side of the bed. It's got a bit of juice left,' she said, checking the level.

'Right, I'll get it if I can. And I'll give you a ring if there's any news.' Sitting down on the bed when he pulled his trousers on and zipped his fly, Joel took a rolled pair of socks out of his case. 'Did you mean what you said?' he asked, slipping his feet into them. 'About looking for an apartment?'

'Absolutely,' she assured him, reaching out to stroke his

hand. 'I don't want to go backwards now we know how we feel about each other.'

'Me neither. So I thought I'd nip into the estate agents while I was out – pick up some brochures.'

'Try Quay Moves,' Maria suggested, remembering that that was where Nigel had gone to get his place. 'They do all those new blocks on Deansgate and overlooking the canal.'

'Where are they based?'

'King Street, I think.'

'Great. I'll be looking all day for somewhere to park.'

'You could always take a cab.'

'No way.' Joel shook his head. 'Had enough of them to last me a lifetime. I'll take the car. Anyway, I'll have to drive so that I can check the house. And I'm going to pop in and see my friend – see if he's seen anything since I spoke to him last night. You'll be all right, won't you? You've got cigs, and your mobile. Why don't you order yourself some breakfast and just relax?'

'What about you? Aren't you going to eat? You've not even had a coffee.'

'I'll get one at my mate's.' Standing up, Joel leaned down to kiss her again, then pulled his jacket on and headed out. Pausing at the door, he said, 'Check the corridor before you leave the room, yeah? And make sure it's really room service at the door if you do order anything.'

'Do I really need to be that careful?' Maria gazed back at him worriedly.

'For the time being, yeah. Sorry for getting you mixed up in this, sweetheart, but I want to know *you're* safe, at least.'

'You'll be safe as well, won't you?'

'Don't worry about me.' Joel grinned. 'I'm a big boy now.'

★   ★   ★

Joel went straight to Quay Moves. His main priority was finding the apartment of his dreams and getting Maria to free up some of her cash so they could move straight in. After that, it was going to be good times all the way.

'We have lots of properties on the market just now,' the salesgirl, Mariella, said, speaking slowly and huskily. 'Let me get the portfolio and show you an example of our most sought-after design.'

Running a hand under her long red hair, she brushed it back, slightly arching her neck, as if it were a sexual gesture. Getting out of her seat, she strolled languidly towards a large filing cabinet, and bent over straight-legged to open the bottom drawer, sending her shapely bottom up into the air and her short tight skirt higher up her long slim thighs.

Joel smiled to himself. She had the hots for him, it had been obvious the moment he laid eyes on her. Her pupils had expanded in her coffee-coloured eyes, and her lips had gone into a pout, bringing her cheekbones into the game.

Coming back, Mariella was smiling slyly, fully aware that he'd been watching her. Taking her seat, she sat sideways-on to the desk and crossed her legs. Taking a page out of the file, she slid it across the desk.

'This is an example of the quayside developments we've been working on most recently.'

'Lovely.' Joel let his gaze linger on her high, firm breasts beneath the silk blouse before actually looking at the pictures she was showing him.

'Everything is included in the asking price – all fixtures and fittings, to the highest specifications. We do have several show apartments in the various developments, which would give you a better idea of scale. Also, if you were willing to wait a little longer, you'd be able to specify colour schemes and work-surface materials. Maybe you'd like to see one?'

'If it wouldn't be a problem,' Joel drawled, giving her his lopsided smile and sexy half-eye.

'Not at all. Would you like me to drive you, or would you rather follow in your own car?'

'You can drive,' Joel said, enjoying himself.

Following her out to the staff car park, he raised an eyebrow when she headed for a slut-red CLK 240. Very unsubtle. Climbing in beside her, he gazed brazenly at her legs. She responded by sliding a little further down in the seat.

The show apartment was great – wide-open lounge space, separated from the ultra-stylish kitchen by a blue glass-brick wall. There was an additional space bordering the two which, for show purposes, had been fitted with a six-seater dining table, complete with adjustable chandelier.

'As with most of these apartments,' Mariella informed him, 'the windows are shatter-proof, and the floors, ceilings and walls are heavily soundproofed. Most of our clients are important in their fields and demand absolute privacy, and we do our utmost to ensure that there are no noise nuisances.'

'Very considerate,' Joel said, following her to the balcony.

Sliding one door open, she stepped outside. 'As you can see, the view is spectacular.'

'Couldn't agree more,' Joel drawled, looking her over blatantly.

Mariella turned to face him, and Joel was amused to see that she didn't twitch or blush, as most women did when he gazed at them so intensely. She was incredibly confident of her sexual allure.

'Quite,' she said, returning his gaze. Then, turning back to gaze out over the city, she said, 'As you can see, you wouldn't be overlooked by a soul in this particular location. That is something we keep in mind at all times, but obviously there are some developments where it can't be entirely avoided.'

Turning back to him again, she rested her elbows on the railing and gave him a pointed look. 'Here, you'd be quite free to roll around naked without the slightest danger of anybody seeing so much as a hair on your chest. But then, maybe you wax anyway?'

Joel grinned and shook his head. She couldn't be coming on any stronger if she stripped naked and laid herself out on the balcony table. Foxy as she undoubtedly was, she wasn't a patch on Maria. But so what? The world was made up of different sights, sounds, smells, tastes, sensations, and he didn't see why he should deprive himself of whatever was on offer. So long as Maria had no clue, it wasn't like he was doing her wrong.

'How about you?' he asked, moving towards her and pinning her against the railing. 'Do *you* wax?'

'Absolutely,' she purred, challenging him with her eyes. 'Question is . . . do you believe me?'

'Only one way to find out,' Joel said, stroking a hand slowly up her thigh and slipping her skirt up around her hips.

'So?' Mariella said when they were back inside, and she had poured a complimentary glass of champagne for him. 'Did you enjoy the viewing?'

'Oh, yeah,' Joel drawled. 'Most enjoyable. I'll be sure to send a letter to your employers praising your sales technique.'

'No need.' She smiled amusedly. 'It's my company.'

'*Yours?*' He raised a surprised eyebrow as his brain ticked into action. She must be mega-loaded, and she fancied the arse off him. And he could have any apartment he wanted if she owned them all. Christ, he was onto something huge here.

'And my husband's,' she added, still smiling as she watched the news hit home. Oh, she did so enjoy this moment.

'You're married?' Joel frowned. 'I didn't realise. You don't wear a ring.'

'Why should I?' She shrugged. 'I don't *belong* to Jeremy. We're equals in every way. Anyway, if you're finished here, shall we head back to the office?'

'Yeah, fine,' Joel said, fully aware that he had just been taken advantage of.

What a bitch!

Still, it had been a nice dream for all of the ten seconds or so that he'd had it. But oh well . . . back to Maria and her measly three-quarters of a million.

On a more positive note, the apartment *was* amazing, and he really could see himself living in something like this. He'd have to see what else Mariella had in her portfolio; get some details to show Maria.

Time to move onwards and upwards.

PART FOUR

26

Maria loved the new apartment. It wasn't too far from Nigel's, but they weren't close neighbours so they still didn't see all that much of each other. But, like his place, hers and Joel's was large, light and airy, with a wonderful view of the city.

They were in the development overlooking the canal at the back of Deansgate, facing away from all the heavy-traffic areas, which gave it the feel of being private and almost countrified, whilst still being within walking distance of the shops and bars.

Not that Maria went out too much. Joel was still highly protective, constantly checking that she was safe when he was out – that she had the front door firmly locked to prevent anyone catching her unawares. She was grateful for his concern, but she did feel a little isolated sometimes, now that he was busier than ever with his tours.

She'd thought about ringing Beth, missing the way they used to chat for hours on the phone. But she'd decided against it in the end. Beth would probably be smarting about Maria's lack of contact; and she'd be even more likely to bad-mouth Joel if she knew the circumstances behind Maria's decision to sell the house.

She did speak to Vicky occasionally, but she kept it to a minimum because she couldn't afford to get back into the best-friends-dropping-in-on-each-other thing – not when Joel had warned her not to let anyone know where they were living. She *had* actually told Vicky – just because she had to tell *someone* – but she hadn't gone so far as to invite her round. She met up with her at a café in town instead – on the very rare occasions when Vicky had enough free time.

Still, weighing the benefits against the deficits, Maria knew that she'd rather endure the solitude than contemplate a life without Joel. And she couldn't begrudge him his time away, because he was working so hard to make his first million. Once he had that, he'd promised to marry her and build her the house of her dreams for herself and their children.

If only Joel would take her money into account, they would be on their way much faster. But he was a proud man, and wouldn't even consider it. He'd allowed Maria to buy the apartment and keep everything running smoothly with the proceeds of the house sale, but he insisted that when they were ready to sell up and move on, that money would be hers to treat herself. It would be his money alone which supported them thereafter.

She wished he'd slow down a bit, though. He was out more often than he was in, these days, and there was a new edginess to him which hadn't been there before. She guessed it was the stress of trying to reach his earning target, but she couldn't make him rest. He'd actually shouted at her a couple of times for going on at him to ease up.

Today, Maria was sitting on the balcony, working on a watercolour of the canal while she waited for Joel to come home. He'd been working in France all week, and his schedule had been so hectic that he hadn't been able to take calls or ring her. The days had dragged unbearably, and she couldn't wait to see him.

The phone rang, making her jump. Laying the pad aside, she reached for it, smiling happily when she heard Joel's voice.

'Pour the wine, babe, I'm on my way home. I should be

about half an hour – fingers crossed. The motorway's a bit chokka.'

'It'll be ready when you get here,' she said, not wanting to let him go. 'Anything else you want? Bath . . . sandwich?'

'Nah, I'm pretty wiped, so I think I'll just jump in the shower, then laze about on the balcony. Anyway, I've got to go. There's a police car behind me and I'm not on hands-free, so I'd best get off before he pulls me. See you when I get there.' Blowing her a kiss, he hung up.

Still smiling, Maria cleared her paints away, and went inside to freshen herself up for him.

'Who were you just talking to?' Angela asked, sitting up in the bed and ruffling her platinum hair when Joel came out of the bathroom already dressed.

She had a sulky look on her face, letting him know that she was still in a mood. She was trying to make him feel guilty, but all it did was make him all the more determined to call it off with her.

Joel didn't know why he'd bothered getting it back on with Angela in the first place. He'd known exactly how it would play out: a couple of nights of hedonistic fun, necking as much coke as possible and drinking themselves stupid, culminating in the wildest sex he'd ever had. Followed by sniping and moodiness, and ending in psychotic jealousy when she would threaten to kill him and any woman she caught him looking at.

Last night had been the beginning of the end. They'd gone to Foxies, a lap-dancing club in town where they'd spent many of their former nights-out together. Joel was going home tomorrow, and wanted to see if they could end on a more positive note than usual. Angela was the freakiest woman he'd ever known, up for anything at any time and, usually, she got off as much – if not more – than him watching all the gorgeous girls with their super-fit bodies do their stuff. She'd get especially wet when the girls were doing their thing up close to Joel, so he'd gone last night with the full expectation of having a night-long hard-on.

First sign that Angela was flipping into the psychotic stage had been when she'd glared at all the girls who were parading up and down. But then she lost it when a particularly stunning girl with even more pneumatic tits than her own got too close. She'd flown out of her seat to physically push the girl away.

They'd been asked to leave then, which had pissed Joel off big time. He should have walked there and then, but, stupidly, he'd gone back to her flat because it was so late and he was a bit the worse for wear. He'd gone straight to bed to avoid the scene that was ready to boil over, and slept right through till now – almost four in the afternoon.

He really had to watch how much coke he was doing. He was having more difficulty getting to sleep in the first place, then it was murder waking up once he had. He'd hit that stage where nothing was ever enough. Before, two lines would have had him buzzing all night. Now he needed a couple of grams just to feel right. And he was getting irritable, too. He'd bitten Maria's head off a few times for absolutely no reason. But, fortunately, she was too caring to punish him for it.

Angela, on the other hand, was about to get her head bitten off, chewed and spat right back up her amoral backside.

'I said, who were you talking to?' she repeated now, her voice rising. 'Don't try to fucking ignore me, Joel. You know I'll flip if you start fucking about with me!'

Turning on her, Joel felt an urge to punch her. His hands actually balled into fists, but he managed to stop himself. Angela was the type to phone the police and scream rape and battery.

'Go on,' she challenged him spitefully. 'Do it! You know you want to. Cut me and bruise me, and show the world what you're really all about!'

'I'm getting out of here,' he said through gritted teeth. 'And this time, I won't be coming back. You are one screw short of a fucking Meccano set, Angela, and I've totally fucking had it with you. Now do me one favour and keep your screeching fucking mouth shut while I get my things!'

'Oh, no,' she snarled, shaking her head, her mouth pursed so tight in her pale face that it looked like an arsehole. 'There's no *way* you're walking out on me! Who do you think you are? You come here and use me for the fucking week, then take off like it meant nothing.'

'It *didn't* mean anything,' he spat back at her. 'I thought you'd have sussed that one out a long time ago.'

'So why do you keep coming back to me?'

'I don't come back *to* you,' Joel said nastily, going for the kill. 'I come to *fuck* you in ways that no decent woman would dream of letting me! You're a fucking *freak*, and I would never be sick or desperate enough to want you in my life in any kind of meaningful way. Now I'm going home to my beautiful girl-friend, to make *love* to her.'

'I'll kill you,' Angela hissed, her wild-eyed stare shooting venom into him as he snatched up his jacket and checked his pockets. '*And* the bitch you're so keen to get back to! Was that her on the phone just now?'

'None of your business,' he said, reaching under the mattress for his wallet.

'Come on . . .' she sneered. 'We all know what a faithless little charmer you really are. How did you get this one? Find her sucking cock in your mother's womb?'

'Fuck you,' Joel snarled, barely restraining himself now. 'Don't you ever fucking talk about my mother. You're not fit to lick the crap out of her toilet.'

'Touched a nerve, have we?' Angela spat. 'Maybe it's *Mummy* you're rushing home to, eh? Got your favourite knickers on today, has she?'

'You sick, twisted piece of shit!' Joel yelled. 'Don't ever come near me again, Angela – I'm warning you. Because I will *really* hurt you.'

Jumping up, Angela flew at him in a frenzy, her naked flesh repulsing him as it brushed across his clothes.

'Give me your phone!' she screamed, struggling to get at his pockets. 'I'm gonna ring the bitch and tell her what you've been doing to me! See if she still wants you after *that*!'

Putting his hands on her shoulders, Joel shoved her forcefully off, slamming her into the wall. The back of her head made a hollow sound as it banged against the hard surface. Collapsing in a heap, Angela started to wail, a horrible thin, high-pitched sound.

Fearing that he'd done some real damage, Joel stood and looked at her for a moment. Then he saw her eyes dart up, checking to see if he was watching, and he knew that she was faking it. Shaking his head, he walked out, slamming the door behind him.

Good thing she didn't know where he lived, because he had no doubt she'd have flown there on her broomstick to tell Maria all about it.

'I've missed you so much,' Maria cried, throwing her arms around Joel and dropping little kisses all over his face. 'Oh, you don't know how much I love you!'

'Not as much as I love you,' he said, lifting her off her feet and walking her into the kitchen. 'Hope you've got my wine ready, 'cos I have had a *mother* of a week.'

'Was she awful?' Maria asked sympathetically. Wriggling down, she went to fetch their drinks and waved him through to the couch.

'Who?' Joel asked, frowning as he flopped down. 'Oh, you mean Cher . . . No, she was great. It was the venues I was having a problem with. They're not too good at getting things ready on time over there. But hey . . . it's over now.'

'Poor baby,' Maria said soothingly. 'Let me run you a bath. I'll put some nice oils in it to help you relax.'

'Go on, then,' Joel said, sighing as the tension seeped out of his stiff shoulders.

He would never go near Angela again. She was bad for his health.

Maria was in the kitchen cooking dinner when she heard Joel's mobile ringing. He usually carried it everywhere he went, in case he missed an important client. But today he'd been so shattered that he must have forgotten, and now he was napping in the bedroom.

Licking garlic butter off her fingers, Maria wiped her hands and went to get the phone out of his jacket pocket, planning to take a message. She was about to say hello when a woman started shouting at the other end.

'Don't you *dare* hang up on me, you bastard! I've got things to say, and you *will* listen, whether you like it or not! I am *not* the kind of woman you can get away with treating like a cheap whore, so here's your ultimatum: you get your arse back here – sharpish – or I will hunt you and that woman of yours down. And I *will* find you, believe me! I know where you hang out, I know which parties you go to, I know *you*, you bastard!'

This was all rushed out and Maria wasn't sure what she was hearing at first. But when the woman paused for breath the words filtered through. Sure that she must have got the wrong number, Maria was about to tell her when the shouting started up again.

'Stop pretending you're not there, Joel! Just because

you're not answering doesn't mean I can't hear you! Joel!
JOEL . . . !'

Disconnecting, Maria stared at the phone. No, she hadn't
just heard that! She couldn't have. It was a wrong number.
It had to be.

But she'd said his name, and how many Joels had Maria
ever met in her life? One.

Shaking wildly, she sat down heavily on the couch. Seconds
ticked by like hours and then, hesitantly, she looked up the
number of the last incoming call. Remembering it, she checked
it against Joel's listed numbers. It was there, under the name
'Angelo'.

But that was a man's name. What was going on?

Glancing nervously at the door, she went into his messages.
There were two that he hadn't opened; they must have come
in while she was out of the room and she hadn't heard them.

The first was short: 'It's in. Call me. Lance.'

The other was longer – and far more upsetting: 'Hey, hot
stuff . . . still in2 dik after all. Fran nitemare – sacd hr off.
Cm rnd 4 fuk. Already wet! Honey Bunny.'

It took Maria a moment to work the text-talk out. But
there was no mistaking the message when she did, and it
made her feel sick to the stomach.

Putting the phone back in Joel's pocket, she went to finish
the cooking. Turning the steak under the grill, the thoughts
turned over and over in her head. Who was the madwoman,
and why had she been shouting abuse at him? And Honey
Bunny, who was still into dick and wanted him to come for
a fuck – what the hell was *that* about?

'Something smells nice,' Joel said, padding through from
the bedroom in his boxers. 'I was having a lovely dream that
I was driving a Ferrari, then all of a sudden I'm at this
barbecue, stuffing myself with sticky ribs. Mmmm . . .' He
looked over her shoulder at the steak. 'Fantastic.'

Sidestepping him before he could put his arms around her, Maria went to the sink and rinsed her hands.

'Something wrong?' Joel asked, picking one of the mushrooms out of the pan.

Still not looking at him, Maria shook her head. Joel gave a bemused smile. What was this? Where were the doting little smiles and hugs?

Moving towards her again, he slipped his hands under her arms and cupped her breasts.

'What's wrong, babe?' He kissed her neck. 'You missed me that much? Aw, don't be sad . . . I'm home now.'

'Don't,' Maria said, wriggling free and going to the opposite counter. Leaning back against it, she looked at him, searching his face for clues. Surely if he was messing about, there would be something in his eyes. But he looked the same as always.

Oh, God . . . maybe she'd got it all wrong.

No! She'd heard it, she'd seen it.

'Who's *Angelo*?' she asked, spitting the name out.

A frown flitted across Joel's brow. Where had that come from? His eyes darted sideways to his jacket on the back of the couch. Shit! The phone!

'A guy I work with,' he said, preparing to get cross with her for prying.

'Oh, yeah?' Maria folded her arms. 'This *guy* sounds remarkably like a woman to me.'

'What are you talking about?' Joel demanded tetchily. 'Shit, Maria, I've been working all week, and this is what I come home to – the Spanish fucking Inquisition. The name is fucking *male*. If you'd bothered looking properly, you'd have seen an O at the end, not a fucking A. Ange-*lo*.'

'Don't swear at me,' Maria said quietly, trying not to cry. 'And I'm not talking about the spelling, I'm talking about the woman who rang while you were asleep. Shouting at you for treating her like a – how did she put it – *cheap whore!*'

'What . . . ?' Joel muttered, looking confused. 'What woman? I don't know what you're talking about.'

Sighing heavily and folding her arms tighter to stop the wild shaking of her body, Maria said, 'You were asleep and your phone rang. I didn't want to disturb you, so I answered it to take a message, and a woman started shouting about how you'd best not hang up, and you couldn't get away with treating her like a whore, and how she's going to hunt you and your woman down.'

Fronting it out, Joel sneered. 'Nothing to do with me. She must have got the wrong number.'

'She said your name, Joel.'

On the ball now, Joel shrugged. 'You probably heard it wrong. Don't worry about it.'

'She *said your name* – three times.'

Turning to pour himself a glass of water from the tap, Joel quickly thought up an explanation.

'I know what it'll be,' he said, turning back. 'Angelo's one of the guys I was working with on the Cher thing. He'll have set this up for a laugh.'

'What?' Maria frowned. 'What's funny about it?'

'It's just the way those guys are,' Joel said, leaning casually back against the sink and crossing his legs at the ankle. 'We were all up to it while we were away – pulling tricks on each other, trying to land each other in it. You get bored, so you do whatever to relieve it. He'll be paying me back for telling his wife he was having a sex change.' Snorting softly, he shook his head and gazed at the floor, a small smile on his face as if he was remembering doing what he'd just said.

'So, you think your friend Angelo got a woman to ring you and shout at you, on the off chance that I would answer the phone?'

'Course. It's obvious now I think about it.'

'But I *never* answer it.'

Joel was getting irritated now. 'So you were lying when you said you just answered it?'

'No, of course not.'

'Well, then you *do* answer it. *Don't* you?'

Maria frowned. He was getting angry now, and she was starting to feel guilty.

'Do me a favour, eh?' Joel said then, tipping the water down the sink and slamming the glass down on the ledge. 'Don't touch it again – not if you're going to start accusing me of all sorts of bullshit! Christ! So much for *trust*.'

'Who's Honey Bunny?' Maria called after him as he stalked out of the kitchen. She didn't want to make him even more angry, but she had to know.

'*What?*' Turning back, Joel was positively scowling at her now.

'Honey Bunny,' she repeated, feeling a little afraid of him for the first time ever. 'You've got a text.'

'You are one step away from me walking out of here and never coming back,' Joel hissed, his expression furious.

'I need to know,' Maria said, unable to stop herself. 'Just tell me, Joel.'

'Another fucking guy off the crew, if you must know,' Joel snarled. 'We all had nicknames. Angel, Honey Bunny, Dipstick, Dogbreath . . . Want me to go on?' Shaking his head when she didn't answer, he gave her a look that made her blood run cold, then turned and walked out.

Snatching up his jacket, he stomped into the bedroom and locked the door.

Dragging his clothes back on, he was still angry with her for snooping. How fucking dare she. And she reckoned she trusted him! Like fucking hell she did!

Checking the texts when he'd finished, he felt a flood

of relief when he saw Lance's. See, the suspicious bitch hadn't bothered quizzing him about *that* one! But at least the gear was in. He'd run out last night and now he desperately needed a line – thanks to bloody Maria pissing him off.

The text from Honey made him smirk. So she'd sacked Francine off, had she. He'd known full well it would never last. Honey liked cock far too much to be satisfied with a finger.

It crossed Joel's mind that he'd been a bit rough on Maria considering she had actually seen Honey's text. If he'd seen something like that on *her* phone, there was no *way* he'd have believed a lame excuse like the one he'd fed her.

But that was her problem.

His problem right now was how to get his hands on some quick cash. Angela had fleeced him this week, so he had nothing in his pockets. The bank was shut, and there was no way he could get enough out of the hole in the wall. He needed two grand, at least, to get a decent score.

An idea sprang into his mind. It was a long shot, but it just might work.

Pulling the chair over to the wardrobe, Joel stood on it and reached to the back of the top cupboard. Pulling Maria's box of bits and pieces forward, he shoved the photo of her father aside and rummaged through the other stuff until he found the small black velvet drawstring bag. Checking that the diamond solitaire ring was still in it, he thrust it into his pocket and slid the box back into place.

'Where are you going?' Maria asked when he came out of the bedroom with his jacket on and headed for the front door.

'Out,' he snapped. 'Don't wait up – I doubt I'll be back tonight.'

He felt a bit guilty, because Maria had obviously been

crying. But he couldn't afford to let it drop right now or she'd expect him to stay in and make up, and he had to get to Lance before he started crawling the walls.

'I'm sorry,' Maria called. But Joel carried on going as if he hadn't heard.

Maria couldn't have felt more miserable after Joel left. She had completely screwed things up. Now he thought that she had been sneaking into his private affairs, and he was offended and angry. And she couldn't blame him. She'd done nothing wrong in answering his phone but, instead of asking him what it was all about, she'd immediately assumed that he was cheating on her. Why did she have to be so damn suspicious?

Her heart gave a lurch when her own mobile began to ring. Running to get it, praying that it was Joel, she was a bit deflated when she saw Nigel's name on the screen. Sighing, she answered it.

'Hello, Nigel, how are you?'

'I'm fine, thank you,' he said, sounding quite serious. 'Am I disturbing you?'

'Not at all,' she assured him. 'I'm home alone, doing nothing. What's up?'

'You're alone?' Nigel repeated. 'Do you think I could pop round for a minute? There's something I need to talk to you about.'

Maria hesitated before answering, and Nigel picked up on it immediately.

'If you'd rather come in to the office, that's fine. It's just that I was on my way home, so I thought I'd save you the trouble.'

'No, it's okay,' Maria said decisively. 'Come round. It'll be lovely to see you.'

Crossing her fingers when she'd disconnected, she hoped

that Joel didn't decide to come back to carry the argument on while Nigel was here. That would be so embarrassing.

'Sorry for this,' Nigel said when he was sitting on the couch ten minutes later. 'I know it's absolutely none of my concern, but I really felt I should check this with you for peace of mind's sake. Because, well, you always insisted that you weren't going to touch the original investments.'

'That's right,' Maria affirmed, frowning. 'And I haven't. Is there a problem?'

'Well, yes, actually,' Nigel said hesitantly. 'Given what you've just said, I believe there probably is.'

'What's happened?' Maria's tone was as serious as his now.

'Well, as you know, investment accounts have a maturity date, after which you either have to empty them or transfer the funds into a new account. Earlier today, it crossed my mind that one particularly large account was due to mature, so I got the paperwork out to check how much we would be talking about when I contacted you to discuss reinvestment. And that's when I learned that a new account had already been opened.'

'By who?' Maria was confused. 'I thought only you or I had access to it.'

'So did I,' Nigel intoned grimly. 'But it would appear not. It seems . . .' Pausing, he put his elbows on his knees and clasped his hands together in front of his mouth. He really didn't want to say the next thing he had to say. It would break her heart if she'd had no prior knowledge of it – which she obviously hadn't.

'Nigel, could you please just tell me?' Maria said, forcing the words out steadily despite her pounding heart. It was obvious from the way he was acting that she wasn't going to like what she heard, but she'd rather know – no matter how bad it was.

'It seems,' Nigel continued, 'that an account was opened in the name of Joel Parry. Then, once the funds were safely transferred, that account was cleared out and closed down.'

'But I don't understand,' Maria said, her face growing ever paler. 'I never signed anything over to him. I never knew anything about it. How much was it?'

'Two hundred thousand,' Nigel told her quietly.

'But I didn't *know*,' Maria repeated. 'How could he have been able to do any of that without me being there?'

'He'd have to have had all the relevant information at hand to organise it,' Nigel told her unhappily. 'Has he had access to your paperwork?'

Maria nodded slowly, her mind flicking back to when they had first got together and Joel had sat down with her to 'help' her through the maze.

'But he still would have needed me to sign things, wouldn't he? It can't be that easy.'

'No, it's not,' Nigel told her. 'But if you didn't sign, he must have forged your signature. I haven't looked into it fully yet because I needed to make sure that *you* hadn't author-ised it and forgotten to mention it to me. Not that you'd have to,' he added quickly. 'But it helps to keep on top of things if I'm kept fully up to date. You have so many different investment accounts, it's actually quite terrifying to think what could happen.'

'Oh, my God,' Maria said, her voice barely audible. 'What about the rest of them?'

'I'm afraid I didn't even think to check,' Nigel admitted. 'I just wanted to know if you were aware of this.'

'So he could have completely wiped me out?' The fear was stark in Maria's eyes now. 'Everything could be gone – and I wouldn't be able to do anything about it, because the account was opened with my apparent say-so.'

Nigel inhaled slowly and deeply. Much as he'd have liked

to reassure her to the contrary, there was every chance that she was right. It would be incredibly difficult to force the bank to repay this money, because Joel would have had all the specific and confidential details that were needed to complete such a transaction.

'I'm so sorry,' he said, feeling utterly helpless to ease her distress. 'This is probably no consolation, but there are several investments that are nowhere near maturity, so they'll be quite safe.'

'Can you make sure they *stay* safe?' Maria asked. '*Please*, Nigel, I couldn't bear it if I lost everything.'

'I'll start investigating at the end of business tomorrow,' Nigel assured her. 'I'll do whatever I can, believe me.'

'Thanks,' Maria murmured numbly. Then, swiping at a tear that was trickling down her cheek, she said, 'I can't believe he'd do something like this to me. I trusted him. I even made my bank account joint so he would know I was committed.' Chin wobbling now, she bit down hard on her bottom lip. 'How could he *do* it? He's supposed to love me. He said he wants to marry me and have children.'

She was sobbing softly now, the tears streaking her face. Her eyes were so full of anguish that Nigel could have wept with her.

'There is a possibility that it wasn't him,' he said gently, wanting to erase the pain, or at least soften it. 'Like you said, he loves you. This could have been done over the internet, or anything.'

Maria shook her head. 'No, it *was* him. And it's my own fault, because I've been a fool. Beth said he was after the money from the start, and I didn't believe her. But it's not just that.' She gazed up at him forlornly. 'He was away last week, and when he came back tonight . . .'

Listening as she told him what had happened with the phone call, and the explicit text message, and how Joel had given that ridiculous explanation before accusing her of spying on him, Nigel felt incredibly sad. And mad at Joel. How could the man treat her so badly? Didn't he realise that the money, the house, the investments, meant nothing without this beautiful, generous, loving woman? Joel must be insane to risk losing her for the sake of money.

But if Joel thought it would go undiscovered while he skimmed the cream off the rest of her accounts, he had another think coming. Nigel would spend however long it took to investigate this. And the moment he had proof that Joel was involved, he would go straight to the police and make sure that the man paid for it – in prison time, if not with money.

'What are you going to do?' he asked when Maria was all cried out.

'I don't know.' She shrugged. 'Kick him out when he gets back, for a start. After that . . . I just don't know.'

'Well, if I can be of any help, you know where I am,' Nigel said. 'You can reach me on my mobile at any time. Please don't hesitate to call – I don't care if it's the middle of the night. If you need me, call. Okay?'

'Okay,' Maria agreed, smiling gratefully. 'Thanks so much for telling me, Nigel. I dread to think what he might have done if I hadn't found out.'

Gathering his things together to go, Nigel looked at her thoughtfully. 'Can I give you a little advice?'

'Yeah, course,' she said, wiping her nose.

'Try not to mention any of this to Joel until I have the proof one way or the other. I'd hate for him to be alerted and cover his tracks.'

'I won't,' Maria assured him.

They both jumped at the sound of a key in the lock.

'It's me,' Joel called, as if nothing had ever happened. 'I can't stay, 'cos I've just had a call, but I wanted to sort—'

Stopping in his tracks when he saw Maria and Nigel sitting on the couch, he narrowed his eyes suspiciously.

Pulling herself together with lightning speed, Maria got up and went to him.

'Are they for me?' she asked, reaching for the flowers he was holding.

'Er, yeah,' he muttered, still eyeing Nigel.

'Thank you, they're beautiful,' she said, reaching up to kiss him. 'You remember Nigel . . . He's just popped in to get me to sign something.'

Patting his briefcase, Nigel smiled nervously and stood up.

'Yes, well, I've got what I needed, so I'll get out of your way.'

'I'll show you out,' Maria said innocently.

Joel was scowling when she came back. 'What was all that about?' he demanded.

'I told you,' she said, carrying the flowers through to the kitchen to put them in water. 'He had something for me to sign.'

'What was it?' Joel followed her.

'Just some paperwork,' Maria said, willing him to leave it alone. She couldn't tell him it was for the accounts, because then he'd know they were on to him. 'Are these for before?' she asked, giving him a shy smile. 'I am really sorry about that.'

'Don't try and change the subject,' Joel snarled. 'And don't fucking lie to me!' He'd had a snort on his way back from Lance's and his instincts were razor sharp. She'd been up to something with that gimpy solicitor, he knew it.

Unnerved by the manic look in his eyes, Maria backed up against the sink and held the flowers tightly, as if they were a barrier.

'You're still mad at me about the phone, aren't you?' she said contritely. 'I said I was sorry about that.'

'I don't give a flying fuck about the phone,' Joel yelled. 'I want to know what you've been up to with your fucking friend *Nigel*!'

'Don't swear at me!' Maria yelled back. 'I hate it when you talk like that. I haven't done anything wrong!'

'Oh, no? So how come he was here the minute I went fucking out? What did you do? Ring him to tell him what a bad boy I've been?'

'Don't be ridiculous.'

'Don't fucking call me ridiculous, you stuck-up bitch!' Rushing towards her, Joel snatched the flowers and threw them to the floor. Stamping on them, he glared at her, grinding his teeth. 'Were you about to jump into bed with him? Did I disturb you? Is that why you were acting all fucking nice?'

'How dare you,' Maria spat, anger overriding her fear now. 'Who the hell do you think you are? Accusing *me* of messing around behind *your* back! It's not me who's getting messages from other people.'

'No, you just bring them to my fucking *BED*!' Joel roared indignantly. 'If I'd known what a dirty slut you were, I'd never have bothered touching you!'

'Yeah, well, I wish you hadn't!' Maria yelled back, her sense of injustice making her say more than she should as she added, 'At least then you wouldn't have been able to steal all my fucking money! Think I wouldn't find out, did you? Well, tough! I know everything!'

Turning on his heel, because he could feel the rage welling up in him and knew that he would probably end up hurting her, Joel stormed out, kicking the couch on his way.

How fucking dare she accuse him of stealing! She'd said from the start that he could take whatever he wanted. Trust a fucking *woman* to throw it all back in your face the minute you had an argument!

Maria knew how close Joel had just come to hitting her, and she was shaking so much that she could feel her legs trying to buckle. Stumbling to the front door, which he'd slammed on his way out, she double-locked it and put the chain on.

God, where had that come from? She'd never seen him like that before. His eyes had been crazy – like he wanted to really hurt her.

Well, there was no way she could let him come back after that. If this was a taster of what was to come, she didn't want to know. She'd wait till Nigel had the evidence and use it to keep Joel away. She'd tell him he could keep what he'd already stolen, but if he ever came near her again she would have him arrested for stealing, and for forging her signature.

27

Nigel concentrated on his work the next day. But as soon as five o'clock came around and everybody else got ready to go home, he started gathering Maria's files and heaping them on his desk.

'Working late?' Adam asked, popping his head around the door.

'Yeah, I've got a lot to do,' Nigel said distractedly.

'Heavy case?' Coming in, Adam glanced at the files. Frowning when he saw the name on the top one, he said, 'What's going on, man?'

'Not sure yet,' Nigel said, sitting down and rolling his shirtsleeves up. 'But it looks like Maria's boyfriend has been helping himself to her money.'

'She probably knows about it,' Adam said, folding his arms. 'They're a pretty tight couple. Don't you think you're treading on toes here?'

'You don't know anything about them as a couple.'

'No, I know I don't. I'm just going by what you've said.'

'I don't remember ever discussing their relationship with you.' Nigel looked up with a frown.

'Yeah, you did,' Adam insisted. 'You told me how smooth he thinks he is, and how he looks like me – thanks for that, by the way,' he said in a less-than-impressed tone.

'I said he looks like you because he *does*,' Nigel said tetchily. 'Or, rather, he *did*, before he decided to dye his hair black and grow that ridiculous goatee. But I know that

I have never discussed their relationship – with you, or anyone.'

Shrugging, Adam said, 'Sorry, must have got it wrong. But I still think you should keep your nose out. Seriously, man. It's her business, not yours.'

Sighing heavily, Nigel ran his hands through his hair.

'Listen, Adam, I appreciate the concern, but you really don't know the ins and outs of this. As it happens, I saw Maria last night and we had quite a chat. I'm checking through this stuff at her request. Okay?'

'Why did she ask you to check him out? Does she *know* he's done something?'

'Not with any proof, as yet,' Nigel said. 'But I discovered something that I thought was a bit suspect, and when I talked to her about it she asked me to check everything else.'

'I see,' Adam murmured, still frowning thoughtfully.

'Look, sorry I can't go into it,' Nigel said, 'but I'm really not sure what I'm going to find yet, so I have to concentrate. I'll talk to you tomorrow when I've got a clearer head – okay?'

'Yeah, sure,' Adam said. 'See you later.'

'See you later.' Nigel waved. 'Oh, and can you make sure that whoever leaves last locks the street door but doesn't put the alarm on? I don't want to be setting it off by mistake.'

'Sure.'

Nigel got his head down when he was finally alone and the night sped along as he pored over the investment files – and over the printouts which had been faxed to him from the various banks and financial institutions that afternoon.

Across town, blissfully unaware of today's developments, Joel was sitting at a table outside the bar below Jippi's place. After storming out on Maria last night, he'd tried to contact Honey to stay at her place, but she'd had her phone switched off.

So he'd detoured to the next nearest place – Rita-Anita's. The poor cow had been so thrilled that he'd dropped in out of the blue that she'd been more than willing to fuck his tensions away. She was no better than before at blow jobs, but that funky clit of hers was quite a turn-on when you got used to it.

Jippi had called Joel earlier to say he was on his way back from Thailand, and wanted him to meet him at the loft, as he was now calling his apartment. The later it got, the less likely it was that he was going to make it before the bar closed. But Joel couldn't stand on the doorstep waiting – the police would be sure to pull him.

Just as he was contemplating where to go, Honey turned up. She was looking for a friend she'd arranged to meet, but she forgot all about that when she saw Joel.

'Oh, my God! I've been like *dying* to see you!' she gushed, flopping down on the chair beside his. 'Why didn't you answer my text?'

'I tried calling you last night, but your phone was off.'

'Oh, shitty shit shit!' she yelped girlishly, pulling the phone out of her pocket. 'No wonder I've not had any calls today! I thought I was just really unpopular all of a sudden.'

'As if,' Joel chuckled.

Switching it back on, she said, 'So, what are you doing here? Waiting for me?'

'No, for Jippi. But it looks like I'll have to leave it for tonight.'

'Great! Let's just go back to mine and shag our arses off.' She grinned naughtily. 'I've been like so *gagging* for it since I haven't seen you. That Francine was a proper nightmare.'

'What happened?'

'Hormones, man!' Honey complained. 'Imagine two menstruating women trying to get it on. You can't do like *anything*, and it's so gross. And the *moods*! Christ, it was like the *Evil Dead* meets *Texas Chainsaw Massacre*! I'm never speaking to her again!'

'Shame. I thought you were good friends.'

'Nah, she's just someone I met at a party. And she *so* can't sing!' Honey bitched. 'So, we going back to mine, or what?'

'Go on, then,' Joel said, finishing his drink. 'As long as you don't try to make me watch the tapes of your show again. Sorry, babe, but it'll put me to sleep.'

'Not got anything to keep us awake?' Honey asked, linking her arm through his and skipping along the pavement beside him.

'When have I ever not?' Joel said, grinning magnanimously.

28

Looking up when he heard a muffled sound outside the door, Nigel felt a throb of fear burst to life in his throat. Who would that be at this time of night? No one ever came in this late. Not even *him* – usually.

Burglars!

Switching the desk lamp off, he eyed the bottom of the door, waiting for the reception light to go on, which would have told him that it was someone with authority to be there. It stayed dark.

Shaking now, he reached for the heavy Blue John paper-weight and edged his way out from behind the desk. Using the faint glow of the street lamp leaking in through the slatted blind to guide him to the door, he pressed his ear to the wood.

A minute passed, then two . . . Hearing nothing after three full minutes, he dared to peer out through the small glass panel. He could just about make everything out in the muted light coming through the smoked-glass street doors – couches, coffee machine, reception desk . . .

There was nobody out there. He must have imagined it.

Exhaling loudly, he flipped the overhead light on and glanced at his watch. It was almost three a.m. No wonder he was so spooked.

Time had a way of running away with him when he got stuck into something – but *boy* was he glad he'd got stuck into this. It had been incredibly revealing. The shit was really going to hit the fan come the morning.

Yawning, he decided he'd best go home and get his head down. Now he knew who he was up against, he needed a crystal-clear head to tackle this.

Putting the Blue John back, he locked the paperwork he'd been working on away in his briefcase, then pulled his jacket on and took one last look around.

Market Street was deserted but for a lazy breeze rifling through the litter bins and scattering loose food-cartons around the walkway. After the bustle of daytime, it felt eerie and abandoned, and the strange orangey glow of the lamps made it look other-worldly. Locking up, he hurried around to the car port at the rear of the block.

Acutely aware of the sound of his own footsteps, he felt the fear prickling the hairs on his neck when he heard a second, slightly out of sync set.

It's an echo, he told himself, quickening his pace. And that shadow he'd just seen from the corner of his eye was only that – a shadow; a nothing piece of missing light.

Reaching the car, he fumbled to get the key out of his pocket, cursing himself for not having it ready in his hand.

Damn! He was all fingers and thumbs.

The shadow took solid form. Feeling the breath on his neck, he dropped the key and turned around, wide-eyed with fear.

'What the hell are *you* doing here?' he gasped when he saw who it was.

Pressing himself back against the car when the hooded shadow reached for his briefcase, he shook his head and gripped the case tighter.

'No. You're not having it.'

'Give me the fucking bag!' the shadow snarled.

'There's no p-point,' Nigel stuttered. 'I know *everything*. This is the end of the line.'

'For you, maybe.'

'Don't be stupid . . .' Nigel said when he saw the knife, his voice betraying his fear as the blade glinted in the dark. 'Put it away, man. That won't solve anything . . . *No*, don't!'

'Shut your fucking whining mouth and give me the fucking bag! This is your last warning.'

'You won't get away with this, you must know that,' Nigel said, trying to inject some sense into him. 'Come on, man – it's over. Just walk away. I won't say anything.'

'Ah, but you will, because you just can't help yourself, can you? Not where *she*'s concerned.'

'There's CCTV,' Nigel reminded him.

Glancing back over his shoulder, Adam looked straight up at the camera, making it look like a furtive gesture.

'So there is,' he drawled, turning back with a smile.

'Oh, God!' Nigel gasped when realisation sank in. 'You wanted to be seen. You want them to think it's *him* – that's why you've drawn the beard on!'

'Round of applause for the smartest moron in town.'

'Why did you do it, Adam? Just tell me.'

'Because it was easy. And she didn't miss it, so what harm was there? She'd be none the wiser now if you hadn't stuck your nose in.'

'It's illegal. You won't get away with it.'

'Ah, but I will – as long as you're not around to drop me in it. Sorry, mate, but you've got to go.'

Plunging the knife into Nigel's gut, Adam yanked it up hard. Then he pulled it out and brought it down into his colleague's chest several times until Nigel slumped to the ground.

Bending down then, Adam wrenched Nigel's watch off and pulled the wallet out of his pocket. Then, grabbing the briefcase, he snatched up the dropped key and jumped into Nigel's car, leaving his body behind in a widening pool of blood as he drove away from the scene.

29

Nigel's office was alive with forensics personnel in full whites, dusting every surface and bagging anything that they thought might be relevant.

In Adam's office next door, Detective Inspector Seddon was taking a statement from Adam.

'So, you were the last one to speak to him?' he said, his eyes searching Adam's face for clues.

'Er, yeah, I think so.' Adam swallowed noisily. 'I, er, looked in on him when I was leaving, to see what he was up to.'

'And what *was* he up to?'

'Looking through some client files,' Adam said, frowning as if he were having a hard time remembering. 'Sorry, I'm a bit shocked. We all are.'

'I can imagine,' Seddon said, jotting something down. 'Approximately what time do you think you spoke to him?'

'Five. Definitely. Because the secretaries had just left, and the receptionist left with me.'

'So who locked the door? Mr Grayson?'

'No, I, er – *me*.' Adam ran a hand through his hair. 'Yeah, me. The receptionist went out, then I locked it, and we walked up to the Corn Exchange together.'

'No alarm?'

'No, Nigel said not to – in case he set it off by mistake.'

'And then what did you and the receptionist do?'

'I went home, and so did she – I presume.'

'And what did you do once you got home, sir?' Seddon looked at him questioningly.

Frowning, Adam shook his head. 'I'm sorry, but what's that got to do with anything? My friend's just been murdered, and you want to know about me eating a bloody microwave meal for one, and watching TV till I fell asleep!'

'It's just procedure,' Seddon assured him. 'We'll be asking the receptionist the exact same questions. And everybody else who was in contact with Mr Grayson yesterday afternoon. So . . .' Glancing down at his notes, he gave Adam another piercing look. 'Anybody have any reason to want him dead?'

'God, no!' Adam protested. 'Nigel's one of the most decent blokes you'll ever meet. I know people always say that, but he is honest and trustworthy, and he's just really decent.'

Noting the use of the present tense, Seddon nodded.

'Where . . . where did it – you know?' Adam said, gulping loudly.

'At the back of the building, getting into his car. Do you know why he would have been here so late, sir?'

'Er, yeah,' Adam admitted distractedly. 'He was looking into something for a client. Can I just ask, though . . . About the car. It wasn't there this morning when I came in.'

'The assailant stole it.'

'So there'll be fingerprints,' Adam said hopefully.

''Fraid not. We found it burned out in Alderley Edge this morning. Nothing left of it to check for prints.'

'Well, what about the CCTV?' Adam suggested. 'It overlooks the staff car park. Won't you find something on that?'

'We're already onto it, sir.'

'Oh, I see. Good.'

'Don't worry, we'll get who we're looking for,' Seddon said reassuringly. Then, 'About this client – must have been pretty important to keep him so late?'

'Er, yeah, he was very fond of her. And he, er, mentioned to me l-last time I saw him that he'd seen her the day before and she'd asked him to look into something for her.'

'Oh, yeah. What's this client's name, and what was Mr Grayson working on for her?' Seddon narrowed his eyes.

'She's rather wealthy,' Adam told him, frowning as if wondering whether he ought to be disclosing this. 'Her name's Maria Price, and she's . . . well, she's got this boyfriend who's a bit dodgy.'

'In what way?'

Taking a deep breath, Adam bit his lip. 'Don't quote me on this, but I think Maria and Nigel suspected the boyfriend of stealing a substantial amount of money from her. She inherited a large estate, you see, and there were some discrepancies with the accounts.'

'Such as?'

'I'm not exactly sure. He only mentioned it for the first time when I was leaving, but he said he'd—' Pausing, Adam gulped again and struggled to control the quiver in his chin.

'Take your time,' Seddon told him kindly. 'I know this is difficult.'

'Sorry,' Adam croaked after a moment. 'He said he'd talk to me about it today. But, obviously, now . . .'

'Okay, I won't keep you too much longer,' Seddon said. 'If you could possibly give us this boyfriend's name . . . ?'

'I think it's Joel,' Adam said, frowning as if he were uncertain. 'Joel Parry. It should be easy enough to find him, because he lives with Miss Price. The address will be on the computer system if you'd like me to get it for you. But I don't know what kind of reception you'll get. The boyfriend and Nigel weren't on the best of terms.'

'How so?'

'Nigel detested him, because he thought Joel was using

Miss Price for her money,' Adam said, shrugging as he added, 'I guess he must have been right if she thought it too.'

'Any idea what this Joel Parry person looks like?'

'Not really,' Adam said. 'I've never actually met either of them.' Then, narrowing his eyes, he said, 'Actually, Nigel did mention that he'd grown a goatee beard and dyed his hair black.' He shrugged. 'Don't suppose that means much to you, though.'

'And what did it mean to Nigel?'

'I don't suppose it meant anything.' Adam gave a soft snort. 'He was just slagging him off for tarting himself up.'

'Thanks for your help,' Seddon said, standing up. 'And I will take that address, if you don't mind?'

30

Joel had just pulled into the car park behind the flats when the police surrounded him.

'Joel Parry?' Seddon said as the uniforms swarmed in from all sides. 'I am arresting you on suspicion of the murder of Nigel Grayson. You do not have to say anything, but anything you do say may be—'

'I don't know what the hell you're talking about,' Joel squawked as his arms were hoisted up his back and the cuffs were snapped over his wrists.

'—Taken down and used against you . . .'

'Get off me!' Joel yelped as he was handcuffed and frog-marched towards a waiting van. 'I haven't fucking done anything!'

Watching from the doorway, Maria shivered.

'All right, love?' the WPC asked, rubbing Maria's arm reassuringly.

'Yeah.' Maria nodded, averting her gaze when Joel turned and stared straight at her. 'I don't have to get in there with him, do I?'

'No, we'll take you in the squad car,' the WPC said. 'You're doing really well, pet. Your statement will help a lot.'

'So, you fell out with your boyfriend yesterday evening, when he came home and found you with Mr Grayson?' Seddon asked when they were settled in Interview Room 3 back at the station.

'Yes.' Maria nodded, holding her cardigan tight around

her shoulders. 'He wanted to know why Nigel – Mr Grayson – was there. I told him he'd brought some papers for me to sign, but Joel didn't believe me. He thought that I was . . . well, he thought I'd been sleeping with Nigel.'

'But you hadn't?'

'God, no!' Maria looked up with a pained expression. 'He was a really nice man, but nothing like that was ever even mentioned. He was my solicitor.'

'And he called to see you because he'd found out that Joel Parry had closed one of your investment accounts and opened another in his own name?'

'Yes.'

'And was it a substantial amount?'

'Two hundred thousand. That's all Nigel knew about at that point, but he said he'd check to make sure the other accounts were all right.' Crying now, Maria swiped at the tears with the back of her fingers. 'Sorry . . . I just can't believe this has happened because of me. I feel so awful. I should have told him to forget it.'

'Mr Grayson was pretty fond of you, by all accounts,' Seddon continued when she had calmed a little. 'Was Joel aware of that?'

'No.' Maria shook her head, dabbing her cheeks with the tissue the WPC had just handed to her. '*I* wasn't. That's why I was so shocked when Joel accused me of sleeping with him.'

'And the argument got pretty heated?'

'Yes. He had a really strange look in his eyes – sort of crazy. I actually thought he was going to hit me.'

'Has he ever done that?'

'No, never.'

'So, what happened after the argument?'

'He stormed out. And I didn't see him again until you came round and asked me to call him to bring him home.'

★   ★   ★

Making his way down to the holding cells when he'd finished with Maria and she'd been taken home by the WPC, Seddon collected two new cassette tapes and headed into the secure interview suite.

'Bring Parry through in five minutes,' he called back to the desk sergeant. 'And the vid. Oh, and a coffee wouldn't go amiss. Two sugars.'

'It wasn't me,' Joel said, glaring at Seddon across the table. 'I don't care *what* you think you know, it was not *me*!'

'Temper,' Seddon drawled. 'Do we have a problem with anger, Joel?'

'You might have, but I haven't.'

'Coke's known for giving you wild mood swings – you do know that, yeah?'

'So, I have the occasional snort.' Joel shrugged as if it meant nothing. 'That's got nothing to do with what you're talking about.'

'The occasional snort?' Seddon raised an eyebrow. 'You had a quarter of an ounce in your pocket.'

'So maybe I was planning to have a party,' Joel grunted. 'It was for personal use. It wasn't cut into deals, so there's no way you can touch me for dealing.'

'I'm not interested in doing you for the coke, Joel,' Seddon said snidely, leaning forward. 'Not when I can have you for murder instead.'

'I wasn't anywhere near the ponce,' Joel said scathingly.

'Can I take it that you didn't like him?'

'Would *you* like the guy that was shagging *your* bird?'

'From what I hear, that never actually happened.'

'Yeah, well, she's bound to deny it.'

'It's the fact that you won't accept it's not true that interests me,' Seddon told him calmly. 'See, that smacks of unreasonable jealousy, and the majority of murders are committed in the heat of passion. Did you know that?'

Looking at him, Joel's face collapsed into a disbelieving frown. 'What the fuck are you talking about, man? I've already told you – I didn't go anywhere near Nigel fucking Grayson. The last time I saw him was when I caught Maria entertaining him in *my* house.'

'After which you orchestrated a blazing row and stormed out,' Seddon promptly reminded him. 'Then stayed out. Hiding in the shadows, watching Mr Grayson's every move until you knew he was alone and vulnerable. And then you killed him. Payback for daring to like *your bird.*'

'Rubbish.'

Sighing heavily, Seddon sat back in his chair and finished his coffee.

'Shall we take a look at this CCTV videotape, then?' he said, as if they were mates watching a movie.

'Yeah, let's,' Joel said, sitting forward and putting his elbow on the desk, quite confident that he was about to prove his innocence. 'Then you'll *know* you've got the wrong man.'

The uniform who was standing behind Seddon pulled the video machine and monitor into position. He pressed the play button, passing the remote to Seddon.

Using it as a pointer, Seddon said, 'Right, this here is the view of the car park at the rear of the building. And that is Mr Grayson's car – but then, I suppose you already know that, don't you?'

'I have seen it before, yeah.' Joel nodded, impatient to get to the bit that would show it wasn't him.

'Anyway, this figure you can see coming into shot is Mr Grayson,' Seddon went on. 'But again, you'll know that, given that you were right behind him.'

'No, I wasn't,' Joel said calmly.

'Oh, but you were,' Seddon drawled. 'See, here you come now.'

'That could be anyone.' Joel squinted at the shadowy figure. 'He's got a hood on, for God's sake.'

'Yes, you did, didn't you?' Seddon agreed. 'But wait . . . *There*!' Pressing the pause button, freezing the frame when the attacker turned and looked at the camera, the detective smiled slyly when Joel gave an audible gasp. 'Camera never lies, eh, Mr Parry? Forget doing that, did you, in your rush to steal Mr Grayson's bag, watch, wallet, and car?'

'But it's not *me*,' Joel bleated, knowing full well that it *wasn't* him even though his own eyes were telling him different. The man on the screen looked just like him, complete with the black goatee . . . But how could a coincidence like that happen?

'I swear to God that's not me,' he said, looking Seddon straight in the eye. 'Please, you've got to believe me. I wasn't there.'

'So where were you?' Seddon sat back casually.

'With a girl,' Joel admitted, his eyes showing his desperation.

'Oh, yeah? So how come you didn't mention that before?'

'Because I didn't want Maria to find out.' Joel ran his hands through his hair. 'Shit! That's what we were arguing about before we got into it about Nigel. She found a text on my phone from the girl, but I denied anything was going on.'

'And you'd still have the text, I presume.'

'No, I wiped it off.'

'Of course,' Seddon said facetiously. 'As if you'd keep something like that. How's about you give us this girl's name, then?'

'Do I have to?'

'Not if you don't want us to talk to her and get you off

the hook.' Seddon chuckled softly. 'Or maybe you'd like us to let you phone her first – so you can tell her what to say?'

'No, of course not. It's just that – well, she's famous. I don't think she'd appreciate getting a call off the police.'

'Famous?' Seddon laughed. 'Jeezus, I've heard it all now.' Then, serious again, he said, 'Come off it, Joel. Quit stalling. We've got your mug on the CCTV. You were there.'

'I swear to *God* I wasn't. Okay, look, her name's Honey Mason, and she's in a soap called *Picture Perfect*. But please don't go and question her on set, or she'll get into trouble with the producer. I'll give you her address and phone number. Ask her about us meeting up at Quiro on Deansgate that night. I was already there having a drink, and she came looking for someone else. Then, when she saw me, she asked me back to hers. Just go and ask her – *please.*'

Seddon left Joel in the holding cell for two long hours while he went to talk to Honey. Bringing him back into the interview room then, he delivered the worst news Joel could possibly hear.

'She hasn't got a clue who you are.'

'But that's not true,' Joel gasped.

Seddon shrugged. 'That's what she said.'

'She must be scared of getting into trouble,' Joel said, trying to think why she would drop him in it like that. 'I *was* with her. I've stayed at her flat loads of times. Go and talk to her again. She'll tell you in the end, I know she will!'

'She says she's never heard of you, and has never been out with you, and that you've never been anywhere near her flat,' Seddon said. 'That's the bad news. Here's the good. We spoke to some of the bar staff at Quiro, and had a look at their CCTV tapes. And guess what? You and Honey were sitting together at a table outside – just like you said you were.'

'So you believe me?' The relief was heavy in Joel's voice.

'I believe you were at the bar with your lady friend when you said you were, yes,' Seddon conceded. 'But I also believe that you said goodnight to her there, then nipped across town to wait for Mr Grayson.'

'But I didn't. I swear—'

'To *God*. Yeah, I know,' Seddon said in a bored voice.

'Look, please just go and talk to Honey again. Tell her that you know she was lying about knowing me. She'll admit the rest then, I know she will. She's just scared.'

31

'I've got it!' Psycho yelled, barrelling into the front room with a jubilant grin on his face.

'Got what?' Eamon glanced up from the couch.

'The fucking address!' Psycho declared, flapping a piece of paper in the air. 'Took me nearly a fucking year, but I *told* you I'd track the cunt down!'

'For real?' Eamon sat up a bit straighter. 'How?'

'With a bit of fucking brain power.' Psycho jabbed a finger at his temple. 'His bird only left a fucking forwarding address for her mail! All I had to do was find out exactly which house they'd sold, and the rest was a piece of fucking piss! Shit, I should be a fucking detective, me!'

'So, what we doing? Going down there?'

'Too fucking right. Bell Jimmy and tell him we're coming for him, then get your shoes on and your arse in gear. There's no way I'm missing him this time. The cunt's arse is mine!'

'Yeah, well, make sure you've got your piece in your fucking hand this time,' Eamon said, getting up. 'I'm taking that other wee cunt right the fuck out if I see him again.'

Still smarting over the last encounter with the 'Bally Boys', as they called Lance and his crew whenever they recounted their last trip to Manchester, Eamon was saving his best bullet for the little one with the big mouth.

'No need to worry about them tossers,' Psycho jeered. 'They only caught us last time 'cos they had a bigger fucking car and surprise on their side. We'll be in Wazzer's fucking jeep this time – and there's no way they're stopping *that* monster in their fucking poncey four-by-four.'

Outside, a horn sounded. Standing face to face in the hall when they were ready, Psycho and Eamon beat their chests, then body-slammed each other. Then, grinning wildly, they set off to pick Jimmy up from his girlfriend's.

Then they headed for Manchester.

32

'Please, babe,' Joel pleaded, looking through the crack in the door. 'Take the chain off. I need to talk to you.'

'Go away,' Maria called from across the room. 'Please, Joel, I can't deal with this. Just leave me alone.'

'I didn't do it! The police have let me out – that should tell you something.'

'They've got you on CCTV. I saw it, Joel. It was *you*. You looked straight at the camera!'

'It wasn't fucking me!' Joel yelled, getting frustrated now. 'Why won't anyone believe me?'

'Go away!' Maria yelped, terrified that he would try to kick the door down. 'I'll call the police!'

Knowing that he couldn't afford to get another pull, Joel gave the door one last kick.

'Right, I'm going. But I'll be coming back, Maria. You're wrong about this, and you're being really unfair. Anyway, you've got all my stuff.'

'I'll pack it for you,' Maria said. 'You can pick it up from the maintenance man's room tomorrow. Now just go.'

Running to the door when he gave up and walked away, she slammed it shut and double-locked it. Reaching for her phone then, she rang Vicky, her hands shaking so badly that it took three attempts to get the number.

'Vicky?' she sobbed. 'Oh, thank God you're in! I didn't wake you up, did I?'

'No, I was watching telly.' Vicky yawned loudly. 'What's up?'

Listening as Maria blurted everything out, Vicky said, 'Right, take a deep breath. I know you're scared, love, but you need to calm down, all right?'

'Yeah, all right,' Maria agreed, making an effort to bring herself under control. 'Can – can you come here for a bit? Just till he's got his stuff and gone.'

'I can't,' Vicky said regretfully. 'I'm waiting for Leroy to come home. But you're more than welcome to come here.'

'It's two in the morning,' Maria said, wiping her nose. 'I can't land myself on you at this time.'

'Don't be so bloody soft,' Vicky scolded. 'There'll be ten to fifteen big blokes all over my lounge in a minute. You don't think your skinny little arse is going to take up much room, do you?'

'Ten to fifteen?' Maria repeated.

'MCs and rappers from the gig,' Vicky explained. 'They like to come back here and set up the decks to work on next week's stuff.'

'Doesn't it disturb the kids?'

'Babe, nothing disturbs my kids. They've heard it all before. So, get your arse round here *now*!'

'Yeah, all right,' Maria said gratefully. 'I know Joel won't come back right away, but I just don't want to be here if he does.'

'Don't blame you,' Vicky said. 'Sounds like a right arsehole. Anyway, call yourself a cab. I'll be waiting.'

'Just a minute,' Maria whispered. 'Someone's ringing the buzzer.'

'Well, at least you know it won't be him again, 'cos he'd be at the door with his key, wouldn't he?' Vicky said. 'Stop freaking out, and go and see who it is.

'Okay, but stay on the phone,' Maria said nervously. 'Just in case.'

'All right, but don't be too long.'

Holding the phone like a kind of good-luck charm, Maria went to answer the intercom.

'Maria Price?' A man's voice said. 'It's the police. Can we come up for a minute and have a word?'

'Oh, yeah, of course,' Maria said, pressing the release button. 'Come right up.'

'It's the police,' she told Vicky, relief rich in her voice.

'Great! They were probably watching him and they've come to check you're okay. Let me know if you're still coming round after they've gone.'

'Okay, but make sure you can still hear your phone if those guys are going to be making a lot of noise.'

Down below, Eamon grinned at the others as the door clicked open.

'That was a bit bloody easy.'

'You know what they say about gift horses,' Psycho said, yanking the door open. 'Kick their fucking teeth in.'

Everyone knew the drill. Fletch went ahead to do his usual with the lights, while Jimmy stayed behind downstairs to watch the doors.

Reaching Maria's door, Gerry gave a couple of knocks, then held his fake badge up to the spyhole.

Maria was smiling when she opened the door, expecting to see a reassuring uniform. She started to tell them to come in, then froze when she saw four large men in dark clothing, their faces covered by masks of famous people. Joel was between Marlon Brando and Ronald Reagan, his face a bloody mess.

'What's going on?' she gasped, terror stealing her breath.

'Inside,' Psycho hissed, giving her a shove that sent her sprawling halfway across the room. Coming after her, he reached down and yanked her back onto her feet before tossing her onto the couch. 'Keep your fucking mouth shut, and you won't get hurt – right?'

Joel was flung down beside her. Landing in a crumpled heap, he gave an agonised moan.

'What have you done to him?' Maria squawked, looking up at the men as they roamed around the room, turning things upside down. 'What do you want?'

'Keep it zipped,' Eamon barked. 'Or we'll finish *him* off, then *you*! Got that?'

Nodding, Maria reached down the side of the cushion and felt for her mobile which had slipped down when the man threw her. Pressing redial, she prayed that Vicky would hear what was going on and not start shouting.

'Who are you?' she asked, speaking loud and clear. 'What do you want? There's money in the bedroom if that's what you're after, but that's all I've got.'

'Ah, but that's not true, is it, love?' Psycho said, coming and leaning right over her. 'See, we bumped into our old friend Kyle outside, and he told us all about your inheritance.'

'I don't know anyone called Kyle,' Maria said, her wide-eyed stare riveted to his. 'Please, I think you've got the wrong person.'

'Oi, Kylie!' Psycho yelled, bringing his foot up and planting it hard on Joel's thigh. 'Tell your bird to stop trying to bullshit me before I give her a good shafting!'

Throwing a hand over her mouth when Joel cried out, Maria said, 'His name's Joel! You've got the wrong *people*. Please, just leave us alone.'

'Oh, fuck, yeah! I keep forgetting he's calling himself Joel these days.' Psycho laughed. 'Sorry for calling you a liar, love.' Squatting down in front of her, he looked her over appreciatively. 'You're a bit of a babe, you, eh? All that lovely blonde hair, and big blue eyes. I think you and me'll go and get ourselves better acquainted when we're done – what d'y' say?'

'Please don't.' Maria shook her head, her expression fearful. 'Take the money – take whatever you want. Just go.'

'Not till we've got what we came for,' Psycho said, running the barrel of his gun up between her legs. 'See, your man *Joel* here got a bit of a battering when we spotted him driving out of this place and rammed him off the road just now. And, cunt that he is, know what he said? He offered to bring us back here and let us have *you* if we let him go. And we're like, why would we want the lassie when we've finally got the grassing cunt we've been hunting down all this time? So then he tells us all about your money, and we couldn't turn that down, now could we?'

'But it's not here,' Maria said, terrified of what they would do to her now. 'Honestly, it's not. There's a bit in my bag in the bedroom, but apart from that everything else is in the bank.'

'We figured you'd say that,' Psycho told her. 'So me and my bro are going to take you round all the banks while the others wait here with your wee man. Do it fast enough at enough different ones and they don't catch on in time to take your card off of you. But see if you try and get away before we've finished, or do anything stupid to draw attention to yourself, your man here's dead. You got that?'

Hardly daring to breathe as he pointed the gun at Joel's head now, Maria nodded quickly.

'Good girl,' Psycho said, patting her leg. 'Then, when we're done, you and me are gonna have a shag or two. So, come on – get your coat and your card, and let's be off before it gets light and people start walking about, eh?'

Down in the entrance, Psycho told Jimmy to stay on guard while he and Eamon took Maria off for a drive.

'Anything happens, bell Gerry,' he said, propelling Maria out of the door. 'And don't *you* forget what I said about drawing attention,' he whispered menacingly down her ear.

Heading for the jeep, Psycho kept a tight hold on Maria's

arm while he waited for Eamon to get the keys out. 'Fuck's sake!' he hissed. 'Why didn't you have 'em ready?'

''Cos I didnae, okay!' Eamon hissed back.

'What the—?' Psycho spun around when something hard jammed into his back. 'The fuck is *this*?'

'This' was a large group of black guys surrounding him, and more round the other side around Eamon, hoods pulled low over their eyes, scarves up around their noses.

'Nae *way* are we getting fucking mugged!' Psycho snorted incredulously. 'What *is* it with us and this fucking place? We cannae move without some arsehole trying it on wi' us!'

Almost laughing now, he made to reach for his gun, but Leroy stepped right up close and stuck his own gun into Psycho's gut.

'Don't even think about it, Jockstrap, or I'll blow y' raas pussy head clean off!'

'Oh, aye,' Psycho drawled, his eyes glinting evilly as he glared down at the smaller man. 'Fancy y'sel a bit, do ye, eh, pal?' He started grinning now, the adrenalin pumping blood through his veins and energising him. 'Come *ooonnnn* . . . !'

He and Eamon simultaneously launched themselves into the surrounding bodies, kicking and butting, punching and biting, like the mad bastards that they were. They knew they stood no chance, but they intended to enjoy every minute while they could.

Luckily for them, Leroy's crew weren't intending to kill them, or they'd have gone down a damn sight faster than they eventually did.

Standing stock-still with fear, Maria almost screamed when someone grabbed her arm and ran her out of the car park and around the corner. Davy was waiting in a car with the engine running.

'Tek her back to Lee's,' her rescuer told him in a thick patois. 'We gon' fuck dem clowns up a bit and be right back, yeah?'

'They've got g-guns,' Maria warned him, shivering as the warm air blasting from the heater seeped into her.

'Me nah fussed 'bout dat,' the man told her with a wide white grin. 'Wha'ever dey got, we got *more*. G'wan back t' Vicky, now, man. She's waitin'.'

33

'Oh, babe, are you all right?' Vicky asked when Davy ushered Maria into the living room with a protective hand on her arm. 'Here, have this.' Pouring a large shot of brandy into a glass, she handed it to her. 'Neck it and let it settle you down, then tell me what happened.'

Sitting Maria down on the couch, Vicky rubbed her friend's arms to warm her up while she gulped at the fiery liquid.

'Better?'

'Yeah, thanks.' Maria smiled gratefully. 'Did you hear me on the phone?'

'Every word, babe. God, you must have been crapping yourself. I didn't know what the hell I was listening to at first. I knew it was you 'cos your name came up, but when I heard you I knew you wasn't talking to me. I thought the police were roughing you up, or something. It wasn't them, was it?'

'No, it was those Scottish guys that were after Joel last year.'

Frowning, Vicky lit two cigarettes and passed one to her. 'How the hell did they find him after all this time?'

'They reckon they ran into him in the car when he was leaving mine. They've really beaten him up, Vicky. He was in an awful state. I feel terrible for leaving him there.'

'Didn't I hear one of them saying something about your inheritance?' Vicky reminded her. 'How Joel had told them all about it and agreed to give you up in exchange for him?'

'Yeah,' Maria murmured, her chin wobbling as the extent of Joel's betrayal sank in.

'Come here,' Davy said, putting an arm around her, making her feel safe and warm. 'Don't go getting upset. Lee and the lads will sort it out.'

'Yeah, and don't you go wasting any tears over *him*, neither,' Vicky told her firmly but gently. 'His kind always comes up smelling of roses. Don't they, Davy?'

'Too right,' he agreed shyly. He couldn't believe he had his arm around Maria. He'd have thought he'd died and gone to heaven if he'd had a chance to do it when he was a kid.

'What should I do?' Maria asked, resting her head on his broad chest, vaguely aware of how fast his heart was beating.

'Wait till Lee comes back,' he said. 'Find out what's going on, then work out your story and bell the police.'

Maria looked up at him. 'You think I should tell the police?'

'You'd be stupid not to,' Vicky cut in. 'Seeing as you're already involved with them over that murder.' Softening her tone then, she said, 'How you doing over that, by the way?'

'Still shocked.' Maria shrugged miserably. 'I just can't believe it's happened. He was such a nice man; really honest and considerate. And now he's dead, and it's all my fault.'

'Oi! You can get that out of your head *right* now!' Vicky scolded. 'It was nothing to do with you. And if he was as nice as you say, then he'll know that, and he won't want you blaming yourself.'

Leroy and a couple of his guys came in just then, panting and sweating from the run back.

'What happened?' Vicky asked, looking him over worriedly. 'Are you okay? Where's everyone else?'

'Gone home,' Leroy said, going into the kitchen for some glasses. Coming back, he poured everyone a drink. Giving Vicky a kiss when he handed a glass to her, he said, 'Don't worry, babes, they've just done a disappearing act so's they don't get connected. They're sound. Nothing major.'

'Did someone get hurt?'

'Just a few cuts and bruises. Nutt'n life-threat'nin'.'

'Dem Scottish dudes was hea-*vee*, guy!' One of his mates laughed. 'You can see why they like all that football hooliganism shit, innit? But they wasn't no match for da *Scarlett Posse*!'

'Seen, man, seen!'

Laughing, the three fight survivors touched fists.

'So what did you do to them?' Vicky persisted. 'You didn't *kill* them?'

'Nah, just roughed 'em up,' Leroy told her cheerfully. 'They had another three friends inside, an' they come out and tried giving it large. But they got what they was lookin' for, so I doubt they'll be trying anything like that again. We warned 'em we won't be quite so *lenient* next time.'

'Thanks,' Maria murmured, feeling a little guilty for getting them involved.

'No worries.' Leroy winked at her. 'Any friend of my lady's is a friend of mine.'

'And ours,' one of his mates added.

'So, you calling the 5–0 in?' Leroy asked, wiping the sweat off on a towel that Vicky had tossed to him off the laundry pile. 'Best had, you know. That other bloke didn't come down, and you still need him out of your gaff.'

'Joel?' Maria gasped. 'Didn't you see him?'

'No offence, darlin',' one of Leroy's mates said, 'but checking up on that dude wasn't part of the bargain. If he got a kicking, it sounds like he deserved it. And I wasn't about to shove no plasters on him.'

'Me neither,' Leroy agreed, kissing his teeth angrily. 'He treated you rough, Maria, man.'

Maria couldn't argue, but she still felt bad for Joel. No matter what he'd done – to her, *and* to Nigel – she had loved him with a passion, and that would take time to completely die.

'What shall I tell the police?' she asked, dreading having to face yet more questioning.

'The truth,' Vicky said. 'Up to the part where you went outside. We'll have to think of something else for after that.'

'You're gonna have to say someone jumped the guys,' Leroy cut in. 'There's too much blood around to say *nothing* happened.'

'And none of it ours!' His mate laughed, sticking a roach in the fat five-skinner spliff he'd rolled.

'Say you were being shoved into the jeep when a gang of men walked past and saw what was happening,' Davy said. 'There's always gangs walking round at this time of night, so they'll believe you. You haven't got a clue who they were, but when they started laying into the men, you ran. You didn't see *any*thing, because it all happened too fast, and you were just glad to get away. And if the police want to know why you didn't ring them straight away, you say you were too scared to stop running in case they came after you. You just wanted to get to Vicky's, 'cos you knew you'd be safe here. Vicky gave you a brandy to calm you down, then told you to call the police.'

'Check brainbox,' Vicky said proudly. 'That's perfect. Just stick to it whatever you do, Maria. Get it tight in your head, and don't change a word – no matter what they say. Okay?'

'Okay,' Maria murmured, her stomach already twisting up inside.

'Say it back to me,' Vicky said.

Listening as Maria repeated the story, she nodded. 'Great. And you're nervous, which is really convincing.'

' 'Cos it's not an act,' Maria said, biting her lip.

'You'll be fine,' Vicky assured her, handing her the phone. 'The sooner they get to your place, the sooner you'll know if Joel's all right. Not that he deserves your concern,' she added scornfully. 'But I know you – you'll get yourself all worked up about him and end up taking him back out of pity.'

34

DI Seddon had asked to be informed if anything came in on his murder suspect. After many long hours of interrogation, Parry had finally gotten smart and asked for a duty solicitor. And it just so happened to have been Dan Reddish who came – one of the sharkiest twats Seddon had ever come across.

Within minutes of arriving, Reddish had insisted that they released Parry, smugly informing Seddon that he had no grounds for holding his client given that the only 'evidence' was a somewhat grainy CCTV image – which, he successfully argued, really could have been anybody and would never be allowed as actual evidence in court. That, and the *unsubstantiated* word of two people that there was animosity between Parry and the victim. And one of these so-called 'witnesses' had reason to incriminate Parry out of spite, having discovered his infidelity earlier that same day, making her testimony unreliable.

Other than that, they had no actual eyewitnesses, no fingerprints, and no DNA to link Parry to the scene. In other words, they had *nothing*.

And, to top it all, Parry's alibi had checked out, because once Honey Mason had been confronted with the videotape of her and Parry quite clearly together and on intimate terms at Quiro she'd finally admitted that he *had* spent that night with her. She'd also begged Seddon not to leak it to the press, or she would lose her part in the soap.

Seddon had had to let Parry go, but he'd warned him in no uncertain terms that there was no way he would let it rest until he'd found something – anything – to place him at the scene.

'I do hope you're not attempting to intimidate my client?' Reddish had said – nearly getting himself a smack for being such a pompous git.

'Not at all,' Seddon had replied, smiling icily. 'Just letting him know that I *never* give up without a damn good fight.'

Ironically, a fight was part of the reason he'd been woken now, as he was about to find out.

'Better be good,' he grumbled when he snatched up the receiver. 'This is the third time this month I've been pulled out of my bed. And if my missus wakes up, I'm putting her on to you, so get ready for a rollicking!'

'Sorry, sir,' the desk sergeant said. 'But you left word that you wanted to be told if anything came up about that bloke you had in yesterday – Joel Parry.'

'Oh, yeah?' Seddon was already reaching for his pants.

'We've just had a call from a Maria Price, reporting that he's holed up in her flat. Seems he had a run-in with some armed men who kidnapped the pair of them.'

'Do what?' Seddon grunted, wondering what the hell that was all about.

'There's a couple of ARUs en route to the scene,' the sergeant went on. 'Girl's pretty freaked, though. Won't go home till we've got Parry out and made sure the attackers have gone. She reckons two of them were forcing her to go round the cashpoints and withdraw money for them, but a passing gang saw what was happening and jumped them.'

'Shit!' Seddon muttered. 'Where is she now?'

'At her mate's . . . Just give me a minute, I'll get the address. There's some uniforms already getting a statement off her. DI Cooper's already at the scene.'

Writing the address down, Seddon said, 'Thanks. I'll go and have a word when I've seen what's going on.'

The car park was off to the side of the block, overlooked by the stairwell, but not by the main apartment windows, and shielded from view of the road or canal side by high hedges. The developers had done this deliberately to give the residents maximum privacy, but they had also created the perfect arena for a crime.

Pulling in by the gates behind the ARU vehicles and the two riot vans that were already there, Seddon got out and looked around. Seeing Sergeant Dalton from his station, he waved him over to get the low-down.

'What've we got, Paul?'

'Lot of blood over there.' Dalton pointed through to where a lot of activity was going on. 'No bodies, though, and no sign of the vehicle that was parked there last. Definitely a mass fight, 'cos we've got plenty of foot disturbance in that general area.'

'People must walk up and down here a lot, getting in and out of their cars,' Seddon remarked, squinting back at the scene. 'Can't be sure it was tonight, can we?'

'Well, it's mainly loose, like this,' Dalton told him, kicking at the gravel underfoot. 'This is still dry and relatively light. But over there, the wet stuff underneath is exposed, so it's a lot darker.'

'And the blood?'

'Most of that's in two areas on either side of where it looks like a vehicle was parked up before it skidded out,' Dalton said. 'Looks like they were jumped getting into it – which is basically what the caller told us. There are a few other patches scattered about, but they're the main bits.'

'Tyre prints?'

'Mainly skid marks, but we've not been here long and they haven't set the light up yet.'

'What about the guy in the flat? Parry. Anyone spoken to him yet?'

'No. There's a unit up there at the moment figuring out a way to get in. They'll let us know when it's safe to go in, but we've been told to stay out till then. And you know how long that can take.'

'Right. Well, I'll nip over and have a word with the girl in the meantime,' Seddon said, gazing up at the windows. Not that he expected to see anything. It was pretty much in darkness, the good residents sleeping soundly in their beds, blissfully unaware of the drama unfolding below. 'Give us a ring if they get Parry, will you?' he said then. 'I had him in as a suspect on a murder yesterday, and I had to let the bastard go. If this is anything to do with it, he's mine.'

'Will do,' Dalton agreed. 'But you'd best have a word with DI Cooper. This is his shout.'

'So I heard.'

The uniforms had finished taking Maria's statement and were on their way down the stairs when Seddon arrived at Vicky's block. He didn't know the bloke, but he recognised WPC Claire Weeks.

Nodding to the lad, he asked Weeks, 'How's the girl?'

'Pretty shaken, sir,' she replied. 'We've said we'll call in tomorrow, go over this again.' She flapped the papers she was holding.

'She on her own?'

'No, she's got a mate with her. Girl whose flat it is.'

'Good. Right, well, off you go, then.'

'Night, sir.'

Seddon got a mouthful of peach air-freshener when he walked into Vicky's flat, and a blast of ice-cold air from the open window. They'd obviously been having a good old smoke of the naughty stuff before calling the police in, but he couldn't blame them. Maria had probably needed something to calm her down after the horrors of the last couple of days.

Maria was sitting on the couch looking completely drained and shell-shocked, her lovely blue eyes clouded with shock and the pain of betrayal. The poor girl had certainly been through the mill, and Seddon felt truly sorry for her. He'd spoken to her at length yesterday and she'd seemed like a perfectly nice, respectable young lady. But that type always seemed to attract the lowlifes like Joel Parry. That kind of man could smell a soft touch a mile off.

'How you doing?' Seddon asked, sitting down at the other end of the couch.

'All right,' Maria said quietly. 'I just . . .' Pausing, she shrugged. Seddon was here to talk about what had happened, not how she was bearing up. 'Joel's at the flat, so I didn't want to go back there,' she said, as if to explain why she was here.

'Probably just as well, under the circumstances,' Seddon said.

'Would you like a tea or a coffee?' Vicky asked.

'Er, yeah, a tea would be great, ta.' Seddon smiled at her. He could murder a cup, as it happened.

Looking back at Maria then, he said, 'I know you've already given a statement, but do you think you could go over it again with me? I'll try not to drag it out, but I just want to get a bigger picture of what's going on; see if it's related to Nigel Grayson, in any way.'

'It's not,' Maria said, her hands still shaking as she reached for her cigarettes. Lighting one, she said, 'Sorry . . . you don't mind, do you?'

'Help yourself, pet.' Seddon wished he could have one himself, but he'd have to wait till he got outside. 'So, you say this is nothing to do with the murder? Sure it wasn't someone trying to get revenge?'

'No, the men that came to my flat have been after Joel for a long time,' Maria told him, feeling guilty for talking about Joel as if he was a criminal – even though he *was*.

'For what?'

'Well, last year when they were following me, Joel said it was because one of the men had thought he was a grass. He wasn't, but he had to leave Scotland because everyone wanted to kill him when the man was sent to prison, but then the man got out and found out where Joel was, and that's when they started following me.'

Seddon held up a hand. 'Sorry, love, but you'll have to slow it down a bit. I didn't really get a word of that. Start at the beginning, and bring it up to date from there. Joel lived in Scotland . . . ?'

'Yeah, but I think he might have changed his name when he left, because the men were calling him Kyle.'

Jotting this down, Seddon thanked Vicky for his tea when she carried three cups through. Then he listened as Maria told him everything she knew, and everything that had happened last night. She'd just reached the part about the gang jumping the men who were trying to take her to the cashpoints when Seddon's mobile rang.

'Excuse me.' Standing up, he took it out of his pocket and answered it. Listening quietly then, he wandered into the hallway to finish the call in private.

'Sorry, ladies, I'll have to leave this till later, if you don't mind,' he said, coming back in. 'Something's come up and I've got to go. You'll be staying here, won't you?' he asked Maria.

'Well, I was thinking I should go back to the flat and get my things,' she said. 'I was just waiting for that policewoman to get in touch. She said she'd find out if Joel had gone yet.'

'Stay here,' Seddon told her firmly. Then, to Vicky, 'Under no circumstances let her leave till I get back, okay?'

'Yeah, sure,' Vicky said, frowning.

'Wonder what that was about,' Maria said when Vicky had shown Seddon out.

'Probably got more questions for you,' Vicky suggested, flopping down beside her.

'Mummy . . .' A little voice called from the hallway.

'In here, Siobhan,' Vicky called back. 'Come and say hello to my friend.'

A beautiful little girl in pink Barbie pyjamas came in, rubbing her huge dark eyes with a tiny hand. Going to Vicky, she climbed onto her knee and looked at Maria sleepily.

'This is Maria,' Vicky said, cuddling her. 'Know how Cerisse at school is your very best friend? Well, Maria was mine when we were little like you.'

Nodding, Siobhan rubbed her eyes again.

'Ahh, did we wake you up?' Vicky asked her.

Siobhan shook her head. 'The man did, talking on his phone. What's a stiff, Mummy?'

'Sorry?' Vicky drew her head back and looked down into her daughter's face. 'Where did you hear a word like that?'

'The man said it,' Siobhan told her innocently. 'He said, "Where's the stiff – inside or out?"'

Vicky and Maria exchanged a horrified look. Then Vicky shook her head, as if to say 'Don't say anything.'

'Come on, sweetcakes,' she said, lifting Siobhan up. 'Let's get you back to bed.'

'But what did he mean, Mummy?'

'Never you mind. That's for big people to know.'

'Oh God, Vicky,' Maria said when her friend came back a couple of minutes later. 'You don't think . . .'

'I don't think anything,' Vicky told her calmly. 'That was probably nothing to do with this.'

Carrying the cups through to the kitchen, she bit her lip. She hoped to God it wasn't, because that meant that Leroy and his mates just might have killed somebody after all. And didn't even know it.

'Where is it?' Seddon asked, finding Dalton by the security door, which was now propped open.

'In the apartment,' Dalton said, indicating upstairs with a jerk of his head. 'Had a hell of a beating.'

'And that killed him?'

'No, the bullet through the head finished him off. Going up?'

'Yeah. I want to know if it's Parry.'

The apartment's lounge area was spacious, but filled with so many people that it looked cramped.

'Where is it?' Seddon asked, flashing his ID at one of the uniforms who was trying to block his path.

'Bathroom, sir.' The copper stepped back. 'Forensics have just arrived.'

'Don't come in,' a white suit called to him as he reached the bathroom door.

Looking through, Seddon saw the body slumped beneath the running shower, a large hole in the centre of its forehead. Bloodstained water surrounded the body which was sitting over the plughole, stopping most of the water from escaping.

It was Joel Parry.

'You are?' the attending pathologist asked, turning round now and pulling on his waterproof shoe protectors.

'DI Seddon,' Seddon told him, wondering how come there were so many faces he didn't recognise around tonight. He'd been in the job too long if the new recruits were overtaking the old crew.

'Derek Corbett. Do you know him?' Corbett nodded towards the body.

'Yeah. I had him in as a suspect for a murder yesterday. Had to let him go for lack of evidence, though, so I was hoping this would have something to do with it and I'd get another shot at him.'

'Ah, well,' Corbett said philosophically. 'At least you can sleep knowing justice was served – one way or another.'

Muttering something incomprehensible, Seddon left Corbett to it and went back down the stairs. What was the point of saying that he wouldn't sleep, precisely because Parry had eluded *his* justice?

'Is it your man?' Dalton asked down below.

Nodding, Seddon sighed heavily. 'Yet another one gets away with murder, eh?'

'You wanted him, huh?'

'Wanted him . . . I wanted to nail his thieving backside to the wall – and Dan bloody Reddish's next to it!'

'I see,' Dalton murmured, understanding his disappointment. Dan Reddish was getting quite a reputation for getting his clients off, only for them to reoffend almost immediately.

'Ah, well . . .' Seddon sighed again. 'Nothing left for me to do here. Do us a favour and let Cooper know I'm breaking the news to the girlfriend, will you? I'm sure she'd rather have me tell her than that cold bugger.'

Epilogue

When Seddon told Maria that no one had come forward to claim Joel's body, she offered to pay for the funeral – even though no trace had been found of the money he'd stolen from her. Bad as he'd been, she couldn't let him have a pauper's send-off when he had once meant so much to her, and an extra few grand on top of what he'd already had was hardly going to kill her. She didn't attend it, though, so the mourning was left to the other women in Joel's life: Angela, Honey – and Jippi.

But she did go to Nigel's funeral a few days later, and was shocked by the number of mourners that turned out. Apart from family, of whom there were relatively few, the rest were friends.

For a man who had thought himself so insignificant, Nigel Grayson had certainly made an impression on a great many people. Throughout the day, Maria heard many of them recounting tales of their own personal encounters with him and the common theme was the level of respect they had all had for him. She was just sad that he had died without knowing the impact he'd had on those around him. Not least on herself.

Or on his workmate, Adam Miller.

When Adam introduced himself to Maria as she was leaving, the first thing that struck her was how much he looked like Joel, when Joel had still been blond and clean-shaven.

Pushing the thoughts from her mind, she shook his hand

and told him how sorry she was that Nigel had been killed by somebody associated with her.

'Nigel would never have blamed you,' Adam told her, echoing what Vicky had already said. 'He was really rather fond of you,' he added with a sad smile. 'If only he'd had the nerve to tell you when he first saw you, you might never have . . .' Tailing off, he shook his head. 'No, I shouldn't say things like that. Just take it from his best mate, he would hate for you to suffer over this.'

'Thank you,' Maria said, taking a tissue from her pocket as the tears welled up in her eyes. 'I really appreciate that. He was a lovely man, and he was so helpful.'

'Wasn't he,' Adam agreed, gazing off into the distance. 'The world lost one hell of a man, and one hell of a solicitor when we lost Nigel.'

'Yes, it did,' she said, smiling sadly.

Maria was much happier at the next event she attended a few months later – Davy's wedding.

Sitting in St Augustine's church, where they had spent many a day playing in the ramshackle old graveyard when they were kids, Maria had Vicky on her left, and Beth – who had come to spend the week with her – on her right.

Davy looked so lovely in his grey morning suit, and Leroy was especially striking in his matching best man's outfit, both turning their top hats around in their hands as if they didn't know what to do with them.

Vicky looked beautiful in a flame-coloured dress and hat, and the kids were so precious: the girls in their little frilly dresses, carrying baskets of flowers, and Luke, the ring bearer, on his best behaviour in his own little suit. Even the baby was dressed up, although he was less than impressed with the bow tie and kept trying to pull it off.

'Doesn't he look handsome,' Vicky said wistfully, her stare

riveted on Davy as he stood at the altar waiting for his bride.

'Amazing,' Maria agreed. 'But how *nervous* is he? He looks like he's about to faint.'

'Probably is.' Vicky chuckled. 'Leroy and the lads got him totally blitzed last night. I was hoping they'd take him to Amsterdam and chain him to a hooker so he'd miss the wedding, but, oh, well . . .'

'Don't be so mean,' Maria scolded. 'He loves her. Be happy for him.'

'Can't help it. I hate her.'

'No, you don't,' Maria said knowingly. 'You're just jealous of her, because you think she's stolen Davy's love from you.'

'Don't be ridiculous!' Vicky tutted. 'I'd rather he was marrying you. He's loved you all his life.'

'He had a crush on me,' Maria told her firmly. 'It's hardly the same.'

Everyone turned to look at the doors when the organist began to play the wedding march and a collective 'Oooh' went up around the congregation when Nicola came in on her father's arm. Her make-up and hair were immaculate, and she looked stunningly elegant in her designer ivory-satin fishtail dress and veil.

Casting a glance at Davy, Maria saw the glow of love in his eyes and knew that she would have to do something about Vicky before her family fell apart. That would be so sad, because Vicky and Davy had been each other's friends and allies throughout the awful days of their childhoods and beyond. They needed each other much more than Vicky would ever admit.

The reception was being held in the community centre attached to the church. Old Father Finlay who had conducted the service popped in for a drink – or ten. He was a funny old man, who obviously didn't remember how many times he'd had to chase Vicky and Maria's gang out of the grave-yard all those years ago – or how much abuse they had hurled at him along the way. Mind you, he'd probably never seen who had said the rude stuff, because they'd only ever dared open their mouths when they were well out of range and knew they wouldn't get into trouble for it. Bad as some of the kids' parents were, they'd have stripped the skin off their backsides if they caught them abusing a priest.

Looking around when the other guests started to arrive for the afternoon buffet, Maria couldn't believe how many faces she recognised. Dragging Beth around the room, she introduced her to some of the girls from the gang, and the lads they'd hung around with. She felt as if she'd come home at last.

'You back again?' Lin Stokes said, giving her a prod in the shoulder. 'Thought we'd seen the last of you last time.'

Turning, Maria saw that Lin was smiling pleasantly – quite a change from the last time they'd bumped into each other. She'd made an effort with her appearance, too, and actually looked quite pretty with her hair loose, and her skin smooth and glowing with make-up on.

'Hi, Lin,' Maria said, giving her a kiss. 'How are you? You look lovely.'

'Thanks.' Lin beamed, unused to compliments. 'You don't look too bad yourself.'

'This is Beth,' Maria said, introducing her. 'She's my friend from where I used to live, in Devon. She's over for the week.'

'Pleased to meet you,' Lin said.

'You too,' Beth replied.

'Our Frankie's over there,' Lin told Maria then, pointing across to the buffet table. 'He's dying to see you after I told him about catching up with you that time. He's on his own, an' all,' she added pointedly. 'He sacked that lazy bitch off last year. Come and say hello. I can't wait to see his face when he sees you.'

Being dragged across to Frankie, who was busy loading a plate up with chicken legs, quiche and sausage rolls, Maria was nervous. He still had all his hair from what she could see, still that little bit longer than everyone else's. God, she hoped he wouldn't give her that uninterested look he'd been so good at dishing out when she'd been a love-struck kid. She wouldn't be able to bear that.

'Frankie,' Lin said when they reached him. 'Look who's here.'

Maria nearly died when he turned round. From behind his beer gut wasn't apparent, but face to face it stuck out like a barrel straining to escape the buttons of his shirt. And his face was haggard, which was a shock, considering he was only a few years older than her. His eyes were droopy, and his jowls were already hanging. He looked horrible.

'You remember Maria Price, don't you?' Lin said, watching both of their faces eagerly.

'Yeah, course.' Frankie grinned. 'How y' doing, Maria? You're lookin' good, girl.'

'You too,' Maria lied. 'So, how's it going?'

'So-so. Got divorced.'

'Did you? That must have been painful.'

'Nah. She was a slag. So have you got a fella on the go?'

'Er, no,' Maria admitted, a thrill of panic seizing her gut. *Please, God, no!* 'I'm kind of off men at the moment.'

'Oh, right,' Frankie said disappointedly, his gaze flicking to Beth.

'Me, too,' Beth said, linking arms with Maria and giving her a secretive smile.

Frankie's eyes lit up. Two for the price of one, and a floor show thrown in. Fuck! He was in heaven!

'Er, I think Vicky's looking for me,' Maria said, spotting

Vicky wandering around with Tyrell on her hip. 'Catch up with you later, yeah?'

'I'll be looking for you,' Frankie said, giving her the grin that she had swooned over when they were kids but which made her feel a bit nauseous now.

'There you are,' Vicky said when Maria and Beth reached her. 'I'm just going home to leave the kids with the babysitter and get changed for the disco.'

'Oh, right.' Maria checked her watch. 'I didn't realise it was five already. Shall we go and get changed, Beth?'

'Yeah,' Beth said, fanning a hand in front of her face. 'I'm boiling in this.'

'Right, well say bye to Davy before you go,' Vicky told them. 'They'll be heading off to the airport in a minute.'

'Where is he?' Maria asked, looking around.

'With the bitch over there.' Vicky pointed across the room.

'Can Beth hold Ty for a minute?' Maria asked, already peeling the boy out of Vicky's arms. Handing him to Beth, she grabbed hold of Vicky and pulled her towards Davy and his bride.

'What you doing?' Vicky squawked.

'Sorting you out,' Maria told her firmly.

Reaching Davy and Nicola who were gazing into each other's eyes in the corner, Maria pushed Vicky down into the chair beside Nicola. Then she squatted down in front of them and put her elbow on Vicky's knee to hold her in place.

'Nicola,' she said, smiling up at the girl who, she had decided, was perfectly lovely. 'Your sister-in-law loves your husband as much as you do – in a different way, of course. All she's ever wanted is for him to be happy, and now she's accepted that *you* make him happy, so she'd like to put the past behind you both and start again – okay?'

'Really?' Nicola said, her eyes filling with tears as she turned to look at Vicky. 'I'd love that.'

Seeing the hope in her uncertain eyes, Vicky sighed heavily. She'd never really tried to get to know the girl, but had decided that she was a stuck-up tart, just because she was a model and spoke quietly and politely. In truth, Nicola had probably been quiet mainly because Vicky had been so aggressive towards her. Davy's bride probably had no clue what she'd done wrong.

Loath as Vicky was to admit that Maria had hit the nail on the head when she'd said that Vicky was jealous, it was true. She'd hated losing Davy – to anyone, never mind to Nicola. But it was time to accept the inevitable. Vicky had her own life with Leroy, and if this was the woman Davy wanted to spend the rest of his life with, then who was she to argue?

'Yeah, I'm sorry,' she said. 'I never meant to hurt you. I was just scared for Davy, 'cos I knew he was mad about you and I didn't want *him* to get hurt. So if you'll forget about all the nasty stuff, I'd really like to get to know you. Just do me one favour, though – stop calling him *David*! It does my head in!'

Feeling very proud of herself when Vicky and Nicola kissed and made up, Maria gave Davy a hug.

'Thanks so much for that,' he said. 'I never thought I'd see the day.'

'My pleasure,' she said, wiping lipstick off his cheek. 'Have a wonderful honeymoon. And don't forget to ring me when you get back so I can come and see the pictures.'

'You're not going, are you?' Nicola asked, wiping her eyes and hugging Maria. 'Leroy's friends are doing a gig later. You don't want to miss that.'

'I won't,' Maria assured her. 'I'm only going to get changed. Have a lovely time. I'll see you when you get back.'

'Proper little matchmaker, aren't we?' Beth said on the way back to the apartment in Maria's new car. 'Shame someone can't do the same for you. That Frankie seemed like a nice man.'

'Don't even go there!' Maria groaned. 'I can't believe how awful he looks. If you'd seen him when he was fourteen, you'd have died.'

'Oh, I can imagine,' Beth said disbelievingly. 'Looks like a regular little sex god.'

'Christ, did you see his eyes when he thought we were together?' Maria laughed. 'He thought he was onto a winner.'

'You never know,' Beth said teasingly. 'Give me a gallon of champers and I might just find him irresistible.'

'If I catch you anywhere near him, I'll have you sectioned,' Maria warned, pulling in to the car park.

Up ahead, a man was leaning against a car. As they got nearer, Beth paled visibly.

'Oh, my God! I thought that was Joel,' she spluttered, turning her head to look back at him.

'It's Adam Miller,' Maria said, wondering what he was doing here. 'He was Nigel's friend at the solicitor's. I met him at the funeral. He's really nice.'

'He's really *fit*,' Beth agreed, getting over the shock. 'And he's actually nicer than Joel. Sorry, babe, you probably don't want to hear that.'

'It's fine,' Maria assured her, activating the central locking when they got out of the car. 'I'm over all that.'

'You look nice, ladies,' Adam said, strolling towards them with a slim briefcase under his arm. 'Been to a party?'

'Wedding,' Maria told him. 'This is my friend Beth,' she said then. 'Beth – Adam Miller.'

'Pleased to meet you,' he said, shaking Beth's hand. 'Sorry for dropping in on you like this,' he said to Maria then, 'but I was wondering if I could have a quick word.'

'Yeah, sure,' Maria said, opening the security door. 'Why don't you come up? We've only come back to get changed, but I'm sure I can spare five minutes.'

* * *

Beth went to have a quick shower, leaving Maria and Adam alone to talk.

'Can I get you a glass of wine?' Maria asked, waving him to sit down.

'Yeah, that would be nice,' he said, looking around. 'Great place.'

'Yeah, it's all right.' Maria handed him the glass and sat down. 'So, what can I do for you, Adam?'

'You had a conversation with Miles Cobb, one of the partners at the firm,' Adam said, 'in which you indicated that you'd like the firm to continue to represent you since Nigel . . . well, since he no longer can.'

'Yes, that's right.'

'Ah, good, just wanted to confirm that,' Adam said. 'That brings me to the reason for this visit. You see, each client is represented by an individual solicitor within the firm, and I was hoping that you would consider allowing *me* to be *yours*. I'm relatively newly qualified, but I assure you I know your case intimately, because I worked very closely with Nigel on it. He was my mentor as well as my friend, and taught me everything he knew – which was an incredible amount. The man was far too modest.'

'He was, wasn't he?' Maria agreed, smiling fondly.

'So, anyway, if you would do me the honour, I would love to pick up where Nigel left off and be the one to take care of you,' Adam said, giving her a piercing look.

Blushing, Maria shrugged. 'Well, I can't see any reason why not, if you've already worked on it with Nigel. He must have trusted you.'

'Oh, he did,' Adam said, unclipping his case and extracting several sheets of paper. 'I just need you to sign these authorisation papers, and we're done.' Handing her a pen, he passed the first of the papers to her. 'I can't begin to describe the sense of loss at the office,' he said as she signed. Taking that sheet, he passed her the second. 'It's so quiet without him. He had a very warm sense of humour – but I'm sure you must have seen it, because I know how much he respected you.' A third, and fourth, then finally the fifth sheet. 'Right, that's it. I'm now your solicitor,' he said, reaching out to shake her hand. 'And if I may be so bold, perhaps I could invite you out for a meal sometime . . . ?'

'What are you looking so pleased about?' Beth asked when Maria had shown Adam out and had come into the bedroom.

'He's my new solicitor,' Maria said, sitting down on the bed to watch as she dried her hair.

'And?' Beth said, squinting at her knowingly in the mirror.

'And he asked me out for a meal.' Maria grinned back at her.

'Oh, no – you didn't say yes, did you?' Beth said, turning round to look at her.

'For your information, I politely turned him down,' Maria giggled. 'You should see your face. You look horrified.'

'Thank God for that!' Beth sighed. 'Not that he isn't a very nice man, and fit as hell, but it's just too soon after Joel.'

'Which is precisely why I said no,' Maria said. 'So stop worrying, and let's get back to the party. I feel like I can finally start to have some fun again – and that's exactly what I intend to do!'

Down below, Adam climbed into his car and put his brief-case on the seat beside him. Patting it, he gave a slow smile. If Maria only knew what he'd been through . . .